# FATES
# DEFIANT

# ALSO BY

## BRIGITTE CROMEY

The Aftermath Trilogy
*The Shattered Ones*
*In the Unbreaking*

Tales of Sea and Skies
*Star of Hope*
*Fires of Freedom*

## C.M. BANSCHBACH

The Dragon Keep Chronicles
*Oath of the Outcast*
*Blood of the Seer*

The Drifter Duology
*Then Comes A Drifter*
*A Name Long Buried*

C.M. BANSCHBACH, BRIGITTE CROMEY

Spirits'Valley Duology
*Greywolf's Heart*
*Saber's Pride*

Drax Guard: Crew Six
*Flashpoint*
*Faultline*
*Conduit*
*Stoneheart*
*Shrike*

# FATES DEFIANT

## BRIGITTE CROMEY
## C.M. BANSCHBACH

BORDERLANDS
PUBLISHING CO.

*Fates Defiant*

Copyright © 2025 C.M. Banschbach & Brigitte Cromey

Published by Borderlands Publishing Co., an imprint of Lux Libris LLC

Cover design by Selkkie Designs - https://www.selkkiedesigns.com/

Character art by Kristin Hildebrand @artkrisma

Interior art & maps by Elisabeth Ward @seeking_stars_studio

Copyedited by Deborah O'Carroll - http://deborahocarroll.com/

ISBN: 979-8-9987782-0-9

www.borderlandspublishing.com

To the reader with monsters still to fight. May this story put strength in your hand when it comes time to slay them.

# AUTHORS' NOTE

Be Advised...

*Fates Defiant* is intended for New Adult audiences. While we did our best to handle certain aspects of the story with grace and understanding, we acknowledge that this is a story that takes place in a very dark world populated with broken people. You can expect to find depictions of violence, drugs and alcohol usage, and mentions of sexual assault/abuse. We don't include these aspects in order to shock or glorify, but in order to tell a very human story of redemption and restoration.

This book gets dark. There's no way around that. But with that said, here's our promise—this is *not* a hopeless story. If anything, the hope, once found, shines extremely bright in the darkness. And when dawn finally breaks, it does so with ferocity.

Promise.

# CYRUS

*"The Golden Sun"*

# BASTIAN LYTOS

"The Starcast Gryphon"

E ndless water stretched before me, sunlight gilding each wave crest in a path that extended to the unbroken horizon. Nothing but exhilaration filled my veins as I skimmed low above the water, scattering droplets from my fingertips before shooting skyward. My lungs burned as I reached the top of my climb, twisted in midair, and plunged back toward the glimmering water with a triumphant yell. I caught myself mere feet above the waves, the sudden weight of gravity sinking my stomach before momentum took over. The wave-etched path gleamed before me, and another yell of pure elation burst from my lips as I increased my speed, streaking toward the horizon as the sunlight kissed my face.

For a joy-filled moment, I was free.

And then I'd wake.

# CHAPTER 1

CYRUS

You could always hear the roar from the stands. It percolated through layers of stone and dirt to reach the subterranean arming room, a constant rising and falling that—if you listened hard enough and were practiced in telling the difference—would tell you exactly what was happening on the packed sand of the Arena floor. To me, the sounds of the audience were a guiding light, an indicator of what type of show they wanted to see.

Today, as attendants cinched my gold-emblazoned leather chest plate around my ribs and tightened vambraces and greaves, the roars were somewhat subdued. I wrinkled my forehead and looked up, as if I could see past the tunnels and white limestone to the ring itself. The massive building towered into the sky, beckoning with a promise of excitement just bearable—adrenaline with no danger to the spectator.

"What was on the list before me?" I asked the attendant in the corner. They always had someone with the day's schedule written on a wax tablet. I didn't usually bother with the man, but the subdued sounds from above were making me curious.

He angled the tablet to catch the lamplight. "A team match. Chimera versus Wyvern."

"But with substitutes on both teams," the boy tightening my sandal chirped. "Domitian got injured two days ago during training."

My muscles tensed at the words. An "injury in training" could mean a hundred things, rarely training related. *Domitian is Wyvern's lead. Their star fighter. No wonder the crowd's quiet. They're bored.*

I straightened my shoulders. Bored audiences I could handle. I'd already been briefed on today's battle, my opponent a convict who'd traded the death penalty for service in the Arena. It was a hollow promise given at every tribunal hearing—impress the crowds, prove yourself worthy, and your crimes would be forgiven. You'd be destined for glory, and eventually you'd be free. Anyone with half a mind could tell a death sentence when it stared them in the face, but it didn't stop most from trying their chances. Death on the sands was preferred to a helpless death at the hands of an executioner.

"Left arm, please," the attendant said, holding up a shoulder guard for my nondominant arm.

I raised my arm to let the man slip behind me and tighten the leather straps so I'd be able to move without worry. Another cheer filtered through the ceiling, and I let the thought of my opponent slip from my mind with a practiced mental shrug. Glorified executioner I might be, but at least I was sending my opponents to a *deserved* underworld.

A rustle of cloth heralded the arrival of Flavius, my former teammate who'd been promoted—or demoted—to my backup. He'd accompany me to the tunnel, watch my fight, and intervene to pull me out if things went poorly—not that I needed it. I was supposed to trust him more than anyone else, but years of parrying his jealous barbs had taught me caution. He lounged against the doorframe, the red stripe running through his off-white tunic already dusty from the afternoon. "They're ready. Are you?"

I took the sword the attendants offered. Its blade—wide at the hilt, narrowing in the center, and flaring again toward the tip—shimmered with wavy patterns, a sign of the magical tempering that ensured this sword would never lose its edge or succumb to rust. Its leather-wrapped hilt felt comfortable in my hand, the blade perfectly balanced as I slid it into the scabbard at my side.

"Ready." I flicked a gaze toward the roof, where the roar of the crowd had increased. "Sounds like they need someone to give them a show."

Flavius grinned, the smile still the same one he'd give me before our team faced our opponents. The expression tugged at the memory of days yearning for glory, when I'd let myself rely on—and even care about—those around me. "Then you'd better make sure you give them a show."

A thin grating of metal separated me from the dazzling sunlight coating the Arena floor. Beyond, I could see clouds of dust swirling as Arena staff finished scraping the sand clear of the blood and debris from the previous fight, hear the building hum of the crowd as the break between the previous fight and mine wound to a close, smell the tang of copper and iron that had become permanently etched into the tunnel walls.

9

The fight coordinator for the day had a crease between his eyes as he gave my appearance a rapid once-over. "Uniform, yes." He brushed a stray thread from the shoulder of my red tunic. "Armor—did they replace the strap you broke last week?"

I grinned. "Of course." There'd been a moment of panic when the strap of my shoulder armor broke under a heavy-handed spear strike, but the crowds had loved my recovery. I rolled my shoulder under the repaired piece, my muscles loose after warming up in one of the practice rings. "Good as new. Can we get on with this?"

"Yes, yes." His eyes flicked to mine, and he gave a slight smile. "Your hair's getting longer. You had to get them to pull it out of your face?"

I chuckled. "Didn't want it getting in my eyes." The hair, golden with lighter streaks from the sun, was the only thing I'd inherited from my mother. The gold specks in my grey eyes had been from my father. Uncommonly good looks were all they'd left me before dying, but I'd managed to take that sparse legacy and turn it into a legend on my own. "Don't worry," I told the fight coordinator. "I'll get them to trim it tonight."

"You'd better. Gods forbid *anything* gets in the way of your pretty eyes," Flavius interjected from the mouth of the tunnel. He was also ready for battle, his armor devoid of decoration and sword forged from plain iron. I didn't expect I'd need his help, but at least he was prepared. "I can get you a helmet if you want. Cover your face. Then we'd see how many of them"—he gestured toward the stands—"are in this just for your looks."

Helmets were almost never used here. The crowds loved being able to see the faces of their heroes. "You just watch yourself," I told him. "And be ready."

10

Flavius snorted. "You won't need me. You never have."

A trumpet sounded, and the grating over the tunnel mouth slid upward with a creak. Golden afternoon light streamed into the opening, bringing with it a smell of dust and blood. I took a deep breath, drew my sword, and ran through the darkened tunnel into the sunlight with my heartbeat rising to thunder in my ears.

The roar of the crowd surged like a wave cresting onto a beach as I emerged, a flag unfurling above the tunnel mouth to display my colors—a noonday sun, white and gold, on a field of red.

For a moment, all I could hear was my own name, with the bygone echoes of my parents' voices behind the adulation of the crowd.

Cyrus. "Sun."

A little while later, I stood with chest heaving and blood spattering my face as cheers resounded through the Arena. Behind me, the scrape of sand spoke of Arena staff dragging the body of my opponent out of the ring. I caught my breath and shook my hair away from where it stuck to my neck. It hadn't been a hard fight, but I'd managed to put a clever twist into my own actions. As far as the crowds could tell, I'd been at my opponent's mercy several times, and their cheers mirrored the feeling of triumph coursing through my bloodstream.

It never got old, this exhilaration of hearing my name shouted from the stands, feeling my pulse pounding in my ears, breathing the dust of the Arena and knowing that I'd been victorious once again. The crowd's cheering grew as I raised my sword over my head, my free hand acknowledging the stands with a wave.

As the cheers reached their height, a shadow crossed the sand.

My grip around the sword had been casual, but I immediately tightened my hand and drew myself into a fighting stance. The golden afternoon light wavered as the first shape was joined by several, a wheeling pattern of ghostly figures painting the bloodstained sand with shadows and blotting out the sun.

I took a step backward and shielded my face to look up. The sky had filled with the clatter of wings as hundreds of doves and pigeons abandoned their perches. Far above, four much larger shapes seared themselves into my vision; copper, brown, and umber feathers turned golden by the sunlight streaming through gryphon wings. Unearthly shrieks pierced the sky, coupled with whoops from the riders clinging dangerously to their mounts' feathered backs.

Longing stirred in my heart as I craned my neck to stare upward. Was it only last night that I'd dreamed—again—of taking flight?

Another scream, this one human, returned my attention to the Arena. The circling riders hadn't made any move into the open-air building, but the crowd was still fleeing. Hands waved at me from the tunnel, someone yelling my name.

"Cyrus! Get out of there!"

With a shock, I realized that some of the crowd had stayed, their faces alight with mixed terror and anticipation as they looked upward.

*They think I'm supposed to fight those things.* Fear crawled up my spine. Forget dreams of flying. Unbeaten fighter or not, I'd only last a minute against that many gryphons.

Sand flew from under my sandals as I sprinted into the tunnel. Strangely, the attendants didn't make any move to usher me farther into the labyrinth. We stood in stunned silence as the stands slowly cleared. After a few minutes, the shadows were the only thing that moved in the entire ring. With a final screech of triumph, the gryphons and their riders disappeared beyond the stony lip of the Arena, leaving me sweaty and tense in a way I hadn't expected on the heels of an easy victory.

"By the gods," someone muttered. "What was that?"

Something twisted in my stomach, like the stirring of the air before a storm. "I don't know." I finally released the hilt of my sword. "Whatever it was, I don't think we've heard the last of it."

# CHAPTER 11

BASTIAN

The Imperial City. You heard it before you smelled it, and you smelled it before you saw it. A feat, since it sprawled and reached with hungry arms. The slave cart creaked and groaned, hitting every rut and rock on the road. In the corner, I kept my eyes shuttered closed, knees drawn up and manacled hands resting in my lap. The others in the barricaded cart with me murmured restlessly to each other, chains clinking as they speculated. For a moment, deserters, thieves, and murderers forgot their disdain of each other, joined together in the shared miserable anxiety of their uncertain future.

I curled my fingers in and out, wrist still aching from fighting off one of those murderers last night. Left forearm still stinging from the rough edge of an improvised weapon from a prisoner of war two days ago. I'd had to rip part of my already tattered shirt to bandage it, rationing a bit of our evening water to splash away the grime coating us all since journeying countless miles from the Chinerean war front.

I didn't begrudge the man the injury. He was desperate and saw in my face a soldier who'd been conquering his home in the wild northern forests. A bit of bone or stick sharpened into a crude weapon was the only power any of us had left. And it wasn't the tribes who'd betrayed me one month ago.

"Hey, traitor," a rough voice sounded. I cracked open an eye. A few dirt-scuffed faces looked at me from the end of the cart. This was the first time an almost civil approach had been taken. "You seen the Arena?"

"Does it matter?" My returning question came in a voice as rough and ragged as the road beneath. I almost winced. I'd not spoken more than strictly necessary over the month's journey, and my voice was paying for it.

"What do you mean?" another asked.

I offered a mirthless smile. "We'll all see it, then it'll be the last thing we know. Why bother wondering?"

A man with a patchwork beard sneered. "Still too good for any of us." He turned his shoulder against me.

I was no traitor. But neither was I Commander Bastian Lytos, leader of a squad of gryphon scouts in the Fifth Legion, anymore. The man who'd betrayed *me* had taken my place.

I tilted my head to look through the iron bars before wishing I hadn't. Farmland spread in golden and green waves, guarded by cypress trees standing in narrow lines. The voices of men and women, and the shouts of children hidden in the depths of the fields, echoed over the constant clattering. Dull red stone aqueducts carried water in rigid lines. Home-sickness and regret slammed into me at the familiar sights, more brutal than an angry fist.

If I looked over the next rise, the city would appear. I should have been returning to this city, to these fields, on the back of a gryphon, leading a scouting squad ready to receive another accolade for service to the Empire. Should have been racing home as soon as I was free of duties to sweep my wife into my arms, where her kiss would have started shaving away the roughened edges I always brought back from war.

Instead, all I had left were torn trousers, a ragged undershirt, and the riding boots that I'd managed to save from the slavers. Tall, supple leather molded to my calves, with small buckles to latch to saddle hooks and stirrups in flight. They were dust-stained and worn now from walking miles behind this cart. Foolish perhaps, to hold on to such a thing when I had no use for them anymore, especially after leaving the dregs of winter behind on the front and slowly journeying back to the milder, southern climes.

But they felt like something of myself to keep in the chaos I'd brought upon me. And a way to hide a more important possession from the greedy eyes of the slavers who weren't content with the gold they'd gain from human flesh, but must strip anything of value from them first. My right boot held my wedding token—a silvery dragon scale pierced at the top to be threaded onto a braided leather cord and worn about the neck. The promise of eternal dedication to my wife, who'd never know what happened to me.

If the gods were just, perhaps Lyra would think I'd died in the latest campaign. It had been one year and one month since I'd kissed her goodbye, a scant two miles from where we rattled. The tiled house would never feel my boot stride again, never hear our laughter mingling in the hazy afternoon. Perhaps, if there was any mercy left, someone would tell her that I'd died, not been sold to slavery for refusing to slaughter innocents over and over.

She'd never know that in the Imperial City, in the famous Arena, I'd be condemned. They said if you won enough fights, killed enough opponents, you'd be given freedom, no matter your crime. Enough of my men followed fights, tracked the rise and fall of heroes in the pits, that my future already felt ordained.

I'd refused to kill innocents. It wouldn't be innocents I'd face on the sands, but it didn't seem like a man could keep killing and killing and retain a sense of what or who he was for very long.

I'd live for a few fights and then die, one way or another.

The carts, three in total, all filled with misery and stench, joined others on the road. More slave carts followed finer carriages with curtain-shrouded windows hiding the wealthy. Men and women on foot or pushing laden handcarts filled the widening road to the city gates. All spilling in together to stuff the city walls with more and more bodies.

I sat taller, taking in the ways the city had changed in the last year. More slums around the outer walls, likely more inside the walls, scents and sounds—almost too much after the empty roads and rigid structure of the army.

Then we were through the gates, lurching through the streets, bracing against the shouts and stares of peasants and the wealthy already betting on our destiny.

Something dangerous started to snare around my heart as I caught a glimpse of towering walls, rounded and spotted with arched cutouts, flags draping from the very top. The embellished cloth declared champions and challengers. The Arena.

They'd refused to kill me at the warfront, instead sending me in the never-ending tribute to the city's entertainment. They'd refused to judge me, but the Arena loomed, and it would remorselessly stand as both judge and executioner.

## CYRUS

The shrieks of gryphons still rang in my ears as I retreated to the armory. There, the attendants set aside the armor to be cleaned and checked my sword for wear and tear before turning me loose. Around me, whispers ran rampant.

Gryphons. Here. Now. What did it mean? What *could* it mean?

"Gryphons, huh?" Flavius commented as we climbed the stairs and left the whispers behind. "You ever fight one?"

"Once," I said nonchalantly. "I won."

I'd been nineteen, and would've died had it not been for the beast's hesitation before the final blow. I'd had time to twist away, but a scar still pulled across the outside of my arm after that day.

"Of course you did." Flavius raised an eyebrow, a challenge. "But I'll bet you wouldn't take on four at a time."

I knocked my knuckles against the rough wall for luck. "That would be a stretch." I laughed. "I'm not saying I couldn't do it, but it would be a battle to remember."

"Then may the gods will that you never have to. Though"—his voice grew touched with sharpness as we came to the top of the stairs and stepped out into the courtyard of the barracks and training wing—"if you ever do, I'd better make sure I lay my odds well. Someone's going to get rich the day you finally lose."

There it was, the bitterness that ensured I'd always be the best guardian for myself, no matter what our respective roles were.

"That'll be the day," I laughed. I took several steps away before turning my back, calling over my shoulder, "You'd better save your money!"

I caught some kind of jeer in return from Flavius before he disappeared into the barracks where new trainees had their quarters. My own path turned to another flight of stairs, leading to a balcony that ran the length of the top floor of the building. The Elite floor was one of the few restricted areas, limited to those combatants who'd proven themselves enough to warrant rooms of their own, personal attendants, and the rare commodity of privacy.

I scrubbed a hand over my face as I approached the end of the balcony, where my room abutted the curved wall of the Arena itself. The blood from earlier had dried and was sticking to my skin, despite the scrub I'd given it with a cloth in the arming room. I stopped and peered over the railing, squinting to catch a glimpse of the sun. It was angling down beyond the stables, and golden light streamed over the roofs to illuminate the complex.

A rumble from below caught my ear amid the ongoing hum of the courtyard. Gates creaked open at the far southern end, and a trio of wagons rattled into the open space. Slavers, bearing the latest crop of new recruits. I leaned on the railing and watched as the wagons halted before the entrance to the barracks. The gates screeched closed, and the drivers hopped down to release the prisoners from their confinement.

I wrinkled my nose. I'd been close to the recruit wagons when they'd arrived in the past, and the stench of fear, unwashed men, and filth was enough to make even my stomach turn. It seemed this would be no different. The men emerging from within the barred cages looked as haggard and downtrodden as ever...

All save one.

I frowned and shifted position so my appearance on the balcony would be less visible, not that anyone in the courtyard ever thought to look up. Among the slump-shouldered, defeated men destined for either death or glory, one man stood with straight shoulders and raised head. There was nothing remarkable about his appearance beyond the bizarrely confident posture—dark hair with suntanned skin, broad shoulders, taller than the others even if they'd been standing straight, ragged clothes with boots that spoke of having hailed from somewhere northward.

It was instinct, I decided, that made him stand that way. Or training. And he clearly had no idea what his posture would signify to anyone who was paying attention.

*Interesting.*

I stepped away from the railing as the door to my quarters opened and an attendant's voice called my name. A party awaited this evening to commemorate the end of the mourning period for the late Emperor, hosted by one of the Senators, and with my name on the invitation ahead of the words "honored guest." The scents of thyme and rosemary drifted through the air as my attendants rushed to ready hot water, drying cloths, scented oils; all the things required to transform me into the type of guest a Senator's rich and powerful friends would fall over themselves to speak with.

"Cyrus," one of them warned with the tone of someone who'd said this a million times. "You're late. You were supposed to come straight here after your match...What took so long?"

With a laughed apology, I complied with their ministrations, filling in those who hadn't been watching about how today's bout had gone. Still, as I scrubbed blood and sweat from my skin, submitted to a massage, and had one of them trim my hair to just below my ears, my memory kept lighting on the unknown prisoner who hadn't bothered to hide his confidence.

*Soldier,* I finally decided as one of the attendants kneaded the knots out of my tired muscles. *Soldier, and he has no idea of what's coming. But of anyone down there, I'd wager he'll at least survive training. Maybe one day we'll meet.*

I dressed in the fresh red-trimmed tunic laid out for me and descended the steps as the sun disappeared behind the stables. The route to the stable went past the archway leading into the barracks. Shouts and the sounds of fighting echoed within—the new recruits, already scrapping among themselves to establish a hierarchy.

I'd fought, and won, my first night in the barracks at age sixteen. Then, I'd been the victim. All the other times, I made myself the instigator, until even the toughest trainees backed away with open hands when I threw a hostile look in their direction. After that, no one bothered me.

I shrugged away the musing and let my attention drift to the evening ahead, golden-hued, wine-soaked, and filled with decadence. Soldier or not, prepared or not, the odds were good that this new combatant and I would never face each other.

And if we did, he'd die by my blade as easily as all the rest had.

BASTIAN

Hangers-on increased the closer we came to the Arena. There seemed to be more boys than men, ruddy-faced youths shouting and swinging at each other with stick swords as they raced and wove. Some wore clothes more ragged than mine, others had longer tunics for higher-ranked citizens. There was a pattern to the boys, mirrored in the men casting glances at the carts and more quietly speculating. Even the women didn't seem to mind talking with baskets on hips or gripping children by the hand.

One woman's dark hair barely contained under a vibrant scarf reminded me of Lyra. The way she'd leveled a flour-coated finger at me days before I'd left, barely masking her smile in the face of my laugh. The way we'd sit and oil saddle leathers and equipment together, quietly sharing dreams of the future or talking of nothing. Missing hit hard enough it felt my heart might start bleeding.

After that, I kept my eyes forward, watching the stone walls come closer and closer. Finally, with more shouts and clatter, we rolled under an arch and into a broad courtyard. The chaos of men, the clatter of training swords from sandy areas cordoned off, the smell of animals...similarity to an army camp stirred for a moment.

Then came the slavers' voices, the crack of whips and verbal threats as the doors were unlocked and we were urged out. I was last out, slowly stretching to my full height, back and legs aching from the day spent cramped in the wagon.

A man in a dull scarlet tunic strode forward, a sheaf of papers in hand. A smile stretched across his broad face, something not unkind but not friendly either.

"Welcome," he said. "To the Arena."

The same stab of familiarity hit, bringing back a memory from years ago of an armored soldier urging uncertain men into ragged lines, demanding names and ages, uncaring for rank or paternal names. All while more confident men jeered from the edges, and animals protested their lack of dinner.

But it quickly faded from something almost gold-tinged to the harsher present where I'd, once again, become a new recruit sent to die for someone else's purpose. But this time, coins were passed from the man to the slavemasters and our wrists released of manacles.

I wondered if we were worth more or less than a soldier.

I rubbed my aching wrists, light and free for the first time in a month, and glanced around. The cacophony came from the west where grooms hauled fresh water and feed, disappearing through barred gates deeper into stables beyond. To the east, stonework buildings rose in three tiers, balconies wrapping the upper. Living quarters by their look.

And to the north, higher and higher than it felt my gaze could bear, rose one wall of the Arena. The same flags draped from the top, flapping in some faint breeze. The center was a bold sunburst on red. The men to my right jostled each other and pointed to it. No doubt someone important in this place. I'd learn soon enough.

I'd been here once, years ago, as a new soldier. I came with other men from my cohort, but the wanton slaughter for the sake of money had turned my stomach so much that I'd never been back or listened to the stories of legends who paced the sands. Fate must have felt cruel the day it decided to send me back.

I turned my attention back to the stream of words our new master was drawling. "You live to serve the Arena now. You fight for honor and glory. The more you win, the higher you climb, until—" He pointed back at that white and golden sun.

A smile tipped the corner of my mouth, but I'd long left humor behind. Still not so different from soldiers, fed the same hope and bravado before being sent to die.

"Tomorrow, you'll be assessed and sorted," he declared. "For now, inside to inspection and to wash the muck off. Those with injuries"—he pointed to me and three others—"will be seen first. We don't want any infection to spread."

A young boy, barely fifteen, stepped forward from behind the man and beckoned to us, carrying the same lofty importance as the adult. He moved with a certain swagger, as if completely unafraid of the types of men who surrounded him. Perhaps he wasn't.

Though if he kept eyeing my boots, he'd get a cuff. I cast one glance behind me, catching what felt like it might be the last light of freedom tingeing the top of the Arena before we disappeared into the quarters.

The boy led us through a main room, down a short stairwell into a long rectangular room with a stone trough filled with water running through it. Enough room for almost twenty men along both sides.

"Strip and wash," he called, and vanished through another door. Two rougher-looking men in leather tunics and bearing knives took his place, glancing from us to the trough and cheap lye soap.

Still not so different from the army. I found a place where a roughly carved gourd hung, ready for scooping water. I doffed my boots, keeping them close as I shrugged free of clothing. A few rainstorms had been the only bath any of us had gotten in the last month, and even before that, it had been quick scrubs in ice-crusted buckets as winter slowly retreated before the Empire's war banners.

A soft-looking man stood at the far end, wringing his hands in alarm at the bathing conditions. I huffed and turned to washing, keeping one eye on my boots and the scale still hidden inside.

But when I retrieved my clothes, one of the guards barked a rough

"Leave it" and gestured to the interior door. For the first time I balked, hesitating at facing some unknown with only my boots.

"Move," he snarled again, miming a lean forward as incentive. I scooped up the boots, ignoring another harsh order to leave them behind. I would not. He paused just long enough at the look I shot him before passing by. Sputtering lamplight illuminated the short hallway before the youth pointed me wordlessly into a better-lit room.

A man in physician's robes checked me over, poking at old scar lines, the fresh cuts, and the scraped skin of my wrists, making sure none of my body carried infection or disease before allowing me to dress in the rough short-sleeved tunic and trousers brought by the boy. The youth eyed the boots again before holding out sandals. I ignored him and shoved my feet into the boots, lacing them up with a daring air of finality. He pulled away, looking to the physician for help, but the greying man didn't care. He only slapped a fresh bandage on my cut and pointed me back out.

From there it was to another room with serving attendants ready to shear hair and beards. Guards stood there too, perhaps to make sure razors weren't stolen for weapons before we killed each other with swords in the Arena.

The attendant finished with me and picked up a slender needle, swiping it across a damp cloth first. He turned to me.

"Hold still."

I jerked away as he moved the needle toward my ear. "What are you doing?"

My shoulders were pinned in answer and newly cut hair grabbed to yank my head to the side, exposing my right ear. No answer came to my second gritted question, only a quick, bright sensation in the top of my ear. Then the man took a thin gold band and threaded it through.

Cold rushed over me, not even broken by the brief heat that was them soldering it closed.

This was a slave mark. The manacles I'd worn for the last month had a brand etched into them. But this was something permanent—a pointed reminder that my life had been bartered away without my consent. And for the first time in my life, I didn't quite feel human.

"There." The man stepped away and I was released. He rapped my hand as I reached for my ear. "Don't mess with it. If it still hurts in a few days, see the physicians."

He didn't flinch before my searing look. "You belong to the Arena now." He pointed to the door and called for the next in line, oblivious to the invisible cords that cinched around me at the words.

The guard who'd restrained me shoved me forward, to a main room where tables and benches were already filled with men, more following behind me from the same inspections and ministrations to be served plain, yet filling dinner. I took mine to the farthest edge I could find. I was used to scouting from above, my gryphon and I taking to perches to observe. This corner was as good as I would find.

And from there, I saw several fights break out. Frightened men masking it with violence, or trying to make a name for themselves already. Like had been decreed to us in the courtyard—our old lives were over. It was us and the Arena now.

I had no true thought for vengeance. It would serve nothing. The betrayal from one of my trusted men still stung, but in the end, he had been a more loyal soldier than me. Reporting my failure of duty as a commander. Empires and armies could not stand if every officer questioned their orders. So here I was. I supposed I could only hope that he cared for our men the same way I had.

At that moment, it was an almost frightening acceptance that filled me. Packing into my corners to steal away the passion that once had driven every beat of my heart. I'd lived in the open air, and now would die trapped within warrens of stone.

Sharpness prodded my foot—the scale shifting in my boot and stabbing the reminder of my wife into me. A shiver ran through me, breaking me free of that terrifying apathy. I could not give up. Not yet.

# CHAPTER III

CYRUS

Not much could compare to the sight from the Arena roof, but I did like this view of the city. Senator Tiberius's villa stood on a rise, flanked by the sprawling mansions of other high-profile citizens and overlooking the temple district. To the west loomed the Arena, distance making it seem normal-sized in comparison to the smaller buildings around it. To the east, not that I could see it now, stretched the sea. I'd seen it at a distance and been there once on a scheduled outing very much like this one. That had been years ago. I hadn't returned since.

Behind me, the villa hummed with gossip, exaggerations, idle chatter, and the more serious discussions of men with too much time and power on their hands. I'd heard it said, years ago, that the most important decisions in the Empire were made not in the Senate Hall, but in villas like these. Based on what I'd witnessed in the last few years, the statement was correct.

I turned away from the nightscape and wandered inside, scanning the crowd for interesting groups to mingle with. These parties were always filled with inane conversations, but today's discussions sounded particularly pointless. Despite this being a commemorative day to end the mourning period for the Emperor, there wasn't a speck of sadness or solemnity in the people gathered here tonight.

"...the wrong color, even after I'd told him *three times* that it should match the others. Ridiculous. I had to..."

I glanced at the speaker, whose clothing already clashed in multiple bright colors, and snorted back a laugh. *The tailor isn't the only one who's been ridiculous.*

"Did you see the memorial wreaths are already gone from the forums?"

"I heard the Empress ordered them to be taken down this morning."

Now that I did believe. If gossip was to be believed—and I trusted the wine-soaked discussions of a party more than the heralded announcements in the streets—the woman had been laying her odds on this eventuality for years.

Another broken phrase of conversation caught my attention as I exchanged an emptied cup of wine for a full one. "...like I'd never seen. I don't know how they manage to stay on those things at that type of speed."

I looked around to pinpoint the conversation, and noticed a pair of men—with physiques that proclaimed their greatest exertion was walking from a sedan chair to a building—standing near one of the tall windows.

*Gryphons?*

Now this was a conversation I could readily join.

"I heard they're adding another event in the mornings now," one of them added as I walked over. "Timed trials, with obstacles to navigate."

"What's this?" I asked. "Anything to do with the interruption this afternoon?"

"New sport," he said. Now that I was looking directly at him, I recognized him as the son of one of the investors who held most of the purse strings for the Arena. Warning skittered down my spine despite my interest as he explained, "The races. Teams of madmen flying through obstacles on gryphons. Like our team trials, but aerial." He twirled a finger through the humid, incense-laden air. "That's what that was earlier, a stunt to draw crowds."

My fingers tightened around my cup. "*That's* what it was?"

The second man laughed and swilled back the rest of his wine. "Sure was! I was sad though—thought for a moment that we'd *really* get a show. How do you think you'd have fared if they'd chosen to attack?"

I plastered a smile to my face. "I wouldn't have survived long, but I'm sure the crowd would've loved it."

This conversation was going sour, and I didn't think I could stomach any more speculation on how badly things might have gone. Irritated, I made some excuse to pull away from the conversation and drift through the party. Wisps of conversation—gossip, really—followed me, as ubiquitous as the strands of incense smoke drifting below the ceiling.

"...could take on five at a time and still win."

So that story was still circulating. It'd been four, not five, but I never minded the numbers added each time the story was told.

"I heard he was in an affair with the praetor's daughter."

"Him? No, he never stays with his partners for that long."

It'd been years ago, when I'd barely gained solo elite status. Her father had paid the Arena a ludicrous sum to secure my intimate company for his daughter, then used the rumors to force her into a marriage she'd never wanted or asked for.

"You see his reaction to those gryphons? I think he was actually *scared*."

"Nothing scares him. They ran when they saw it was him they'd have to fight."

This last tickled my fancy, and I laughed into the dregs of my wine before draining the cup and passing it to a servant. That was the part of my reputation I had no difficulty with. The more people who viewed me as fearless, the easier my wins became.

"...there he is. Cyrus!" A hand waved across the room, and one of the Arena servants wove his way through the crowd to stand before me. "Octavian sent me to find you. He and the others are waiting."

*Others.* I cast a quick glance around the room. Sure enough, the fight coordinators and overseers had disappeared from the party. And given that Senator Tiberius was one of the board members who governed the Arena, this could only mean one thing.

A meeting. During a party. How boring.

"Cyrus, thank you for joining us." Octavian, the lead fight coordinator and my trainer since age twelve, greeted me with a smile as the servant left the room and shut the doors behind him. "Enjoying the party?"

I took in the occupants of the room in a heartbeat. All told, five of the six board members were present, along with several more Arena staff that hadn't been at the party. Flavius smirked at me from the opposite side of the room, where he stood alongside one of the team trial coordinators. I knew he hadn't been invited to the party itself, but no doubt he'd take this inclusion as a sign that he was moving up in our cutthroat world.

"The party's wonderful. You really know how to entertain, Senator." I dipped my head in the direction of the host, who raised his cup in acknowledgment. "I don't think I've ever heard so many people complimenting the host. And the vintage you chose? Absolutely perfect for the weather."

"Speaking of," one of the trainers said. "How much have you had?"

I shrugged. "Some." I eyed the group again, this time not disguising my growing unease. "Though, maybe not enough, depending on the topic of conversation."

The man laughed. "Better sit down, then." He gestured to a spot on the couches and I sat, lounging against the cushions like I'd been anticipating this the entire evening. Inside, my nerves were beginning to thrum with the same energy that surged in the tunnel before a fight. This wasn't the sand of the Arena, but there was risk here nonetheless.

"Is this about the gryphons this afternoon?" I asked before anyone could say anything. "Because if that's all, I think we can agree it didn't mean much. All they did was circle a few times."

"Perhaps, but this incursion is the symptom of a larger problem," one of the board members said. "Their...races are drawing more crowds every week. Last week, the revenue drawn between ticket sales and wagers almost doubled ours from the same day."

I smirked. "I wasn't fighting that day, that's why." I didn't pay attention to the attendance of other events or solo fighters' matches, but I knew enough to be assured that my fights always drew the highest numbers.

"Yes, but even your matches have been declining in revenue over the last six months." One of the board members, a former soldier, leaned forward in his seat. "They're no longer as exciting as they used to be."

"You're saying I'm boring?" I scoffed and shook my head. The haze in the room spiraled in my vision as I did, a warning that there shouldn't be any more wine consumed tonight if I wanted to keep my reflexes intact. "It's not me who's boring, it's my opponents. My skills have only improved over the years, it's not my fault everything's easy." I turned my attention to the fight coordinators. "If you want a show, you'd better give me something I can work with."

Almost as soon as I'd said it, the grim looks from the trainers across the room informed me that I'd said the right—which meant wrong—thing. I'd never learned to hold my tongue under pressure, and it seemed like this was another instance where it was about to get me into trouble.

*Idiot,* I chided myself as the board and supervisors exchanged knowing, approving glances and Flavius grinned maliciously. *You had things exactly as you wanted. Why jeopardize it now?*

"More difficult opponents?" Octavian nodded thoughtfully as I shot an uncertain glance at him. He gave me a smile, and I straightened under the approval as he said, "We can try. But"—he was addressing the board members now—"will it be enough?"

"Revenue's down in all events," Senator Tiberius said, eyeing me over the rim of his cup like he was calculating how much of that deficit I represented. "There might be other ways to raise it, and we'll look into them. But the fact remains that our 'people's hero' isn't drawing the attention he used to. Perhaps it's time to let your many admirers know that you're open to their intimate company again?" He gave me a knowing grin. "It's been a while, but that selectivity only makes you all the more desirable."

My skin crawled at the thought, and I quickly schooled my features to stay composed. The praetor's daughter hadn't been the only time someone powerful paid for my romantic company. When I'd been younger, the idea had held allure, but over time the appeal had soured. It'd been a long while since I'd had to trade intimacy for gold, enough that I'd thought I'd managed to dodge the threat permanently. But now...

"Trust me," I said, forcing a chuckle to cover the unease spreading through my limbs. "I'll do whatever's necessary to prove myself. But let's try with a sword first."

"Well and good," Octavian said. "I'll keep my eyes open for anyone that might prove a challenge." He gave me a look that was almost a warning. "But you'd better be ready."

Worry spiraled in my stomach to match the unease. Octavian's warnings were infrequent occurrences, and the appearance of one here confirmed that my life was about to change dramatically—and not for the better. I pushed myself up from the couch and took my leave, as the conversation turned to adjustments being made to the team trials.

Flavius slipped out the door behind me, his smile doing nothing to settle the uncertainty that had been churning ever since the gryphons' shadows wheeled over the Arena. "Brace yourself," he warned with a smirk. "The odds aren't with you anymore."

The ride back to the Arena was quiet, as I thought over what I'd been told and tried to shake off the fear brought on by Tiberius's suggestion. By the time the bulk of the Arena loomed overhead, I'd concluded there was nothing I could do but accept whatever lay ahead. I'd told the truth, mostly. Octavian's relentless training in my youth had molded me into exactly the type of combatant the crowds loved to see: fierce, lethal, and entertaining to watch. But lately, my fights *had* been too easy, my opponents too unskilled, to provide the epic battles the crowds longed to see.

The loss of revenue wasn't my fault, but apparently the regaining of it had become my responsibility.

The night was wearing on as I bade goodbye to the others and climbed the stairs to my quarters with unease dogging my steps. The rooms were dimly lit with flickering oil lamps, a sleepy attendant there only long enough to take my incense-tinged clothes for laundering. He departed after a moment, leaving me alone for the first time since I'd woken that morning. With—finally—no eyes on me, I ducked out the door and hurried down the steps.

This compound was a maze of corridors and covered walkways, but I'd had a lifetime of traversing them and quickly found my way to a courtyard near the infirmary where herbs grew in raised beds. A grape arbor shadowed one corner, and there I waited, silent and still, until a slight figure in grey linen appeared from the archway on the opposite side of the courtyard.

Callista. A worker who served the infirmary, and the only person other than myself who knew how often I dreamed of flying or suspected that I harbored sentiment for anything other than the adoration of the crowds. I wasn't certain why she tolerated me, or this life, or anything about this place, but I was nonetheless grateful at the presence of one—just *one*—person who'd known me before fame struck.

The moon was rising, and silvery light cast across Callista's delicate face, sweeping brown hair, and graceful figure as she stopped at the edge of the grape arbor. A smile that could rival the dawning sun crossed her face as I stepped from the shadows. "Cyrus."

Relief flowed through my limbs, undoing some of the knots brought on by the chaos of the day. "Lis."

A few hurried steps brought her close enough to hug me. I closed my eyes and let her, the smell of herbs and clean linen washing through my senses before I released her and stepped back. "I didn't know if you'd be here. It's later than I expected."

"I heard the gathering might go late," she said as she looked into my face. The bright smile that had greeted my appearance now changed to concern. "And I heard what happened this afternoon—are you all right?" Her hands reached for mine, but I stepped out of her reach. Initial greeting aside, there were too many ways in which someone could touch me that I wanted no part of, especially with the wine-daze from earlier still wearing off.

"I'm fine. Don't worry about it." I crossed my arms. "It wasn't even because of me. It was a publicity stunt for the gryphon races."

"At least they didn't try to attack." Callista raised serious eyes to mine. "Was there some important meeting at the party? Octavian and the others weren't anywhere to be seen, and I heard Flavius bragging that he'd been invited."

"He *would* say that." I sighed, information coming together in a different way now that I'd had more time to think about it. "I think they had him there because of me." I pressed my lips together, unsure if I should tell her about the increasing odds. Callista already worried about me each time I stepped onto the sands, and I didn't want to add to her burden with the knowledge that my survival was no longer guaranteed. "They warned that revenue is falling as the races gain popularity, and they want me to help hold public interest."

Her dark eyes widened, then narrowed. "Which means..."

"My matches are going to be more difficult. Different opponents, more frequently. They want the odds to be steeper; make it more uncertain if I'll win every time. And if that's not enough, they're—" I scuffed a hand through my hair. "They're talking about...other things."

I wished I hadn't said it. Callista's jaw clenched and she flinched, as if the very words had hurt. And they likely had. I could still remember how shocked I'd been, the first time someone had paid for a night with me.

Gods, there were tears in her eyes.

"Please don't." Her words came out a desperate whisper. "Not this again."

I closed my fingers into a fist. "I swear, Lis, I'm trying to discourage them. I don't want it any more than you do."

"Promise?"

It broke my heart that she even needed reassurance. When we'd met, I'd been so wrapped up in the pursuit of fame and glory that I'd obey the board and sleep with anyone who paid highly enough—even if it wasn't exactly my choice. That willingness hadn't been part of me for years, not after I'd paused long enough to see Callista's gentleness, her cleverness, and how she held her sorrow and my fears with steady hands.

I *couldn't* promise, not really. She knew as well as I did that there were no refusals here, with every part of our lives overshadowed by the Arena. But still...

My hand skimmed to brush a wisp of hair from her face, lingering for a moment before I pulled away. "I promise. I'll do whatever it takes."

# CHAPTER IV

BASTIAN

I could hear it. The crowd. A throbbing, pulsing sound reverberating through layers of stone. It was echoed in the lower murmurs of the three other men in the armory as we prepared for our first battle. Somewhere across the Arena, four more men were doing the same.

The last two days had been fighting in sandy pits, being driven to show strengths and weaknesses to the trainers and affluent men who owned everything in the Arena down to the very breaths we breathed. And now, eight of us had been placed into teams and were preparing to fight.

An attendant slouched against the stone entry of the tunnel, looking boredly over us without seeing. I focused on cinching the poorly fitting leather breastplate, sloppily painted with a burst of yellow. My fingers worked out of long habit, some part of me feeling just as distant as the gap between the armor and my tunic. Like I hadn't decided yet if I was afraid of stepping onto the sands.

This was different from the restless energy and pooling adrenaline that sank into muscles right before a sure fight from the back of a gryphon, or in the moments before my boots touched down on bloody earth to continue the violence that came after first lines clashed and gryphons followed in a charge.

Vambraces snugged against my forearms. I had to work a little harder to get greaves over my boots. The molded piece was meant for bare calves. Small nicks in the leather and surface cracks around the buckles announced that they were also meant to be passed man to man as they died or lived. These were not the combination leather and metal armor pieces meant to keep a gryphon rider alive for more than one battle.

With the left greave finally in place, I dropped my foot from the low bench and straightened. There was nothing left on the table before me but a sword. I glanced left and right, but no other man had what I looked for. I frowned.

"Helmet?" I called to the attendant. In three days, my voice had not improved, still barely taken out unless to warn others away.

The man chuckled like I'd told the best joke he'd heard in days. "Helmet?"

Even some of the other sacrifices laughed.

"Hardly anyone wears a helmet. The crowds love a face."

*They love blood.*

"It's about recognition. If you start to win, they'll know you instantly."

*To win, you have to stay alive,* I thought bitterly. "Helmet," I repeated.

40

A bemused look creased his features, perhaps surprised that he hadn't swayed me with the eloquent description of a faceless crowd who were only here to witness violence. If they'd been to war and back, spending the last eight years of their life broadening the Empire's maps, they might not crave it so deeply. The attendant pointed to an arched door leading to another arming room.

I took my sword with me as I went. One touch to the handle and a scowl creased my face. Metal cheaply forged, with more cracked leather around the hilt. I was starting to think they were trying to hasten our deaths as much as possible.

The next room held stacks of armor against one wall and racks of weapons against another—swords, spears, flails, anything a man could want. And finally, helmets. I stayed in the center of the room, eyes sweeping over the array of helmets hanging off hooks. What should have been a simple task was now distorted by seeing helmets from every territory in the Empire. Different styles and needs. Simple infantry from the main forces, the shock troopers from the distant Egyean Mountains with bulky forehead pieces. Swooping lines of cavalry helmets. Dragon wrestler helms from the distant sands with a movable visor, their shimmering metal treated with dragon blood to protect against fire.

My lip curled. None of these would suit me.

*Goddess, help me,* I thought, surprised that the faint curse felt more like a prayer. The first to cross my thoughts in a month and three days.

And then I saw it. Tucked among the dragon wrangler helmets, similar enough that no one had known where to sort it. I crossed with quick steps to free the gryphon rider helmet.

This was kept in better condition, the leather more supple, the surfaces burnished even if no one cared to use them. The leather and cloth lining the interior was also fresh, no hint of mustiness. Now to pray that it would fit.

I pulled it on, and the sounds of the crowd muted. My next exhale dispersed some of the tremoring in my fingers, the following inhale bringing something steadier in its place.

It fit. The helmet flared a little at the nape of the neck, allowing for some protection for the space between breastplate and helmet. The attached faceplate angled like a low mountain peak to allow for wind to break across the face and not blind. Hidden slits where it was set over the main helmet, allowing the rider to breathe. A continuous eye slit over the faceplate allowing for full range of vision to the periphery—a must for aerial combat. And another small, angled piece over the eye slit to help funnel wind away from the eyes. The inch below my chin was protected at least, but the armor didn't match the helmet in protecting my throat. I fastened the strap and picked up the sword, weighing it in my hand.

Perhaps I'd die today, but at least I felt halfway like a soldier again.

The attendant shouted, and a surging roar came from the crowd in response. It was time.

I returned to the main room, bootsteps feeling lighter and more purposeful than they had in days. A hush followed my entrance before the murmurs returned, now edged in more nervousness. The attendant looked me over and shrugged before urging my team to follow him into the main tunnel.

Somehow I became positioned just behind the attendant as we marched up the sloping tunnel to the Arena gates. Perhaps it was long habit that sent me to the front of the line. One month and three days cannot kill two years of commanding squads.

"You four are out first." The man spoke. "Crowds feel restless today, so give 'em a show and really warm them up for the big fights after."

Anger tried to rise up and scorch the last of the apathy trying to cling to me. We'd received our instructions when selected from the mess hall yesterday. Four men against four, fight to the death, no holds barred. And a battle like that was not what the masses were truly here to see. We were bait, scraps dangled to whet appetite for the higher-profile fights that'd take the sand later today.

The brief thought of refusing teased, until the pressure of the scale against the top of my foot reminded me. I didn't know if I'd ever see Lyra again, but giving up now and dying pointlessly in the sands did not strike me as the way I wanted to enter the afterlife. Not without fighting to live, and seizing any small chance to see her again.

The gate creaked upward and I strode out, borne on the restless surge of the men behind me and the increasing roar of the crowd at the promise of battle.

Instead of open sands like I'd expected, jagged stone outcroppings stood in the center of the Arena, piled within jumping distance of one another. Larger constructions like wooden walls were scattered about, set at angles to the rocks and each other. And in a broad ring around it all, spears had been thrust point down in the sand.

We did not have time to scout and fortify it or make any sort of plan, as from another entrance to the Arena, our opponents charged. "Team" was a pitiful word, for as soon as combat approached, it became each man for himself, some racing to meet each other, others sprinting for the rocks. A man with a blue-spotted breastplate charged me with a wordless scream. I weighed the sword in my hand and settled to a ready stance, no time to get to the rocks myself. Instead, I set my back to the nearest wooden wall. There was no one to watch my back, so I had to trust in what I hoped was something sturdy.

The first clash of blades sent an unsteady shiver through the sword in my hand. I gritted my teeth in annoyance and set to trading blows as fast as I could. The man fell back before me, frantically parrying, until he overstepped a lunge and I kicked his feet out from under him. A more warlike cry jerked my attention up to another blue team member charging me with a spear.

I barked a curse, pivoting out of the way of the incoming strike and retreating. It gave the fallen man time to scramble to his feet and set against me once more. I retreated again, dodging spear strikes until my boot hit a rock. The men exchanged a slight glance of triumph at seeing me cornered. I dropped to a ready stance, waiting.

The spear snaked out again. I swiveled, catching the haft as it whispered by, driving into my own turn and yanking as hard as I could. The weapon joined me through the motion, a surprised cry from its former wielder coming after. As soon as I faced the rock behind, I started scrambling, spear in one hand, sword in the other, trying to gain altitude and distance.

Their cries came after me, and scuffling announced them following. Another prayerful curse toward the goddess and I leapt to the next set of rocks, mounded higher than my previous perch. My boots settled onto a flat enough space and I twisted, shifting my grip on the spear and throwing it once I had the men in view. One had started to straighten as he got his feet, only to receive the spear through his chest and hurtle to the sands. The second man backed off, sliding down with new caution in his eyes.

I took a moment to scan the battle. One yellow and one blue were down. Another man from my team engaged the fighter I'd just driven off. They set to chasing each other around the walls, caught in cat and mouse with sloppy sword strikes keeping them on equal footing.

Shouts announced another uneven pairing. Two blue were going after the third man from my team, sprinting and leaping between rocks. He was barely staying ahead of them. I headed for them, not stopping to overthink each jump and step on the uneven rocks.

My teammate's ankle twisted on his next landing, sending him to the stone with a panicked cry. The sound drove me faster, the memory of another red-haired soldier in trouble spurring me on. One more dangerous leap to a lower surface before I slammed my sword through the blue team's man who'd been about to stab down. My momentum and his weight took us dangerously close to falling to the sands, and I almost desperately threw myself backward.

My sword came free, and my knee stung where I hit the rock. The sound of another man dying drew me back to my feet, but it was due to the man I'd saved, now upright and dispensing of the last threat. He turned to me, eyes wide and lips parting as if to say something. But I turned away, bringing the last two men into view down below.

They still ducked and wove, bleeding in dozens of places. The noise of the crowd came rushing through my ears, rising and falling in eager and disappointed pitch as the men traded blows.

Another spear was angled on the next set of rocks. I jumped there and scooped up the spear. Jubilant shouts heralded one of my other allies finally falling to his opponent. The victor stood over the dead, shaking and not appearing to notice that he was the only one from his team still standing. Not noticing myself and my teammate on the rocks above.

But the crowd did.

They roared louder, and I could almost pick out what sounded like urging to turn, to take caution, for me to throw the spear.

Finally, the man turned and looked up. Panic set in before he raised his blade, thought better of it, and tried to run. I threw the spear and was rewarded with applause.

Bile rose in my throat as I slowly turned and saw cheering faces, disappointed expressions, money changing hands.

*This* was what I'd been kept alive for? I'd rather have had my head removed in a forested wilderness, left for wolves and crows. That seemed like the better end than this.

I made my way down from the rocks, striding toward the gate.

"Hey!" The other survivor dogged my heels. I ignored him. Ignored the attendant's almost mocking "congratulations," and turned into the arming room. Stripped off the armor and helmet and left them in a haphazard pile.

"Hey!" The red-haired fighter snagged my arm. "Thank you."

Confusion chased the gratitude when I didn't answer.

"What's your name?" he asked. I pulled my arm free and left, finding my way back to the courtyard and open air. Already becoming like the other servants and veterans here.

*If you're still here next week, I'll learn your name.*

I burst into the sunlight, weaving through men and chaos, another wagon already bringing in more bodies, and searched until I found the quietest corner I could to fight through the crushing sickness. I'd always served the gods, trusting in their mercy and guidance, knowing that a life of faithfulness would lead to an afterlife of peace. But this? What twist of fate or divine justice had sent me here for refusing to slaughter innocents hundreds of miles away? It was enough to keep my limbs shaking and eyes stinging for terrifying moments, until I mastered them and slid to the ground.

I'd survived today. But I was suddenly staring down empty days until I met my fate on the Arena sands and passed into obscurity. Name not even known, except on a list somewhere. Leaving behind a wife who might always wonder what happened to me.

She'd waited for me. Always waited. From the first time I'd seen her outside her father's stables caring for a gryphon, I'd been awestruck. But she hadn't spared me a glance, used to ignoring admiration and varying words from soldiers of all ages, hopeful trainees, and full-fledged riders. It wasn't until I'd happened to cross paths with her inside the stables, where she was attempting to treat a gryphon who'd slashed its leg in a scuffle, that we'd spoken. Years of gentling horses carried over to gryphons, and in return for my help, I got her name. And Lyra waited. For me to attain the Fifth Legion's colors and my own gryphon.

To fly to war and come back on short leaves over the next two years. For me to muster the courage to ask her father for her hand. And then after we'd tied dragon scale necklaces around each other's necks, she waited each time I left, and welcomed me back with open arms. Patient, as I shrugged off war and settled back into an easy routine at each other's side. The brightness she kept in our home as we laughed and lived for however long it was until I was called back to the skies always lingered with me. Latching into some corner of my heart to keep me moving through one day and the next, until I could make my way back to her.

But this time...she'd keep waiting, and wondering. And after what I'd just done on the Arena sands, I was almost glad that she'd never know. Fear threaded my mind. Perhaps I was already losing myself, and in another seven days, if I survived, I'd become something unrecognizable even to the gods.

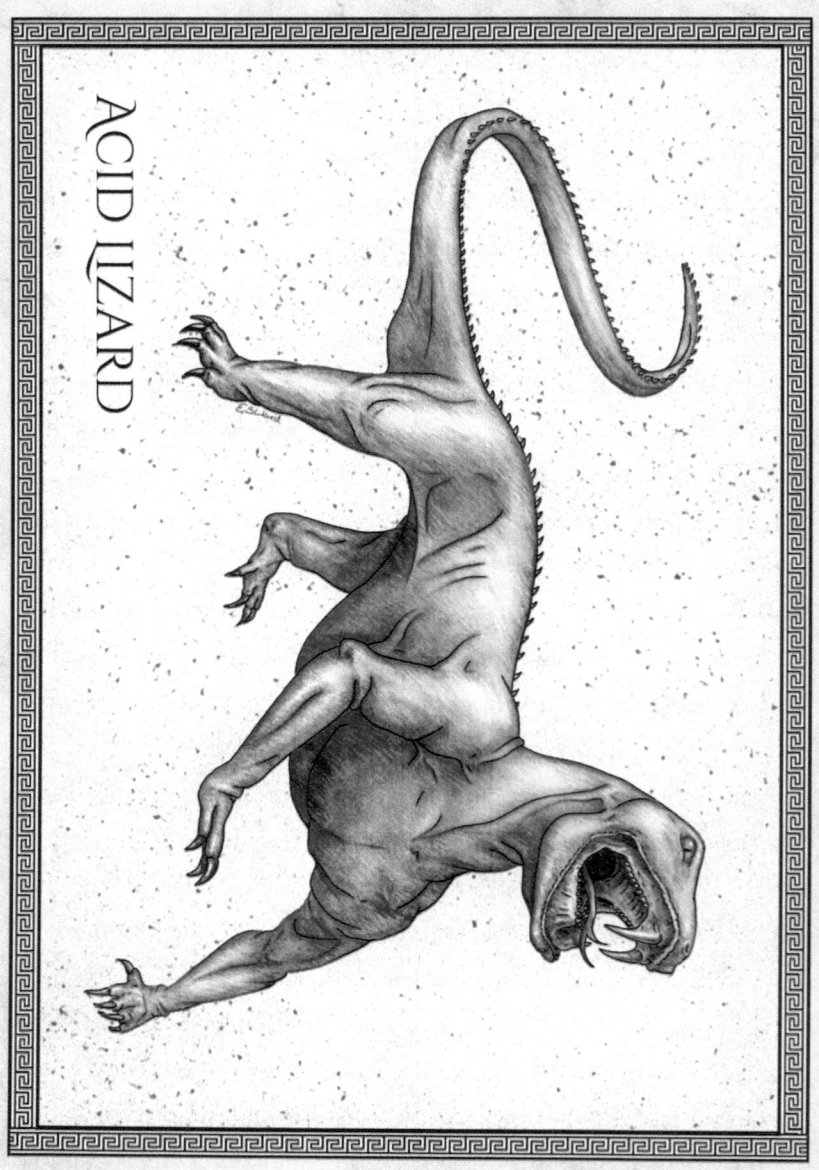

ACID LIZARD

# CHAPTER V

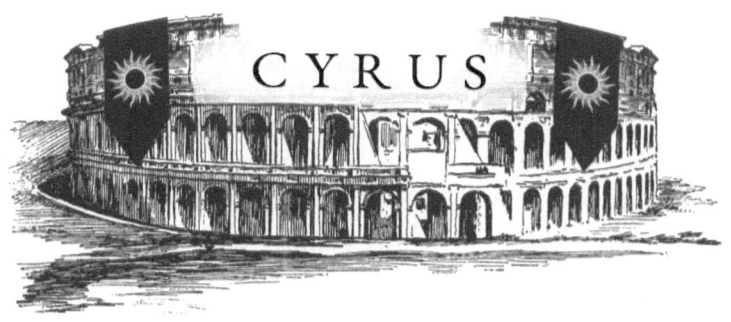

CYRUS

"That was...spectacular." Senator Tiberius sat back in his canvas chair with a satisfied sigh. "These were trainees? That one didn't even hesitate."

"I suspect this was their first fight." I leaned an elbow on the arm of my chair and balanced my chin on my hand as I stared down into the Arena. The board's private box was the best in the house, and I had a perfect view of the structures arranged on the sandy floor. Staff were already coming to clear the bodies of the fallen, consisting of the entirety of the blue team and two of the yellow. I shook my head dismissively as they pulled the first corpses out of view. "Most of them panicked and their organization fell apart. I don't know what they were thinking, but

I suspect it was just 'hit hard and try not to die.'"

"As opposed to..."

"Hit hard and try not to die, but faster than everyone else," I said with a laugh. "And keep out of the action until it's the right time. Only one of them thought to do that."

The Senator frowned. "Which?"

I pointed to the victorious team's tunnel, through which the two surviving yellow players had vanished. "The one in the helmet. I was watching him for most of the match."

"Ah, him." Tiberius nodded. "Whoever that was, he's ruthless."

I had to agree. I knew the look that said someone was considering mercy, and there hadn't been even a fraction of hesitation in that fighter's body language before pinning his last opponent to the ground. With that confidence, I wondered if it was the same man I'd caught sight of in the arrivals courtyard. Whoever he was, he'd catch the attention of someone more powerful than him with actions like that.

I had, once.

I'd advanced to a spot on the Dragonesque team, scale patterns etching my breastplate in iridescent blue-green. That day, before charging from the tunnel to face the Chimera team, Octavian pulled me to the side with specific orders. The following moment on the sands forever altered the course of my career.

*"No, Cyrus! Don't!" The disgraced Chimera player scrambled backward, feet kicking the sand as I resettled my sword in my hand. "Mercy!"*

*I hadn't realized that battle could be cold.*

*"You want mercy? Ask the gods."*

"Cyrus?"

A twist of surprise went through my stomach. How long had Tiberius been talking, while I'd been sitting here staring at the Arena?

"Sorry, I was trying to remember something." *Trying* not *to remember.* "What were you saying, sir?"

He laughed and nodded to the stands. "I was just saying that the crowd liked his decisive action. Maybe we'll be seeing more of that player—do you have any idea of what type of helmet that was?"

I shrugged. "I have no idea. I haven't worn a helmet since a teammate choked me with mine." It'd been years ago, during one of those moments in training when both Flavius and my tempers had flared. He'd later said it was a joke, but I hadn't trusted him the same way since—or afforded him the chance to do it again. "It looked like it could be a dragon wrangler's helmet? Don't they have full face coverings?"

"I'm not certain." The Senator stood easily from his chair with a nimbleness that belied his advancing age. The sight reminded me again of his background, the only Arena combatant in over a decade to survive a five-year solo career and live out all of our dreams of fame and fortune. "But I'll look into it. There's something about that one." He made to leave before half-turning to me. "You're fighting this afternoon?"

I threw a glance at the sky. The sun was approaching its zenith, casting shadows around the feet of the Arena obstacles. The Senator's invitation to watch the morning match had been a stroke of luck, and now I knew the arrangement of rocks and barriers as well as I knew the layout of my own quarters. Even with the promise of a greater challenge, I'd retain the advantage.

"I have some time. But you're right." I stood and rolled my neck, testing muscles that had gone stiff from sitting. "If you'll allow it, I'll report to the armory. Octavian told me that this will be an interesting one, so I hope you'll be impressed."

"I'm sure I will be." Tiberius tipped me a casual wave as I stepped out of the box. "May the odds be with you."

I ducked and weaved through staff corridors into the depths below the Arena. Another hour later, I'd changed into my match uniform, let the attendants check my appearance, and gotten something in my stomach that would help me last but not weigh me down. Practice was next, warming up my muscles and reflexes in a subterranean court with a trainer to coach me. Flavius was nearby at this point, also in uniform and looking unusually interested in the process—especially when the trainer handed me a shield.

"What's this?" I demanded, weighing the unfamiliar equipment in my hand before turning it over to examine the front. The circular boss in the center was painted gold, with rays of paint spread all around it. A sunburst, of course. I raised my eyes to the trainer. "I don't use these. I never do."

"You might want it today," the man warned, affixing it to my non-dominant arm. "I was told it would come in handy to block things."

His tone was mild as he said it, which only made my suspicions grow. "Fine." I shifted my feet to let him adjust the straps. The weight dragged at my arm, and I worked my hand in and out of a fist. If there was a chance I'd have to drop this thing, I wanted to ensure the functionality of my fingers. "Refresh my memory, then. How am I supposed to use this?"

Another hour and several frustrated moments later, I stood in the mouth of the tunnel. Outside, the crowds roared as my standard unfurled above the entry, and afternoon sun streamed in to paint the roof of the tunnel gold.

"Remember, Cyrus," Octavian said from behind me. "They're here to be amazed. They want a show, so give them one."

My temper was already fraying from the unexpected equipment change. I settled the shield on my arm and glared at him from behind it. "They'll get one." I turned my head to pin Flavius with a similar look. "You'd better not let me down if I need you."

"Wouldn't dream of it," he replied with a saccharine tone. The trumpet sounded, and he knocked my shoulder. "But you won't need me."

There was no time to reply. I hefted the shield, unsheathed my sword, and ran out of the tunnel to thunderous applause. The circle of rock formations and cantilevered wooden walls crouched in the center of the sand, and I made my way toward them.

The roar of the crowd had subsided, and a thread of uncertainty sounded from the stands. I knew why, and the knowledge sent me sprinting to one of the tallest rock formations. By this point, another armored figure should have emerged from the opposite tunnel to the same thunderous reception as I'd received. None had.

Which meant—

I heard it over the noise of the crowd, felt vibration under my feet as a trap door slammed open. A sibilant hiss wound through the field of obstacles, as from around the edge of the farthest wooden wall came a creature I'd never seen before. It stood almost as tall as my chest, a lizardy thing with dull, mottled brown-green-grey scales, hulking shoulders and head, and a tail that stretched a body length behind it. A line of barbs ran down its spine and continued along the tail, and suddenly the shield made sense.

Not that I could climb or maneuver with a massive wooden object weighing me down. And—gods, this thing was *fast*.

I'd already been halfway up the closest rock, but in the time it took to clear the distance, the creature had crossed the ring to snap at my sandaled foot. Without thinking, I twisted and swung the shield down to block the monster's advance, almost losing my balance as the thing slammed equally into shield and rocks. I lurched backward with a yell, bringing my foot up to slam into the creature's blunt snout and sending it flailing to the ground below.

*Height. Get height.*

I stepped back, then back again, feeling my way up the pile of rocks as the crowd roared. Another step brought me to the highest point, more than ten feet above the ground. Already the thing had regained its bearings and was scrambling upward once more, mouth gaping to reveal wickedly curved fangs and a forked tongue.

*It can't climb well.* Another step. *I'm better up here.* Resetting my feet to keep myself balanced. *Keep knocking it back, unless I can...*

My eyes lit on something atop the next formation over. A spear, left on purpose or missed during clean-up. A scrabble of claws and corresponding yell from the stands warned that the creature was almost to the top of the rocks. Adrenaline churning through my veins, I drove my sword down into its shoulder as its clawed foreleg came over the lip of the rock. The monster hissed and recoiled, giving me enough time to launch myself across the open space and land on the shorter rock formation.

I twisted my left arm and shook the shield straps loose. *This thing is useless.* The straps came free as the beast scrambled to the top of the rock opposite me, and I hurled the shield away before taking a knee to snatch up the spear—and not a moment too soon.

The creature gathered itself and sprang impossibly high, clawed forefeet reaching for me as it flew through the air. With no time to jump,

I dropped my sword and wrapped both hands around the spear shaft, angling it up, up, up to jam it through the creature's chest and out its shoulder as it plummeted over me.

We both toppled off the rocks and I landed with a gasp in the sand, wind driven from my lungs. The creature landed, thrashing, scarcely a foot from me. A curved set of claws raked across my shoulder and arm, and I yelled in shock and pain as something else scorched the outside of my shin.

*Sword.* I caught my breath and rolled frantically to the side. My sword had fallen with me, and lay at the foot of the rocks with its blade coated in wine-dark blood. My shoulder burned as I rolled again, enough to get a hand on the sword hilt and pull the weapon toward me.

The beast's breath was rattling in its throat, but it was still thrashing. The crowd's roar had reached a fever pitch, and I realized there should now be another fighter in the ring to distract or destroy my opponent.

Flavius.

I spat a curse onto the bloodied sand and hauled myself upright. The creature's tail lashed as it rolled to its feet, jaw sagging open and a horrible gurgle coming from its mouth. It charged, reeling. I thrust my sword through its neck before yanking the blade free and scrambling back.

Gods and monsters, it was still moving. And where was Flavius?

With a ferocious cry, I swung the sword as hard as I could. The first strike must've done more damage than I'd thought, and the single blow was enough to decapitate the creature. Exhausted, in pain, and with adrenaline pounding through my blood, I raised my sword and yelled at the sky. The crowd answered, the roar almost drowning out the sound of footsteps as Flavius—finally—jogged to my side.

"That enough challenge for you?" he shouted over the crowd, sword angled at the decapitated head with its still-snapping jaws.

"Yes." I slammed my sword into its scabbard and stalked to collect the shield from the dust. *Let the armory staff worry about the blood.* "No thanks to you."

The roar followed me into the tunnel, where Octavian greeted me with a proud smile. "You did it!"

I dumped the shield and sword into the attendants' hands, frustrated enough to snap, "Where in the skies was my backup? Was this part of your plan?"

By the look on my trainer's face, it might have been. I didn't wait for his answer, pushing through the curtained door of the armory and making for the infirmary.

Let the crowds cheer. I'd given them the show they were looking for.

And evidently, I'd be doing it alone from now on.


The adrenaline took a shockingly long time to wear off. By the time it did, I became acutely aware that I hurt all over, from aching ribs and back, throbbing pain in my shoulder, and a burning sensation everywhere the creature's blood touched.

The infirmary was cool and relatively quiet, but its white-linen, herbal-smelling expanse quickly became filled with onlookers as word spread of how the match had gone. I sat, exhausted, on a padded bench with my tunic off and teeth clenched as the grey-haired head physician—Atticus, I thought his name was—prodded the wounds across my arm and shoulder.

"We need to get these cleaned," he muttered. "And the blood has to be neutralized before it burns you. Let's have you lie back."

"No," I said immediately. There were too many people crowding the room, all looking at me with amazement and assessment in their eyes. I hadn't been badly hurt in almost a year, and I could only imagine what conclusions they'd draw if they saw me lying injured on a bed. "I'll be still. Just do what you need to do."

Atticus nodded understandingly before sweeping the room with an icy-eyed glare I wished I could rival. "If you don't have a reason to be here, get out. Yes, even you." He pointed at Octavian, who'd just stepped into the room with an attitude like he deserved to be there. "This wouldn't have happened if you'd done your job correctly. You might have command down there"—he gestured contemptuously in the direction of the armory—"but this is my domain. Get out, all of you."

The room began clearing with irritated murmurs as the physician returned to my side. "Give it another moment, then we'll get this taken care of. Not all monster blood burns, but..." Atticus frowned, lines creasing around his eyes with concern. "Have you had any experiences with our neutralizer agents?"

I shook my head. The last time I'd gotten this covered in monster blood, it'd been while facing a juvenile dragonesque at age eighteen, and I hadn't ranked high enough to warrant the usage of expensive medicine. The soap in the team barracks had worked to remove the caustic blood, but the burn scar still marked my leg.

"Well, it reacts with the blood to stop it from burning you further. It can be surprising the first time. I wanted to make sure you were forewarned." Atticus gave me what I assumed was meant to be a reassuring look before walking away to collect supplies.

I let my head fall back against the wall. Without the buzz of adrenaline or acute awareness of watching eyes, all I had left was exhaustion and trepidation. *This* was supposed to be the new level of ordinary for me? By the way Octavian had acted when I'd confronted him earlier, it seemed so. Though—I watched the infirmary staff as one emptied purplish earth into a bowl, then stirred while a sparkling cloud rose from it—the crowds *had* loved the intensity, both of my match and the trainee fight that preceded it this morning.

Maybe this *was* the best way to ensure the attention of the crowds. I just hoped the board would consider it enough.

"All right," Atticus said, returning with a handful of linen as his assistant brought the bowl of neutralizer. "Now that there's no one watching, you might want to lie down. This is going to hurt."

Gods, did it. I didn't know what alchemy inhabited the contents of the bowl, but it fizzed and stung anywhere that the creature's blood had touched. It was worst against my shoulder where the monster's blood and mine had mingled, and I struggled not to lash out at the physician's assistants as they held me still so their master could work. Finally, the wounds were clean and my skin was free of blood. Atticus painstakingly stitched the trio of gashes across the outside of my right arm before applying salve and a bandage. "There. You weren't hurt anywhere else?"

I stared at the ceiling, running the fight over in my head. It'd scratched my shin with its tail, but those cuts hadn't even bled. "I don't think so. Unless you count the fall."

"I do, but rest is all that will help with that." The lines framing Atticus's eyes crinkled as he said it, making me almost laugh at how absurd all this was. "You'll have to be more careful jumping around like that, though it's what saved your life this time." Atticus set the needle and thread to the side. "You'll have a lot of bruises, but I expect you're used to that. Let's get you a clean tunic and see if you can make it to your quarters. Callista, could I please have the—yes, thank you."

My breath caught in my throat with a quick indrawn gasp. Callista. Here. Of course, she would be—this *was* where she worked—but...

I pushed myself to an elbow as she handed the physician a folded stack of clothing. Our eyes locked, and not even a professional demeanor could hide her deep-seated worry at the sight of the new injuries.

I hadn't realized she was in the room. If I had, I'd have made sure I was sitting up, keeping silent, *anything* so she wouldn't see how much pain this was causing. I grabbed the tunic off the stack the physician offered me, sitting up and yanking it over my head with more energy than I felt. The motion pulled at the new stitches, and I swore as a spasm crossed my shoulder and chest.

The next moment, a pair of gentle hands slid between my hair and the neckline, tugging the tunic down without pulling the bandages.

"Easy," Callista murmured, her voice brimming with everything I knew she wished she could say. "Let me help you." Her hand skimmed the tunic sleeve and dropped to graze my fingertips before pulling away. "You've had a hard one, and there's no need to hurt yourself over something this small."

I could hear the words as clearly as if she'd said them out loud. *Take care of yourself. Don't take unnecessary risks. Stay alive. Promise me.*

"Thank you." I swallowed, risking a quick glance at Atticus. His back was turned as he dropped used equipment into a basin, and the other attendants had left the room. My hand closed over Callista's, fingers squeezing with all the reassurance I possessed. *I promise.* "Hopefully this is the last time I'm here for a while." I dropped her hand and laughed, "Maybe they'll let me have a few days off!"

"That doesn't seem likely," Atticus said with irritation. I tore my gaze from Callista's face as he said, "You were a bit distracted earlier, but a messenger came to ask if you were fit enough to attend some kind of gathering tonight."

I swore under my breath. "They want to make a statement. Fine. I'll play." I pushed myself up and nodded to the physician. "Thank you, sir. Your skills are exemplary, and I'm sure I'll be fighting fit in no time."

He inclined his head, accepting the compliment while understanding filled his eyes. "I'm certain."

I straightened my spine, raised my head, and stepped out of the infirmary without a backward glance. Sure enough, several pairs of eyes watched as I walked down the hall and into the sunlight. One of the men I recognized as Octavian's personal attendant, meaning my condition would be officially noted soon enough.

I could hear the gossip already. *He survived increased odds and won without a backup. The golden sun still reigns.*

They could say whatever they wanted. For now, I just wanted to rest.

# CHAPTER VI

BASTIAN

T he early morning air greeted me with the wisping tease of the sea. Barely there, but enough to stir up the notion of freedom and memories of the Meridian Islands, where I'd been born and lived five years before the Empire convinced my father to bring his family to the mainlands to train their long-limbed cavalry horses.

This was the first time I'd sensed anything like salt in the air. But this was also the first time I'd heard the Arena mostly silent, pretending to be abandoned in the minutes before the sun rose.

It was only because I had chased sleep all night, fending off the memories of the fight, the way I'd thrown that spear without hesitation. There were so many other memories from eight years of war trying to claim space in my tired head that I finally gave up and went outside. The barracks were lines of men against the wall on rough sleeping pallets. I'd slept in more comfort in my two years as an infantry soldier than I did here.

Talk ran that if you impressed both the crowds and the board in fights, you moved out of the main hall into rooms with more privacy, cots, different bathing areas, climbing your way up the building levels as you gained more fame. The top floor held the solo fighters, the men with the bright banners that hung from the Arena top. At least one had already been removed in my four days here, marking the fragility of both life and fame.

I glanced at the banners stirring idly in the tempting breeze. Talk had run wild yesterday, until even my numbed senses attuned to it. The fighter with the golden sun had barely survived a battle yesterday against some new lizard-like creature. Some claimed to have seen more like it in the bowels of the Arena, others whispered that the fighter was barely clinging to life in the infirmary. Still more said that he'd walked back to his quarters with barely a scratch.

A few said that after almost five years, his sun might finally fade.

A clanging screech echoed and I instinctively looked up. The sky was empty, but my heart raced. *Gryphons.* It came again, bouncing off the stone. The voices of men followed it, calmer and unpanicked. My feet moved before I realized, carrying me toward that sound.

Another cry guided me toward the stables, through a narrow tunnel that ran along the Arena wall. An archway led into another courtyard, barricaded from the stables by walls of iron bars reaching well above my head.

A flash of golden red heralded a mass of fur and feathers launching forward to sink claws into a practice dummy. It knocked the stuffed armor over and settled to tearing away the head, raw meat spilling from the broken fabric.

I settled back on my heels, almost smiling at the sight of the gryphon contentedly tearing at the meat. Some of my former men followed the Arena fights when we were stationed outside the city, and enough of them cared that rankings and results were carried out to the front. I knew gryphons were used in the fights, I just hadn't seen them before now. Hadn't heard them.

It finished off the meat with a gulp and pushed to its paws, tail lashing and wings spreading as it looked around. Something rolled from another gate and it crouched, head tilting as it regarded the wooden sphere. My hand curled around one of the bars, and I smiled softly, watching it pouncing and batting until the ball broke apart along a seam and more meat was revealed.

Even though horses were what I knew best, I'd avoided the cavalry legion in some stubborn attempt to prove I was making my own way. It didn't take long in the infantry for my feet to regret that decision. I'd started to consider talking my way into the cavalry, when I'd seen the gryphon scouts up close for the first time. Until then, in all my twenty-one years, I'd never considered *flight*. But after watching the golden creatures soar that day, it was all I could think about.

Another screech sounded, this time above us. I looked up, catching sight of two winged figures sailing overhead. More gryphons. I'd heard the talk running about the gryphon racing sports and the mock attack on the day I'd arrived. But this was too early for attention-seeking riders, and these gryphons flew at a relaxed pace. Out for an early morning flight, or warm-up.

Rustling returned my focus to the Arena gryphon. It crouched, head tilted up, a softer rumble breaking as it watched its kin above. It gave mighty flaps of its wings, and breath caught in my throat for a moment, thinking I'd see it take flight. But its paws remained firmly on the ground, and it gave another mournful cry as the others disappeared from sight.

My heart fell. "What have they done to you?" I murmured, seeing it even as I asked. The flight feathers were clipped, keeping the creature bound to the ground and the Arena.

It tore at some place deep inside, though I should have expected it. They weren't here for riding, they were here for sport and slaughter.

"Commander?" a hushed voice asked.

I turned, habit sending me to acknowledge the title before I thought better. A familiar face looked back, a little more lined than I remembered from two years ago. Titus wore the sandy brown and red tunic of the stable workers. A former gryphon rider too injured to fight could still find work caring for the beasts.

"I thought I'd caught a glimpse of you yesterday, but thought my mind was surely playing tricks," he said. "What are you doing *here*?"

The scents and sounds of gryphons and face of a former soldier combined to bring something familiar and prompt an answer. "The army no longer had need of me."

Titus crossed his arms, scarred face twisting in disbelief. Some warmth sparked in my heart, that even with two years between our last meeting, he believed me to be an honorable man. "You should have been commanding the entire Legion, not fighting for your life here," he said stubbornly.

The last three days had seen the more vocal trainees trading stories, trying to outdo one another with reasons they'd been sent. Some tried to protest their innocence, but were quickly drowned out. I'd not been asked, and was not jumping to offer my story.

But to Titus, perhaps I would. "They thought differently." The faint scoff that now passed for my laugh escaped. "Soldiers are meant to obey orders, and not even commanders are exempt from that rule."

Disbelief edged his short laugh. "I'd never have thought it." His face fell quicker than the man yesterday. "What about your wife?"

Any remaining shreds of warmth left from seeing the grounded gryphon and a former soldier vanished. I turned away.

"Commander." He stepped after me.

I whirled, halting him with the sudden ferocity of the movement. "I am no longer a commander, Titus. I'm a slave, and doomed to die here. Lyra will never know."

He didn't flinch from my intensity. "What if she could?"

I didn't dare parse through the meaning. If there was a way to get a message to her, Titus might be it. Like others here, he had no slave earring and would be free to come and go. But for what? To see Lyra, then die on some nearing day? Let her see what I might become with more fights? I couldn't bear to see horror in her eyes directed at me instead of gentle laughter and love.

"She will *never* know," I said and strode away. The cry of the gryphon chased after me, and I tried to outpace it.

I retreated into the barracks, the inhabitants barely beginning to stir. The open air no longer offered sanctuary and the mass of bodies here would only make me feel more trapped. Instead, I found the narrow stairs that led below, risking the feeling of certain entombment in the dark, silent tunnels.

The painted marks on the walls were the only way I felt confident

I would not lose my way. A few lamps were already lit, likely by early-rising servants who kept the Arena running. My fingers traced stone as I walked, my boot steps whispering back at me. Voices stirred from another hall, but I had no desire to run into anyone here. I ducked down the nearest split. Gentler light flickered and danced deeper in the corridor. Keeping fingers on stone, I crept farther down the passage to investigate.

Wide niches had been hewn into the walls. Candles burned before small, carved wooden figures, surrounded by offerings. I stepped closer, drawn like a moth to the sight.

The gods. Someone, sometime, had found a way to bring the gods into this place. I almost retreated from here too, but the part of me that had always left offerings at the goddess's shrine, praying for her winds to uplift wings, bade me stay.

I found her among the niches, bits of food offerings—bread, lumps of cold pottage—intermixed with small shells from the coast, their interiors painted blue to mark her favor. She was the patron of the sea, and the winds and rains that came with it. My parents had kept her practice once leaving the Islands, passing it to me. Sometimes my mother spoke of an older god, but my father would dismiss the idea with a wave, saying the goddess had always looked out for us.

There were men and women in temple robes who came to the exterior wall, bartering and passing tokens through the iron bars to those who had something to give. I had nothing, not even a bit of bread to lay at her feet as I asked her *why. Why did this happen to me? What law did I break?*

Or did the gods sometimes seek entertainment the way humans did?

I scanned the line—some niches were full, bursting with offerings mounded around the statues. Others were sparse. The gods all had temples in the city and ones scattered through the Empire's territories. Some of the deities had even been taken from conquered lands and given places like they'd always belonged.

They all stared serenely out, faces blank. It wasn't like it would be different at a temple, except the figures would tower in carven marble. Perhaps I was just looking for something more real, something I could grab and shake and demand answers from.

I turned back to the goddess, fury masquerading as despair hitting me harder than a charging gryphon.

"*Why?*" It ripped hoarse and strangled from me.

She did not answer.

My hands curled into fists. I wrenched away, striding deeper into the hall to lose myself in the Arena underbelly, when a faint flick of motion sent me whipping toward another alcove. It was just a mouse, whisking away as soon as it had my attention. It had knocked over a stub of a candle, and the light guttered weakly.

My rage vanished as I took in the statue with one meager offering of herbs that retained scant freshness.

"Forgotten too?" I whispered. I righted the candle, and the light cast onto the statue. A craggy featured man, eyes wise even carved in wood. The draping robes of an emperor covered his broad-shouldered frame, and his hands cupped like he wanted to reach out and carry something for me. This was the First God. The one they said had made the world and brought the other gods to being. Some even claimed the others weren't gods at all, but servants. Either way, the First had been lost in the multitude.

And he had been lost here too. My mother would wave incensed prayers in his direction if she felt the goddess wasn't enough. *They say he sees everything, Bas. That he still watches us even if we don't look back at him.* I'd nodded, wide-eyed at the thought of someone more powerful than the goddess. *Don't forget him,* she'd say, almost fearfully reverent, like she wasn't sure if he was safe or something to frighten children with.

A scoff caught in my throat. "I don't think anyone's looking," I told the statue, and left the forgotten god behind.

## CYRUS

My words to the physician proved overly optimistic. I survived the society event on will and charisma alone, repeating the story of fighting the lizard until my voice wore out and my ears rang with the accolades of the admiring. As far as anyone knew, I'd come through a high-stakes fight with minimal damage, proving, unfortunately, that the board's plan of having me appear in public so soon after victory was a success.

Once returning to my quarters, I collapsed into bed. I'd hoped to fall asleep immediately, but that proved more difficult than I'd expected. The gashes across my shoulder throbbed incessantly, and the warmth of caustic burns was slowly spreading to encompass my whole body. Eventually I fell into dreams where the monster slashed my skin over and over until I woke, gasping, only to plunge again into the dark.

I didn't mark the passage of time—or realize I'd become feverish—until a cloth pressed against my face and the voice of one of my attendants sounded from nearby. "He's burning up. Someone get the physician."

If Atticus was seen coming or going from my quarters, rumors would spread faster than news of my injury had. Perception of weakness was something that could spell destruction, and with how narrowly I'd won this match, it was the last thing I could afford.

"No," I mumbled. "No physician. Water?"

The edge of a cup pressed against my lips, and a hand slid behind my head as one of the attendants pulled me upright enough to drink. "You're scheduled to fight again tomorrow, Cyrus. We have to get you on your feet."

I struggled to an elbow, then sat up. Hunching into myself and containing a shiver, I looked for the sun outside the latticed windows. "Wait, what day is it? How long ago..."

"Yesterday." The attendant handed me the water, watching me carefully as I drank. "And it's afternoon now. They already posted the lists."

"Tomorrow?" I opened and closed my hand. Stretched my arms, then wished I hadn't. "I..." A shiver seized my limbs. Perception of weakness or not, if I walked onto the sands like this, I'd be dead. "Fine. If you can get him here without anyone seeing. No one else can know."

"I'll be discreet," the man assured me. "But would it be so bad if it was known...no?" He stepped away as I shook my head. "I'll go, then. Please try to rest."

I lay back and—for once—did as I'd been told. That fact alone told me how bad this really was. Ordinarily, I'd have been up as soon as possible, ready to prove that I could absorb a blow and keep fighting.

Atticus arrived an hour later, accompanied by one of his assistants—and Octavian.

"Gods," the fight coordinator swore as soon as he saw me. "What happened?"

I wasn't sure if the concern in his voice was over my well-being or the possible failure of his plans, but it was at least a *little* reassuring.

Atticus knelt beside the bed and ran his fingers across the bandages that hid my upper arm. "These shouldn't be causing this...we cleaned everything." He frowned and rested a hand against my right leg. "You're *absolutely certain* that nothing else happened during that fight?"

"Nothing!" I protested, more than a little fearful now that I couldn't hide how I was feeling. "I fell, it fell with me, its claws got my arm, I—ow!" I gritted my teeth against a curse as the physician removed his hand from my shin. "All right, its tail did scratch me, but that didn't even hurt!"

Atticus gave me a scathing look and pulled the blanket away from my legs. An immediate chill washed over me, and I wrapped my arms to keep myself from shaking. The scratches that had hardly bothered me yesterday were now angry red, some weeping clear fluid.

Atticus narrowed his eyes at the wounds. "This," he said, "is what I meant when I asked yesterday if you'd been hurt anywhere else, you idiot."

I had to laugh. It made my head ring, and the room spun in response.

Octavian's eyes widened, and he asked, "Will he be able to fight if he's like this?"

"No!" the physician snapped, already pulling off his wide-sleeved robe and making for the washbasin. "Look at him! You want the public to see their hero like this?"

Time was beginning to shred apart again, no matter how hard I tried to keep a grasp on the words flowing around me. They were arguing, I could tell that much, but I was beginning to find it difficult to care. If anything, it was hilarious.

"All right," Octavian finally huffed. "We can push it by a day. Cyrus..." His voice drifted to me from a long distance away. "I'll see what I can do. Just get better. We still need you."

# CHAPTER VII

BASTIAN

T he throbbing roar of the crowd followed me into the tunnel. Even with only two fights to my name, I was starting to learn the pitches and sounds of the spectators like I might learn the cues of a temperamental gryphon. They were pleased.

Two men followed me inside, the only ones left of another eight who'd stepped onto deceptively open sands.

I ripped off my helmet, spattered with blood and crusted sand. My team had discovered the traps first. One released pressurized acid to a wild gasping roar from the spectators. Later, I'd been driving an opponent back until steel jaws clamped about him. Killing him had been mercy rather than survival.

Each step had turned to panic, unsure if or how another trap would be triggered. Wild blows were traded. I'd been knocked to the ground as it shuddered and opened up around another man. I think I'd triggered that trap, faintly remembering a *click* and pressure under my boot before I'd been cast to the sand. A red team fighter had set upon me, but even with the numbness around my heart I'd still been quicker.

My bloody sword clattered to the table, my helmet slammed down after. I'd had to go looking for it again, and the same attendant as two days ago hadn't jeered as much.

"Bastian." The red-haired man, still alive, spoke. I don't know how he'd gotten my name.

I kept my back turned.

"Him," another voice interjected. I pivoted as two armed men rushed me. Fight still racing in my veins sent me lunging for my sword. Before I could reach it, one grabbed my arm and yanked backward. A blow glanced across my face, stunning me enough for both arms to be wrestled behind me.

The stocky man I recognized as Octavian, overseer of every fighter and battle, stonily regarded me. "Who are you?"

My arms were pulled tighter. The other two men still in yellow-blotched armor had pressed to the side, watching warily. *What is happening?*

"Someone looking for honor and glory in the Arena." I spat at our feet.

He smiled thinly and reached to the arming table to pick up my helmet. "What is this?"

"A *helmet.*"

He set it aside and turned to undo the straps of my breastplate. Having

72

so many men crammed close, my limbs helpless, sent me jerking futilely against them. Remembrance of another moment like this kept my anger hot. Octavian pulled the armor away and tossed it carelessly aside. Then punched me hard in the stomach.

I cursed as I was yanked upright.

"What *kind* of helmet?" Octavian searched my face, looking for *something*. When I didn't immediately answer, he struck again.

"A gryphon rider helmet," I said, and wheezed another curse on him and his mother.

"Where did you get it?"

"Your cursed armory," I spat.

He looked over his shoulder. The attendant must have nodded, since Octavian settled back to regarding me. "And the boots?"

"*Mine.*"

"It's a poor disguise then." He appeared to think before punching again.

"Disguise for what?" I was hauled back upright.

"You'd think the gryphon races would have sent someone smarter."

"What?" Perhaps my head had been hit in the Arena.

"Who sent you?"

*The Gryphon Legion Commander and a traitor.* I didn't speak it even after another blow, this time to my face. The man on my left wrestled my sudden weight off him, pushing me onto unsteady feet. They were looking for some spy, honing in on me for being stupid enough to reach for remnants of my past and not thinking of anything broader like the rising competition.

"I was sent by my Legate from the Chinerean front lines," I said. "The Empire has no need of a disgraced gryphon rider beyond *enter-*

*tainment."*

Octavian smiled thinly. "A likely story."

"It's true, sir," one of the yellow fighters said cautiously. "I was on the wagon with him."

I looked at him to actually *see*, and recognized him as a man I'd spent weeks crammed into a cart with.

"All the way from the north," the slave said.

Octavian huffed. "Well, perhaps instead of a plague, the gods sent us a gift." Calculating shone bright in his eyes as he returned his attention to me. "You've gained the attention of high men," he said. "Keep fighting like you have and you might find that disgraced soldiers can find new life."

He gestured to his men, who slammed me against the wall and left me to crumple as they stepped away.

Octavian loomed over me. "I will still verify this story against the intake lists, Bastian Lytos," he said, seeming to relish having my name without my consent. "And remember that I can help you rise or I can see you killed like that." He snapped his fingers. He turned away, pausing by the attendant only long enough to tell him, "He keeps that helmet." Then he and his men were gone.

I coughed as I slumped against the wall, turning my head to spit out a bit of blood. The two men regarded me in wary respect.

"You fought on gryphons?" the red-haired man asked.

I nodded, too weary of everything to bother ignoring him. This story would likely spread, and perhaps I *did* care enough to make sure there were elements of truth in it.

"What did you do to be sent here?" the other asked, seeking answers like a hound.

"Disobeyed orders." I dragged my foot to set it against the floor, preparing to push into standing. A deeper ache bloomed in my stomach at the movement.

Later. I'd stand later.

"You're not from the races?" Red Hair asked.

I scoffed. "It's a poor plan to send a scout into certain death. How would you get a report back?"

He nodded and turned to divesting his armor. After a beat, the other did the same.

"It's been two fights I've made next to you on the sands," Red Hair said. "Octavian said you'd drawn notice. Perhaps they'll make us a team with your lead." *And the rest of us will rise too.* It was clear in his voice and the way confidence returned to his body.

I shook my head, slowly climbing to my feet. I'd been wrong yesterday. Someone *was* looking, and perhaps they thought to make me a god myself, or leave me as a bloody offering to the Arena.

The next day seemed to fulfill the red-haired fighter's expectations. The three of us surviving from the yellow team were called to training in the early morning hours. Another man was brought to join us, returning us to a team of four. Octavian stood at the end of the sandy, cordoned-off area. His assessing eyes swept over me, searching for any sign of weakness from the bruising darkening my stomach. I stared back until he perhaps found what he was looking for by the slight smile he gave.

"You will fight again tomorrow as a team, and it won't be human opponents." He gestured to the burly trainer standing next to him and the spears lying on the ground. "He'll teach you what you need to know." And then he was gone.

We'd been given our armor for training, and wielded blunted swords. My helmet had been wordlessly handed to me. I couched it against my hip as the trainer started outlining our next fight.

There was still no word of what we'd be fighting, even two hours later when we were soaked in sweat and some frustration. But he seemed pleased enough that we could work together long enough to fight some creature and perhaps even give the crowd enough of a show.

I pulled off my helmet, working muscles in my jaw that were stiff with bruises from Octavian yesterday and clenching today. The three other men moved off after slight nods to me. It had not been lost on me either that I'd been positioned as the leader. It was also not unnoticed how many men were hanging around to watch, and how the whispers had changed through the barracks as the men I'd fought with made sure to sit closer to me at dinner. Perhaps I should not stand like a commander anymore, but my muscles wouldn't let me slouch.

Lower-level servants in simple tunics took our weapons and armor before we were pointed in the direction of the bathhouse. My feet dragged across the bustling courtyard, my body too alive from the movement, my mind spinning too fast from the way things were changing by the minute to settle yet. I wanted height, some quiet to think over it.

By the sounds, the crowds were happy with whatever was happening inside the Arena. There were people aplenty outside the gates too, peering through the barred wall to get a glimpse of the exterior training courts, women coyly gaining men's attention and temple servants trying to barter offerings. I glanced up at the towering edifice, wondering if there was a way to climb over the barracks and escape from the constant press and noise that only faded in the dead of night.

"Bastian!" A wild cry wrenched my focus to the external wall, searching in frantic hope for the owner among the clustered groups.

"*Lyra!*" I found her and ran, shoving around men until I practically slammed against the iron bars.

"Bastian!" she half-sobbed, half-laughed. The bars were too thick and closely set for me to kiss her, but I could reach through to press hands to her suntanned cheeks, wipe the tears streaming from her deep blue eyes. Her hands clutched at the front of my sweaty shirt.

For a moment, we just soaked in each other's presence, and everything faded out behind me. Then reality crashed over me. "What are you doing here?"

She released my shirt and reached up to brush sweaty hair from my forehead. "A man named Titus came last night. He said you were here." Her voice was low and clear, often pitched in singing as much as talking.

"He what?" Anger started to rise again, until her touch against my cheek stilled it. Even with bars between us, she was still tempered steadiness.

"He said you'd saved his life years ago, and he thought to try to save yours now. What happened, Bas?" she whispered.

"Lyra..." I closed my eyes, resting my forehead against the bars.

A soft squawking sound answered me, something like an affronted gryphon kit. I opened my eyes in surprise to take in Lyra's shy smile, finally noticing the scarf wound about her chest. And when a small hand reached from under the dark green wrap, I thought my heart might give way.

Lyra pulled down a fold of the scarf to expose a chubby face and slowly blinking eyes. "Meet your son."

"My..." Shock still chained my movements.

"I knew only a few weeks after you left. I almost ran after the army to tell you myself." She laughed softly as she angled her shoulder to the bars and tilted the babe to face me.

He had a thatch of black hair from me, his mother's deep blue eyes, his grandfather's chin. I reached tentatively out to brush his hand. His fingers closed around mine and a smile split his face, beaming like he knew who I was.

A year and a month, and in that time I'd had a son. It cracked through my heart sharp enough that it seemed like the sound should be heard even in the Arena.

My vision blurred precariously as my son kept hold of my finger. "I missed it." The words tremored from me.

Lyra's laugh soothed some of the ache. "I was unattractively swollen and grumpy for most of it. And said some uncomplimentary things of you. You didn't miss much." A tear lingering on her lashes belied the light words. "I named him August."

The babe looked at her at the sound of his name, giving her another bright smile. He released me to reach for her face, cooing softly.

"It's a good name," I said.

She smiled and adjusted him so she could face me again, features falling to seriousness. "Bastian, what happened?"

"Does it matter?" I asked, some of that earlier dull acceptance falling over me.

"Yes," Lyra said fiercely. "Yes, it does. I know *you*, and you would never do anything dishonorable enough to be sent here. And if..." Her jaw trembled. "If, someday, I have to tell August of his father, I want him to know the truth."

*If. Someday.* She naively hoped I would walk out of here, be there for the life of our son.

My forehead rested against the cold iron. If someone should know the truth of what happened, best it should be my wife, who could then remember me as I was.

"There were several villages causing trouble. Raids. Ambushes." Not ready to lay down weapons and surrender to the Imperial standard. "We were ordered to put a stop to it. To remove the threat."

A small gasp let me know she understood. Her free hand slipped through and squeezed around mine.

"When we arrived, it was old men, women and children. Babes." I looked to August. I hadn't known it then, but I'd had a son much like the one a defiant woman had clutched to her chest when claws settled and boots thumped to the ground.

"I couldn't give the order," I whispered, and the pressure of her hand tightened. "I warned them to submit instead. My disobedience could be ignored one time by my men. The second time, some murmured. But a third, and fourth?" I shook my head slightly. It was my second-in-command who'd made the report, a man I'd trusted with my life for two years. "After that, I was questioned. My men were as well, and the truth came out. I was stripped of my armor and rank, and shoved into a slave wagon bound here."

"Bastian."

I shook my head. "I spared them and for what? For a few more days before someone who wouldn't hesitate brought more troops? To be sent here to die while losing myself?"

Her hand found my cheek again, brushing more gently as she finally saw the bruised skin. And I could not look at her when stillness fell over her and she touched the slave earring.

"They cannot do this!" Anger overlaid the sorrow in her eyes as I finally met her gaze. "You are a free man. A soldier."

"They can, Lyra. They *did*." I inhaled sharply to rein in the anger and helplessness I'd already battled against. I wouldn't let her be bruised by it. "There is no choice for me here." A half lie closer to ashy truth after the quick kills I'd willingly made in the Arena. No choice if I wanted to keep surviving. And looking at her, *at my son*, I desperately wanted to.

"You've already fought?" she asked quietly, and I nodded miserably. "When do you again? I'll come—"

"Lyra, no. I don't want you to see. I don't want him anywhere near this place." I'd beg if I had to. And I'd already stood here too long, and too close, that it might be noticed that this was more than just bartering for gods' offerings.

"Then I'll come and find you again," she said stubbornly.

"No, don't. I..." My traitorous hand reached up and brushed her jaw. "I don't want you to one day come and wait endlessly. I don't..."

She caught my hand and pressed a kiss to it. "I won't leave you like this."

I shook my head. "If, someday, you tell him about me, tell him I died on the front lines. Tell him I died a proud gryphon rider, not trapped here."

"Surely there's some way to get you out?" She caught my hand as I tried to withdraw.

In all the tales, in all the rumors, it was only how to rise. Never how to leave. Even the champions at the top were not free. But looking into her eyes, at my son grabbing a fistful of her dark, wavy hair, I could not manage yet to tell her the truth.

The only way out was death.

# CHAPTER VIII

CYRUS

W hen the dreams changed from death on the sands to flying over them, I knew the fever was breaking. By the second day after being injured, the sun no longer felt too bright, the air no longer stifling or freezing, and I was able to get up and work the knots out of my muscles. By the third day, I was holding my sword in hands that didn't shake, and Atticus's admonitions had returned to, "Be careful today."

"I will," I promised, wincing as I worked my arm back and forth. The bandages rasped against the edge of my tunic sleeve, and I considered removing them before reason asserted itself. The crowds knew I'd been injured. There was no reason to hide the facts.

"Do you have any idea of what you're facing today?" Atticus asked, an edge to his voice implying he was as frustrated by the coordinators' course of action as I was. "Not another of those *things*, I hope."

I shook my head. "Another solo fight, to the death." A flash of amusement came with that thought, and I smiled—maybe I *was* feeling better. "I just hope it's not mine."

Atticus snorted before making a mark on the tablet he'd brought with him. "Glad to hear you sounding like yourself. You're reporting downstairs soon?"

"I am." We'd followed the usual preparatory routine—massage, food, appearance check, warming up—in my quarters. "I'm not worried." A lie, but better than the truth. I'd felt fine an hour ago during practice, but now I was as tired as if I'd spent the whole morning training.

"Well, here." He reached into the bag of supplies he'd brought from the infirmary and handed me a clay vial sealed with wax. "They told me to make sure you drank this immediately before reporting. It'll help hold off the fatigue."

"Thanks." I pried the wax off, but hesitated before downing the liquid. "You're sure it's all right?"

"I'm sure. Octavian gave the order himself. I think you had him worried."

Worried, like he had been other times when he'd pushed me too hard and I'd broken under the pressure. The moments were rare, but the worry—the regret—that he showed then was enough to convince me to get up and press forward.

*Rise or die trying.*

Even now, with the promise of harder fights to come, and even worse for me if I couldn't keep up. With a grim mental shrug, I swallowed the tart, salty liquid and made a face as a resinous aftertaste coated my tongue. Whatever it was, I hoped it would help.

Normally, my passage to the armory only garnered a few stares, but today it felt like everyone in the southern courtyard was watching as I left my room. I kept my head high and my shoulders straight, only letting myself slouch once I'd gotten into the stairwell leading to the tunnels.

I was halfway to the armory when a familiar voice fell on my ears. "Feeling better?"

"No thanks to you." I'd been steadying myself against the wall, but now I pulled my hand away from the stone. "You'd better be on your mark today."

Flavius sauntered down the steps to walk ahead of me into the tunnels. "Course I will. Why would you ever doubt?"

I snorted. "Why ever." I eyed him as he went around the corner. *You're just disappointed I survived.*

The atmosphere in the armory was tense today, the hum of the crowds overhead already reaching a fevered pitch. I stood in silence as armor was tightened and checked, my sword inspected. The medicine the physician had passed me was doing *something*—at least, I didn't need to stabilize myself against the wall any longer.

"All right," the fight coordinator told me. It wasn't Octavian today, which, given how concerned he'd seemed earlier, had me confused and a bit worried. "One opponent, to the death. And"—he caught my eye with something like concern—"some of the board are here. They heard what you did with the lizard and are hungry for more. Don't take foolish risks, but give them what they want."

*So that's where Octavian is.*

Anger stirred in my blood. "Concerned", indeed. It seemed his *concern*

83

had only lasted long enough to ensure that I'd muster the strength to keep fighting.

It shouldn't have surprised me, but the reality still stung.

The gate swung open. My feet moved on their own, carrying me into the sunlight. I immediately cast my gaze at the board's private box. Sure enough, there sat my trainer, along with several of the others who'd conspired four days ago to throw me into a match with no backup. Only the gods knew what new things they were concocting to make my life more interesting. If the gods were watching at all.

*You want a show? Try this.*

"What were you thinking?" Octavian demanded. "What type of show was that?"

"I won! What else did you expect?" My muscles ached, but I pushed the fatigue away and retorted, "You trained me to be ruthless, to end the fight before it got too dangerous." I flung a hand in the direction of the Arena, where scarcely a quarter hour prior I'd annihilated my opponent within the first few minutes of the match. "I did that—I *won*, just like you taught me—and they loved it! How can you be unhappy about this?"

Octavian gave a deep sigh. "Yes, win. Always. But not like that." He reached out to flick the top of my ear. "You killed him before the people had the chance to see who you were facing! Where's the showmanship in that?"

"I won," I insisted, rubbing my ear with a grimace. "I got him, then I got his second. That's two on one, and you know they weren't easy marks, either."

He opened his mouth to yell at me again, when a clatter of footsteps on the stairs announced one of the other trainers. "Cyrus, I—oh." He pulled up short when he saw Octavian. "Sir! I was going to find you next." He flipped a tablet from under his arm and presented it to the fight coordinator. "Look!"

Octavian took a few steps into the pool of light cast by the lamps, angling the tablet to see better. I shifted from foot to foot, unsure if my jumpiness was stemming from leftover adrenaline or whatever had been in the medicine I'd taken.

Finally, Octavian raised his head, something like pride in his face. "You win this time, Cyrus. We haven't had so many bets placed on one of your matches in a long time."

"Meaning..."

He returned the tablet to the trainer and smiled. "This week they saw you get knocked back, then rise to defeat your foes with ferocity and precision." He raised an eyebrow. "Crowds love to see a return against the odds."

A shiver of relief passed through my chest. *Maybe the gods are watching after all.*

Octavian turned to leave, beckoning me to follow. "Let's go. If the public is watching, you need to be in their eye as much as possible. There's a private concert at the praetor's home tonight, and I want you there. Don't worry," he added. Apparently, he'd caught the exhausted shift in my posture at the thought of putting on the public face after a week like this. "It's not going to be a lot of socializing, just a quiet gathering of old friends. Besides," he cast over his shoulder, "everyone knows how you felt about his daughter at one time."

It was a threat. Cleverly veiled, but a threat nonetheless. *Play along, or there's worse things in store than an uneven match.*

I raised my head and forced a nonchalant note into my voice. "I do love a nice evening with quiet conversation and music. Sounds like just the right way to celebrate another victory."

"That's the spirit."

He left and I left, returning to my quarters to wash, accept another dose of the horrible-tasting medicine, and change into clothes more suited to a party. The evening itself was exactly how Octavian had promised: a quiet gathering of the influential and their honored guests.

*Play along.*

I chatted, listened appreciatively to the music, and maintained a casual, charismatic manner with the guests vying for my attention. No hints of exhaustion escaped through my demeanor, not in the villa nor as we bade the host a good evening and departed for the Arena. As darkened streets closed around us, I let myself relax into the carriage cushions until a splash of color caught my eye.

I twisted to get a better look, wincing as bruises reminded me of their presence. Sunset-gold lettering was scrawled across the dingy plaster at the foot of a building, its brilliance already marred with street dirt. Before I had time to properly comprehend it, it was gone—disappeared as we turned a corner.

"Was that my name?"

Flavius's mouth twitched in a smirk. "Looked like. And a sunburst." He raised a jealous eyebrow. "You're getting popular again."

*Graffiti with my name?*

It wasn't a new occurrence, but certainly the first in a while. Which meant that Octavian's plan to bring in spectators and revenue was working.

The thought should have settled my nerves—public opinion was everything, after all—but instead something sank in my stomach as we entered the Arena gates. It might have been exhaustion, but it wouldn't go away—not as I left the others and shut the door of my quarters, not through washing the incense smell from my skin and hair, and not as I wandered onto the lattice-enclosed balcony that adjoined my quarters.

The Arena was never quiet. There were always the sounds of fights, shouts of workers, and roars from the beasts housed in the lower levels. Add to that the rumble of carts, hiss of metal being tempered, and thumps of training, and you ended with a place that sounded like the constant hum of blood in my ears. Most of the time, I didn't mind. It was easier to stay in the very center of the noise, creating it myself if necessary, than it was to face the gaping silence that waited when no else was present.

And reminders like this week of how alone I really was didn't help.

Stone scraped my skin as I slipped through a gap in the lattice to stand on the narrow ledge beyond my quarters. The architects of old had constructed the Arena with multiple decorative facings, fashioned in such a way that someone determined could climb them with ease. I grabbed for a handhold and scaled to the top of the Arena, muscles burning and the risk of falling spurring me on. It wasn't until I was sitting with my feet dangling precipitously over the edge of the roof that the urgency fell away and bone-numbing exhaustion crept in.

*Graffiti with my name.* I rubbed a hand through my hair, the dampness from washing it clinging to my skin the same way as the sweat from today's fight had. *No doubt there are also stories, songs, people talking about me in every forum.*

"It's working," I told myself. The thought of the public talking about my successes would ordinarily have cheered me up. Tonight, the thought brought nothing but uncertainty. "There's nothing to worry about. It's working."

*Until it doesn't, and then what?*

The thought lanced through my skin faster than any monster's claws. This evening wasn't the first time I'd seen my name splashed across a building, and stories about me—most wildly exaggerated, others eerily close to the truth—had circulated ever since I'd gained public attention at age nineteen. I'd used my sword blade to reflect light into my opponent's face, and the tale of a fighter who wielded the power of the sun had spread like wildfire. Over time, my name became intrinsically linked with the sun itself.

Golden. Powerful. Glorious and beautiful.

Unfailing.

"I won. This time." The healing gashes across my arm burned as I buried my head in my hands. "What if I can't keep this up?"

## BASTIAN

I lay curled on my side, the small whelk shell Lyra had slipped me before I tore myself away from the wall clutched in my hand. She'd brought it for me as a reminder of the goddess. The interior was painted blue with small flecks of pale white—sea foam or stars, depending on who you asked. My thumb ran across the smooth surface over and over. I'd had a similar shell among my possessions at the front. Who knew what had become of the spare clothes, cloak, weapons, or monthly wages saved to send back if I could?

The money was likely divided among the men, the clothes and armor taken to the quartermaster to be given to the next unlucky man. They'd also wanted my boots, much like the slavers. Boots of this quality leather were valuable enough to keep and pass on to another soldier, or to sell. I'd still managed to keep them despite the continued interest, only taking them off to wash. Not even to sleep, for worry they'd be stolen or the more precious item discovered. The shell had been tucked into my left boot as soon as I had a moment, but my scale necklace had yet to come out.

I should have given it to Lyra, I'd belatedly realized. But now having seen her, my heart rebelled at losing what felt like a renewed link between us.

*Keep trusting,* she'd whispered, not knowing that I doubted everything I'd ever known. But I hadn't given the shell back, nor had I cast it away.

I'd fight again today, in a matter of hours. Lyra coming through the aid of Titus seemed almost like a sign. My lips pressed together, wanting to refuse. But I pushed aside the blanket and rose in the dark silence of the barracks. The underground tunnels were silent and cool, broken only by pooling light. My fingers traced the stone again as I made my way to the gods' hallway.

But this time, it was not empty. I heard her before I saw her, her presence marked by shaky inhales around a murmured prayer. I softened my stride, easing around the corner to see a young woman in a light grey dress standing in front of a niche. I halted at the sight of the First God and the fresh bunch of herbs she'd placed at the base of the statue.

Suddenly noticing my presence, she jolted back a step, apology forming on her lips. I waved a hand, keeping back a few paces and resting my shoulders against the wall to show her I was no threat. She hesitated, eyes flicking to the altar, perhaps wanting to finish her small worship but not wanting to in front of me.

"Does he answer?" I almost startled myself at the sudden question.

The woman glanced at the First God. "Sometimes. And sometimes not in the way I expected."

I huffed. "But is that just the way of the gods?"

A small smile quirked her lips. "Perhaps. My family always worshiped him. I've prayed to the others, but with him…" She lifted a shoulder. "He seems to always care."

I shook my head. "I'm starting to think none of them do."

*He watches us, even if we don't look back,* my mother's words seemed to echo in the hallway, flicking at the candles.

"They do," she said almost fiercely, and softened almost instantly. "They have to, or nothing makes sense."

My lips pressed tight, not wanting to destroy her faith so strongly spoken. For the first time to me, nothing *did* make sense, and it felt like they'd turned away.

"Don't give up," she said. It felt like she might not quite be saying it to me. She gave a slight nod and vanished down the hall, leaving me with her god.

My hand clenched tighter around the whelk shell, its point driving into my palm. The goddess's shrine was filled with offerings. She stood above them all in flowing robes, holding a staff adorned with albatross wings. The shell could be wedged amongst the offerings, easily overlooked even if the temple attendants always taught that each offering was weighed along with the supplicating heart.

In contrast, the First God with his meager bundles of herbs kept drawing my eye. If the goddess had turned from me, perhaps I should also look to someone else.

*He seems to always care.*

I thought the goddess had as well. *And here I am.*

Though if legends and lesser staffed temples spoke true, perhaps this one had created the goddess, the earth, and us.

It felt almost like a dare as I set the shell down in front of him. "Then show me." The whisper cut between my teeth. "Show me you care."

Something caught my eye behind the statue. A crook in a stone in the farthest corner. Hesitating only a moment, I slid my boot off and pulled out the scale necklace, weighing it in my hand. The sharp edge had poked and prodded me for days, almost dangerously distracted me in training the day before. I didn't want to risk it happening again in a few hours, and didn't want it to be stripped from my bloody corpse and sold without care if the worst happened.

I coiled the braided leather and tucked it behind the stone. Some part peeked out, but this shrine clearly wasn't visited often. I stepped back, and the distance better concealed it from all but a sharp look.

A faint bit of guilt stirred for practically daring a god to give me a sign, then using his shrine as a hiding place. I adjusted the shell a little closer to the statue base.

"Even if you don't care about me, care about Lyra and my son. Please." And then I left the First God behind me.

RACING GRYPHON

# CHAPTER IX

BASTIAN

A bit of leather flaked off against my fingers as I adjusted the shoulder strap of my breastplate. I frowned, brushing it away and looking for the attendant. As much as I didn't want to be here, I didn't want to die from faulty equipment either.

"These straps are close to breaking." I knocked a fist against the yellow-painted leather.

He shrugged. "Just get your helmet and be ready to go."

The three other men of my team exchanged a glance as I scowled. This appeared to be the same armor set I'd been using for the last two fights, and no care had been given between. I didn't need to step closer to the others to see the same issue.

"Are they ready?"

I tensed as Octavian stepped into the arming room. But no thugs followed him.

"Almost," the attendant said. "That one is complaining about the armor." He pointed to me.

"It's close to failing," I said.

Octavian offered the same lift of his shoulders. "Winning this fight, and winning it well, will bring things like better armor your way." He seemed to look longer at me when he spoke, and I offered a thin smile, letting him know I saw through the paltry promise.

I belted the sword around my waist and pulled the helmet on. As we passed the attendant, he handed us spears. Octavian followed as we made our way up the tunnel to the gate, but gave no other word as we were urged out onto the sands.

This time it was empty space, though last time that had held traps. My muscles seized for a moment at the memory, until I forced myself to keep walking. They'd prepared us to fight *something*. Hopefully that meant there would be no sabotage beneath us.

I detected a spike in the crowd noise, something interested and almost excited. I glanced around, but saw nothing. It seemed to be *us*, possibly even *me*, that intrigued some small part of the crowd.

A creaking and groaning announced a gate opening in the curve of the Arena to the right of us. A wild screech tore from the dark tunnel, and my heart fell.

No.

Not this.

A gryphon raced out, pausing to whip around and snap its beak, swiping its claws at the men who drove it out with spears.

My fingers turned cold around the spear. He'd forced a confession of my past from me, then sent me to kill it. *Bastard.*

"Spread out," I said hoarsely. If this had come two days ago, I might have hesitated. But not now. Not with my son's face in my mind.

Our movement attracted the gryphon's attention and it turned to us. This animal wasn't like the glossy, muscled creatures I'd ridden for the last six years, or even like the one I'd seen in the stables. This male, young from the slope of his haunches, was wiry, ribs one or two more missed meals from standing out. Its clipped wings were dull and un-preened. A dangerous, wild light shone in his eyes as he dropped to a crouch and lashed his tail.

Captivity had broken him. Likely he could not be brought to heel, and had been sent to die instead.

The new man took the farthest point to the right. But his spear wavered, and he shook. The gryphon's attention fell to him. Finding the weak spot in the herd of prey.

Sand stirred to a storm as it launched toward him. I raced to intercept. A wild cry broke from the man, but to his credit, he stood his ground.

The gryphon swerved aside to avoid my spear thrust.

"Stand!" I shouted to the man as the creature wheeled back, lashing out with extended claws. We retreated, returning with spear jabs as the other two men raced up to assist. It was quick and agile, somehow avoiding all of us before retreating. We settled back to a semicircle and reset our spears. They all seemed to have settled a little, but the crowd was working into a frenzy.

The gryphon screamed a new challenge and leaped over my former wagon-mate at the farthest left. He turned too late, and claws bore him to the ground in a spray of red. We charged again, but it was only enough to drive the gryphon away. I thrust out and my spear scraped across its shoulder, enraging it.

Wings flared and the red-haired man stabbed. It whipped around with a wild shriek, ripping away the spear still caught in its wing. I pushed forward, jabbing at the softer spot in its neck as it lunged at him.

My aim was off, or it moved too fast, and my spear passed underneath the neck as my feet bore me too close. It pounced, paw slamming me to the ground. I flung sand up as the head came down, and it cried again as its vision was obscured. It tried to retreat, but its claws were punctured into my breastplate. I did not share the crowd's excitement as I was dragged along.

I tried to dig my feet in to resist, one hand fumbling at the straps to see if I could get out of the armor. Each move was disrupted by another yank.

The crowd warned me before I saw, and I curled closer to the leg as the beak swept down, impacting the sand just behind my back. I cursed and yanked backward, desperation propelling every muscle.

The breastplate ripped free, and I blessed the ragged leather that had just bought me a few minutes' more life. Yells announced the surviving men jabbing out, giving me space to scramble away and leave the leather to the beast.

Roaring filled my ears as I drew my sword.

"Target the wings!" I raced back to the fight. One man obeyed, stabbing the uninjured wing instead of the snapping beak.

"Left paw," I screamed at the red-haired fighter, hoping he'd understand to stab at the claws still tangled in leather. Together, they were able to drive the gryphon back and back toward the nearest wall. It sensed the danger and pushed to another leap, trying to clear us. Its tattered wings spread helplessly, and it tumbled in a rush. We followed, closing in as it tried to scramble back to paws.

Its forepaw jabbed out, snagging my trouser leg and tearing. Fire followed in its wake. I screamed back and swung the sword, landing a blow across its leg. It buckled and a spear sank into its right shoulder, further pinning it.

The gryphon screeched and thrashed for a moment, then sagged to the sands. I limped closer. Its golden sides heaved and the wild light had faded from its eyes, something closer to resignation shining there instead.

"I'm sorry," I whispered before I plunged my sword through its throat, finally stilling it.

I closed my eyes against the approval of the crowd, opening them only to reach out and place my hand in the space between the gryphon's eyes. Then I turned and made my way to the tunnel entrance.

It was only once inside, facing Octavian's pleased smile, that I realized I was bleeding. My back stung, and my leg shook under my weight. The tunnel tilted for a disconcerting moment before I ripped my helmet off to gasp for air. My shoulder slammed against the wall.

Octavian leaned closer, inspecting. "Get him to the infirmary, and tell them to make sure he's ready to fight again in two days."

Some noise broke from me and he held my gaze.

"You did well. Don't throw away this opportunity. You see what we do with defiant animals." He tilted his chin toward the Arena entrance, where the crowd still shouted acclaim.

I had no answer. Nothing that wouldn't immediately get me killed. I accepted help to the infirmary, where blessedly shallow cuts on my thigh and back were treated and I was given something to numb the pain. But no medicine could numb the tangling anger and fear.

I'd won again today, but what would I now become?

CYRUS

A gryphon rider. That's who this unknown fighter was, or *had* been. Rumors had circulated earlier this week to that effect, though opinions varied as to if he'd been sent here as a spy by the races. I didn't think that was the case. I'd met some of the racing competitors at a party, and they didn't have the same mannerisms as this man. "Soldier" had remained my guess despite the rumors, though I hadn't realized there were gryphon riders with the army. The whispers had finally piqued my curiosity, and I'd come to watch this match to see things for myself.

It *was* the same man I'd seen in the arrivals courtyard, I was certain of it now. He hadn't lost that straight-shouldered confidence—or the ruthlessness that'd first drawn the attention of the crowds. I'd seen it again in this fight, an unwillingness to hesitate or give under pressure, even when facing something he'd once loved.

Exactly the type of fighter the Arena craved.

I pushed away from the grating of the stables' tunnel with a sigh. Undefeated or not, he'd soon learn there was more to this life than just confidence and ruthlessness. This place took stamina and grit above all else, a fact that was becoming more and more apparent to me since my encounter with the lizard monster.

"He's sharp," the trainer said beside me. "And he's managed to keep some of those men alive for more than the average number of trainee fights. They might actually have a chance to ascend, thanks to him."

I shrugged. "Time and fate will tell. We'll see how much longer he lasts." I gave the animal handlers a salute as I left the room. "Thanks for the show."

The sun was dazzlingly bright as I emerged from the underground on the far side of the stables. There was another courtyard here, hidden from the public by a solid wall and overlooked by a building that housed offices, the team barracks, and another row of elite solo combatants' apartments on the third story. More to my interest were the practice courts that lay beneath several ancient olive trees, reserved for elite fighters and teams.

I stopped in the shade of the trees and adjusted the straps of my practice armor. It still bore traces of the paint that'd marked my team affiliation when I'd fought for Dragonesque, and the faint outlines of blue-green scales shimmered in places where the leather was less battered. Weighted practice sword in hand, I set up a dummy at the center of the ring. It was easy, almost a relief, to fall into my usual routine with most of my awareness absorbed in the patterns of motion and only a small piece set aside to warn me of anyone approaching.

I'd finished warming up and was taking a moment to breathe before starting afresh when a quiet voice interrupted. "You're back."

My breath caught in my chest, and I spun around. "What are you doing here?" Practice forgotten, I stepped over the rope barrier and into the shadow of the trees, where Callista stood with a basket of laundry on her hip. "If someone sees—"

"No one's looking," she said stubbornly. "And I stayed away while all eyes were on you last week." The linen of her dress brushed against my shins as she came to stand before me. "I can't avoid you forever, Cyrus. Not when I know what that fight cost you."

"Lis, we can't." I instinctively looked up to check the balconies, the arched entries, the Arena rim itself, before returning my gaze to her.

The midmorning light cast dappled shadows across her face, blending with the scattering of freckles over her nose. Even in her work clothes, and with frustration and worry in her warm brown eyes, she was the most beautiful thing I'd ever seen. "If anyone sees us, if anyone sees *you*, they'll—"

Her mouth tightened, and I cut off the fearful words that'd been about to spill out. Atticus, who'd long positioned himself as a guardian for all his workers, was a more than adequate deterrent against threats to Callista as she went about the compound. But there was no such deterrent for me, and not even Atticus was powerful enough to oppose Octavian, should my trainer learn of this relationship and determine that I needed a reminder of who truly stood in control.

I banished the thought with a shake of my head and insisted, "It's not safe for us to be seen together. Not here. Not in the open."

Callista gave an irritated sigh and swapped the basket to her other hip. "Then come with me, and we'll go somewhere where no one will see us."

I hesitated, the urge to pull away for her sake surging through my mind almost as fiercely as battle adrenaline. Then, a tiny spark flared deep inside. If Callista dared to be defiant, so could I. And if things went the way that Octavian and the rest of the board were threatening, I might not get another moment of peace for a long time.

I leaned my practice sword against one of the trees. "All right."

Callista knew the corridors and tunnels beneath the Arena better than I did. Still, it was a surprise when she stopped in the alcove dedicated to the First God, a broad-shouldered man with a kinder face than many of the others. A candle burned there, guttered down to a puddle of wax, and I wondered who else would honor a god who was all but forgotten.

"I think we're safe here." The gold of her slave earring glinted in the light from the candle as she pulled a sprig of rosemary from behind her ear and laid it at the foot of the statue, alongside a tiny, blue-painted shell left by some other worshiper. She closed her eyes for a moment in prayer before turning to me. "Are you all right? The injuries, the illness—"

"—haven't affected me much," I lied. I couldn't admit the truth, not while she was already so concerned. I twisted my arm to show her the cuts across it. "See? They're healing. And I didn't get in trouble for finishing my last match too quickly. I'm all right, really."

"But for how long?" she pressed. "And when will it finally be long enough? You keep saying—"

"I know." The question she'd just asked had chased my every footstep since she and I had confessed our feelings to each other, when I'd first contemplated a future that might hold something other than sand, blood, and death. "I've been solo for four and a half years, Lis. Half a year more, and I'll be free."

That was the promise dangled before all of us who achieved solo combatant ranking. Survive elite combat for five years, impress the crowds, and at the end you'd be offered the chance to retire and live comfortably off your winnings to the end of your days. So far, only a handful of fighters had made it—Senator Tiberius the most recent in decades—and no one had come close since then until me.

"You think they'll let you go?"

I had to consider the words carefully. Did I believe it? I had until this month, when things had gotten so much worse than I'd expected. But public opinion was a powerful thing, and for that reason alone, I suspected the board would *have* to comply with tradition. Finally, I nodded and said, "I have to believe they will. If not, all that's left for me is death on the sands, which would leave you with no future at all."

She gave a short laugh. "*My* future? You'd take me with you?"

"Callista!" I quickly lowered my voice and glanced down the corridor in case anyone was coming. "*Yes*, I'd take you with me." I lifted empty hands to her. "I don't have a token to give you, but I've saved every scrap of earnings they've given me. If they won't let you leave right then, I'll buy your freedom. Even if it costs everything I have."

She blinked hard. Tears welled up in her eyes, catching the spare light from the candle in the First God's shrine. "You mean it?"

"I mean it. When I picture the future, the most beautiful thing in it is you."

Before I could react, her arms were around me, and the scents of soap, herbs, sunlight, and linen filled my senses. "I want to see that future," she whispered into my chest. "Please stay alive."

I carefully wrapped my arms around her, her hair so soft under my palm that I forgot how to speak. After a long moment, I released her and stepped back, capturing one of her hands in both of mine. "I'll do my best, Lis. But listen," I warned, squeezing her hand tightly. "You might need to keep your distance over the next few weeks."

A flash of uncertainty went through her eyes. "Why?"

"I don't know what's going to happen. The rules I've played by until now are changing, and I don't know what anyone might do if they found out about us." I looked over my shoulder, acutely aware that anyone could come down this hall and instantly have a weapon to wield against the only soft part of me. "Just know that whatever happens, I'm trying my hardest to keep the future—*our* future—secure." I squeezed her hand again before letting go. "Even if it becomes brutal, I need you to trust me."

"I...I will. I'll keep back, but I'll be watching." She glanced behind me at the altar to the First God. "And I'll pray. Maybe you aren't as alone as you think you are."

Maybe it was desperation, maybe frustration, but for whatever reason, the suggestion didn't sting the way it would have a month ago. I took a deep breath. "Maybe. Maybe not."

# CHAPTER X

BASTIAN

I'd survived my first week in the Arena, and another began. And things had changed. I now had a private apartment on the opposite side of the stables from the main barracks, fresh food, armor that fit, and trainers who took more care and attention.

Octavian circled, hovering like a vulture or running training bouts in enclosed courtyards. His bulk wasn't for show, and he moved quick and relentless when he picked up a training sword against me. He picked at strengths and weaknesses, and left no excuse. And I disliked the pleased look on his face when I withstood his attacks and training regimens.

No more did I have a team. It was me against whatever they placed in the Arena. I had a second to watch my back. The red-haired man. I learned his name was Phestus. And true to his word, Octavian placed me in the Arena two days later. I won, and the days fell to training and fighting and killing. Injuries bandaged, salve spread, all to keep me walking out over and over.

Four days after I killed the gryphon, I walked along the barred wall from the stables toward the main barracks, ordered to return to the infirmary by the grey-haired head physician, who possessed a glare more ferocious than any legion commander's. I'd told Lyra not to come back, but I couldn't help but scan the faces on the other side of the gate.

And standing in the exact spot she'd first called my name, she waited. I glanced around, but no concerted focus was on me as I quickened my steps and reached through the bars. Her smile settled me on my feet; the warmth of her hand clasped around mine felt like it could hold me back from the brink.

"You shouldn't have come," I said.

"Would you have stayed away?" she asked, laughing softly as I kissed her fingers and declined to answer. "How are you?"

I tipped my head against the bars. "Alive."

Her slender features tightened as she freed her hand and tugged at the wide collar of the tunic, exposing a bandage. Then to my upper arm, which I'd been trying to hide with how I'd positioned myself to the bars.

She gently adjusted the tunic to cover the bandages. "I'd heard rumors that a man in boots and a gryphon rider helmet had been winning against the odds."

"I killed a gryphon."

Lyra pressed her hand over my heart, hearing those few seconds of heartbreak when I'd killed it.

"They also moved me to solo fights."

"Is that good?" she asked.

I lifted a shoulder, let it drop, and focused on the green scarf wrapped around her. "How is he?"

"Asleep. He screamed almost all night." She shook her head, tugging away part of the scarf for me to see August's profile.

"I'm sorry," I said.

Lyra blinked hard, then forcefully brightened. "Someday I'll happily hand him off to you."

"Lyra..."

"There has to be *something*," she whispered. "What if...what if we could be here with you?"

The same desperation in her eyes filled me, but the days here showed that was a dangerous road. "No," I said, shaking my head when she opened her mouth to protest. "Lyra."

She subsided, her fingers clenching in my tunic again as she almost glared at me.

"The only women here are slaves," I said. "*I* am a slave." My hand over hers barely stilled her vengeful protest. "I meant it, Lyra. I don't want you, or August, anywhere near this place. They mark everything that comes through these gates for some sort of use. And if something happened to me, I don't think they'd let you go again. That's not worth it for a little time together without bars."

She shook her head, barely masking the tears glistening in her eyes. "Bas..."

I gently squeezed her hand, my heart shredding further at what I was going to tell her next. But it was the only sure future I saw for them with me trapped here. "Lyra, you should take him to the coast, back to your family..."

Lyra's blue eyes snapped to mine, steel filling them. "Don't say that. I've waited for you for years, Bastian. At least...at least this time I know where you are while I wait."

"My love." I rested my hand against her cheek, but she only returned my look with the stubbornness that sometimes exceeded my own.

"Don't ask me to leave, Bas. Not when there's still something for me to come find here." She softened slightly. "You wouldn't leave me, so I can do no less."

I shook my head though some small selfish part of me was glad that, if I survived, this was not the last time I'd see her. But I didn't have anything else to give in the face of her hope.

The other soloists, and sometimes team fighters, talked. They said if you survived five years, you retired. But I was *days* into that and too much could happen. In the end, all that mattered was that Lyra would leave and walk the two miles home, to return in two days as she promised to see if I was still alive.

But before she left, she pressed another shell into my hand and made me swear that I wouldn't give up.

The golden-haired fighter was fast. He commanded the training court, practice sword flashing against other similarly armed men. I watched from the deeper shade of the olive trees that ringed the grounds. Phestus stepped up beside me. He'd taken to life as my second well. It was the better place to be. Hanging back from the most dangerous parts, getting all the same benefits as me.

"Have you seen him fight before?" he asked.

I shook my head. "He's fast." And strong. His wiry frame delivered louder strikes than those of the bulkier men training opposite him.

"He's—" Phestus's jaw dropped. "Bastian, that's *Cyrus*, the golden sun." He spoke the name reverently. "He's undefeated for four years. Last week he took out a solo fighter *and* his second in a matter of minutes. And then went to some party that night."

I didn't know what was more impressive to Phestus—the speed of killing or the invitations to parties in the upper villas.

"That could be you someday," he said, perhaps content for now to ride at my wing.

I shook my head. I had been a soldier before, and the son of a horse trainer even before that. I did not belong in villas then, and I did not now. Not like this.

Something shifted on the court. Something in the way the golden sun moved. I stood frozen, staring in awe as he launched an attack, seeming to move three steps ahead of the men surrounding him. In moments, they were defeated.

And he smiled.

It had taken days to learn the tunnels from my new quarters to the gods' altars. But by the end of the second week, I was familiar enough to move from one end of the Arena to the other on the main paths. Lyra had come the day before to quietly tell me that news of my fall had finally been brought to the city. She'd gone with my stamp to the standing encampment's quartermaster to claim the bit of wages set aside for her every month. They'd turned her away with nothing, telling her that I was a traitor.

She had enough to live on for the next few weeks, she'd said. But if I knew her and the way she tried to lie, it was only for a week more. I had some small earnings promised to me in my new position, but I would not see them until month's end. I didn't know if it would be quick enough, or if I would be alive to try to slip it through the bars to her.

The young woman had beaten me to the First God's altar again. She'd brought more herbs, and stood aside for me to place the bit of bread I'd brought.

"Did you get your answer?" She pointed to the two shells, softly laughing when I glanced at her. "I only know one other person in this whole place who prays to him, and they don't bring shells."

I huffed, regarding the statue. "I'm still trapped here, so perhaps he doesn't like the sea."

She slipped hands across her waist. "I don't think he cares about what you bring, just about your heart."

"I'd lay it out bleeding for him if it got me an answer," I said. How to protect Lyra and August, how to keep any part of myself.

She shivered. "Don't say that." After a moment, she turned to me. "You're the one with the gryphon helmet." She smiled slightly. "Everyone also talks about the boots, and you're the only one who wears them."

I glanced at my feet. I'd been able to get oil to keep the leather fresh, and was now able to take them off without fear of them walking away. "You notice many things, then."

"You learn to watch things and people," she replied, an edge to her voice. I tensed, but she did not seem wary or afraid of me.

"Are you all right out there?" I asked, my chin tilting to encompass all of the Arena.

Surprise fringed her look. "Yes, I am protected."

I relaxed a fraction. These encounters had been odd, some sort of brightness clinging after, like her faith rubbed off on me to carry for a little while. "I don't know how much I can do, but if you need anything, let me know," I said.

"What's your name, then?" she asked.

My lips turned up into a faint smile, something almost real. "Bastian."

"Callista." She inclined her head, then was gone.


Two days into the next seven, I exited the Arena. Another victory after a soloist and I had been paired up to take down a lizard-like thing. Once it was dead, he'd turned on me. I stepped into the arming room, the attendants coming over to help. One took my sword and helmet, another turned to divesting my armor.

"How was it?" the man working to release a blood-stained greave from my leg asked.

I didn't answer, yanking at the bracer on my left arm. I often didn't reply, too unsteady from the adrenaline and not wanting to risk saying something foolish. Each meeting with Lyra gave me caution and brought to mind Octavian's threat about defiance. I could not do anything about the risk on the sands, but in the walls and courtyards, I needed some caution.

They were used to me by now, and didn't press.

"Well done." Octavian strode in as the breastplate was lifted away. I fought a grimace. I had dozens of small injuries, and a knee that ached from being pinned beneath an opponent four days ago. Octavian sounded jovial enough that perhaps I'd dare ask for a few days away from fighting.

"There's hot water waiting in your room, a massage, and fine clothes." He crossed arms and regarded me with a pleased expression.

I faced off with him warily. This did not seem like the start of anything good.

"Why?" Unintended contention filled my voice.

The attendants eased away. For a moment, I almost wished for Phestus to come in from divesting his own armor, better to watch my back.

"You caught the eye of a wealthy patroness. She wants to know what's under the helmet." Octavian smirked. "She paid for a night with you. Almost as much as we get for the top-tier fighters."

"What?" My brain refused to understand, but my entire body tensed. Ready to flee.

Octavian smiled, tolerating the sharpness for now.

"Good food, expensive wine, silk sheets, and a beautiful woman who wants to be pleasured in them," he explained like I was slow. "If you do well enough, perhaps we'll let it be known that you're available. The helmet is a mystery and women are simple."

Dread hit harder than any opponent. The residual roar of the crowd seemed to fill up the small room, drowning out noise, but funneling his words to me nonetheless.

"You were a soldier, so I assume you know your way around a woman. She is wealthy and refined, so treat her better than a camp whore. You'll be back in the morning, and with the money this brings in, you won't fight until the end of the week."

Shock and revulsion hit me so hard I couldn't breathe. From the way he spoke, the way the attendants listened, this was not uncommon. This was...expected. My blood wasn't enough, they were going to sell my body too. My heart pounded, every beat screaming "*Lyra, Lyra, Lyra!*"

"Bastian?" Octavian seemed genuinely confused.

"Come." An attendant placed a hand on my shoulder. He reeled back as I batted it away and struck the center of his chest with the heel of my hand.

"No."

I would not be complicit in this. Would not dishonor Lyra or myself.

"No?" Octavian arched an eyebrow. Warning filled his tone. *Remember.*

I was too angry to be afraid of what might happen. "No."

He reached slowly to the wall, pulling down a plaited whip best used for driving away chimeras. "One chance, Bastian."

The attendants scurried to the farthest corner of the room, leaving me to face off with the fight coordinator who blocked any escape.

"I'll tell her you were injured in the fight. Too much to be any good tonight, but you'll be ready tomorrow." The almost kindness in his voice didn't match his eyes.

"No." My right foot slid back. I needed a weapon, and my sword lay on the table two paces away.

He let the whip uncoil. "If you had anyone outside, forget about them. This is it for you."

I lunged for the sword, my hand about to close over it when a crack broke against my side. I slammed against the table, its edge driving into my ribs and stealing my breath in tandem with the bright pain across my side. I clung to the wooden surface, new shock slowing my movements.

Octavian knocked the sword out of reach. I tried to shove myself to my feet, but the butt of the whip cracked across my temple. He yanked my shoulder, hitting my knee as he did and sending me to the ground.

"Not too late, Bastian." He backed away a pace, leaving me to feel dampness trickling down my jaw.

"I won't be sold like meat," I gritted, shoving up to an elbow.

He kicked at me, cursing as he did. "Your face is ruined," he said like it had been my fault. "No matter, there are ways to make you comply."

I clenched my hands against the stone as I turned a furious glare at him. They'd have to kill me, and he knew it. As I pushed upright, he swung. My arms shielded my head, barely smothering the half scream as the leather bit into my side again.

"What a waste!" Octavian shouted with another strike. "What a *waste*!" He tossed the whip aside. "I told you, Bastian. Defiant animals have no place here. You'll fight Cyrus tomorrow." And he was gone.

I couldn't feel anything but the heat of blood at the news that I'd be sent to my death tomorrow. The golden sun was undefeated. Unmatched by any other solo fighter. Anyone who faced him was killed without hesitation. I tried to get up, but slumped even farther, my forehead pressing against the cool stone.

"Bastian." Phestus's voice was accompanied by a hand on my shoulder. I jerked away from him. "Come."

The second time, I let him bring me to my feet. "We'll go to the infirmary."

I didn't want the faint respect in his face. Even if I didn't regret defying *that*, I regretted not being able to see my wife and son one more time before I died.

Dawn had yet to break on my last day. I sat on the edge of the bed, scale necklace clenched in my hand. I left it at the First God's shrine before every fight, then made my way back to reclaim it after. Now my desperation to keep it would rob Lyra of it.

Or perhaps not. I cursed as I pulled on a clean tunic, the motion tugging at my bandaged side. The physician had been visibly confused as he tended the long cuts, somehow shallow enough to only need salve. If they had needed more care, I might have told him not to bother. Not to waste the materials on me.

If Octavian had declared me facing anyone else, I wouldn't have been this resigned. But after seeing Cyrus in training, and catching one of his fights from the other side of a gate, I did not have high hopes. "Sun" was not an accurate description of anything but the brightness of his hair. The young man was a demon—fast, calculating, merciless.

I shoved my feet in my boots and pulled out a small bag of coins from under the mattress. I'd won them in a card game a few nights before with the Dragonesque team, with nothing to wager except my boots. I'd walked away with both them and some money to pass to Lyra until I saw my first earnings.

Hopefully it would all still find its way to her. Each step came easier as I left the room and made my way into the tunnels. It was about the time when I'd seen Callista before. I prayed for the First God to show some of his legendary mercy, and was finally rewarded for one prayer. Callista was there before his shrine, laying down fresh rosemary. Her smile of greeting faded as she saw me. "Bastian, what happened?"

I could not manage any reassurance.

"Rumors in the infirmary were that you came in with injuries that you couldn't have gotten from the sands." Her gaze tracked to the shallow cut and bruising on my temple from the whip's handle.

My lips barely tilted. The physician had pressed, but there was nothing to say.

"Nothing for you to worry about," I finally said.

The way she tilted her head, mouth pursing, loudly declared that she would anyway.

"Can you do something for me, Callista?" I asked.

The young woman stepped closer, halfway reaching out. "What?"

I swallowed hard and extended the bag and necklace. "I need you to get these to someone, if..." I cleared my throat as she took them, the marriage scale glinting in the candlelight. Understanding flashed and she looked at me in compounding worry.

"My wife." My voice failed. "She's been coming to the wall. Her name is Lyra; dark hair and eyes bluer than a summer sky. She'll have a babe with her." Wistfulness stabbed my heart. "She was supposed to come tomorrow, but I..."

"Bastian." Callista freed a hand to place it on my arm. "You're fighting someone today?"

I nodded.

"I can keep these for you, but you've been winning. Everyone says it."

My mouth twisted in a poor smile. "Today I fight their golden god."

Her face paled and she fell back a step. "Cyrus?" Her whisper cut between us, faith in my skill fading before the name.

I nodded. "I don't have anything to give you for this, but can you give that necklace and the money to her? Or if you can't...Titus from the gryphon stables can." I hoped. I hadn't gone to speak to him again, either to thank or curse him for bringing Lyra to me. Perhaps he'd honor a request from a dead man, who wouldn't be able to even the debt between us.

"I will. I'll make sure she gets it." Brightness filled her eyes, and I wanted to tell her not to weep on my behalf. "Bastian, why are you fighting him?"

I didn't want to tell her, but she likely knew of this side to the Arena. Hopefully it didn't extend past the men whose blood wasn't enough to sate the thirst of the powerful. I didn't want Lyra to know. Some part of me couldn't bear to give voice to it.

It wasn't like I hadn't seen this sort of slavery before. It followed the army, lurked on street corners under painted stones telling men and women what they could get for a price. I had a rule in my squad; any man who'd use wages for something like that would be reassigned. And it felt like, even a day later, I couldn't wash off the filth of the idea that *I'd* be bartered in such a casual way.

Her fingers touched my hand again.

"I wouldn't allow myself to be sold like an animal," I finally said, regretting the way she blanched at the admission. "Defiance has no place here, Callista. Maybe there will be some honor in my death."

She squeezed my hand, trembling lips pressed together. "You're a good man, Bastian. I'll pray for the fight, and for you after."

Someone would remember me with kindness if I wasn't granted immediate entry to the gods' halls. If either the goddess or the First God didn't speak for me against the god of judgment when he weighed my life on his scales.

"Thank you," I said, voice close to shattering. "Look out for yourself."

She nodded, tears beading her lashes.

"Tell Lyra to take the money and go to her parents' villa on the coast. Leave the memory of me behind. Maybe tell our son of me one day." My eyes stung, even more when she threw her arms around me.

Callista pulled away, hands closing around the necklace and coin purse, offering another promise with a firm nod.

"Thank you," I whispered, and left after one more glance at the god. I didn't bring anything to offer him except the tears I took with me. Perhaps in the afterlife I could look down and see my son grow up, for it didn't seem like I'd have a chance to on this earth.

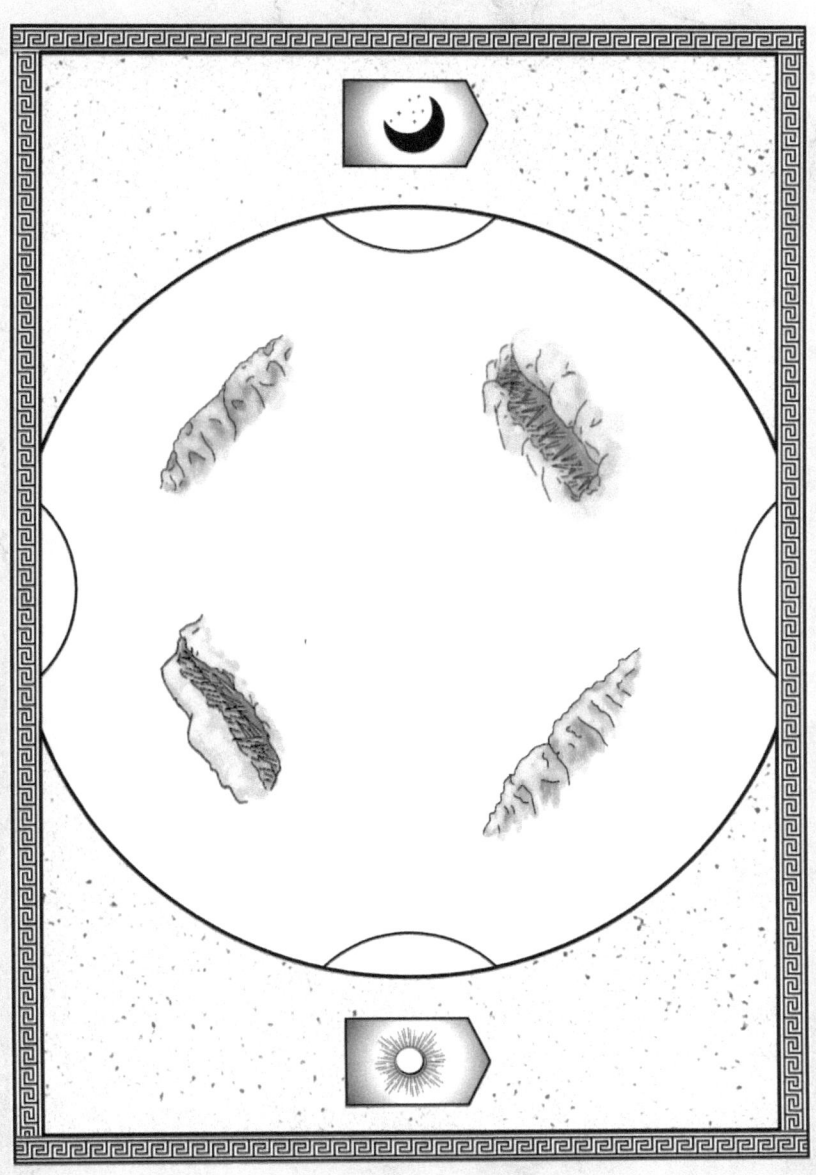

# CHAPTER XI

CYRUS

"We'll need to replace this piece soon," one of the attendants warned as he adjusted the straps holding my shoulder armor. Overhead, the crowds were taking on a note I'd never heard before, a suppressed hum that had me more than a little distracted.

*Something's different today.*

I returned my attention to the room as the man explained, "We did what we could with the blood from that *thing*, but it's done something to the leather." He gave a smile that held little mirth. "Assuming we get more than a day or two to replace it, with how often you've been taking the sands."

"That's not likely to change anytime soon." I tipped my head back to examine the ceiling, as if I could see beyond it and assess why the crowd sounded so off. "Is...is something happening out there that's unusual?"

"We have a special guest joining the board members in the box today," Octavian said as he came in. Every eye in the room turned to him as he said, "Word of our champion's almost-defeat reached Imperial ears, and we've caught the attention of the Empress." He nodded in the direction of the sand—and the spectators. "She'll be watching this match."

Astonished mutters broke out all around me. So that was it. The attention of a patron with a hundred times more influence and power than any celebrity. Try as I might to hide my surprise, the tone still came through as I asked, "What do you want me to do?"

"You?" Octavian seemed genuinely perplexed. "Do what you do best. Defeat your opponent and make it look good. Win!"

He waved me toward the tunnel. Flavius came to hover behind me, and I turned to give him a deadly look. "Leave me in the dust again, and you won't see another sunrise."

"If I do, there won't *be* another," he shot back. "You fall, and everyone falls with you."

So maybe the earlier failure to respond hadn't been *entirely* planned. Not that it made me feel any safer. I turned my shoulder to him, ears keen for any sign of him deciding to rid himself of me as the gate creaked open.

"By the way." Octavian paused my advance with a hand to my breast-plate. "You're fighting that gryphon rider. I don't care how you kill him, but make sure he feels it."

I gave him a grim nod. It wasn't the first time I'd heard that order, and not likely to be the last. And if I didn't comply, *I'd* be the one to feel Octavian's wrath, even with my opponent dead. I drew my sword and ran out of the tunnel mouth, the roar of the crowd breaking on my ears. A goldenrod-colored banner unfurled from above the opposite tunnel entrance, blank with no emblazon, and my heartbeat immediately surged at the sight of another fighter in a helmet and knee-high boots emerging from the entrance.

That posture. I'd know it anywhere. It was the same man I'd seen two weeks ago, ascended unbelievably fast...but facing me now.

I didn't know what he'd done to make Octavian hate him, but I almost pitied him.

I'd paused to let my senses get accustomed to the noise and light in the Arena, but now I started running, my eye taking in the obstacles arranged around the sands—a pair of long earthen rises the height of my shoulder and a corresponding pair of ditches, set to form a square of obstacles for us to navigate.

As my feet landed in the center of the open space, my opponent moved, dust rising from under his boots as he sprinted behind the berm nearest him. I couldn't see much more than his helmet, but it looked like he was trying to get to the end of the ditch that ran perpendicular to the berm. The opening of the ditch sloped, but the sides were steep—and fenced with spikes.

*Make sure he feels it.*

I quickened my pace, cutting off his trajectory at the mouth of the ditch. The gryphon rider skidded to a halt, his sword impacting mine with a *clang* that sent a shudder up my arm as I blocked.

Gods. He was *strong*. Strong, taller than me, and almost as fast.

I blocked another blow and took a step to the side. If he took the bait, if he pressed the advantage, I could get him with his back to the sharpened wood stakes lining the ditch. Impalement would be sudden, terrifying, painful—Octavian should be happy with that. The crowd would love it. It might even secure the patronage of someone with so much money that the board would ease the pressure against me.

Another step. Another block. To the crowd, it must've looked like I was afraid, retreating before an anonymous opponent. He might've thought so too, until his advance halted. The helmet swiveled to one side, and I caught a flash of eyes widening behind the visor.

He brought his sword smashing against mine, the impact forcing me back one more pace—no longer a feint, but a true retreat. I threw my full weight and speed into a counterattack, and this time it was him who was forced back, back, back toward the spikes. The crowd's yelling increased, like they could sense the death approaching.

The gryphon rider twisted to the side, dodging both my blade and the spike I'd been trying to drive him against. A startled yell met my ears as his foot slipped over the edge of the ditch. The rest of the lip gave way beneath him, and he landed in an ungraceful tangle at the bottom.

Now that, I hadn't been expecting.

## BASTIAN

A curse wheezed from me as I impacted, finding my way to the bottom of the ditch in the last way that I wanted to. Goddess, he was fast. And smart, trying to lead me forward and then drive me into the spikes. It was only a ripple of warning that had slowed my advance, reminding me that the surest strategy for staying ahead of him was to keep distance.

I scrambled to my feet, tightening my grip on my sword and casting about for anything useful in the pile of weapons that rested against one side of the ditch. The crowd changed pitch, now urging and excited. A rattle marked the golden sun's lithe figure slipping through the spikes. I retreated a step and grabbed the nearest weapon—a long staff with a metal-encased end.

He jumped into the ditch, landing in a crouch like a showy gryphon coming to land. Behind me lay an escape. I just needed to hold him off long enough to get there.

I backed up, and he closed the distance. The staff weighed awkwardly in my non-dominant hand, but there was no time to switch, only time to jab out.

*Sorry, Bastian, Octavian ordered me to keep back,* Phestus had apologized in the tunnel. I'd reassured him not to risk himself on my account. Better that only one of us died.

I swung again and my opponent twisted, sword clattering against the wood in an attempted block. *Curse this place.* I heaved the staff at him, not watching the ungainly arc or for any block he might make, instead turning and sprinting.

An enraged cry told me I'd managed a hit. I still didn't stop, boots digging into the rough incline and propelling me out. At the top, I swung around and dropped to a crouch.

He strode toward me, blood pouring from his temple and vengeance in his eyes. It felt like the stone might split under the force of the crowd. I lunged forward, dragging my boot through the dirt and kicking toward him as he ascended the ramp.

Sand sprayed and he floundered, arm up, with the dust already in his eyes.

*Move.* I obeyed the instinct and headed into the center of the sands. Face-to-face, I had some height and bulk against him. I'd rather this be settled in open space than with me trapped in a corner.

## CYRUS

My tunic was covered in blood from the lucky strike of that gods-forsaken staff, but it was better than nothing. I swiped furiously at the dust obscuring my vision, blinking until the world resolved around me. The gryphon rider had made good use of the time, and was already halfway into the center of the ring. With a yell, I shook the last of the dirt from my eyes and charged.

He stepped back, bracing himself to meet me, and our blades clashed together with a ring that almost drowned out the roar of the spectators.

Forget Octavian and his orders. I was going to end this however I wanted.

Dust rose around us as we circled, trading blows as the crowd's yells and cheers resounded throughout the Arena. In the open, we were as evenly matched as possible, him taller, me faster, his unyielding power against my cold fury as my head rang and blood streamed down my face.

That last was enough to make me even more determined to end this quickly.

I slammed my sword into his once more, angling the next cut for his neck. He raised his free arm in time to block, and the edge bit into his skin above the bracer. A curse burst from behind the helmet, and I laughed at the realization that he was as unsettled by this match as I was.

In the never-ending circling and jockeying for position, we'd almost reached the rise nearest the tunnel I'd entered the Arena from. The gryphon rider was forced to step up, his balance dangerously thrown as I aimed a cut at his feet. Another step back, and he'd regained his footing. What had been a disadvantage instantly turned to advantage, as his strikes changed from sideways slashes to overhand cuts that fell against my sword with added power.

I blocked once, twice, then a third time, my own balance shifting farther back with each clash of sword against sword. The last blow landed awkwardly, sliding against my blade to strike my vambrace. I frantically threw my weight into pushing the gryphon rider's sword away, lurching backward despite the rise under my feet.

Before I knew what was happening, a booted foot caught my ankle, yanking it from under me and sending me backward to the sand. It wasn't far to fall, but the impact still rattled my vision and sent my arms flailing wildly. I tried to roll, to get to my feet, to get *away*, but it was already too late.

The gryphon rider skidded to land with a knee against my chest, one hand pinning my sword arm to the ground. The crowd had been yelling furiously, but now an eerie silence descended over the Arena until the loudest sound was the blood pounding in my ears. For the first time we locked eyes, as he leveled his sword at my throat.

Five months till freedom, and now this?

Impossible.

## BASTIAN

An appalling hush fell across the sands as I steadied my sword. I'd never once considered winning. Only hoped to die with some shred of honor. It had been sheer instinct that drove my limbs into the attack meant to give space for mounting a gryphon in battle. As I finally looked down at my intended executioner, I halted.

He looked shocked. Terrified. And young. *So young*.

For another two heartbeats, nothing moved. We barely breathed. A tremor rocked through my muscles.

I hadn't given orders to kill children months ago. He was grown, only a few years younger than me. But it was still the helpless look in his eyes, the frantic shock I'd seen in other bloody young soldiers realizing they'd never see the sunset.

And I couldn't.

Gods, I couldn't.

What this would bring on me next, I couldn't guess. But at least I'd enter the afterlife with my head a little higher.

I lowered my sword, gently tapping the point against his breastplate. Done.

Then I pushed to my feet and scrambled to put distance between us.

And the Arena erupted.

# CHAPTER XII

BASTIAN

Two men charged from the far end of the Arena. I braced for another attack, but a "Bastian!" barely made it over the noise before Phestus grabbed my shoulders and shook me. The same disbelief covered his face.

A figure moved toward us. Octavian. I raised my sword, but he didn't even look at me, halting by Cyrus in a burst of sand.

"Get him out of here!" He pointed at me.

More attendants swarmed around, hands pushing me backward. Others helped my opponent up. His armored second glanced at me, his dark look...disappointed. The golden sun moved shakily, and I caught something caged about him before I was turned and hustled toward the

Arena underbelly.

Something like fear.

I understood. The same had sunk its claws into me. I'd survived. I wasn't supposed to have survived, to have *won*. A glimpse of purple and heavy gold in one of the spectator boxes caught my eye before I vanished through the gate. The Imperial colors.

I stumbled against another rush of fear.

I'd likely only heightened Octavian's fury at me. And now, in sparing Cyrus, had gained another powerful enemy. He'd been undefeated until now. And I'd humiliated him in front of the Empress herself.

They pushed me past the arming room, past the wide-eyed arming attendants. Shouts filled the tunnels, other men jockeying for position as they rushed to see the aftermath of the fight. Phestus had been shoved away, but I could still feel him at my back.

Arena guards gripped my upper arms, maneuvering me through the press until I was thrust into a smaller room. The door slammed behind them, and I was left alone inside. Small slits on the upper wall let in some threads of light, along with the continued roar of the crowd. A table and some benches were the only furniture, the stone wall opposite the door painted as a gladiator locked in battle with a chimera.

I yanked off my helmet and sent it clattering to the table. My sword had disappeared from my grip at some point, and I stared down at empty and shaking hands. The left was covered in blood, the stinging injury above my bracer finally getting past the raging adrenaline and fear to announce its presence.

My forearms slammed to the table, and a sobbing mix of curses and prayers escaped me. *What would happen now?*

They left me wondering for what felt like hours. Only broken by a physician coming to tend the wound and blessedly ordering some water for me to drink before he left. I remained in armor but otherwise defenseless, as somewhere my fate was decided.

Finally the door swung open and Octavian pushed in, flanked by another man trimmed in wealthy robes. I caught a glimpse of Phestus's worried features before we were shut inside. I braced myself, hands curling to fists as I faced off with them.

Octavian looked me up and down, shaking his head with barely concealed annoyance that I'd survived. "This is Senator Tiberius. He is a member of the board that governs the Arena." *Don't cross him,* the warning came clear.

Tiberius stepped closer and I gave a pace, sidestepping to keep the length of the table between me and them.

He raised an eyebrow. "That was...unexpected, what you did," he said. My jaw was still so clenched that I couldn't ask when they planned to kill me. "Cyrus always wins. He's the sure bet, even when the odds seem stacked against him."

*And I upset it all.*

"Right now, there are some very content people leaving, but others think we swung the match." Tiberius watched me. I could assure him that Cyrus had not been pulling his blows.

Silence lingered just long enough for me to grit out, "And?"

Tiberius smiled like he'd figured out something. The sharpness of his eyes, the bulkiness of the chest and arms under soft cloth and a slight paunch, bespoke his past of *fighter,* if not quite soldier. "And you've just proved to the board, and the crowds, that things can always change. It seems that you're a contender."

I did *not* like the way he said it, evaluating, calculating.

"You'll be given a room on the upper floor, a personal attendant, higher-profile fights. There might be space for two champions, as long as the Arena can hold both of you."

I swallowed hard. *Until we kill each other.*

"Octavian says you were a soldier."

I nodded and offered nothing more.

"He also says that defiance is what placed you on the sands against Cyrus to begin with. He suggested being done with you once and for all," Tiberius said.

I flicked a look at Octavian and the hand he placed on his knife, ready to get rid of me immediately.

"But." Tiberius smiled thinly. "Some competition would be healthy for Cyrus, and with him more focused, we can look to you. There's money to be made from you yet. And make no mistake, *Bastian*, money is what matters here."

Octavian's irritation at me faded, only for some new calculation to cross his face at the mention of Cyrus.

Tiberius continued, "You'll go on the lists as a wild card, a rogue, a challenger. You'll keep fighting, and you'll do it with the same tenacity you showed today and in your other fights. But if you can't follow orders, you'll find mercy is in rare supply."

From the way Octavian's lip curled, he would be all too happy to illustrate that point if I stepped too far out of line.

There was nothing for me to say. So I tapped a fist against my chest, a soldier's salute, but the defiance they warned of was already creeping back. Defiance was what had brought me to the Arena, and it echoed in the sharpness of the salute and my unflinching stare. I would not die today, but their hold had only tightened around me.

## CYRUS

*I lost. How did I lose?*

I was aware of footsteps running to meet me, of being pulled up by my arm while someone scooped my sword from where it'd fallen. Flavius. His face was painted with the same shock that had affected the crowds in the heart-stopping moment when the gryphon rider's sword had been aimed at me.

This wasn't supposed to have happened.

I cast a glance at the board's box, where the purple and gold of the Imperial standard was visible. The Empress had come to see a show, but I didn't think this was the type of show she'd wanted. There would already have been repercussions—there always were with my missteps—but her presence had just guaranteed they'd be ten times worse.

A pounding headache struck as I got to my feet. The head wound was still bleeding, and pain combined with the ear-splitting roar from the stands to make my head ring as Flavius and the other attendants ushered me into the shelter of the armory. I stood, numb to everything, as my armor was shucked away and the rumble of panicked and surprised voices filled the room.

*I lost.*

The thought stayed with me all the way to the infirmary, where the wound was swabbed clean with stinging disinfectant, dust rinsed from my hair, and my head bandaged. I pulled on a clean tunic, concern breaking through the frozen feeling as my hand brushed the bandage. "Is it going to scar?"

Atticus tipped his head to the side, a faraway look directed at the ceiling before he answered, "I could've tried to stitch it, but it's not a clean cut." He sighed and met my gaze apologetically. "It likely will. I'm sorry."

*"I told you to be careful of his face!"*

Octavian's furious voice broke through my mind, the image of him standing over a combatant who'd landed a lucky hit in training coming to the front of my memory.

*"How's he supposed to attract women with you ruining his looks?" He grabbed my chin, scrutinizing the growing welt across my face with concern. "At least it won't scar."*

"Perfect," I muttered, the cold chill of renewed fear creeping down my spine. I looked around the room, the sunny exterior and prying eyes of the courtyard too much to bear. I didn't want to ask, but the only person to hear was Atticus. And he'd been the one to patch me up for the last three years, for injuries sustained both on and off the sands. "Can...I stay here for a bit?"

Atticus's eyes flicked first to the door, then the windows, outside which the usual noise of the Arena was filling with sounds of surprise and excitement as news of my defeat spread. "It might be wise. I have no doubt the fight coordinator will want to speak with you, and it might be best that he do so here." Flinty strength filled his ordinarily placid gaze. "He'll hesitate to take out his frustration on you if I'm here." He crossed the tiled floor to pull shutters over the windows, returning to hand me a folded blanket. "I know it's the last thing on your mind, but try to rest."

It *was* the last thing on my mind, but I pulled the blanket over my shoulders and curled with my spine to the wall. Tremors shivered through my core, and I tensed my muscles in an effort to hide them. Alone in this room I might be, but *no one* could know how terrifying those last moments had been.

*I lost.*

By the time Octavian finally appeared, the clamor outside had died down, and the light faded beyond the shuttered windows. I'd—miraculously—fallen asleep for an hour, but had spent the rest of the time alternately sitting and pacing, feeling like the room was fast becoming a cage. The numbness had worn off, and all I could think of was the odds I'd stacked against myself.

It would've almost been better if my opponent *hadn't* shown mercy.

The door closed on Octavian's heels with a rattle. Gods, he looked...tired. And angry. I wasn't sure which was worse.

"Where've you been?" he demanded.

"Me?" I got up from the bench with frustration overriding the fear. "Where have *you* been? Normally you're on me as soon as I take so much as a *step* wrong."

"That was before you lost a fight that ought to have been an easy win!" He shook his head with disgust, and I remembered his earlier sadistic order regarding the man who'd almost killed me. *Make him feel it.* "Don't you have *any* idea of the type of trouble this could cause for you?"

"Yes." The word snapped from me. I'd built a pattern of victories as a solo fighter, become known for them, but I hadn't been undefeated the *entire* time. There had been plenty of times where my losses had come with steep repercussions on and off the sands. "But I'm still alive, and one loss doesn't finish me."

"It almost did," Octavian growled. "You're just lucky your opponent is a more honorable man than you."

"Gods all bless honorable men," Atticus said without turning around.

He'd kept his back to us, working at the table beneath the window, but I knew he'd been alert to everything. I'd never been so grateful for his presence, or for the fact that he'd kept the other infirmary attendants away. With the way Octavian's anger sometimes went, it was better for everyone to keep their distance.

Octavian sighed, and his features relaxed into something more ordinary. "Fortunately, the spectators appreciated the twist in events. Her Radiance, in particular, was taken with the drama of it all." He gave me a calculating look. "You're so close to retirement, and they want to see you rise to the very end, whatever it may be."

There it was, the hollow sense of my future—and Callista's with it—slipping from my grasp like Arena sand through my fingers. I straightened my shoulders and looked Octavian square in the eye, like I had other times in the past when he'd challenged me to live up to my potential.

"Rise again or die trying? I'll do it. Just watch."

He smiled grimly. "That's more like it." A flicker of movement was all the warning I had before his hand whipped through the air to crack against the side of my face. I recoiled from the blow, ears ringing with shock as he snarled, "But don't you *dare* fail me again."

# CHAPTER XIII

CYRUS

T he next morning, my attendants had to wake me, when normally I was up with the sun. I swung my legs over the side of the bed, wincing as muscles twinged and my head started throbbing. By the worried looks on their faces, Octavian's blow from yesterday had left quite the bruise.

*Just watch,* I'd promised him last night. *I'll rise again or die trying.* A statement that had all but guaranteed fiercer and fiercer odds against me until I either impressed him or finally broke. And with the way he'd lashed out, I wouldn't bet on myself, especially now that the light of day was illuminating my reckless words from the night before.

Another cautious look from the attendants warned me that I'd spent too long sitting, frozen, at the edge of the bed. I reluctantly got up, washed, ate—all too stiff and without the engaging personality that I normally displayed, but enough to set their fears aside. Ordinarily, I'd go to training next, but hesitation slowed my hands as I reached for practice armor and weapons.

By now, everyone would know I'd lost. There was no hiding that, or the bruise I'd gained as a result. And much as I wanted to hide in my quarters—or better yet, atop the Arena where I could at least enjoy the *illusion* of freedom—every hour hiding would only weaken me in the future. For that matter, the time I'd spent out of training after fighting the lizard might have contributed, however indirectly, to my performance yesterday. And I couldn't afford to let anything like that happen again.

My hand closed on my practice armor, and I slipped it over my head and did up the buckles. No hesitation. No backing down. No mercy. I'd survived this long on those terms, and I'd have to keep my guard even higher if I wanted to continue.

Shoulders straight and chin high, I made my way to the practice courts. Sure enough, whispers followed as I crossed the courtyard, ducked through the stables, and stepped into the shade of the olive trees.

"Cyrus!" The current lead for the Wyvern team paused mid-swing to raise his practice sword in salute. "You're still alive!"

A laugh cracked through my chest. "Guess so."

"When you didn't show up this morning, we thought Octavian had killed you himself." His eyes flicked to the bruise on my face and his smile became strained. "Seems he thought you were worth another chance."

"For now." I nodded at the ring. It looked like he and the other Wyverns were finishing their practice with sparring drills. "Have room for another?"

"Only if you go easy on us," one of the others said with a pointed grin. "*We're* not the ones who sent you flying yesterday."

Some of the tension in my muscles relaxed. Wyvern wasn't too bad, as far as named teams went. At least among them, I didn't have to immediately keep my guard up. "I'll try to remember."

They rearranged themselves, and Domitian, the leader, assigned a new drill. I started slowly at first, letting the repetitive motions settle before allowing muscle memory to take over. Soon I was breathing hard, and by the end of the drill the Wyverns were looking suitably impressed.

"Nicely done," Domitian congratulated me. "I *knew* yesterday was just a fluke."

I frowned. "Who's saying it wasn't?"

His grin sobered and he nodded at the other training ring, where several of the lower-ranked solo fighters were sparring. "They're mostly talk. But they were saying earlier that you're getting slow and yesterday was a long time coming."

"Interesting..." I examined the other combatants between sips of water. Two of Flavius's friends who fought for Dragonesque, and three others who'd barely made it to solo matches.

Easy.

"Hold this for me." I passed the water I'd been drinking to Domitian and stepped over the ropes of our practice ring. The *clack, clack* of practice swords slowed as I approached, and I raised my voice to be heard over the noise. "I heard someone thinks they could match yesterday's performance."

The men in the ring halted, turning to me with expressions ranging from bravado to all-out fear. One of Flavius's friends squared his shoulders. "That sun of yours has to set someday. Maybe yesterday was just the beginning."

I stepped over the rope that separated us. "Say that again."

A flicker of hesitation crossed his face before he raised his chin defiantly. "You couldn't even hold your own against a rookie fresh from the wagons. You're done."

I'd seen the shift in his weight before his feet moved. I took a half step to the side, and his headlong rush took him past me. A quick, two-handed strike to the base of his neck with my practice sword, a sweep of my foot around his ankle, and he pitched to the ground just inside the ropes. I twisted to slam the pommel of my sword against his temple, and he lay still—unconscious, or pretending to be.

A furious yell warned me to beware the others. I turned in time to block a blow aimed for my head, catching the blade against mine and using the momentum of standing to throw its wielder back a pace. He cut down at me again, and this time I sidestepped, dodging the blow and darting inside his reach to bring the weight of my sword with a crack against his wrist. He yelped, a startled, pained sound that drew all eyes within the courtyard, and staggered away with his sword falling from tensed fingers.

One left. He'd hung back, unwilling to work with the others to take me down. His eyes darted to the others, then me, and he turned to run.

Mistake.

The practice swords were heavy, and a blow to the hip was enough to send him pitching into the ropes. They collapsed under his weight, stakes pulling free from the ground. It was the work of a moment to close the distance, and even less time to bring the pommel of my sword down on his head.

Silence rang through the courtyard, broken only by the whimpers of the man whose wrist I'd just snapped.

I leveled a glare at the other two who'd been in the ring. "You as well?"

They shook their heads and backed away, showing me empty hands as they went.

"Anyone else?" I yelled.

Silence.

*Good.* I put up my sword and stepped out of the ring, past the man who'd first insulted me. I spat in the sand near him. "Idiot."

A ripple of laughter went through the courtyard as I returned to Domitian and the other Wyverns. Behind me, the men I'd downed were slowly stirring, the one with the broken wrist helped by the two who'd possessed *some* common sense.

"Thanks for not interfering." I reclaimed the water from Domitian and downed it gratefully before setting the cup aside.

"I feel like you had to take care of this yourself," he said. "Though, did you notice..." He gestured at my forehead, where the bandage covering my injury from the previous day had slipped.

"Oh." I pulled the bandage off and crumpled it in my fist with satisfaction. Now there'd be fewer doubts as to the danger of crossing me, even when I was obviously injured. "Oh well. Could be worse."

Domitian laughed, respect clear in his eyes as he turned to survey the courtyard. "You won't get in trouble for this, will you?"

"Over them?" I shook my head. "Doubt Octavian values them that highly. But if anyone else asks, make sure you tell them about this." I picked up the rest of my gear and slung it over my shoulder. "Let them know that one defeat isn't going to take me down."

Something twinged in my temple as I crossed the courtyard, warning that my casual dismissal of the bandage had been premature. After leaving my practice gear in my quarters, I turned to the infirmary, finding Atticus decanting glowing green liquid from one jar into another. He looked up in surprise, which quickly changed to exasperation.

"When I apply a bandage, I expect it to remain longer than a single night." He tipped his head to take in the rest of my appearance, from the sweat soaking my hair to the dirt smearing my tunic. "I take it you've been putting rumors in the ground?"

"There were some loudmouths at training. I took care of them." I nodded to the jar, which I now recognized as disinfectant. "You might need that. I didn't leave them looking pretty."

"More work for me? How kind of you," he said dryly. He set the jar on a shelf and pointed to the side door. "There's a basin in the other room. Go wash—quickly. I don't want you crossing paths with them again so soon."

I followed his instruction, returning a minute later with wet, clean hair. The disinfectant stung as it went on, but the sensation quickly mellowed under a new application of salve and a clean bandage.

"There," Atticus murmured, tucking the end tightly. "You look silly, but something tells me you don't mind that."

I smiled. "I just put two over-confident idiots on the ground and broke the wrist of another, all with a bandage wrapped around my head." I ran a finger across the band of linen. "I'll take the attention if it reminds them that I'm not going down easily."

"Understandable. But if I were you, I'd avoid the more crowded training times for a bit." Something angry shadowed his eyes. "I've seen enough 'accidents in training.'"

*So have I.* I nodded. "I plan to. I won't back down from fights like this, but I don't want to get hurt in one, either."

"Speaking of," Atticus said, eyes flicking to the door. Outside, I could hear the sounds of several people approaching, and not quietly. "You'd better go. Use the other door, and may the gods grant you luck."

I left the infirmary and rejoined the sunlight—and stares—in the courtyard. Word of my thrashing Flavius's friends was already making the rounds, and I felt all the better for it. Hopefully, others would take the hint and leave me alone. With more pressing matters taking the forefront of my mind, I made for the herb garden where I sometimes found Callista.

"You told her to keep her distance," I admonished myself as I turned a corner. "She'll understand if you don't find her after all that."

I paused at the entrance to the sheltered courtyard. Callista was there like I'd hoped, working in one of the planting beds with another girl. The sunlight shimmered against her brown hair, illuminating each strand with gold more pure than anything that flowed through the Arena coffers.

*I have to let her know I'm all right.*

A moment later, my decision was rewarded. The other girl got to her feet, hoisting a basket of cuttings to her hip and leaving Callista alone.

Gravel crunched under my sandals. "Lis!"

She gasped, looking up with a mixture of surprise and joy. "Cyrus." The herb shears fell with a *clunk* into the basket at her feet. "You're safe, you're—"

"Alive?" I came to stand beside her, daring to quickly wrap an arm around her shoulders before withdrawing. "I don't understand why. He's never hesitated in his other matches. I don't know why he did this time."

"I've crossed paths with him once or twice," she informed me. "His rise to fame hasn't been easy."

I nodded soberly. She likely meant in the infirmary. And the fact that he'd been facing me was evidence enough that the gryphon rider had made at least one enemy in a very short time. "And?"

"He's more compassionate than his fights indicate. And he has a wife out there." Callista nodded in the direction of the city. "She's been here at the gates, looking for him."

I wasn't sure why, but that knowledge struck painfully in my chest. "Well, I hope for her sake she forgets him and moves on." I crouched to run my hands through the shorn stems of the lavender. "Even if he survives, he won't be the man she once knew."

"But what if he is?" Callista asked. "And what if she still wants him, even after knowing what he's done to survive?" She knelt and picked up the shears to begin snipping again, angling a look at me. "This place is horrible, but it only changes you if you let it."

"Trust me, it's not a choice," I said. The *crack* of bones breaking under my practice sword was no easier to forget now than it had been the first time it'd happened. "Everyone here becomes a monster in the end."

A slender hand covered mine. "Not everyone. Some men see the things no one else sees, and decide they're worth fighting for."

Warmth spread through my chest. "I'm not the only one who's defied this place." I reached down to gather a handful of lavender sprigs, weaving them through the braids that bound back her long hair. "And not all fights are won on the sand."

She blushed. "I'd still wait for you."

I ducked my head to hide a smile. "Good thing you won't have to."

Callista began collecting lavender into her basket. "You'd better go before June gets back. She'd faint if she saw who I was talking to."

The reminder scorched across my skin with the realization that we'd been standing in the open this whole time. *I didn't mean to stay so long.* I stood, closing my hands into fists to cover my sudden panic. "Let's avoid that. I...I don't know what the next few days will hold, but remember me when you visit the altars."

"I will." Her voice followed me as I left the garden. "Gods all bless, Cyrus."

The corridor was cool and quiet, and I paused for a moment to let my eyes adjust. With blood humming in my ears and warmth lingering in my chest, it was a cold shock when a familiar voice greeted me from the dark.

"Never stays with his partners for long, hmm? *And* hasn't taken a lover in a long time. If only they knew why."

I stiffened, a hand instantly rising to guard. "What's it to you?"

Flavius pushed away from one of the arched windows, his gait like that of a chimera circling its prey. "She's lovely, I'll grant you. But you really could do so much better." He stopped a few feet from me, loathing in his eyes as I slid my foot to a ready stance. "I heard what you did at training today. You'd better watch your back." He glanced at the garden, where several other workers had joined Callista. "Or perhaps it's not *your* back you should be concerned with."

I closed the distance between us in a furious rush, one hand catching under his chin to hold him against the wall. "Touch her and it's the last thing you'll ever do," I gritted into his face. "Let the gods be the ones to grant you mercy."

I shoved him to the floor and walked away, ears sharp to the sounds of him wheezing, spitting. A quick glance through the window he'd been lurking by told me that Callista had left the garden, but my heart still pounded with terror.

*What have I done?*

For years, we'd been so careful—*I'd* been so careful. *How could I have been so foolish?*

I rounded the corner and descended into the tunnels below, dropping to my knees as soon as I was certain no one was watching. My breath came as hard and fast as it did in the middle of a fight—only, there was no winning this.

"Callista," I whispered into the silence. "I'm so, so sorry."

# CHAPTER XIV

BASTIAN

Nothing, and everything, had changed. I was moved to the third floor of the building I'd been housed in, given a room abutting the curve of the Arena itself and passing ragged men who dreamed of such status every time I left its relative safety. I had three days away from the Arena sands. Days spent training, visiting the armorers, taking vague warnings from Octavian as he oversaw everything. I could not get away from the eyes. Could not find a moment of peace for myself, or to go to the exterior wall and try to find Lyra.

Days had passed since we'd planned to meet again. I had a faint hope that Callista had gone to see her anyway, even after news of my victory, but I didn't have time or space to go to the altars. If it wasn't some guard posing as an attendant, it was Phestus, and I did not want even him intruding on those moments.

I wasn't sure why I had the guards. Unless they worried Cyrus might seek me out and gain his revenge. I had not seen him, and that gap left a constant buzzing over my skin, wondering when he, or someone else, might make their move. If I'd upset more than just him in my unwanted rise.

But nothing came, except a summons on the third day. To an arming room, where newly crafted armor sat on the table. A pile of cloth lay beside it and two attendants waited, Phestus with them. He seemed pleased, but then he didn't seem to fully realize the scrutiny on me, only that he had risen as well.

Octavian pushed in, ignoring the way I immediately tensed. "Get changed." He pointed to the cloth. "Then they will arm you."

None made a move to leave, and I finally grabbed the top piece and shook out a short tunic of black with a pale stripe sewn down the length. I exchanged mine for it, then looked at the remaining clothes. Dark grey pants, with a black stripe down the sides.

"What is this?" I asked.

Octavian smiled mirthlessly. "Fighting is only part of the show."

I scowled as I doffed boots, habit keeping one eye on them while pulling on the new trousers. Even if I'd wear tunics and sandals if I were home, part of me was glad they'd let me keep some semblance of the gryphon rider's uniform. I felt more comfortable fighting dressed like this.

I lifted arms from my sides once everything was tugged and laced into place. Octavian shot me a warning look and gestured to the attendants. One came forward with the breastplate, swatting away my hand as I reached for the straps. I frowned, but he glared back. They took their duty seriously.

I looked instead at the surface, catching a glint. I finally had armor that fit correctly, but it looked ridiculous. A pale arc embossed the right side of my chest, and on the left? My fingers skimmed over seven dull scales tacked on. I shook my head, recognizing the pattern. The gryphon constellation.

"What is this?" I demanded again. I almost punched an attendant as he grabbed my arm, but it was only to drape a bracer over and start buckling. The other knelt and fastened on greaves made for fitting over boots.

Octavian didn't answer, just smiled again. My helmet, burnished and oiled, was handed to me as the other man showed me a sword of fine steel, blade treated with something that sent it shimmering in the lamplight. He sheathed it and would not let me buckle on my own cursed sword.

"Carry the helmet and come with me." Octavian strode out, and I had no choice but to follow. Two men fell in behind me. Perhaps Octavian did not trust me to be armed at his back without his own seconds.

We wound through the tunnels, finding stairs and climbing up and up until we came out onto a higher level of the Arena. Wide walkways looked out on the city through arched cutouts to my right, and the distant sight of a gryphon in flight woke a deep longing inside. A hand against my back kept me moving as my feet paused for a moment to take in the sight.

Octavian pushed through another door and I entered behind to find a room full of wealthy men clustered around a table laden with delicacies, stuffed meats, and plentiful wine. My stomach might have grumbled at the sight if it wasn't so tightly wound.

Senator Tiberius set his wine down and slowly clapped, a few gold bands around his wrist jingling as he did. "My compliments to the armorers."

I snugged the helmet against my hip, left hand clenching tight as the other men looked me over like they were inspecting a stallion or full-fledged gryphon for sale.

"He certainly looks like a challenger. But is the moon motif too much?" one asked, refined features creasing in disdain.

"The only thing that can truly defeat the sun is the moon. It wouldn't make sense to make him *clouds*, would it?" another asked in a nasally pitch.

Tiberius circled me, reaching out to tug the tunic sleeve so it sat more evenly. If he noticed my forearms tensing, he didn't say anything.

"He knows his part?" a younger man asked, leaning on the swooping low back of a chair.

"He's about to," Tiberius answered, finally giving me space. I searched for a way out, but the only way lay in the door behind, guarded by the two men. Or to the left, where an open curtain exposed a wide balcony that likely looked down over the Arena itself.

"There is considerable interest from the public for a rematch between their beloved hero and the unknown challenger." He pointed to me like I hadn't been at that fight. "Our interest lies in making that as profitable as possible. So we build your reputation up. You'll have a string of easier fights to get more victories under your belt. Cyrus will have to prove himself again, and you? You just keep winning, until you get a chance to beat him once and for all."

I glanced around the room. None seemed to mind that Tiberius had practically put a price on their golden sun's head.

"It's no secret that the gryphon races have been pulling attention from the Arena. But between Cyrus and you, we have a chance to quash their attempt at relevancy. A rivalry will keep attendance up and bets flowing in."

This was no more than he told me in that room levels below, but it still felt raw and bitter.

"Now," Tiberius continued. "Octavian has told us the root of your obstinacy."

My hand brushed my sword hilt and Tiberius tilted his head, the gesture warning me just as loudly as Octavian's sudden step forward. "You'll remain anonymous for now. Helmet on for each fight. No parties, no women. Yet."

The younger man scoffed from where he still leaned carelessly against the chair. The others just looked annoyed they couldn't sell me yet.

"Our previous conversation still stands, Bastian. Deviate in any way, and you'll bear the price."

I had nothing for that except another salute. Tiberius dismissed us with a tilt of his head, already turning to wine and conversation before I stepped out the door.

Octavian grabbed my upper arm and shoved me until my back touched the wall. "I did not want this," he hissed. "I've spent too long training Cyrus to see him upset by an unknown contender. *You* are not my choice, but I still oversee your training and every aspect of your life. Remember that."

I jerked my arm away and offered the same abrupt tap to my chest, letting it look like the curse that raged in my head. He smiled thinly and did not stop me as I turned and made my way below.

The armorers wordlessly helped me out of the armor and I changed into the simpler tunic and trousers, somehow feeling safer in them. No one followed as I left the arming room, and I was alone for the first time in days.

My feet took me to the quiet hallway lined with altars. It felt a small mercy that it was empty except for flickering candlelight. I stopped in front of the First God.

"What do you want from me?" I whispered. No answer came and I slumped against the opposite wall, sliding down to sit under the crushing weight of the last few days.

"What purpose does this serve?" The question wrenched from me, hot frustration trying to push from my eyes. I felt like a child again, trying not to cry when Father had forbidden me from the stables. Later I understood it was because he did not want me around the soldiers who tried to take more than what they were promised. But this? This did not seem to serve any greater purpose.

My knees pulled up and I rested my arms against them, sinking hands into my hair. *Trust the gods,* I'd been taught over and over through all my twenty-eight years. Trust was easy when you were free. When things made sense. I scraped a hand down my face, dismissing a few tears as I did.

I leaned my head against the wall, regarding the First God's statue. He looked back in gentle solemnity. Who'd decided that's what he looked like? Unless it was just a sculptor also looking for a bit of hope.

"I cannot do this," I whispered to him. "I cannot..." The only way to defeat the men who held all the power was to let my next opponent kill me. Not fight. But as soon as I thought it, the faces of Lyra and August flashed and I rebelled against the thought of lying down and dying. I smiled mirthlessly. Another thing that felt raw. Lyra and I had been married for almost four years, and in that time, had never had a child. It had started to weigh on her more than me. And it wasn't until I left, maybe to never come back, that we'd finally had a son.

"I don't..." *Believe? Trust?* But still the god looked back. Not that a carved statue would change or speak. But maybe some part of me had been hoping for an answer, a sign from the god the carving represented.

"Bastian?"

I jolted at the voice, relief breaking over me as Callista rushed to my side. "Thank the gods! Are you all right?" She knelt beside me, one hand on my forearm. I nodded, tears still stinging my eyes, maybe more at the friendly face.

"I've been coming as often as I can, hoping to find you here," she said.

"They kept me busy." My smile held too much misery.

Her arms circled my shoulders. "I'm so glad you're alive. Both—" She cut off and pulled away. "What will happen now?"

I scrubbed under my eye and let my arm fall across my knee. "From what they told me, they intend to set me up as a contender. Until I face him again and one of us dies."

Callista's faint gasp drew my focus to her suddenly pale face. She pressed hands against her chest, fear shining again in her eyes. My head rested against the cool stone. I'd been too caught up in my own fear days ago to catch it. Now I wondered if the golden sun cared about anything, or if she just watched wistfully from afar.

"It sounds like it won't be for a while yet. We both have to prove ourselves," I said, and her worry receded slightly.

"I have something for you." Callista rose to her feet and went to the niche, returning with something in cupped hands. "When I didn't find you here the morning after, and no one knew where you were, I went to the wall. I found your wife."

I sat a little taller. She smiled and pressed braided leather into my hand. "She took the money, but told me to return this. She said you needed some part of them with you."

My fingers curled over the marriage scale, its edges sharp and cool. Lyra had been lightly frustrated with me when I'd spent months of purposefully saved wages to buy them. Most others of our status had simple tokens to give each other, but I'd wanted something bold and lasting for us. She'd forgiven me quickly for the expense, and I'd laughingly teased her that she'd rub hers away with her habit of messing with it when in thought or frustrated.

"She also said she'd be back. She seemed so determined, I didn't think I could convince her not to. Sorry."

A laugh barely stirred my chest. That sounded like Lyra.

"I left it there for him to watch over." Callista pointed at the god. "I didn't have a good place to keep hiding it, or carry it if I saw you again."

My smile wobbled, but it felt more real. "I put it there before each fight. If...if I..."

Callista nodded. "*If* the worst happens, I'll get it to her." She paused. "Your son is beautiful."

I turned away, hiding another rush of emotion. "He is." My voice still betrayed me.

A rustle and gentle pressure against my shoulder marked her sitting next to me. She tucked her grey dress over her knees. "I got you this." She handed me something else. I tugged the strings of the small bag, and the sharp smell of incense rose from it.

"Callista, you shouldn't have." Incense could be expensive.

She shook her head. "I know someone from before I came here. We

151

served the same house. She was taken to the temple when I was sold here. Sometimes she comes by with the temple attendants."

I closed the bag, folding both it and the necklace between my hands.

"It felt like you needed something," she said.

"I..." A faint scent of incense still lingered. "How do you have any faith in this place?"

She smiled softly. "I've been a slave my whole life, Bastian. My mistress was kind enough, but I won't say it wasn't hard to watch free men and women every day. When she died, there was no one to inherit, so all her possessions were sold away and I came here. This place is...cold. But I have to believe in something. Pray to someone, because otherwise it's just misery after misery, isn't it?"

Eight years of war had shown me some of the worst humanity had to offer. Not so long ago, I'd been like her. Stubbornly clinging to some belief that there was something better, or some greater purpose besides blood and muck. Perhaps the gods should have turned from me with how easily my faith had been shaken. I'd only been marked a slave for weeks, but she'd borne it her entire life.

"Does anyone ever answer?" I asked.

"The people I care about are still alive, and perhaps I can help one's family find some peace if I need to." She nudged my arm.

I smiled faintly. "Caring seems dangerous in a place like this."

Callista looked at the First God. "Caring is never really safe."

"No," I agreed. I studied the First God. Perhaps he'd given me some sort of answer after all. Callista had told me he was unexpected, and this friendship certainly was. I'd feared I'd leave Lyra always wondering, but perhaps this was an answer to my desire that she'd find peace. Perhaps prayers weren't answered in showy flashes, in bright signs. Perhaps they were answered in people, in pockets of warmth in cold places.

I pushed to my feet and pinched a few grains of incense to place in a small pile before the god. Callista joined me and offered a sprig of lavender from her hair. I lit it in the candle and touched it to the incense. Fragrant smoke rose as the burning herbs flickered to embers, but the incense smoldered on.

"For hope, then." I glanced at her. Callista smiled back.

I closed my eyes. *Then please, if I'm here for some reason...help me do it well.*

# CHAPTER XV

BASTIAN

*R*idiculous.

I tested the buckles on my new breastplate, turning to the bracers after. This was my first fight as...whatever they wanted me to be. Besides the armor, a new banner had been made. It hadn't been unfurled yet over the entrance. They waited for me to run out the tunnel onto the bright sands. Phestus stood by me, holding my helmet as I checked armor like I might before climbing on a gryphon and flying to battle.

"What do you know about him?" I tilted my chin to the tunnel entrance. I didn't much trust Phestus's swordplay, especially after seeing him engage in a few fights, but I did trust his penchant for gathering information.

"Mid-tier. They all say he's showy, plays to the crowd." Phestus handed me the helmet. "Crowd seems to like it."

"And they'll like it more if you play along, draw it out," Octavian growled. I glanced over my shoulder at him stalking forward to join us. He still had not forgiven me for survival, and the last two days as he'd taken over my training had felt like he'd try to end me before I had a chance to fight again. The only benefit of this new station was the attendant who knew how to work a numbing oil into sore and bruised muscles to get them healing faster.

I pulled on my helmet, meeting his glare again through the narrowed slit. Lying down and dying was not an option, open defiance would be punished. I drew my sword and turned to the entrance. This fight was only to the first injury. I allowed a mirthless smile as I broke into a jog, bursting into the sunlight and being greeted by the swell of the crowd. Playing along had never suited me.

My list of sins only grew in Octavian's eyes as I aimed only to end every fight as quickly as possible. The "string of easy fights" became only that first time. Then it turned to death matches against higher-ranked fighters, sometimes two at a time, across an Arena shaped into dunes with stake-lined pits on one side, across wooden frameworks that would collapse without warning, or into mazes that housed traps in corners.

I was a mess of scrapes and cuts from fights, and bruised from training and Octavian's fury at my continuous refusal to make a spectacle of things. His men were all too happy to restrain me like they had that day in the yellow team's arming room. Phestus almost gleefully brought the rumors, only building after each fight. Oddly, it felt like I passed invisible through the courtyards, as most eyes were on me in fights or training when the helmet obscured my features.

I still had not seen Cyrus except for distant glimpses. His legend was gaining power as well, growing with each fight he won. My banner sat beside the sun atop the Arena walls, and every time I glanced up, it brought back the sickening knowledge that they intended me to face him again someday. Perhaps soon. And they might hope that one or both of us would not survive.

Time not spent fighting was spent learning the mazes beneath the Arena, trying to find any other space hidden from eyes. I hid and re-claimed my scale necklace from the First God's altar four times. It'd been days since I'd seen Callista more than in passing. Days since I'd been able to go to the courtyard wall to look for Lyra, though I had no doubt she was coming every two days. Once I thought I saw her, but I'd not dared to stop and look, only walked on with the heat of Octavian's glare against my back.

The morning of my fifth fight, I burned a small bit of the precious store of incense, bracing hands against the stone altar and whispering a prayer for strength. I tucked the necklace away, along with a small bag of coins. It had been begrudgingly given to me three days ago, but there seemed no point as I was not free to step outside the Arena like some of the other fighters. Even if I was, I'd still save it to be passed to Lyra if I didn't come back.

Today was to be a chimera fight, alongside another higher-level soloist. It hadn't been stated, but I assumed it would be the same pattern as last time I'd been paired with a fighter against a creature. Kill the animal, kill each other.

The attendants silently armed me. Phestus paced with restless energy like he was going out first to face the thing. As minutes passed, the breastplate felt like it cinched tighter and tighter against my chest, until a forceful exhale relieved the pressure.

I buckled on the sword and took the spear handed to me. My partner had the whip, I had the spear. After feeling the other weapon used against me, I'd no desire to train with or use it.

"Good luck, Bastian." Phestus shifted beside me in the tunnel entrance. I pulled on the helmet and did up the strap, only slightly settled. Even though I was sure he'd help if I needed, his words still felt a little final.

"Giving up on me?" I asked.

He smiled faintly.

"We took down a gryphon, the two of us," I said.

"With two other men and the god of luck."

I chuckled, the sound almost carrying the emotion. I'd almost rather fight the golden sun again than the creature waiting for me. But the god of luck wasn't getting my prayers. I stepped closer to the tunnel entrance and glanced at the sky like I could see all the way to the afterlife, maybe glimpse the First God looking down. Hopefully he was.

"Hold him steady!" the head physician barked. One of his assistants threw his weight against my lower leg, jostling the bleeding wounds across my thigh. I jerked again, barely pinned down by another assistant. The damned chimera had finally gone down. *After* my ally had shoved me perilously close to its claws. I'd barely dodged, the claw marks not as deep as he'd intended, but gods it *hurt*. The stinging pulsing through my leg felt almost metallic. It throbbed in tandem with the bleeding wound wrapped around my left forearm from the whip.

Cloth ripped and I craned my head to see the physician readying a vial of fluid above my exposed leg.

"This is going to sting," he warned, eyes full of grim resolve. He poured, and I screamed through clenched teeth. He swiped a cloth across the injuries, then relentlessly poured again. "Can't be too careful with chimera claws," he said, ignoring my cursing. "They're so dirty, this'll get infected if we don't get it clean."

The pressure on my chest and leg let up, before they ambushed me with something bitter to drink. At least it started numbing things as the physician poked and prodded at my thigh.

"Get the rest of the armor off. Some of this will need stitches." He glanced up briefly. "Soldier, were you?" he asked, pushing clean cloth against the injury.

I nodded, tipping my head back against the thin pillow.

"I've found it's usually soldiers who curse so creatively. Tunic off," he told the assistant. I levered up enough to let him get it over my head before I sank down. The physician wrapped a cloth around my forearm and directed me to hold it in place. A frown only made his features more stern as he looked over me and finally shook his head. "You're the gryphon rider?"

I nodded again.

"Octavian still doesn't realize you'll live longer if not treated like a piece of meat?"

I huffed. "I think he's trying to get rid of me."

"He's going to be successful." The physician let go of my leg long enough to nudge my head to the side, revealing a two-day-old bruise across my jaw. Octavian usually waited to hit me until I was out of helmet, preferably armor, depending on how much I'd frustrated him. Or used blunt staffs that could still sting through the leather.

"Don't encourage him," I mumbled.

The man scoffed under his breath. "I rarely do."

I didn't feel much of anything as he treated my leg, finally wrapping clean bandages around. "Let's see." He gently took my arm and pulled away the temporary bandage. "What caused this?"

"Whip," I replied. His eyes narrowed, and I could see him comparing the slash to the bruised welts he'd treated over a week ago. "You're lucky," he finally said. "Those who survive a chimera fight usually come to me with many more injuries."

It felt more like incense burned and a faint thread of faith clenched in a bloody and bruised fist than luck.

He eventually helped me sit up, and an assistant came to remove my boots and help me out of what was left of the trousers and replace them with new clothes. Exhaustion slammed into me so hard that my eyes watered as I sat there, right hand clenching the cot's edge. The distance back to my room felt like miles.

"Lay back." The physician nudged me. "Rest for a few hours at least."

I obeyed, and a blanket was pulled over me as I turned onto my side. "Thank you," I mumbled. "Gods all bless." The familiar words slipped out, more than halfway a prayer of thanks that I'd survived another day with the physician's help.

A hand pressed my shoulder. "They do, lad. They do."

# CHAPTER XVI

A few days after Flavius's threat against Callista, another upstart fighter attempted to catch me unaware as I went from my quarters to a society event. I dodged his attack, broke his arm, and left before anyone else could try their luck. The main training times were no longer safe after that. Too many measuring glances, too many whispers.

And over it all loomed the darkened banner of a moon cradling a constellation of stars—a gryphon cast in silver and bound to the heavens.

The symbolism wasn't lost on me. The new banner was placed in opposition to mine on the Arena wall, after all. Nor was it a surprise when stories of its bearer began circulating the courtyards and city beyond.

"He's destroyed every single opponent he's gone up against."

"He doesn't hesitate—not ever!"

It was true from what I could tell, which made his earlier refusal to end my life even more disconcerting. Most of his fights were over in minutes, but the crowds couldn't cheer loudly enough each time he defeated an opponent.

"Does anyone even know what he looks like?"

No. Hardly anyone did. He wore his helmet to train and kept to his quarters the rest of the time. My memory of his arrival didn't serve me well, merely reminding me of what I'd already determined. From what I could remember, he'd had dark hair, but so did almost everyone else. And any other memory of his face had already disappeared.

"Did you see him against that chimera? He walked away without a single scratch!"

That part I didn't believe...I'd been watching the fight, and both he *and* the man he'd been partnered with had stepped wrong near the thing's claws. There'd been blood, but the crowd was in such an uproar when the two men turned on each other that the injuries had gone unnoticed.

"I think he's better than the Golden Sun..."

Octavian rarely trained me himself, these days. But one afternoon, he'd ordered me through my paces in the training courts, brow furrowed and face unreadable. "Look at them, Cyrus," he said between strikes of a practice sword, daring my attention to the men crowding the practice yard. "They think you're doomed to failure." A blow that rattled my teeth, barely blocked. "They think your sun is setting." He sidestepped my counterattack, got inside my guard before I could twist away. "Are you going to prove it"—he halted his sword an inch from my throat—"or prove them wrong?"

He was right. The measuring looks couldn't be cowed, no matter how many times I won my matches or flattened opponents in training. After that day, I avoided the training yard entirely, practicing late at night or early in the morning when there was no one else to see. I avoided other combatants, avoided the staff and trainers. Avoided Callista, though it tore through my heart each time I caught a glimpse of her.

"I can't predict what Flavius will do," I'd warned, the one time we'd crossed paths without anyone seeing. "It might be that he'll wait until he knows it'll hurt me the worst, or he might strike at any time. Just please." My voice had broken on the words, and I'd held her like there was a chance, even in that moment, that something would happen to leave her undefended. "Be careful. Be watchful. Please try to stay safe."

Careful. Watchful. Words that now made me curse my earlier carefree mannerisms.

And I had reason. Since my loss, I'd faced monsters I'd previously only had nightmares of, and my opponents were better equipped and trained than ever before. I'd always prided myself on my ability to recover quickly from combat, but I'd never realized how *exhausting* it was to use all my reserves of strength and cunning time and time again. Even with the growing weariness, I kept training, practicing old skills, climbing the Arena to scrutinize obstacles from the roof—only to fall into my bed each night after yet another public event.

For that reason alone, I envied my opponent. At least an anonymous fighter wasn't forced to socialize when he'd been fighting for his life three hours previous.

And it all kept returning to these moments, with the pulse of blood matched by the roar of the crowd. Flavius and I exchanged murderous glares with each other before stepping out of the tunnel.

"Try not to stab me," I said. "It'd be so hard to explain."

His eyes narrowed. "Don't get in my way, then."

Well, that settled things.

This match was one of the new ones the board was trialing, with teams sent into a maze to retrieve banners in their color while their opponents attempted to stop them. Incapacitate your enemies and the odds of success swung in your favor. It was supposed to be a test of teamwork and skill, but today?

Today, I had Flavius on my side. And the entirety of Domitian's Wyvern team as my opponent.

"Don't kill them," Octavian had ordered, warning clear in his voice. "That's not the purpose of this match. Get the flag and make it look good. They all know you're smart, so impress them."

*Impress me. Rise or die trying.*

As if I *hadn't* been trying.

I set my jaw. "I will."

No sooner had we exited the tunnel and stepped into the maze than an explosion sounded nearby. A puff of smoke rose into the air, coupled with a clatter of wood, and I immediately knew that the first hazard in the labyrinth had been triggered.

"Find the banner!" I yelled to Flavius. "I'll keep them away!"

He scoffed but obeyed, disappearing around a corner. I ran toward the center of the maze, where I suspected Domitian's men would hold their ground in an effort to prevent me from exploring their side of the sands. As I ran, a now-familiar hiss came to my ears, and I swore at the sound.

Lizard. It hadn't been in the maze when I'd scouted last night, but the sound was a dead giveaway. They must've moved it in early this morning. And if I were to hide an item in a labyrinth, I'd make sure it was well guarded.

I turned toward the sound, the pitch of the crowd telling me that I was going the right direction for...something. Heart pounding, I skidded around a corner, stopping with just enough time to skip out of the way of a lashing tail as the monster wheeled on itself.

There. Beyond the lizard, at the farthest end of the maze, pinned to a wall and flapping feebly in the disturbed air. A red flag.

These lizards couldn't climb well. I'd established that in my first fight against one. Before the monster had time to gather itself, I'd backed up and gotten a running start. My sandals scraped against the wall, and I hoisted myself over the top. Once I got my feet beneath me, I was able to keep my balance, running along the tops of the walls with enough forward momentum to keep upright.

A yell sounded nearby as I snagged the red banner from the wall it'd been tacked to. It sounded like one of the Wyverns. I caught my breath and tucked the flag into one of my bracers, its red tail flapping as I jumped from the wall to land in a crossroads.

Almost as soon as I did, voices broke into my ears.

"There he is!"

"He's got their flag. Get him!"

A chill ran down my spine, breaking the elation that'd come with retrieving the flag before Flavius had gotten a chance to find it. I didn't know what Domitian had been told, but I wouldn't put it past Octavian to order some targeted twist against me.

I tipped my head one direction, then the other, mind flicking through what I'd seen from above the night before. The earlier explosion had made one side impassable. The other had already been demonstrated to house a lizard. I'd crossed to this side of the maze over the walls, but there was no time for that now. That left this avenue as the only open path to my own tunnel, with four Wyverns fast approaching to stop me from reaching it.

But there was something about this path that only I knew.

I took off running toward my side of the Arena. The hum from the stands grew louder at my retreat, the spectators' roar drowned out by the yells of my adversaries.

Thirty feet. Twenty feet. Ten.

Behind me, voices. I was used to hearing them in training, and for a moment it almost sounded like the days when both Flavius and I had fought under Dragonesque. Like friendship, twisted by being set against each other too many times.

"Nowhere to run now, Cyrus."

"Come back and we'll make it easy on you!"

Eight feet. Seven and a half.

The Wyvern players charged around the corner.

I skidded to a stop. Took a half step back, a subtle click tapping the bottom of my sandal as my foot landed on the arming mechanism for a buried explosive charge. My heartbeat thundered in my ears once, twice, three times—as the first Wyvern stepped over the ten-foot mark.

Triumph overtook my voice. "Oh, you lose. You lose!"

My foot came off the pressure release, and the sand erupted beneath their feet.

Once in the tunnel, Flavius wheeled on me. "What was that? 'Go find the flag' and you send me down a dead end?"

"Would you have done anything if you'd found it yourself?" I retorted, keeping my distance. "Spare me the anger—you know I had no idea where they put those flags."

I allowed myself a moment of satisfaction as I doffed my armor and chatted with the attendants. Four versus one, and I'd still won. The Wyverns had been blinded, dazed, thrown from their feet, and I'd sprinted for my own tunnel with the flag held high over my head. Even without seeing Octavian's grudgingly proud face, I had no doubt that this story would spread.

"Impressive," Octavian said. "I'll be consulting with the others, but I think this style match may serve us well in the future." He raised an eyebrow at me. "Did you know the trap was there?"

I shook my head. There was no need to tell him that I'd known the entire layout of the maze, down to the exact placement of each hazard. "I felt it under my sandal." I shrugged, the movement as casual as I could make it. "The rest was just luck."

"Well, luck or not, you may have won yourself a few days of reprieve." Octavian turned to leave. "Maybe the sun still rises after all?"

*Maybe.* I took a deep breath as he vanished around the corner. The triumph of victory was already fading under the venomous looks Flavius was giving me, further solidifying the knowledge that the sands were the *safest* place for me right now. I could only hope that when his wrath finally broke, it would do so against me and nobody else.

# CHAPTER XVII

BASTIAN

Resting for a few hours turned into waking the next morning still in the infirmary. I came awake with a slight inhale, pulled from dreams of racing across wave-crusted sands on horseback, trying to outrun something behind me. I hadn't dreamed of horses in many years.

The physician had given a brief smile and introduced himself as Atticus, checked the bandages, and declared me no worse for wear. He sent me back to my quarters, where I washed, ate, drank what felt like half the Arena's water supply, and fell back to sleep.

Octavian had been none too happy to find me asleep again, perhaps hoping to find my leg amputated. He grudgingly agreed to the physician's demands for rest, but by the second day after the chimera fight, I was back to training.

I was to report to the courtyard by midday and I slowly pulled on armor, testing weight on my leg. It ached, but two days of rest had my body feeling almost brand-new. I sat to adjust the scale necklace in my boot, and paused. If I'd calculated correctly, the odds were good I might find Lyra at the wall. And Octavian had indicated that it would be a different trainer that afternoon.

Only a moment's more hesitation before I grabbed the small bag of coins and tucked it into my belt. I made my way to the courtyard, adjusting my stride to hide the limp as much as I could. Phestus had reported that some had tried to attack Cyrus in training. I might not have his status, but I was making myself enough of a threat that someone might do the same if there was a sense of weakness around me.

No one stopped me. Most barely spared a glance. Though they might start to notice the helmet I carried as I made my way across the courtyard. I looked to the wall, scanning the many faces lining it who spoke to the men clustered in small groups.

And my heart threatened to leap out of my chest when I saw her. I fought to keep the smile off my face, drawn there just because I'd finally seen her again. I didn't go straight to her, moving to a temple attendant in the light blue robes of the goddess. I plucked a coin from the bag and picked out two painted shells in return. Lyra waited patiently for me to make my way to where she stood in the shade where two walls met.

I leaned against the bars, back to the stone, and kept one eye on the courtyard.

"I was starting to think you might have forgotten me," she said lightly.

I tipped my head a little closer, daring to place all my attention on her. "Never."

Lyra studied my face, anger stirring again in her blue eyes as her look darted from bruises to scrapes. "Bastian, you wear a helmet to fight."

I glanced away, having no voice to explain what battles I had off the sands because I wouldn't treat life and death like a game. "I do," I finally said. A whispered curse almost as rough as a soldier's came from her. It made a slight smile appear on my face and I arched an eyebrow at her.

She pursed her lips and slipped a hand through the bars to squeeze mine. "You scared me, sending that young woman to find me. I thought you were dead."

My heart twisted and I gently brushed my thumb against her hand. "I should have been. Did you get the money?"

"I did. Bastian—"

"Lyra, listen," I interrupted. Seeing her had salved some injuries, but threatened to carve more. "You can't keep coming back. There are too many eyes on me. And if they see you and me, or figure out who you are..." I shook my head. Octavian was happy to use brute force to try to wear me down, but if he knew about Lyra, I'd break like he wanted me to. "They'll use you against me any way they can. I can't see you—either of you—hurt."

There was only resolve in her face as she looked steadily back. "No, Bastian, listen. Your men are back."

I startled despite myself. "What?"

She nodded, pressing closer to the bars and casting a cautious glance to make sure we were still unheard. "They came back from the front days ago. Some came to tell me about you. They brought your things." She smiled softly. "And more money than they said you'd saved. I counted, and it's more than the year's wages I know you get."

"All gods bless those idiots," I whispered.

Lyra chuckled softly. "That's what I said. I'm taken care of for now."

"Good." I straightened slightly. "Take it and go to your parents on the coast. Get as far away from here as you can. Tell my father…" My voice caught. My mother had passed five years before, and Father had turned to his horses and training, putting up a gruff shield to the world. Losing me as well might shatter him. "He'll want to meet his grandson."

"No."

"Lyra." I was nearly begging.

"No, Bastian, *listen*." She gripped my hand tighter. "When I told them where you are, what is happening…they want to find a way to free you. Maybe we can buy your freedom."

I scoffed. "The Arena makes too much from one fight to even consider whatever a squad of soldiers and an almost-widow could scrounge."

She scowled and reached through the bars to hit my arm. I narrowed my eyes back.

"Then we find another way." Lyra studied the Arena like she might figure out how to crack the fortress.

I shook my head. "The only way out is in five years, *if* I keep winning and manage to stay alive."

"I find I cannot wait that long." She lifted her chin, but it trembled. "I need you, Bastian. He needs you." Her free hand pressed to the sleeping bundle wrapped against her chest. I reached through the bars to brush a finger against the tiny hand barely visible. August twitched, but stayed asleep.

"I don't know if there's a way out. They don't even let me out of here like some others. Too rebellious," I said at her questioning look.

She smiled. "That sounds more like you."

I shook my head.

"Then we find a way, Bastian. Most of your men, they say they'll do anything to help. That they shouldn't have let you be taken in the first place."

"They would have ended here beside me, or worse. Tell them to stay away," I said.

Lyra only smiled again. "I will not."

I fought a smile and lifted fingers to her cheek. "I have to go. If you come back, space it longer. Every four days. I can't risk you."

Blessedly, she agreed. I passed her one of the shells. She took it and the small bag of money, and tucked them in with August.

"I can bring you something next time." She indicated the shell that remained in my hand.

"Save the money," I said and stepped away.

Her hands closed around the bars, like she held herself back from reaching for me. "Stay safe. I love you."

I could only smile back, lips soundlessly moving in the same promise before I made for the training courts.

The small blessing of Octavian's absence vanished when he arrived an hour into easy routines to test my leg.

"You fight tomorrow," he announced, seeming pleased. He couldn't see my curse behind the helmet, so I let him have another wordless one. "Start again," he ordered.

By the time he declared himself satisfied, I was limping and had taken multiple new bruises from hits landed against me. I gained my feet after the lower-level trainer slammed me to the ground. Octavian was gone, and the sun slanted heavily toward evening. I pulled off the helmet and gratefully drained a waterskin.

"Get to the infirmary, have your leg checked again," the trainer said. At least he offered a shred of compassion. I gave him a more respectful salute and made my way across the main courtyard, barely able to mask the way my muscles clenched around the injury.

I circled to come through a different entrance, avoiding the main barracks hall. Shorter corridors would take me into a smaller courtyard of herbs and plants. I leaned a shoulder against the wall, taking a breath to steady myself before going on. I hoped the slashes on my thigh hadn't broken open. Something told me Octavian wouldn't care, and would drag me into the Arena himself if I couldn't walk.

A sharp crack and feminine whimper sent a jolt through me.

"I'm done with him making a fool of me," a man hissed. Another fearful sound followed. "Cyrus shouldn't have let me see he has a heart. How do you think he'll break when he finds *you*?"

"Please..."

If I hadn't already been moving, I would have then at the sound of Callista's voice.

A few feet ahead was a nook shaded from both corridor and courtyard. In the gathering dusk, I could barely make out the grey of Callista's dress behind a man's bulk.

"Let her go," I snarled.

The man whipped around with a surprised grunt. My own shock nearly matched his when I recognized Cyrus's second. His hand pressed against Callista's neck, pinning her to the wall. Tears streaked her face and blood beaded her lip.

"This doesn't concern you," he sneered. "Move along or I'll deal with you after I'm done with her."

I smiled thinly. "Let her go."

He only pressed harder against her throat, daring me. I hefted the helmet still in my hand and caught the moment he realized who I was. I hurled it at him, and he flinched enough to loosen his hold on her. Enough for me to grab his tunic and haul him away.

He came around swinging, catching my side with a fist. I staggered a step before throwing my weight against him, slamming him into the wall. He grunted and swung a hand at my face. I pulled my shoulder up, deflecting most of it. Another blow came and I caught his wrist, twisting and yanking, the joint breaking in tandem with a harsh scream from him. My elbow slammed into his with another pop. He folded and I threw my entire strength into three vicious blows across his face. He fell to the ground, spitting out blood.

I glanced over my shoulder to find that Callista had fled. When I looked back, the man was trying to lurch to his feet.

"Do you know who I am?" he slurred, swiping blood away. I did, only by virtue of the man he was supposed to protect. And even if I cared, I still would have protected her.

"No," I spat. It only enraged him like I'd intended.

He never got to his feet. I kicked out, connecting with his stomach and flinging him to the ground. He tried to retaliate, to get up, but I kicked again.

He tried to curse me, but I just yanked him up by his bloody tunic and bent close. "Don't ever think about coming near her again," I warned. "And if you try to come for me, I won't be merciful." I delivered one more blow, sending him to the stone and unconsciousness.

I stepped away, the frightening coldness that had swept over me evaporating into the panic that had been recognition of Callista's voice. I left him in the corridor for someone else to discover and went to find her.

Callista hadn't gone far. She'd stumbled into the small courtyard, hands pressed over her ears, hunched shoulders shaking.

"Callista." I circled around, trying to meet her eyes. She curled away from me. I tried again, gentling my voice as much as I could. She stumbled back with a short cry, fear fading only a little as she saw me.

I reached out slowly, stopping just short of touching her. "Are you all right?"

"B-Bastian?"

"Yes. It's safe, it's just me."

She shivered, the motion pulling more tears from her eyes.

"Are you all right?" I repeated.

"I..."

I eased forward another step, and she threw herself toward me with a sob. It rocked me back a step, and I gently rested my hands on her shoulders. If protecting her in that moment was the only reason I'd been brought here, I'd gladly accept it.

"You...you were here?"

"I told you I'd help if you needed," I replied gently.

Callista pushed away, clutching at her upper arms. "Where...?"

"Don't worry about him." It came out harsher than I intended.

"Is he..."

I huffed. "Not yet." It had briefly crossed my mind, held in check only by the knowledge of who he was. "Callista, that was Cyrus's man."

She swallowed hard and backed away, new paleness chasing across her face. There was new fear in her eyes. Of me.

"Did he hurt you in any other way?" I asked.

She shook her head violently, eyes wide at the thought.

*How do you think he'll break when he finds you?*

174

I hesitated, wondering if I'd accidentally unearthed her secret. Maybe the golden sun's too. "Callista, has Cyrus ever done anything to you?" I asked carefully.

"No, he'd never dream of—" Her lips clamped shut.

I offered a faint, rueful smile. Her words at the altar before made more sense now. I didn't know a thing about Cyrus other than his ruthlessness, but I wouldn't betray Callista. And I'd still protect her if she needed it.

"You have one of my secrets, and it looks like I have one of yours," I said softly. "We're even, the two of us."

She only stared at me, still trembling. And for the first time, I seriously considered the foolish idea of escaping. If only to bring her to freedom and safety too. I retrieved my helmet and gently touched her elbow. "Come, let's go to the infirmary, make sure you're all right."

"No, I have to..." One hand fluttered toward the overturned basket, trimmings scattered everywhere.

"You, or someone else, can get it later." I set my hand on her upper arm and turned her away from the basket. She let me nudge her toward the side entrance, and we stepped into the quiet cool of the infirmary.

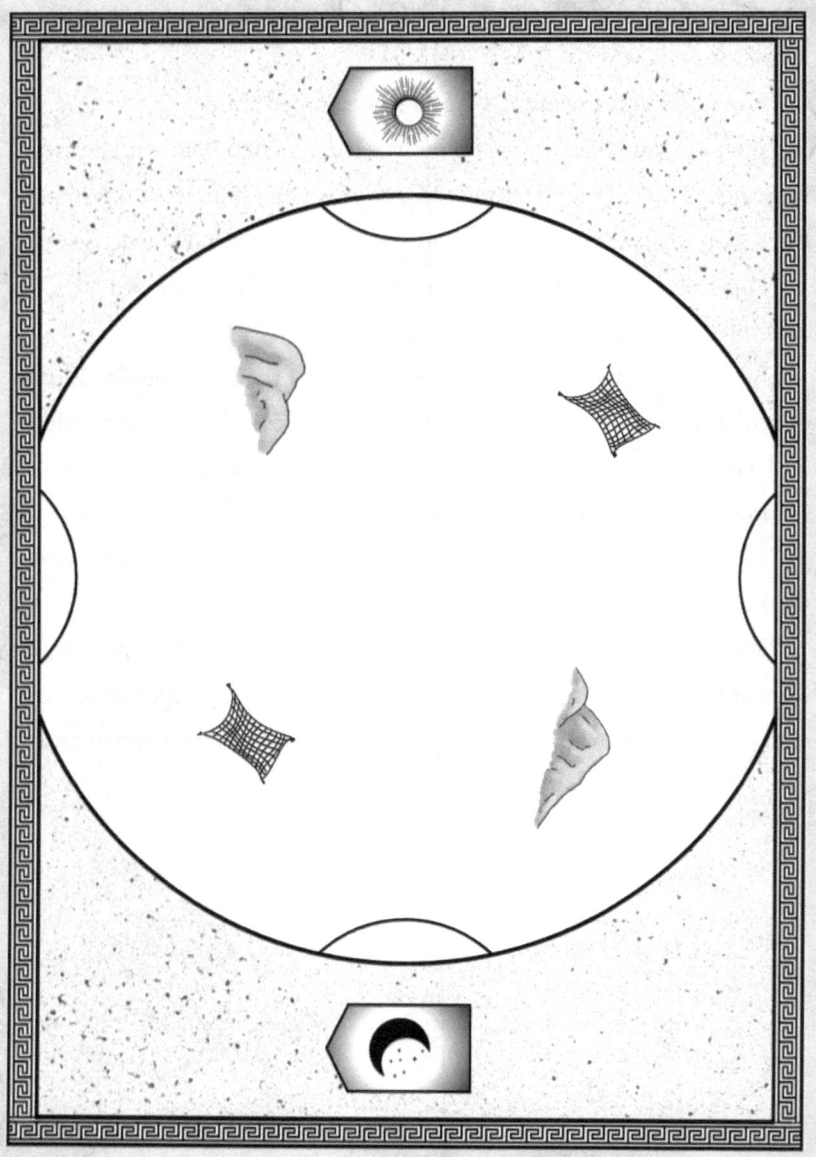

# CHAPTER XVIII

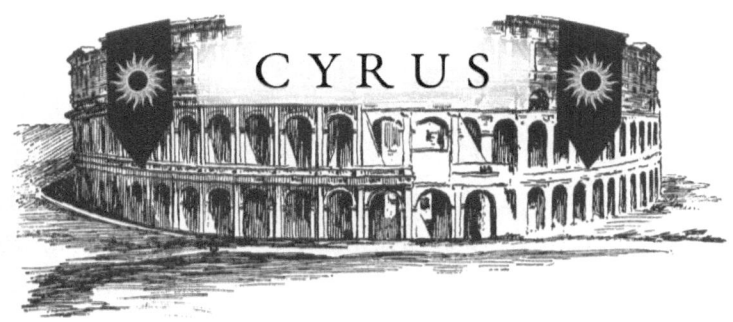

CYRUS

The board was pleased with the results of the skill-based matches. The gathering in their private box the night after the maze trial was jovial, almost celebratory. According to the tablet they'd shown me—not that I understood, but I nodded and smiled nonetheless—revenue was skyrocketing on the days when either I or the gryphon rider fought. The odds had never been more profitable, and the whole city was talking of us.

I took the news with grim satisfaction, even if outwardly I showed the board the same carefree, confident face I'd always presented. The longer I kept this up, the closer we drew to the month that marked five years since I'd taken solo elite status. All I had to do was stay ahead of the odds, keep winning, and—

"...we've realized the spectators want more," the man who oversaw the ticketing office and publicity said. "They've gotten a taste for drama, and we plan to give it to them."

"We're going to face each other again?" The words slipped out before I had the chance to contain them, and I swore at myself inside my head. *Don't seal your own fate.*

"Not yet," Senator Tiberius said. "It's too soon."

"We're keeping eyes and ears on the public." The first man laid the tablet on the cushions beside him. "They love each of you separately. To put you in the Arena together would put an untimely end to this rivalry."

I forced my face to remain in a neutrally friendly expression. *Rivalry.* No one had so openly acknowledged the truth to me until now, but hearing it spoken was leaving a bitter taste in my mouth.

"Then, what?" I crossed my arms, hiding a wince as a bruise ached beneath my tunic. "I've found my pacing again, the public is taking notice...so what now?"

"Revenue is up, and has been since your loss. We want to try an experiment." Octavian met my gaze without flinching. "You've been winning against every opponent, and the crowds are convinced you're unbeatable once more." His fingers twitched as he counted silently. "In a week, there's a contender coming from Sieneca's arena for a match against you. You're going to lose."

"*What?*"

"You heard me. Lose. Throw the match. Let the public wonder if you can keep the pace." He gave a dangerous smile, one of someone who'd calculated the odds and found them to his liking. "They love their heroes, but they want to see them fall."

"But—but, I'll—"

"You might get hurt," he agreed. "I'd almost expect it. But you've taken hits before."

"Of course!" I snapped, irritated now. "*Many* times. But never on purpose!"

"If that's too much, we could draw attention another way," one of the younger board members put in. "I've got a long list of wealthy women—and some men—who'd give their right hands to say they'd spent a night with you."

I closed my hands into fists, the gesture no longer one of frustration but of panic. "Don't. I'll lose, fine. I'll make it as dramatic as you want. Sieneca will be proud of their hero, and the people here will flood the gates to see if I can recover." I forced myself to stand straight. Almost five years of fighting stretched like waves behind me, the end like the sun rising over the ocean. *I have to hold on.* "I won't let you down."

I stayed late at the gathering that night, trying to repair whatever bridges I'd destroyed between me and the board before returning to my quarters with the feeling that I'd done everything I could. That night I couldn't sleep. Instead, I slipped from my room and climbed to the top of the Arena, lying on the tiled roof and staring into the sky until dreams of flight took me.

The clatter of pigeon wings woke me in the early light of dawn, and I scrambled down before anyone saw. It was almost past my usual time to train, so I quickly gathered my things and hurried to the courts. My movements were sluggish with exhaustion these days, and I was sweaty and tired by the time I finished training. The complex was still waking as I returned to my room—gryphons screeching in the stables for breakfast, recruits stumbling out of the barracks for training, and staff hurrying between morning tasks.

I was halfway across the arrivals courtyard when one of the staff caught my eye. Callista, head bowed, was carrying a basket of linens toward the laundry. I started walking toward her without really meaning to, pulled by the need for something stable in a world that felt like it was falling apart.

She raised her head as I approached, and my heart almost stopped. Bruises marred her fair skin, and her lip was swollen and scabbed where the skin had split.

I ground my teeth. *Flavius.*

"Callista," I whispered. Then, louder, "Callista!"

She jumped at the sound, her eyes locking with mine. With an almost panicked look, she freed a hand from the basket and gestured for me to follow.

We stopped in the stables, where the animal handlers were seeing to their charges with no mind paid to the two interlopers. I stopped in an alcove half-filled with hay, no longer able to bear the silence. "What happened? Who—" I gestured helplessly at the bruises, my voice cracking. "Who did this?"

Callista hugged the basket tight against her chest, her gaze resolutely on the floor. I dared to reach out, laying my fingers against her hand. "Lis, please. Talk to me."

A breath shuddered from her. "Flavius. Like you said. I—I think he must've been angry at you defeating the Wyverns without his help... He said he was tired of you making a fool out of him."

I ducked to better see the bruises. Gods, there were more across her throat. My fingers closed into a fist as I withdrew my hand, and I fought to keep the shaking out of my voice. "Did he do anything else?"

She shook her head, slowly at first, then faster. "No, he didn't have the chance. Cyrus—" She looked up at me, wonder shining in her eyes. "The gryphon rider saved me."

"What?"

Callista sniffled and brushed away a tear. "I was in the courtyard alone when Flavius cornered me. Bastian must've been in the corridor and heard. He—Cyrus, he didn't hesitate. Not a moment. He pulled Flavius off and had him on the ground, and—"

"Bastian." I repeated the name flatly. "How do you know his name?"

Callista took a shuddering breath. "I told you, we've crossed paths. In the infirmary, and again at the First God's altar." She paled at the sight of my expression, but continued, "I offered to take news to his wife when he thought he was going to die facing you."

I groaned. "You... Callista, that was so foolish. He could've... *You* could've..."

"But he didn't. And then he saved me." Callista's shoulders straightened, and she took a deep breath that steadied her words. "I still don't know why he spared you, but I don't think I've heard anyone as angry as he was when he realized what was happening to me. He was *furious*."

"I'm going to kill Flavius," I informed her, the reminder of who was responsible for this sending cold through my veins.

"He probably wishes you would," Callista said with a snort. "His arm's broken in two places, and his nose too. He might never be able to stand at your back again." At my sharply inquiring look, she explained, "Bastian brought me to Atticus as soon as he could. I overheard them talking."

A low whistle escaped me. "You're serious?"

"I'm serious." She gave a short laugh. "I didn't think anyone would see, and certainly no one would stop. But he did. I know I helped him earlier, but—"

"You would have done that for anyone—you never learn." I rubbed my forearm, where a scar crossed under my bracer. I'd been dizzy from blood loss and sick with worry after a hard fight when a slave girl with more compassion than common sense had stopped to help me. I'd later learned that her name was Callista, and ever since had lived with the knowledge that I owed her a debt.

Debts were dangerous things, best repaid before they became a vulnerability to exploit. Surely that's all this incident had been.

Though perhaps now *I* owed something more to the man who'd spared my life.

"I'm glad you're safe," I finally said. "I'm so sorry I wasn't there. I wish—"

She put a hand on my wrist, silencing me. "I know. I know, but I'm also glad it didn't have to be you. Flavius might keep quiet about this, but he'd have retaliated if it'd been you instead of Bastian." Something like fear crossed her face, and shame twisted in my stomach that *she* should be afraid on *my* behalf. "It's bad enough that he struck once; I don't think I could bear it if he lashed out at you as well."

"If he did, I'd end him," I promised. "Are you *certain* you're all right?"

She nodded. "I'm all right. And I don't think Flavius will try anything again." A smile ticked at the corner of her mouth. "He's scared of more than one person now."

"So it would seem." I took a deep breath, tension ebbing from my muscles. Whatever the motives behind the gryphon rider's intervention had been, Callista was safe from Flavius. And by some twist of fate, perhaps I was as well.

## ◆———— BASTIAN ————▶

The crowd was more eager than normal. I leaned on the crossbar of the gate that usually spat creatures into the Arena, glad I was not going out. There was something restless in the air, something that would make me hesitant to take flight if I still had a gryphon. Something that had me checking over my shoulder, checking the sky, looking for what was amiss.

Even I'd heard of the visiting gladiators from Sieneca. Octavian had made sure to let everyone know of it, making sure everything in the Arena was polished and pristine. To impress or overawe, I hadn't decided.

Cyrus was fighting today, and the Empress herself had come to see, Imperial banners draped from the upper balcony. I silently cursed her—and the late Emperor's—ambition that had turned from defending borders to ruthlessly expanding them.

There would be no creatures for this fight, billed as to the first injury. No point in battering—or killing—prized fighters.

The announcer raised his voice, calling through a dragon horn to amplify to the highest rings of the Arena. Lauding each fighter, building lists of victories to cheers or boos from the crowd. I rolled my eyes, imagining the man on the front lines declaring, "The elite gryphon riders of the Fifth Legion of Her Imperial Majesty, coming to decimate the backward savages who don't find as much joy in killing."

I scanned the walls—over thirty feet from sands to spectators, sheer, with no way to climb into the stands and disappear into the crowd. No other way to the benches and sweaty press from the side of the Arena I was contained to. I'd been hauled up to the board's private box after my last fight to be paraded again, praised for the money I was bringing in, and given another warning to keep following orders. The way there had been marked by guards. No way to sneak unseen.

A frown twisted my lips, even though I had already known the answer.

Ever since finding Callista and hearing of my former men's idiotic loyalty, the idea of escape had seized me. I hadn't been able to shake it, no matter the bleak reality staring me in the face. The same that I'd already told Lyra over and over. There was no way out.

I hadn't been able to speak with her again. Days had passed painfully with one sighting of her at the wall, but I was unable to go with Phestus dogging my heels and two trainers beside me.

I was still a scout, and I needed to see it all for myself. Prove my suspicions to the hopeful nudge trying to prod me. The underground tunnels ran to rooms, the Arena, or dead ends. There were other gates from the stables allowing for new animals to be brought in, along with the never-ending train of food to keep them. One question on how the gryphons were kept fed to Titus, and he'd shaken his head.

"Don't even think about it, Commander," he'd said. "Anything a desperate man claims he can pay once he's through the gates will be matched, or paid over, by the Arena. Or anyone stupid enough to listen dies when the unlucky man is hunted down and confesses accomplices. I've seen it happen both ways in the last two years here."

I'd just tilted a nod and asked where they got the gryphons. There was a small part of me relieved to know that they didn't get any from Mursa, where Lyra's father still trained gryphons for the Fifth Legion or for racing.

There weren't many other places to look, and I'd brought myself here to watch the fight and see if a different vantage brought any new information. The handlers hadn't argued, just given me a wide berth. Either my reputation from the sands, or what I'd done to Flavius. A name to finally match the unfortunate face that looked even worse now. Speculation was rampant, most thinking I'd done it to try to sabotage Cyrus, but he hadn't sought me out. To fight *or* thank me. It seemed unlikely Flavius would return to fighting, not after the way I'd left his dominant arm. Something I'd not regret, even once standing before the gods and answering for it.

The tunnel behind Cyrus remained empty as he ran onto the sands, the sunburst flag unfurling above him. A hill banked against the southwest curvature, another at the opposite wall. It blocked just enough of my view as the challenger strode out.

He was bulky, built like an oak, with armor barely latched over him. I rubbed my thumb across my chin. This wasn't going to be much of a match. Not with the golden sun's speed and wiry strength. He'd spin circles around the man and hamstring him in the sand.

Like our fight, and the other two I'd watched, Cyrus charged immediately. No hesitation, no fear. I crossed my arms and leaned against the bars. If he was a rider under my command, he'd have learned restraint a long time ago, to be an asset rather than a danger. But he didn't move like he'd thought about a team in years.

His opponent swung and hacked. Cyrus blocked each strike. My thumb skimmed over a newly forming scar on my chin, slashing upward to my cheek. This should have been over already, bare minutes in. The challenger was already moving a half-beat slower, his endurance waning.

Cyrus kept moving, feinting, stumbling a step here, twisting like he could barely match a blow there. He could have injured the gladiator a half dozen times, while the other man had come nowhere close to landing a blow. A humorless laugh burst from me. *They told him to lose.*

I glanced at the stands. No one seemed to notice the obvious. They leaned forward, almost piling on one another in places, shouting, waving scraps of cloth with the fighters' colors. A bit of gold glinted near the Imperial banner far above, declaring where she'd placed her odds today.

It felt painful, watching this. *Phestus* could take this man, apparently the best Sieneca had to offer. They circled a little closer, and I caught a glimpse of Cyrus's face. Nothing but grim concentration. Then he wobbled to the side, and I caught it, a flicker of irritation.

"Are you tired yet of the show?" I murmured. There was nothing obvious in the Arena other than the hills. Nothing to use against each other. Yet.

They wove back, closer to the tunnel Cyrus had emerged from.

"This is ridiculous!" Octavian's shout had me glancing over my shoulder and down the tunnel. "Give them another minute and it'll be obvious Cyrus is pitching it. What can you throw out there to liven it up?"

"They'll find the traps eventually," came the answer, almost pleading.

"Get something ready," Octavian snarled. "If this isn't over soon, I'm going to push something out. It'll be you if we have to."

I turned back to the fight. Cyrus stumbled back and back, giving a good show of desperation. The other gladiator shouted incoherently, sensing some sort of victory. I almost hated that he'd be able to brag about defeating Cyrus.

It happened in a second. Cyrus gave one more stride, then froze, true surprise filling his face. The sand exploded upward, thrown by the violent release of a net. Cyrus was wrenched to a knee, rope coiling around his leg. I pushed away from the bars with a curse. One end of the net enveloped him, small weights on the corners whipping around to ensnare his shoulders.

That warning hum in the air from before the fight built higher. Lightning about to strike. *Get out of the sky.* My hands swept to my sides, ready for...what?

Cyrus thrashed and swung, each movement guided only by panic. I felt I could almost see the whites of his eyes. The gladiator stepped forward, raising his sword to deliver the winning cut.

*Don't try to fight a caged animal.*

Cyrus flung off the part of the net that had trapped his shoulders and head. Another curse slipped from me as I saw it happen, almost *before* it did. His eyes widened at the threat looming. He jabbed up, lunging to his knees. His sword plunged under the man's breastplate, deep into his gut.

They toppled, Cyrus with legs still partially tangled in the ropes. Uncertain cheers started, then built higher. But it was just horror in his face as he stared at the man he wasn't supposed to have killed.

He scrambled to his feet, then squared his shoulders, lifted his bloody sword to the crowd, and strode toward the tunnel. It was the same tug that had urged me to spare him that sent me striding down the tunnel, turning the corner that would lead me to the fighter entrance.

*To do what?* I argued with myself.

"What did you do?" Octavian practically screamed. I turned away from the sound of it, hating myself a little as I did. Telling myself there was nothing I could do this time. Hardened already by the Arena, where there was no mercy for anyone. Not even their golden sun.

# CHAPTER XIX

CYRUS

I 'd won.

I hadn't meant to, had been steeling myself the entire gods-forsaken match for the moment when I'd have to let my opponent's weapon find a mark. The brute would have something to brag about to his friends. An injury scored against the golden sun, and gods grant that it'd be something I could recover quickly from.

Then that net had caught my feet, entangled me so fast I'd had no time to dodge—and for a terrifying moment, I'd been stuck. Pinned in coils of rope, blinded by sand, and I'd forgotten everything other than survival.

The crowd loved it. They surged to their feet, scraps of cloth in my colors and his raining down onto the sands. I struggled to my feet, drawing back my blade in horror. The announcer's voice rang strangely through my ears, the roar of the crowd like the rush of waves behind it.

Instinct had never failed me, until the moment I'd been ordered to ignore it.

I shook my feet free of the net. Stepped off. Raised my sword in acknowledgment of the crowds. Strode to my own tunnel and into the relative safety of the armory, where I collapsed, shaking, against the wall.

*Fearless,* the stories said. *Undefeated.*

Those who repeated that legend hadn't seen the countless times I'd been pinned under opponents larger than myself, hadn't witnessed when I'd gotten sick from training harder than the other recruits, hadn't seen the bruises from Octavian's relentless drive to make me the best there was.

They didn't see the fear that lurked every time I stepped out of line, even now.

*Especially* now, as Octavian's furious voice resounded through the armory and attendants scattered out of his way. "What did you do?" He hauled me up by my breastplate and shook me like I was fourteen. "Don't you have any idea how much this is going to cost? We promised them their people would be alive at the end of this, now we'll have to pay out for their blood!"

I got my feet under me and stood upright. "I know—I'm sorry. I don't know what happened. The net was a surprise, and I—" I caught the twitch in his shoulders, and dodged a slap that would've surely left a handprint across my face. "I panicked! I'm sorry!"

"What am I going to tell the board?" he growled. "You've ruined *everything*! What am I going to *do* with you?"

I backed up another step, the panic that'd seized me on the sands now screaming at me to run. Forget losing when I should have won. Winning when I should have lost would have consequences worse than anything I'd ever experienced. I was almost ready to return to the sands, where hopefully the thousands of watching eyes would be enough to dissuade Octavian from whatever he was about to do, when a wide-eyed runner burst through the armory door.

"Sir!" He held up a message tube, sealed in purple and gold. Mouths dropped open, and an awed murmur spread through the room at the sight of Imperial colors.

I kept edging away, hand fumbling behind me for a weapon—anything to protect myself from the fury about to be unleashed.

Octavian composed himself. Took the message from the runner and broke the seal. When he looked up again, his face held a mixture of awe and cunning, a combination I'd never in a million years thought to see on the heels of his anger.

"What is it?"

I didn't even hear who'd said it, but it *was* the only question worth asking.

Octavian lowered the message. "It's the Empress," he said by way of explanation. "She loved the show. She's asked us—well, you specifically—to a victory celebration."

I'd finally gotten my back to the wall. It still took me a moment to find my voice. "...And?"

"And you're going," Octavian informed me with a smile that said my penalties had been delayed. "The city wants to celebrate their hero."

The Empress had been planning this invitation in advance. The villa—a few miles from the city at the base of a vineyard—was decorated in the colors of both Sieneca and the Arena. My sunburst and the starcast gryphon were displayed prominently near the entry, and more fighters' banners lined the portico.

The Imperial hostess was nowhere to be seen as we entered the lushly decorated space. Other guests *were* in abundance, and soon I was the center of an admiring crowd. Across the banquet hall, a similar knot of people surrounded a pair of other fighters sent from Sieneca for this week's matches. I wasn't sure what their attitude toward me would be, since I'd just obliterated someone they'd probably known or looked up to. To my surprise, their greetings were almost jovial.

"Been telling him for years that rushing in like that would get him killed," one of them said once I'd made my way over. "He's been top for so long, he's gotten sloppy."

"*Was*," his partner corrected. "No longer." He tipped his cup toward me. "Thanks for today. You've done both of us a favor."

*Favor.* I scanned the room for those who were angry with me after this "favor." A handful of board members clustered around the tables of food, and Octavian was in conversation with the well-dressed man who'd welcomed us to the party. I returned my attention to the Sieneca fighters without much enthusiasm. "You'll be able to rise higher now that he's gone, is that it?"

"Something like that," the first one said. "A number of us will be able to advance now, and maybe some other things will change as well."

The conversation continued along similar lines for another few minutes, until the pair looked over my shoulder and excused themselves with respectful nods. I turned to see Octavian approaching alongside the man he'd been speaking with. Fresh panic crawled up my spine—he looked far too cheerful for what I feared he was planning for me as soon as eyes were off both of us.

"Enjoying the party?"

"It's beautiful." I crossed my arms to hide the fact that my hands were shaking. "Interesting conversations, lovely decor. A really festive evening."

"I'm glad to hear it. Have you met the hostess yet?" Octavian nodded to a doorway at the end of the banquet hall. "Apparently she's become quite the follower of your matches, and would love to have a word."

"The Empress—I—" The words froze in my lungs. I'd spoken with Senators, generals, other public figures, but never someone with this amount of power.

"Yes, Cyrus. Her Radiance would like to meet you in person."

I forced the tremor out of my hands. Put a smile on my face, and followed Octavian and the Imperial attendant out of the hall. I'd expected we'd be shown to a smaller room and more private gathering, but instead the attendant led us deeper and deeper into the villa. Soon, I'd lost all sense of direction, and it wasn't until he stopped before a carved door that my reason returned—and with it, a sudden, crushing sense of doom. This was all too similar to other encounters. Ones where gold had changed hands, and I'd had to submit to others who didn't care about me beyond what my body could offer them.

"Why are we here?" I asked, taking a step back.

Octavian turned to face me, the sharp edge in his voice returning full force. "I told you. She's taken with you. She has a liking for powerful men, as long as they can be broken."

Terror pounded in my ears. "You wouldn't."

"It's already done." A horrible light glittered in his eyes. "You've been forgetting your place, golden boy. It's time someone reminded you of it."

My attention had been fully on him. I didn't see or hear the men who appeared out of the shadows until my arms were pinned behind me and a strong hand clamped something rough and acrid against my face. I tried to twist away, to fight, but already the world was going fuzzy and golden around the edges.

The door opened with a smell of incense and perfume, and I caught a glimpse of a tall woman draped in purple linen. Her voice sounded strangely through my ears, luminous and compelling as she asked, "Is this him?"

Someone answered, a familiar voice that sent fear streaking through my limbs as I struggled to keep my feet under me. "The golden sun himself, Your Radiance. All yours, as promised."

She smiled and extended a hand. "Come in, Cyrus." I found myself pushed forward, and her fingers wrapped firmly around my wrist. "I've been so eager to meet you."


I'm not sure if I slept. The night blurred into morning, and morning blurred into the rocking of a carriage with heavy curtains. I felt dizzy. Sick. Sore, but not sure how I'd gotten that way. My head rang with images half remembered—awful even when viewed through the foggy mess that was my mind—as the carriage rumbled through the city.

I could tell the Arena was nearby even before we stopped. Sounds hit my ears—the roar of a crowd working itself into a frenzy, the screeches of gryphons in the stables, the bustle of hawkers peddling pennants in our colors. Some part of me urged me to show a good face to whomever was waiting behind the complex's walls, but I couldn't muster the strength to care. I glared at the curtains that shrouded the carriage. The gods-cursed things were woven with gold and purple threads. Anyone clever would know where I'd been, and the rumors would only grow from there.

*I heard you slept with the Empress.*

No one would believe that it hadn't been my idea. The legend would grow—*my* legend, the fighter who'd faced countless opponents and come out victorious, survived longer than any combatant in this generation, bedded the most powerful woman in the world, only to...

Only to what?

Die when Octavian decided I wasn't worth tormenting any longer?

The gates creaked open, and I recognized where I was by the sound of the hinges. The western gates. Near the officials' quarters, the guest barracks, and the tunnel where my opponents always appeared during our matches.

"Come on, let's go," a voice commanded from outside.

The curtains parted and light spilled in. I swore and covered my eyes as the sun streamed over the edge of the Arena, blinding me for the moment it took to stumble from the carriage to the arched gateway.

Like I'd expected, a handful of guards waited to usher me into safety. The sound of the gate closing behind us sent a shock through my ears. Then, cool air and the familiar smell of dust and iron marked the Arena outbuildings. I followed the guards almost blindly, content for now to let them guide me into the tunnels. There must've been instructions given to keep me out of sight, I realized as we turned a corner. It would've been quicker to cut across courtyards, not to—

I pulled up short as the man in front of me stopped.

"What's going on?" I peered around him, eyes widening as I realized where we were. The doorway to an arming room, with the mouth of a tunnel that sloped to the sands—but not the one I usually emerged from.

"Welcome back, Cyrus."

Defiance flared along with fear, and I spat in Octavian's direction. "Bastard."

"Hmm. Not your best insult." He stepped around the guards to examine me, a cruel grin sliding across his face. "I trust you enjoyed your night. Given how much funds arrived this morning, I believe your hostess was extremely pleased." He gestured sharply at the guards, and two of them grabbed my shoulders. "But there's still the matter of the disobedience." His voice pitched louder, echoing through the tunnel as, beyond it, the roar of the crowd surged. "I've told you before, crossing me has its consequences."

I threw my weight against one of the men holding me, but it was no use. My reflexes weren't working, my limbs too slow to fight. A fist slammed into my stomach, another into my side, and I yelped as I hit the floor. Weight pressed against my shoulders, my hips, pinning my limbs and leaving me immobile. I tried to breathe, to find the clarity that fueled each ruthless counterattack or clever evasion, but all I could find was the same emptiness that greeted me with each kill.

Frozen.

Helpless.

I ducked my face into my shoulder. Time stretched as blows rained against me. Finally, they let up, and the pressure on my limbs released. The world spun as I struggled to my elbows, sobbing out a breath and spitting blood onto the stone. Darkness was creeping into my vision, my ears ringing with the roar coming from the tunnel.

*Get up.* I had to get up. I had to—

Another blow fell against my ribs, eliciting a scream that was more of a whimper. The light from outside wavered, and I blinked hard as a figure stepped from the tunnel, wearily undoing the straps of a helmet with embossed stars and pulling it from his head. He turned to the armory—and froze.

The gryphon rider. I'd know that posture anywhere. But the expression? It was shocked, confused—then furious.

"Get him out of here," Octavian ordered. "I think he's learned his lesson."

Something struck the back of my head, and I collapsed to the floor with the roar of the crowd fading from my consciousness. The last thing I saw was the imprint of stars against the inside of my eyelids—a captive gryphon, bound to the heavens.

*You should've killed me when you had the chance. It would've been kinder.*

# CHAPTER XX

BASTIAN

I lurched toward the crumpled golden form, but Octavian's hand slammed into my chest.

"You'll get your chance," he said, misreading the iron fury spreading through me. "Until then, here's *your* reminder that defiance and disobedience do not go unpunished. No one is exempt." His men hooked arms under Cyrus's and started dragging him away. Octavian smiled thinly. "Maybe someday soon I'll be giving you the order to make sure Cyrus doesn't make it off the sand." He pushed me back a fraction and then was gone.

Air rushed viciously into my lungs. *No one was exempt.* It was the talk of the Arena how Cyrus had gone to one of the Empress's villas for a celebration last night. Octavian had waited for me to see before he fully punished their sun. Reminding me. They wouldn't hesitate to strike their champion, so what would they do to me? A curse hissed between my teeth and I strode into the arming room. Attendants appeared as if from nowhere, wordlessly taking armor, laying out fresh clothes so the black and silver uniform could be washed of victory.

"Bastian," Phestus said as I laced my boots. He must have seen some of it too, and knew by now to give me space if a fight had been bad. I didn't want to say anything. Especially not as I saw a gentler form of the same warning in his face. *Keep following orders.* He might have cared a little bit for me, but I think he worried more for his place, what might happen to him if I fell.

"I'm going to the infirmary," I said, mind made up in seconds. "Training injury pulled in the fight."

He nodded, accepting the lie. Restlessness chased and I would not be content until I...what? Made sure the man who was meant to be my rival was all right?

I headed for the stairs, chased by the truth. It was the helplessness in his face as he lay bleeding on the floor—the same that circled me like a vulture. The panic and fear in his face in that moment after we'd fought, more prominent after he'd killed the gladiator yesterday. Someone with his skill didn't need protection in a fight. But battles weren't always on sand with a sword in hand.

The physician turned from his workbench as I pushed in, poised as his attention swept over me, assessing for injury. There were a few forms on cots near the far wall, none of them the person I sought. Perhaps he was in one of the smaller, private rooms.

"How is he?" I asked, voice low.

"Who?" Atticus frowned.

Frustration hissed, but why would I be here asking for *anyone*, much less him? "Cyrus."

He looked at me like I was stupid. "Why would he be here? He didn't take an injury yesterday. And surely not at the party, or I would have seen him already."

I don't know why I was surprised. "They didn't bring him here?" I cursed again. "Octavian and his men just beat him into the ground for killing that gladiator yesterday."

I was angry, but for a brief moment it seemed like Atticus might strangle *me* simply for being the messenger. He shoved past me and I followed. Up to the third level, down the balcony to the biggest rooms.

He shoved open a door and pulled up short. My gut wrenched at the twisted form left on the ground. Scarlet matted the back of Cyrus's head, and he barely stirred as Atticus knelt beside him to place a gentle hand on his cheek.

"Cyrus?" he asked gently. No response. The same almost feral protectiveness as earlier flared in the physician's eyes as I knelt beside them.

"I only want to help," I said. "I swear by the First God."

Atticus nodded. "Let's get him on the bed to start."

Cyrus blinked slowly, eyes still unfocused from the head blow. He made no resistance as I got arms underneath him. A groan broke as I pulled him to sitting, and his head thumped back against my shoulder. Atticus took his feet and together we lifted, bringing him to the bed.

Atticus tried to pick through the bloodied hair to find the injury, giving up after a moment. "Get his sandals off and wash your hands. I'll be back."

I obeyed, barely finished when he shoved through the door.

"Attendants are nowhere to be seen," he growled. "Cowards." We got Cyrus out of his tunic and onto his side. Atticus doused a cloth, handing it to me. "Try to clean away some of the blood on his head and find the injury."

As I reached for it, Cyrus came more awake, an arm jerking to knock the cloth away from his face.

"No," he mumbled. "Tell them no. Not again."

Both the physician and I froze. My fury was nowhere as close to being spent as I'd thought. The tunic was too fine for daily wear, spun in his colors. He must have just returned to the Arena.

Atticus grabbed the discarded tunic and sniffed. He cursed roundly, taking another cloth and dabbing it to the inside of Cyrus's cheek. My hand clamped on Cyrus's shoulder as the physician poured a drop of some tincture on the cloth. The fabric turned green, and his cursing almost made my hair curl as he left the room.

Cyrus mumbled again, trying to pull an arm over his head. I gentled my hold on his shoulder and settled my hand against the side of his head. "You're all right, Cyrus. It's safe here." My voice felt too tight to be reassuring, but he seemed to understand. The glint of gold on the rim of his ear sent another flare of anger again. *Doesn't matter how high anyone rises, we're all just slaves.*

Atticus returned with a cup. "Drink this, Cyrus. It'll settle you." He looked to me and I slid an arm underneath Cyrus and lifted. The young man slowly drank, the dazed expression starting to recede.

"What did they do?" I asked as he settled back.

"That's expensive perfume and incense on his tunic." Atticus sighed. "He was at a party last night. They must have drugged him to make him more compliant. First time they've had to." If I'd given him a sword,

Atticus likely would have followed me to war right then. "I've seen the effects on women more than men in my time but—" He cursed again.

I pressed Cyrus's shoulder like I could protect him from what had already happened. Bitter realization swept over me. He was at the *Empress's* villa...

They said his five years were almost up...

*First time they've had to.*

Gods, he was so young.

Atticus put the cloth in my hand and I resumed trying to clean away the blood in Cyrus's hair as the physician inspected the bruising already showing on his back and sides. He pressed carefully over Cyrus's ribs, eliciting a pained sound and a panicked motion from the young man.

I caught Cyrus's arm as he blindly swung. "Easy, Cyrus. It's all right." I kept gentle hold of his arm as Atticus prodded, not flinching as Cyrus jerked again. "You're all right," I murmured again. Apparently satisfied, Atticus turned to mixing something new.

"Soldier, were you?" I finally asked, almost unable to take the silence. He'd been right before. It was usually only soldiers who cursed so creatively.

Atticus huffed. "I was."

"Why are you here?"

A bit of calmness had returned to him. "The First God has sent me many places over the years. Always where I need to be." The look he gave was challenging, almost. I had no argument. It had started to feel like the god had a plan after all. "Why are *you* here?" He turned it to me.

In the room. Helping. I pressed the cloth against fresh bleeding as the gash was finally exposed. Cyrus's eyes flew open and he cringed away with an incoherent sound that turned to something agonized as the movement aggravated his injuries. I grabbed his shoulder again, my other hand resting against his hair, a soft *shush-shh* sound escaping me out of reflex. But it wasn't a spooked gryphon in front of me.

Cyrus settled just as fast as he'd startled. His eyes flickered open, briefly exposing a bit of gold in their unfocused depths before closing. I stared down at him as Atticus's question hovered between us. There was less barbarism in the wild lands I'd been sent to conquer over the years than there was here.

"This place is miserable enough without me adding to it," I finally said.

"No one goes out of their way to help. Certainly not twice like you have."

I smiled faintly. "Maybe the First God uses even blunt instruments."

Atticus's short smile gentled him. "Indeed he does."

I helped lift Cyrus again as Atticus wrapped a light bandage around his bruised ribs. The young man seemed to be truly asleep as we finished.

"He'll be all right?" I asked.

Atticus pulled blankets over Cyrus. "Physically, yes," he said grimly. "Best make yourself scarce, Bastian. No one needs to know you helped."

I reluctantly stepped away. Cyrus's face twisted for a moment, some dream trapping him in its hold before it passed. Atticus pointed to the door and I obeyed, slipping out and returning to my room. No one needed to know, not even Cyrus. But maybe I'd find a way to talk, face-to-face. Just to make sure he wasn't finally defeated.

 CYRUS

Days passed.

I didn't leave my quarters. Not to train, not to fight. Not even to climb the Arena and end it all, though the thought crossed my mind more than once. It'd be a poetic end that storytellers would spin over and over, how the golden sun plummeted to earth and died on the sand. The only thing keeping me from the heights was the knowledge that someone would have to bear the news to Callista—and low as I was, I couldn't bring myself to break her heart so badly.

My attendants were noticeably scarce after the first day. They brought food, fresh water, and clean clothes each morning, cleaned and aired the room, then departed without saying anything. I didn't know what they'd been told, or what they'd inferred from when I returned from...wherever I'd been. Memories of that night were blurred, but the pieces of recollection I had were enough to make my stomach turn, my muscles seize.

In winning when I should've lost, I'd failed Octavian badly enough that he'd turned against me. That much I *could* remember, along with the freezing helplessness and shame I'd suffered under the hands of his men. In all the years of training under him, he'd always been the type to punish me himself. Not this. Never this. The realization that he'd so completely cut me loose should have been disheartening, even angering, but all I could feel was lost. Numb.

Atticus came each day. By the fourth day, he eased the bandages away from my ribs and said, "It'll help if you move. You're so accustomed to being active that you'll stiffen if you stay like this." He gave me a deeply sympathetic look as I shrank from the suggestion. "I know you don't want to. You don't have to be near anyone, or face any of the rumors. Are you sleeping at all?"

I nodded, then shook my head just as fast. I'd spent so much time asleep the first two days that the previous night had seen me staring aimlessly through the latticed windows into the early morning hours. "Couldn't last night. I don't know why."

"I'm not surprised." Atticus gave a deep sigh. "Tonight, if you can't sleep, go down to the tunnels and walk. Take one circuit of the under-layer, then come back." He gave me a firm look as I began to shake my head. "You know as well as I do that no one goes down there that late at night."

"I..." I looked at the floor, unable to vocalize the crawling sense of shame that came with the idea of anyone seeing me. "Maybe."

"Please try." He smiled gently. "I promise, it'll help."

That night, I tossed and turned, cursing bruises and almost crying with frustration over the blank spaces in my memory. Finally, I swung my feet out of bed. By the noise—or lack thereof—it was past the middle of the night, and the Arena was quiet.

*One circuit of the tunnels,* I told myself. *Just one, then back to where it's safe.*

The tunnels under the Arena were always chilly and dark, but even more so in the dead of night. Perfect if you didn't want anyone to see you, terrible if you wanted to see where you were going. Fortunately, my feet knew the way even if my eyes were betraying me. I put a hand to the wall and walked, counting steps in my head each time I passed a corridor to make sure I didn't run headlong into stone.

One turn. Two. Three. Four turned into five. My eyes had adjusted fully to the darkness by the time I made the sixth turn, when a flicker of light caught my attention. A glow, illuminating the mouth of a tunnel with warmth.

Curious, I followed the glow and found myself in the same corridor where Callista had brought me over a month before. The altars looked as they always had, some lavished with offerings and others almost barren. I passed the statues of the gods of battle, luck, chaos, and tide, my feet drawing me almost irresistibly to the candlelight flickering upon the altar to the First God.

I stopped in the pool of light and examined the altar. A bundle of lavender tied with string sat at the god's feet. Three tiny, blue-and-white-painted shells clustered at his side. A smudge showed where incense had smoldered to nothingness.

It should have been pathetic. The other altars showed clear signs of visitors, offerings piled at the feet of the statues and the scent of incense hanging in the dry air. But for all the attention, their statues' gazes were hollow. Empty. This one should have been the same, but instead...

I raised my eyes to meet the god's. He stared back, his expression full of life, compassion, understanding, despite being rendered in the same painted wood as all the rest. Standing there, it was like I'd been...seen.

And for once, I wasn't afraid.

"The One Who Sees," my father had called him. An old, old god, who he said had created all things and breathed his own life into them, who was always watching and could never be deceived or frightened away.

I crumpled to my knees, hot tears filling my eyes. For all my prayers, the gods had never responded with anything more than silence. After years of looking for answers that never came, I'd concluded that I was alone. And I'd never felt more alone than over the last few days.

"Did you see?" I whispered, my voice thinning on the words. "Did you care? Where were you when—" My voice choked against the memories, so many tumbling through my head that I curled into a ball and sobbed under the weight.

All those years, no one had seen.

Or if they had, no one had cared.

I didn't know how long I stayed like that, tension dissolving into salt water and spilling onto stone, but after a while I was able to take a shaky breath and sit up. A deep stillness had settled in my heart, easing the pain where memories were failing me and the future had crumbled.

"Do you see me?" I asked again, a little less desperately. "Are you watching?"

There was no answer, not to my ears. But as I slowly got to my feet, the candlelight glimmered off something on the statue's face. Dampness.

I raised a hand to my own face, fingers brushing lingering tears. And somewhere, certainty took hold. *I think he might actually care.*

I returned to my room in silence, the quiet from the First God's altar lingering as the Arena began to wake and the eastern sky lightened. When a messenger arrived that afternoon with the news that I'd be taking the sand in two days, I only nodded.

I'd fight. I had to. But the lesson Octavian had hoped to teach was now the farthest thing from my mind. If there was any chance for me to survive now, to gain my freedom, I couldn't rely on impressing him. I'd lived by one set of rules most of my life, but perhaps it was time to break them.

An "accident in training," the official word said. The explanation for why no one had seen or heard of me in almost a week. And the absence, after such a high-profile victory, brought spectators swarming to the Arena on the day I returned. The fight, versus a pair of convicts who had more desperation than teamwork, was meant to be an easy win.

It was, but not as easy as it ought to have been. My reflexes were slow, the clarity in my mind dulled. Muscle memory was forced to carry me through the match, and if I'd been feeling more myself, I'd have shaken my head at the sloppy showing.

It would have to do. I didn't have it in me to perform today.

Both men fell in the end to a rush of applause from the crowd, and I returned to my tunnel amid a shower of red pennants.

"Good, Cyrus!" My new second was enthusiastic, wide-eyed, and a little starstruck. I hoped his placement would be permanent, given that Flavius had been reassigned to training new recruits while his broken arm healed. This youngster wouldn't be any help in a fight, but at least he wasn't looking to stab me in the back. "Well done!"

His enthusiasm was the only such in the room. Everyone was jumpy, tense like they were expecting a fight to break out between the match ending and my departure. I couldn't blame them. Word of Octavian's punishment had spread and nobody wanted to be on the receiving end of anything like that. I swapped into plain clothing, swearing as a bruise pulled, and shook dust out of my sandals before heading toward the courtyard and the safety of my room.

Loud talk and banter met my ears as I left the armory. One or two of the lower-level solo fighters and a few team players, returning from viewing the match through the disused stables' tunnel.

"Cyrus! Good show out there today!" A Chimera player raised his hand in greeting. "Nothing knocks you down for long!"

The others laughed. "I didn't see the Empress today," one of them said. His smile sharpened. "She's already tired of you?"

I sucked in a sharp breath at the mention of the Imperial banner. Half-recalled images churned in my head, threatening to break loose from where sleepless nights had held them at bay.

"No, no, she's letting him rest." The other team player gave a knowing wink. "You would know, Cyrus. Is she as relentless in bed as you are on the sands?"

Pain tore through my chest as the events of that night rushed back.

*Purple and gold.*

*Incense.*

*Terror.*

*Pain.*

The others' laughter dwindled as my foot slid back, their expressions freezing in panic. "Hey, it's a joke!" one of the Chimeras stammered. "Cyrus, don't—"

A hum built in my ears, vivid recollection filling the spaces left in my memory, and I backed away. Two steps, three, four. Once I'd put distance between us, I turned and ran like I'd never run before. Through the corridors, past the turn for the surface, increasing my pace like I could outrun the awful memories snapping at my heels.

A surprised curse greeted me as I swerved around a corner, and I all but crashed into someone on the other side.

"Careful!" he snapped, grabbing me to stop both of us from plummeting to the ground. Then, recognition spread across his face. "Cyrus?"

I wrenched myself free and reeled back. My breath froze in my chest.

I knew that voice. Had heard it, protective and calming, in the middle of a drugged and semi-conscious fog. And suddenly, I had a name to go with it.

"...Bastian?"

# CHAPTER XXI

BASTIAN

I wasn't sure what was more shocking. The almost-collision, or that it was Cyrus and he knew my name. He hadn't been seen in days, and Atticus hadn't told me anything other than he was recovering. I'd gone to watch the fight, just to make sure he really was on his feet again.

"You all right?" I almost blurted the question. There were no evident bandages, but he hadn't fought with his normal fearless speed.

He didn't answer, just kept staring at me.

"Cyrus?" I dared reach a hand out between us. He took a sharp breath, stepping back another pace, and his expression became more guarded.

"...Why do I know your voice?"

I don't know if I was relieved or not that he didn't remember. Wasn't sure if I wanted to tell him if he didn't.

"We've never met. I only saw your face for the first time last week." An empty, panicked look shot through his grey eyes, and I knew immediately what moment he was referring to. "We've never spoken before—*how*?"

My fingers curled into my palm, and I took a short breath. "I helped Atticus," I said. "I saw what happened." I gestured vaguely toward the tunnel. "I just...I wanted to make sure you were all right. I went with Atticus and he found you, and...I helped."

I didn't know if he'd believe me. Like I'd been told by both the physician and Callista—no one ever intervened.

A shudder ran across his shoulders, but the panic was giving way to confusion. "You...you helped? You realize that *no one* does that."

"So I've been told." Another bitter smile twisted my face. "Maybe it's just another way for me to defy these bastards."

Cyrus laughed at that, a short, sharp sound that echoed what passed for mine these days. "Defiance doesn't get anyone far here, but thanks. It seems I keep ending up in your debt." Finally, he met my eyes. "I don't understand, but thank you."

I shook my head. "No debt," I said. "And you're welcome. Now...are you all right?"

"I'm fine. Not hurt. Just—" He looked over his shoulder at the tunnel he'd been running through. "Avoiding something I can't fight." Another half-laugh burst from him. "Things are simpler on the sands."

"Maybe. Feels like barely a breather in the middle of the bloodiest fight." I watched the way he warily sized me up, waiting for some sort of attack, not realizing I wasn't here for any other reason than potentially misguided concern. "Gods, this place is miserable, isn't it?"

"You get used to it." He pushed away from the wall and took a few steps down the corridor, keeping an equally watchful eye on me and the hallway.

After a moment of hesitation, I fell in alongside him. "Hopefully not."

He scowled in my direction, but kept moving.

"It feels like my existence is just a bane to Octavian, but what did *you* do?" I asked. I already knew, but it still didn't make sense for the trainer to so brutally punish their champion.

"Did the unexpected," Cyrus said, his voice matter-of-fact. "Defied him. Twice." There was silence as we turned a corner. He paused at the junction, darting a quick glance around the corner before turning into the new hall. "Both times it cost the Arena money and embarrassed him. The board doesn't care how the money's made, but he can't handle being made to look foolish. He takes failure personally. And out on me." His steps slowed a fraction, and he tipped his head toward me. "What did *you* do?"

I huffed another laugh. "Which time?" I'd lost count of how many times Octavian had threatened or struck. I didn't really want to taste the bitterness again, but wanted him to know he wasn't completely alone. "Started weeks ago, when I told him I wasn't getting sold for some woman's pleasure."

I tried to shove down the intense anger at them having done the same, and maybe worse, to him. Octavian had threatened to try to make me *compliant*, and clearly hadn't thought twice about doing the same to Cyrus. Taking a gamble, I stepped through the door of a smaller, deserted arming room.

Cyrus paused at the entrance. It almost felt like trying to lure one of the half-wild island ponies to the stables as a child. A long moment later, he stepped through the door to stand with his back to the wall. "That's fast," he said. "Normally, it takes a few months before—wait, you said 'no'?" His head tipped with surprise, and he stared at me like I'd claimed to have flown last night.

I took a seat on a narrow bench set against the wall. "I did."

"And you're still alive?"

I flashed a faint grin. "I was assigned to fight you the next day, so I'm not really supposed to be."

A more genuine laugh broke from him. "Makes sense why he hates you now. He can't control you." The grin sobered, and a flash of that earlier emptiness went through his face. "You shouldn't have hesitated."

I studied my hands, picking at a bit of dirt around a knuckle. I hadn't been sure why I'd hesitated weeks ago. Not until I'd seen him in a bloody heap. I wasn't sure if, or why, *I* was the one the First God might have sent for Callista, or for him. I'd gladly have turned over the duty to someone else and been home with Lyra and August instead.

"You just..." I stopped. "I've been a soldier for years. You see many, many faces—dead, alive, wanting to be dead. Trying desperately to live. Sometimes you wish you hesitated more."

My fingers clenched for a moment before I opened my hand again. Even though it had sent me here, I didn't regret sparing those villages. Didn't regret sparing *him*, though it had been dogged survival since.

"Hesitating will end up getting you killed here," Cyrus said quietly. "But that moment meant I could have another chance at surviving." His eyes went to mine. "I can't promise, but if the time comes I might hesitate before striking against you."

"I wouldn't blame you if you didn't." I rested my head against the wall. "But you're close to the five-year mark, aren't you? What are the odds of you making it out after that?"

Some part of me wanted to know if the promise would be honored. If someone *could* get out that way. Just in case there was no other means of escape.

I hadn't found one yet, if there was.

"They're supposed to honor it," he said, something lost appearing in his expression. "But after last week, I'm not certain. If I do make it there, it'll be public pressure that forces them to keep their word." His jaw tightened, and he looked away. "It's not long. I'll survive, and they'll *have* to let me leave."

I rubbed my chin, not liking the amount of *ifs* that lingered in his words. "But what if they don't?" He was right. After the Sieneca fight and the way Octavian had punished him, the arc of his sun felt uncertain.

"They will. I'll make them." A fist closed, and for a moment I thought he'd bolt out the door. "I've done it before. I've risen against the odds and made them all take notice. I just...have to hold on and keep the crowds' attention until the time runs out." He looked up at me, a challenge flashing through his eyes. "Rise or die trying."

Perhaps, but I wanted a third option, and it seemed he desperately wanted the same. And the part of me that couldn't kill helpless innocents, and couldn't kill him weeks ago, flared to the surface. "What if you didn't have to do it alone?" I asked. "Rising, not dying." I managed a faint smile.

"You can't be serious. That's insanity—they'd *know*." He shook his head. "No. That's even more of a risk than we face on *or* off the sands."

"I'm not saying we make a visible alliance," I said. "I don't know...maybe there's some way we can stay even with each other. It's no secret they're pitching us against one another out there." I lifted my chin in the direction of the Arena floor.

"Which means everyone is watching us." He settled his feet more firmly, crossing his arms like he braced against the very thought. "I've seen others try things like this in the past. It never ends well. They end up betraying each other, or are killed once things get discovered." He nodded at the tunnel entrance. "It's all a show out there, but only if the coordinators approve. Anything else gets snuffed out."

Mirth avoided my low chuckle. "You'll find I'm *very* uninterested in making it a show. Octavian and the board can pound sand for all I care."

Cyrus snorted at that, the tension in his shoulders relaxing a bit. "*If* I weren't to do this alone, what would that look like?"

I lifted a shoulder. "Training together, making sure there's no surprises between matches. You could have easily beaten me that day. Twist of fate." I shrugged again. "If we make sure we match each other in skill, then we'd be unbeatable on the sands, and you get to your five years and walk away."

His eyes narrowed, but it looked like he was considering my words. "And with no clear imbalance, they might not act to end either of us."

I leaned on my knees, hands brushing together. "I'm also interested in the 'not dying' part."

"Most people would be," he said before adding, "I haven't seen you fight much. I've been too focused on staying alive and ahead of you. But I'd prefer not to be surprised again." A sound that could almost have been a laugh came with that admission. "Even if we manage to stay out of their vision, they'll throw us against each other again. We'd need to be able to control that match."

I nodded. "I've got some advantage, having seen a few of your fights. And have the honor of walking away from one." I flashed another slight smile. "Surely there's some place up there where we could train without anyone seeing. I don't much like being underground."

Cyrus sighed and leaned his head back against the wall. His focus pierced the ceiling like he could see the courtyards and tunnels above. "There's the courtyard where the apothecaries grow their herbs. No one visits at night. Or the stables, but the gryphons might make noise and give us away."

"I might have someone who can help with that in the stables," I said. Titus hadn't offered, but training in the stables wasn't the same as trying to escape. He'd probably take the money and keep his mouth shut. "Barring that, I have some experience with gryphons." Just the thought had my hands itching to touch feathers, heart thumping a little harder at the memory of climbing in a saddle and pulsing up into the sky. But stone still pressed around me, and all I had left of that life was boots.

"Stables, then." Cyrus stepped away from the wall and toward the door. "If I read the schedule right, you're on the sands day after tomorrow. That night, I'll be at the stables. If you're there, I'll know I can trust you."

I met his gaze. "If I'm not, it means I'm dead."

Cyrus smiled a little at that. He stepped through the door with a heartbeat pause before disappearing around the corner and leaving me alone. I scrubbed my hands against each other again. It seemed like some life had returned to him with our words. I had only wanted to make sure he was all right, but now I might have made an unlikely ally. If it meant one of us might survive, if someone might escape, then...*please. Let me be strong enough.*

## CYRUS

I left the training room with my mind spinning in a thousand different directions. How could one conversation leave me feeling so alive, when this morning I'd fought to keep my head amid something I'd trained for my entire life? One part of me pushed against the growing hope, though, as I ascended the stairs. My memories were spotty enough that there was a chance I'd been lied to, that I was about to lay trust with someone who wouldn't hesitate a second time when it came to ending me.

But then, Bastian had laid claim to another name, someone else who might verify how truthful he'd been about his involvement.

I pivoted and made for the infirmary.

The fights today had ended with no casualties requiring treatment, and I hadn't heard of anyone else being injured. Still, sounds of activity came from the side room, and it was long minutes before Atticus emerged, cleaning his hands on a cloth before throwing it into a basket. Surprise crossed his face as he saw me, mixed with the same sympathy that I'd seen other times when I'd been under his care.

"Cyrus...everything all right?"

How many times were people going to ask me that today?

"Fine." I'd been leaning against the wall beside the door, but now I stood upright to address him. "I just had the most interesting conversation with someone in the tunnels. I wanted to check some details with you."

"By all means." He crossed to a peg hammered between two stones to retrieve his robe. "But don't take offense if I immediately claim ignorance and send you packing."

I rolled my eyes. *Physicians.* "Suit yourself." I went to sit on the bench where I'd lain far too many times while receiving treatment. "It's about earlier this week. When Octavian's men pinned me down and pounded me into the stone."

Atticus's face tightened as soon as I mentioned Octavian's actions. That fact alone told me that my memory hadn't exaggerated how bad things had been as I continued, "I woke up in my quarters, with a bandage around my chest. I don't know how I got there, but just now I ran into a certain gryphon rider who claims to have helped me." I raised my head to look the physician straight in the eye. "I need to know. What was his involvement that day?"

"*Bastian's* involvement?" Atticus asked incredulously. "You might owe him your life, lad. I didn't even know what'd happened until he came looking for you."

"Here?" I interrupted. "I didn't think—" I stopped as Atticus held up a hand. "Go on."

"Well, he told me what had happened. Apparently he'd seen?"

The reminder sat bitter in my stomach. "He saw. Octavian made sure of that."

Atticus nodded, anger tensing his jaw. "He was furious—no, not with you," he clarified. "With Octavian. He swore that he only intended to help, and I was grateful for it. When we found you, you were..." His face shadowed, and I wondered if his duties ever weighed heavy on his shoulders. "You were conscious, but not enough for reason. Bastian held you still while I worked, calmed you when you would've lashed out, then left with no argument."

"He says it's his own way of defying the coordinators." I laughed shortly. Now that I thought about it, there'd been a stiffness to Bastian's

217

movements and bruises that spelled having been in more than one scuffle. And Callista had said that his rise hadn't been without enemies. "I almost believe him."

"He's gods-touched, that one," Atticus said, his voice taking on a thoughtful cast as he leaned against his work table. "The First God has a way of choosing the least likely vessels to show his will."

Interest sparked at that statement, the memory of candlelight on an altar making me ask, "Does he? I didn't think he cared enough to involve himself. No one else ever has."

"Don't mistake his patience for apathy, lad." The physician raised an eyebrow. "He works in ways we don't understand, and sometimes we behold him in others before growing brave enough to meet his eyes. Once we do, he has a way of enabling those he chooses to defy even the greatest odds."

"You think the odds can be defied?" The question escaped before I could rein it in.

Atticus gave me a dry smile. "Of course they can. Make no mistake, he sees."

The One Who Sees. And hadn't I defied the odds my entire life?

I stood from the bench with a sigh. "Thank you. I think I know what I need to do now—or at least what's less likely to get me killed." I laughed at his exasperated snort before adding, "I know it's a lot to ask. But the next time you see Callista, will you tell her I've been thinking about her?"

Warning narrowed Atticus's expression. "Don't break her heart, lad. You'll have more than one person after your blood if you do."

I shook my head. "I have no intention of hurting her. Ever. She's the only good thing in this place, and I'd give my life to see her protected."

A faint smile crossed Atticus's face. "I thought so, but it's good to hear you say it..." He straightened from the table to give me a nod. "I'll let her know you're all right. She's been worried sick; I don't think I've ever seen someone as distressed as she was that night."

My skin crawled at the reminder. What must she have heard? What must she have *thought*? "It wasn't my choice," I blurted. "Please tell her. *Please*."

"Believe me, I know," Atticus said. The anger had returned to his voice, but I didn't think it was directed at me. "That was clear to anyone with a scrap of sense. I'll tell her." He nodded to the door. "Go do what you need to do. And let me know if there's any way I can help." A dangerous light flickered in his eyes. "Defiance isn't limited to the sands."

# CHAPTER XXII

CYRUS

R umors spread, like I'd known they would. The whispers that
followed my footsteps were different in tone now, more jeering
and speculative than anyone had dared to be in years. At the same time,
the others in the courtyard shrank from my path as I did my best to
resume my usual routine—like they were afraid to cross paths with a
higher authority than even Octavian and the other coordinators.

Bastian fought two days after our chance meeting in the tunnels.
I'd retreated to my quarters, telling the attendants I needed time alone
before turning them out. They left with only a few backward glances.
Apparently the change in my demeanor had been noted by more than
one person. Once they were gone, I squeezed through the lattice sur-

rounding my balcony and climbed the Arena—not to the top like usual, but to one of the arches that supported the roof. Its position, high above the stands and with a good view of Bastian's gate, gave me the perfect spot to watch his match.

Now that I was watching carefully, I could tell that my earliest assessment of the former soldier hadn't been wrong. It was difficult to tell with his features hidden behind that helmet—Gods, that had to be difficult to fight in—but I thought he was keeping as close an eye on his surroundings as I did. And his strikes, brought against his opponent with the power of a taller fighter, were precise and intense in a way that spelled a dislike of expending too much energy.

I laughed at that. *Octavian must be furious after each match, if this is how he fights every time.* The laughter died in my chest at the thought of what might be occurring out of the Arena in between fights. I'd assumed that the bruises I'd seen had been from scrapping with other combatants, but there could be another reason for them. If Octavian hadn't hesitated to take out his anger against me, what might he be doing to someone who so frequently disobeyed?

I shifted positions as Bastian successfully trapped his opponent against a rock. An unflinching swing of the sword, and the convict dropped with his blood streaming into the sand. An unremarkable ending, but the reaction from the crowd as Bastian returned to his tunnel was anything but. Scraps of black and silver rained into the Arena, and even from here I could hear chants and cries of his name. I hadn't heard that type of enthusiasm from the crowd for any other combatant in a long, long time.

*Please,* the plea went up from my heart to the First God, *if you're really there, don't let me have made a mistake.*

That night, I waited until the clamor in the courtyard had died before buckling on my old Dragonesque armor, taking up my practice sword, and going to the stables. The corridor where Callista and I had talked after Flavius's attack had come immediately to mind when I'd been thinking of out-of-the-way places, specifically the gryphon training pen that it bordered. The place was surrounded by the stable building, open to the sky, floored in sand, and away from the more trafficked paths through the complex.

The stables were quiet when I arrived. Either the gryphons were sleeping, or were so used to the passage of their handlers through the building that one more person wasn't a surprise to them. The gate to the training pen was unlocked, so I pulled it halfway open before retreating to the shadows of a crate-filled alcove to wait.

*He might not come.* And if he didn't, I'd have to consider my next move.

It wasn't long before a shadow crossed the arched entry to the corridor. A figure in dark clothes and plain training armor appeared between me and the bars of the courtyard, a sword in one hand and a helmet cradled under the other arm.

I dropped from atop the crates to the floor of the alcove, raising my voice just loud enough to be heard. "Didn't think you'd come."

Bastian jolted, pivoting until he marked me in the shadows. His shoulders sloped down. "Told you I'd either be here or dead."

"Not much of an option." I went to pull the gate open, wincing as the hinges gave an awful creaking sound. Somewhere across the stable, one of the gryphons stirred at the sound, and a curious clucking sound came from an enclosure on the far side of the training yard.

Bastian slid through the opening, making for the sound with something light about his steps. I tried not to laugh at the throaty cooing noise he sent back. It settled the gryphon, and nothing else stirred.

"Used to calming those things?" I followed him into the gated yard and leaned my practice sword against the bars, close enough that I could reach it in a hurry if necessary. "I guess that persona they've got for you isn't all for show. Does that explain the helmet too?"

The faint huff that seemed to pass for his laugh escaped. He set his sword within reach and hefted the helmet. "I fought in the Fifth Legion for four years, and was a commander for another two. This is what I know."

"That thing?" I had to halt a scoff before it emerged. "How do you see?"

He tapped the front of the helmet. "It has an eye slit," he said, then tossed it to me. "Full range vision if it fits correctly."

I turned the helmet over in my hands, taking a few steps into the moonlight that spilled down through the square of roofs that framed the sky. There *was* an eye slit, and bigger than was apparent at first glance. But the weight... "There's no way I'd be able to fight in something like this." I made sure Bastian was looking and tossed the helmet back to him. "A helmet is a liability when you have to move fast."

He caught it, turning it over in his hands to look down at the faceplate for a moment. "You'll change your mind the first time on a gryphon." He tilted a glance up. "And first time in the mess of flying into battle." He rapped his knuckles against the surface. "My old helmet had a divot the armorers couldn't get out after it saved my life."

*Gods, what must that have been like?* I crossed my arms and shook my head. "Mine almost killed me," I said shortly. "I've never worn one since."

He studied me for a moment longer than felt comfortable. "Then you didn't have the right kind of helmet."

"Or the wrong kind of teammate." I shook away the memory and went to grab my practice sword. "I'm never letting myself get put in that spot again."

Bastian stretched an arm across his chest. "Speaking of teammates, I take it you're not too upset about what I did to your second." It didn't sound like he was concerned if I was upset or not. Maybe he'd guessed who I'd been referring to just now.

"Flavius?" I spat in the dust. I'd seen my former second berating new recruits. He'd eventually regain the ability to fight, but I hoped he'd never serve as a secondary again. "Would've been better if you'd killed him. He's been after my blood for years, since I ascended to solo and he stayed with the teams."

"He seems an odd choice for your second then." Bastian took up his practice sword and moved opposite me, settling into a loose stance.

I moved to face him, bringing my sword to a guard position. "It wasn't my choice. Nothing really is."

"I've noted it once or twice." A faint smile stirred as he began an easy sequence to warm up. A few muted coos from the gryphons followed the clack of the swords, but nothing else stirred. It only took a few moments for us to fall into a familiar drill pattern of strike-block-counterstrike, both of us moving slowly and keeping an eye on each other.

It was as I'd noticed earlier, both in fighting him before and watching his match this morning. Downward blows held more weight, and he kept more distance than I did. The imbalance, as I pushed forward and he gave, meant that soon we'd circled from the shadows cast by the buildings and into the central patch of light.

The pace had increased by this point, but as I looked up to block a blow, something made my reflexes stutter. The moonlight had shifted in the short time we'd been here and cast silvery across a new bruise on Bastian's cheekbone—exactly where it would be if someone had struck him with all their strength.

I stepped back and lowered my sword. "I thought you won your match today."

Confusion furrowed between his eyes as he also disengaged. "I did."

"Then what happened here?" My hand went to the same spot on my own face. Even as it did, things fell into place. "The helmet. The crowds won't see the bruises." I stepped closer, peering at the rest of his face. Now that I was looking closer, more bruises mottled the skin under his jaw. My hand tightened on my sword hilt. "The bastard."

Bastian scoffed. "He's not doing much to try to save me for anything. Except taking you down someday." He glanced above the roof before focusing on me again. His sword swept up into guard. "I'm fine. Keep going."

I shrugged and resettled my hand on my sword hilt. "Faster this time. Don't hold back."

I caught the hint of a smile across Bastian's face before he readied himself and swung at me. No more careful back-and-forth, this was more like the speed and accuracy I'd seen from him this morning—sharp, intense strikes that had me using more of my weight to block than I usually needed.

*Finally.*

I pushed back, settling into the cold, sharp clarity that only came when I had my entire mind focused in one place. Strike versus strike, dodge, block, counter and sidestep to get inside his reach and—

*Crack.* My blade came down against the outside of his sword arm. The impact immediately saw him twist away, a string of curses coming from him as he switched the practice sword to his other hand, grabbing it by the blunt blade and letting it fall. Another curse came as he pressed his arm to his ribs, eyes closing.

"Gods and monsters." I let my sword fall and reached out to grab his wrist. He tensed, but didn't pull away as I angled to avoid casting a shadow. A long, angry-looking welt ran across his forearm and disappeared beneath his vambrace, the skin already bruised and swollen.

This wasn't from us sparring. "Gods. He really does hate you."

Bastian gently lifted his arm from my hold, working his hand in and out of a fist. "It's fine."

I stepped away, leaving my sword in the dust. "I don't think we should continue. Not tonight. Not if…" I shook my head.

I'd assumed that Octavian was angry after each of Bastian's matches, but seeing the proof was another thing altogether. No matter that I'd been on the receiving end of such anger in the past.

Bastian's shoulders rose and fell, and he cast another look up at the sky. I caught the same yearning for freedom as earlier in the sharp profile before he shifted to motion again. He dropped his sword and went to sit against the bars, arm still cradled against his stomach.

I bent to collect both practice weapons before joining him, tipping my head to stare at the sky. It was difficult to see the stars from here even at the best of times, but one or two pinpoints of light were visible near the moon.

"You're a lot faster than I expected," I told him after a moment. "Does riding a gryphon make you that way, or did you have to learn?"

"I started as a foot soldier. Fought for two years on the front lines," he said. "If you're fast enough, the Fifth Legion is always looking for a specific kind of crazy that'll climb on a gryphon." Something closer to a real smile flashed. "Then it's months of training on foot until you're ready to do it on a gryphon."

"And then in the air?" I couldn't remember when the dreams of flying had started, but I was sure fighting in the air would always beat being stuck on the ground.

Bastian tilted a glance at me. "Then you're grateful for the helmet. It directs the air around you—aerial patterns, dives, grappling." He tapped a finger against one of the buckles on his boots. "You'll want these too. Some of the squad uses bows, the rest of us have swords. Most blade work doesn't come in until you set on the ground, but once you land—" He snapped his fingers. "Seconds to get off before you get a spear in the gut. Especially when you're the shock troops."

I frowned. Scouting from a gryphon made sense, but dropping into a battle sounded like a tactical nightmare. Then again, being able to see the whole battlefield before landing *would* have its advantages. "You were in command? What happened to put you here?"

He stared across the courtyard, jaw tight. "Have you ever killed defenseless women and children? Old men who can't walk without a crutch?"

"No," I answered honestly.

"I haven't either," he said. "I disobeyed orders four times. Four times refused to slaughter villages that had no one to protect them. I tried to make a choice, to hesitate for once." He glanced at me. "And here I am instead."

"Where there's no reward for hesitating," I agreed. "Until the one time when it raises you to the public eye."

"*That* I surely could have done without," he said wryly.

"Maybe, but it's the attention from the crowds—well, the money they spent *after* you got their attention—that ensured you stayed alive after you defeated me. Otherwise, trust me, you wouldn't have lasted another night." I got my feet under myself and stood, offering him a hand up as well. "I know you hate it. It's obvious to anyone looking closely enough, but you might consider letting your fights last longer, at least."

Bastian flexed his wrist again. "And let Octavian win?" One eyebrow quirked.

"He only wins if you die. And letting him continue to drive you into the ground won't give you any advantage on the sands." He gave me a narrow look, and I had to smile. "I didn't say play to the crowds, sell your sweaty tunics to adoring fans, or bed every woman he dangles before you. Trust me, he'll still find ways to make you miserable. But you might be able to get away with fewer bruises."

"Where's the fun in that?" he asked, scooping up his sword and going to retrieve his helmet.

"If that's what you call fun, I'd hate to see what you consider misery." I stepped out of the training court. "Three nights from now," I told him. "If I'm not here, it means I'm dead."

## BASTIAN

*"When will you learn?"* Octavian's furious question echoed after he and his men had left the arming room. I braced a hand against the table, empty after the attendants had whisked everything away and retreated in the face of Octavian's advance. A few spots of red dripped to the surface and I lifted my other hand from my stomach to wipe my bleeding nose.

When *would* I learn?

"Bastian?" Phestus's cautious voice drew my attention. He lingered in the doorway, a tamer version of the coordinator's frustration in his eyes.

"I'm fine," I said. A disbelieving noise came from him, and I pushed from the table, with my left hand returning to my stomach. "I'm fine. Go get your arm checked."

He'd been pulled into the fight from the beginning, a two on two against fighters from another city, and the rough bandage he'd wrapped was showing bloody spots. He should have already gone to the infirmary. I wasn't sure why he insisted on hanging around and making sure I was still standing after Octavian left.

Phestus hesitated a moment longer before I impatiently pointed him out the door. He tapped fist to chest like he'd seen me do and retreated. I shook my head, waited until I was certain he'd left, and started limping forward.

I wasn't leaving the tunnels yet, not until I'd walked some of this off. Octavian had injured me worse than the fight. All I had from that was some scraped knuckles and tired muscles. Now, I had a bloody nose and an aching stomach. And the lingering question—when would I learn?

A faint curse broke as I leaned my shoulder against the wall and tried to staunch another drip of blood. I worked my scraped hand in and out of a fist. I might not learn until I'd done something I'd be proud to tell my son about one day.

"You look like you're *trying* to make him kill you himself."

I lifted my head, searching the darkened tunnel for the gladiator to match with the voice. "I'd hate to see him actually try."

Cyrus emerged into the light cast in the juncture of two corridors. "He'd win. And I thought I told you you'd only get worn down trying to beat him at his own game."

I shifted to lean my back against the wall, a second away from sliding down to sit on the floor. "I'm not trying to play his game. Life and death isn't a *sport*."

Exasperation crossed his face. "Maybe not, but it is to those who hold our lives in their hands." He gave me a sharper look, maybe noticing my unsteadiness. "Let's get the blood off your face. Then you might make it to your quarters before word spreads that you've gotten hurt again."

I tilted my head. "Concerned for me?" I kept it light, still trying to figure out my new ally.

"I can't amaze the crowds by myself, not with how they're setting us against each other. And you obviously don't care enough about yourself to stay alive." Cyrus nodded down the corridor. "This way."

I shoved away from the wall, arm pressing tighter against my stomach as I followed him, not trying to hide the limp. Another curse hissed between my teeth. "Has he always been this much of a bastard?"

Cyrus brushed through a curtained doorway and into a room filled with medicinal smells and stillness that spoke of being disused. He rummaged in the dark before the click of a firestarter brought a lamp to life. "There's a reason I know how to get into this." He gestured at a locked chest on one of the stone counters. "He's always been one to take out frustration personally."

I leaned against the counter opposite him, gingerly dabbing away some more dampness. "Sounds like a 'yes' then."

Cyrus tossed me a cloth from one of the shelves before ducking to search for something under the counter. "He wasn't like this when I was younger. I suppose he has some limits."

I arched an eyebrow as I pressed the cloth to my face. It seemed like

I was helping Octavian find those limits. Though from the way he, and other men I'd crossed paths with in the army, grasped for power or fame...those limits weren't far at all.

Cyrus emerged with something that glowed purple clutched in his hand. He pressed it to the lock on the chest, which swung open to allow the lamplight to fall on a collection of bottles and jars. "Here." He passed me a stoppered bottle. "Get that on the cloth. It'll stop the bleeding."

I slid up to sit on the counter before obeying. And wrinkled my nose at the liquid's scent. It came with a bit of familiarity, especially as I doused some over the cloth. I'd used this on him not too long ago.

It did stop the bleeding, and stung a little while it worked before chasing after with enough numbness that I breathed easier. I swiped it over my scraped knuckles next, setting the cloth beside me as Cyrus continued rummaging through the chest. After picking up and setting down a handful of smaller jars, he passed me a vial sealed with red wax. "If you want. Deaden some of the pain from that." He nodded at my stomach. So he *had* noticed the unsteadiness as we'd been walking.

I rotated the vial in my hand before prying off the wax. "If this doesn't taste terrible, I'm going to assume you're poisoning me."

He smirked at that. "It tastes terrible."

One quick tip of the vial and I agreed, coughing as it burned its way down. Residual bitterness swept back up, feeling like it was trying to sting my nose for good measure. "I'd dislike physicians if this didn't work every time." I managed another mouthful before setting it aside and taking up the cloth again, using it to scrape away the drying blood. "Thank you," I said. "You didn't have to help."

"Letting favors go unreturned is as dangerous as needing them in the first place," Cyrus said, shutting the medicine chest and dodging beneath the counter to replace whatever had unlocked it. "I don't leave debts unpaid."

I shook my head, even though his back was turned. The misery in this place extended down to the warped form of currency. "There was never any debt between us."

"Well, this goes a short way to covering things." Cyrus nodded at where he'd hidden the purple object. "The key's stuck under the counter, if you need to come back here another time."

I eased another breath as the knots in my stomach started to relax. "Do all top fighters know about hidden keys and medical chests?" I asked. I wouldn't be surprised. And also wouldn't ignore the small gift of knowing it was here.

Cyrus's shoulders tensed and he quickly said, "Not everyone. I...I had someone else to show me. Someone whose job it is to restock whatever goes missing."

It was the difference in his tone, the way his sandal almost scuffed at the ground. The way someone else had talked about *him*. I almost smiled. "Callista?"

The shift in his posture at her name was instantaneous. His eyes narrowed, the angle of his shoulders changed, and a foot slid back. I stayed where I was and kept talking.

"She's been kind when she didn't have to be. And very worried about you," I said. I'd seen her once at the altars in the days after I'd helped tend Cyrus, tears streaming down her face. She'd accepted the shoulder to cry on, even if she never said what she wept for. "I told her I'd keep her secret, since she's keeping one of mine." I held his stare, letting him see it was only truth.

The razor sharpness began to fade from his eyes, replaced by something thoughtful. "That's why you intervened when Flavius attacked her."

I shook my head, anger stirring again just thinking about it. "I intervened because no woman should be so hurt or helpless because of a man."

"She told me about it the next day," Cyrus said. "I couldn't believe it. No one..." He looked at the floor and a shudder crossed his shoulders, like he was hearing the awful reality of the words for the first time. "No one intervenes in things like that."

"There are many things I refuse to learn here." My words came soft but still wrapped in steel.

"You're not the only one. She's stayed kind, even after all these years." Cyrus raised his head. "When I leave, I'm taking her with me."

"Good." I eased to my feet. "I'll help keep an eye on her until she follows you out. No debt."

A slight smile pulled at the corner of Cyrus's mouth. "We need to survive until we reach that point. You think you can keep this up for three more months?"

"If it means freedom for you and safety for her, then yes," I said. I'd find my own way after, no matter how bleak the chances looked. But it was starting to feel more and more like I might have been sent here to help the two of them. Somehow. I also hoped there was some sort of divine plan for me to survive after I discharged that duty. "Don't worry about me. Besides." I pointed to the chest. "Now I know about this."

"If they don't realize you're hurt, they'll target you less," Cyrus said. "I can't speak for Octavian, but you might be able to escape others if it's less obvious that you walk out of each fight injured." A noise in the corridor made both of us look to the curtained door. Cyrus snuffed the lamp, leaving us in the dark. Despite myself, a jolt ran through me at the abruptness. A moment later, the voices faded, and Cyrus warned, "They're always watching. Don't give them anything they'll be able to use against you."

The curtain swished on the heels of his words, and he was gone.

I remained in the darkness a moment more, until the intense discomfort that came with its suppressive cloak drove me into the lamplit hallway. I hated the stillness of the underground corridors, but right now they were one of the safer places to be. I already knew the truth of his warning, and I wished Lyra wasn't so stubborn with staying. A faint smile tugged my mouth at the thought of her—we were well matched, the two of us, in that regard. Likely, our son would follow in our footsteps.

Just as fast, the smile faded. Five years was the only certain escape for me. The one pain medicine couldn't reach was accepting that my son might never know me. But maybe Cyrus or Callista could carry a story to be told for him one day. One where I never learned to play by Octavian's rules.

# CHAPTER XXIII

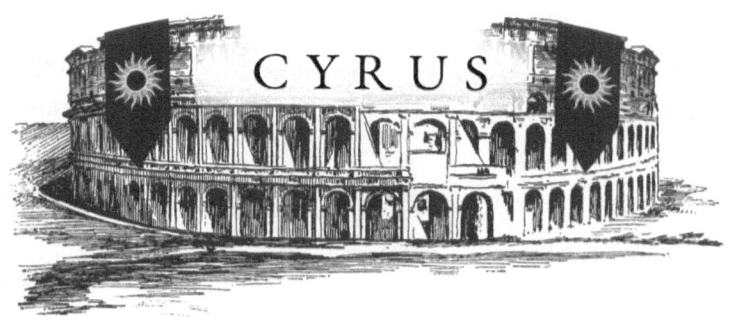

Almost a week later, and I was still alive. Somehow.

"Quite the party, don't you think?"

"Different," I agreed, setting my empty cup to the side. "Refreshing, really."

Gossip and talk floated around me, echoing through the high-ceilinged marble halls of the University's reception building. They'd hosted this event to draw attention to their students' breakthroughs in mechanical and alchemical research, and I'd been invited as part of their efforts to showcase how research could be applied—the obstacles and traps common to Arena fights wouldn't be possible without such breakthroughs, after all.

The invitation made sense, but I didn't enjoy the reminders of how the Arena itself had tried to kill me. At least these conversations didn't require me to flirt with anyone. The academics were overjoyed to ramble at length about their areas of expertise, and all I had to do was maintain a suitably interested demeanor.

Like this fellow, an astronomer from a province southeast of the capital. I'd asked a simple question, and he'd hardly needed prompting to commence a detailed explanation of how his field of study was mapping the heavens to predict seasons, weather, and events that the common people would attribute to the workings of the gods.

From his dismissal of such superstition, I assumed he didn't ascribe to faith any more than I had until recently.

"...been able to predict such things as the rising and falling of the moon, in accordance with its path across the sky and its inherent ties to the sun." He nodded to my tunic, the gold stripe in it a constant even when I wasn't on the sands. "You know something about that, I assume. The sun and moon are always connected, and at times their paths through the skies align."

"Is that so?" I scanned the crowd, uneasy at the sight of Octavian talking with one of the demonstration engineers. After the Sieneca fight, there'd been something cold in his demeanor toward me, and I couldn't help but tense each time he came near. "What would that look like?"

The scholar's dark eyes lit up, and he snatched two oranges from a nearby table to demonstrate. "Like this." He held one fruit at arm's length above his head, describing an arc like the sun through the sky. "The sun keeps to the same predictable path, straying only as the seasons dictate. But the moon"—he held the other orange closer to his head than the "sun" one, its arc lower and less steady—"it keeps to its own path and time, and sometimes..."

His hands stopped moving, and I stepped around him to look from his perspective. From here, there appeared to be only one fruit held aloft, one orange completely blocking out the view of the other.

An unsettled feeling stirred in my stomach. Up to now, this conversation had been a rote thing, meant to fill the space until it was time to leave, but now...

I angled my head to see around the "moon" orange. "So, how would this appear from the ground?"

The scholar lowered his hands to hold one of the oranges between him and I. "When this event—it's called an 'eclipse'—occurs, the moon's path will take it before the sun, passing between it and us. The sun's light will be blotted out until their paths across the sky diverge." He grinned triumphantly, unaware that my smile had been fading with every word from his lips. "It'll be like night in the middle of the day."

"That's...fascinating," I managed to say. "And you've managed to predict the exact date of this?"

"Not just the date!" he blurted. "The time!" A stream of explanations issued from him, numbers and dates combining in an enthusiastic rush as I did my best to nod along and pretend I wasn't feeling sicker by the moment.

The date he'd mentioned was this summer, a handful of weeks from now.

*The sun's light will be blotted out.*

I didn't know if the board knew about this, but it felt like too perfect of a coincidence. The rest of the astronomer's explanations whirled past, only the smallest part of my awareness focused on keeping a smile on my face and an interested tone in my voice. The rest of my mind stayed busy, putting together dates and times in conjunction with the rumors I'd been hearing but refused to acknowledge until now.

*A rising elite fighter as unknown as the night.*

*He's fast. Strong. Ruthless in battle.*

*The Arena's rising champion.*

I made my excuses as another academic approached, and strode away with my mind spinning. My time as the Arena champion was meant to end with the onset of autumn, but this event, this "eclipse," would occur long before then.

I needed answers. And for that, I needed to talk to Octavian. I just hoped he'd consider me subdued enough—*broken* enough—to answer truthfully.

Speaking with Octavian was easier decided than done. I had to wait until the following day, when another skill trial saw me returning to my tunnel exhausted and covered in mud from the rain beating down into the Arena. I'd expected, upon waking to a leaden sky, that the spectators would seek their entertainment in drier quarters. I was proven very wrong. Evidently, the crowds' enthusiasm couldn't be dampened by rain, and the skill trial went on without modification.

The scramble for flags amid mud and half-triggered traps had seen me flying into a wall after an explosive triggered beneath my foot. Luckily, the damp had smothered its full fury, and I'd escaped without burns. My second was likewise battered—he'd run afoul of the Dragonesques and was now limping. In some ways, I pitied him. Most backup fighters were able to enjoy the extra training and equipment of a second's post before ascending to a solo position of their own. This youngster—I hadn't even learned his name—had the dubious honor of being adjacent to my fame, but also to the rumors that hadn't stopped flying since my encounter with the Empress's "favor."

And today, as he sagged against the wall favoring his right leg, I couldn't help but say, "Well done today. You were a big help."

"I was?" His eyes shone under the praise, and he stood straighter despite the grime streaking his face. "All I did was get knocked down, but thank you."

For a moment, he sounded like I had, years ago. I'd spent months taking hits meant for my primary fighter, until the rescue that'd catapulted me into fame myself. "You bought time for me to find the banner. Couldn't have done it without you."

"I almost wonder if you *could*," Octavian said from the armory door. He gave me a measuring look as the attendants scurried to get my armor off. "Maybe we'll give it a try."

"You weren't pleased with the show?" I asked, accepting a cloth to scrub mud from my face and limbs. The carefree mannerisms I used when speaking to him were coming less readily as I commented, "I think the crowds like this new feature. We should petition the gods for more rainy days."

"May they hear your prayers," he said, rolling his eyes. "The crowds do like these skill trials, though. And it saves us time and money in training."

I slung the muddied cloth into the basket that already held my filthy red-and-gold uniform. "Tired of me killing all your combatants?"

"Tired of things not going according to plan." He turned dark eyes to me as I pulled a clean tunic over my head. "You need to come with me. The board wants to see you."

My fingers closed involuntarily into fists. "Now?"

"Now." Gods, he sounded entirely cold. "There's some things we need to lay out."

Heart pounding, I followed, running through the last several days in my head. I'd won my last fight in spectacular fashion, been the life of the two parties I'd attended, and only broken one person's nose when the jibes about my reputation crossed a line. If there was a time to approach him about my suspicions regarding the eclipse, it was now.

Not all the board members had been watching the skill trial. A handful of them lounged in the open area behind the balcony, watching the rain pounding on the emptying stands. Perhaps the others had sought their entertainment elsewhere, even if the spectators had not.

"Oh good, you're here," the box office manager said as Octavian and I came around the corner. "Here." He passed Octavian the tablet, where early revenue numbers for today's fight were displayed. "Even with the rain and the new format of skill trials, it's promising." He glanced at me. "Have you told him yet?"

"Tell me...what?" I tipped my head to give Octavian as severe a look as I dared. "What's going on?"

"Nothing, Cyrus. Calm down."

"I'll be calm when you tell me what you're planning," I insisted. "What is it?"

"We only wanted to update you," one of the other board members said with exasperation. "And to give you advance warning of the rematch against the starcast gryphon next week."

"A rematch? So soon?"

It wasn't soon, not really. I'd suspected this was coming, had warned Bastian of as much. It'd been over a month since we'd faced each other, practically an eternity given the frenzy the crowds had worked themselves into. I'd heard absurd things, like how followers had gotten into brawls with members of opposite groups. And I'd personally seen more than one person wearing boots that matched—or attempted to replicate—the ones that Bastian had worn since his arrival.

"The crowds love seeing you independently," the board member said. "But the most ardent devotees on both sides are becoming impatient. Some are claiming you'll remain undefeated, others that your sun is about to set permanently."

I would've laughed, but the scholar's words rang in my head.

*The sun's light, blotted out.*

"They'll have to wait and see." I raised my head to meet his eyes grimly. "I take it this isn't going to be to the death?"

"Not this time," Octavian answered for the others. "Just to the first injury. The people want to see you face each other on equal footing, to better lay their odds." He pinned me with a look that promised torment if I disobeyed. "*Don't* kill him."

"And ruin the show?" I scoffed. "I know what you want, and I won't step out of line again." It didn't take much to let my confident smile slip. "I've learned that lesson."

"It can be taught again." A cold threat, and one he meant wholeheartedly.

"I *know*." I shook my head fiercely. "It won't happen again. Clearly, you have other plans for him." This time it was my turn to glare, if only to cover the nerves churning my stomach. "And those plans had better include me walking out at the end of my five years."

"They do, assuming you can prove once and for all that your reputation is deserved." Octavian nodded at the rainswept balcony, where Bastian's banner hung alongside mine in a contrast of black and silver. "Defeat this upstart, and you'll be at the height of your fame. *Then* we'll speak of retirement. You'll go down in memory as the people's hero, immortalized with barely a defeat to speak of."

I'd have been thrilled to hear it, two months ago. But now, between Octavian's harshened demeanor and the furtive glances being thrown around the room behind him, I couldn't deny the truth any longer. If I killed Bastian and was sent into retirement, there'd be no champion to bring in crowds and fill coffers. A hero was only as valuable as the money they brought in, and with how readily the crowds had flocked to Bastian's name, banner, *legend*, it was clear.

They'd weighed my life in gold and found it lacking. Now my only escape from this place would be death.

# CHAPTER XXIV

BASTIAN

I hit my knee. Again. Sheeting rain had slackened to a drizzle, but the trainers hadn't cared. Thankfully Octavian was nowhere to be seen, but his replacement had been just as intent on keeping me moving no matter the mud and pooling water. My clothes and armor were soaked and stained. I'd had to take my helmet off at least twice to clear mud that had caked around the eye slit or clawed its way inside. Phestus was in no better condition. Maybe worse, as he chose not to wear a helmet.

I wrenched to my feet, and the trainer must have finally read my frustration as he quickly announced we were done. I ripped off the helmet and tilted my head to the sky to let the rain wash away the sweat brought by training and humidity.

Phestus tried to wait for me, but I impatiently waved him on. The attendants had been waking me late the last two mornings, and no amount of ointment or massage could banish the perpetual ache. I didn't want any more gossip or encouragement from him, and the rain driving almost everyone inside promised a quiet walk to my quarters.

Despite the weather, a few people still hovered on the free side of the barred wall. I glanced that way, hoping to see Lyra but knowing she'd be smart enough not to come in this weather.

A flash of red hair caught my eye instead. My feet stuttered for a moment in disbelief. A familiar smirk flashed, and its owner made his way to the sheltered nook where bars met wall. I kept moving as well, making sure my path was unnoticed.

"Commander." His husky voice greeted me as I leaned against the bars.

"That title was taken from me, Felix," I said.

"We shouldn't have let it," he returned, guilt coloring the rasp left from being trapped under a downed gryphon as a forest burned around him.

"You all would have died." I matched his stubborn glare. "Why are you here?"

Felix rested his shoulder against the stone. "Lyra said you're being stubborn, so I volunteered to come today instead."

I shook my head. "There's no way out except death."

"There was no way out but death in Laecanthum too. And remember what you did?"

I focused into the courtyard, making sure the rain kept obscuring me. Laecanthum had been a foolhardy plan with no chance of success, plunging on loyal gryphons who'd clung to the side of a rocky cliff for hours with their riders gently shushing them the entire time. It shouldn't have worked.

"Some of the men have been coming on days you fight," Felix said.

I shoved arms across my chest, watching the way the scattered runoff from the wall above had begun washing some of the armor clean. I wasn't sure what my heart felt—shame at them seeing that side of me, or relief that there were friendly eyes in the stands.

"Not like you to have nothing to say, Commander." Felix's wry words drove a harsh sound from me.

"There is nothing to say, Felix. I've looked for a way out, and there is none. Go back and tell Lyra to stop clinging to foolish hope."

"No." His refusal came almost immediately.

I glanced at him. He was in a simple tunic and trousers, and like me, like other Legion riders, more comfortable in boots than out. A cloak hung loose around his shoulders, the hood long tipped back to let the rain drench his red hair. This weather was milder by far than what they would have come from. And the expression? The same stubborn loyalty that had taken my orders without flinching for two years, and had flown steadily at my right wing for two years before that.

"Thank you for taking care of her," I said, throat tightening. They'd planned to look after her long before they'd returned to the city.

Felix nodded. "Least we could do," he replied quietly. "We followed your orders, Commander, though maybe we should have questioned the Legates sooner like you did." His arms crossed like mine as he leaned against the wall. "They sent us back to those villages after you were taken."

My heart froze, but his mouth only twitched up. "By the time we got there, they were empty. Everyone had fled deeper into the forests, feeding the resistance that's brought the Legions to a standstill."

I shouldn't have felt so relieved to hear it. If I were still at the warfront, maybe I'd be frustrated that we couldn't find the enemy. Or maybe I'd still be questioning orders to wipe out innocents just as much. Either way, all those people had lived, and it made the lingering bitterness of what had happened to me fade.

"Then why did they send a scout squad back?" I asked. The Fifth Legion was renowned for discovering secrets and breaking ranks. They were often the last to be recalled.

"We were sent for additional training," he said. "To see if milder climes would brush the edges off. To get a new commander."

"What happened to Camillus?" I asked, my jaw clenching around the name.

"Dead," he said flatly. "No, we didn't kill him," he reassured at my quick look. "But we didn't try to save him either." He seemed grimly pleased that the man who'd reported me to the Legate had met his end. "And to bring back Tertius. He refuses to bond with a new rider."

A faint smile flickered. My gryphon had stayed loyal.

"Where did you take him?" I asked.

"Home."

He didn't mean a tiled house in the fields outside the city. He meant the emerald hills that rolled into mountains on a wave-swept coast. The place where Lyra's father had bred and trained Tertius before passing him to me.

"We saw your father," Felix said quietly.

I blessed the rain for hiding the strike at my heart. "How is he?" I asked thickly.

"Angry." Felix's chuckle didn't hold much humor. "Leonis practically had to sit on him to keep him there."

A sound escaped me. Lyra's father and mine were close as brothers. Had been since Lyra and I had brought our families together four years ago.

"Will you make sure Lyra takes August and goes home if..." I faltered.

"I will," he promised softly, and some steadiness returned. Felix's promises were more valuable than gold. "But what if you were there with them?"

I shook my head. "There's no way out," I said.

"There has to be." Felix was also more stubborn than a mule.

"I've looked, Felix."

He *tsked*. "Too long as a commander has you missing things all over."

I threw a glare his way, and he smirked. "There's always a way." He straightened. "We'll keep coming to the fights, see what we can scout out. Make sure we keep winning good money off you."

I treated him to another narrow look that only had him laughing.

"It's not just that," I admitted. "There are two people in here who are just as trapped."

Felix pushed away from the bars, triumph sparking in his green eyes. "I *knew* it. I *knew* there was some other reason you're dragging your feet."

I rolled my eyes. A reason, but no good way to ask Lyra to keep waiting for months while I helped make sure Cyrus gained his freedom. Made sure that Callista followed after him. "One's a fighter. He has only a few months left before he gains his freedom."

Felix rocked back on his heels. "And you're thinking of making sure he gets there?"

I lifted a shoulder and tilted my face for him to see the bruising. "There's more fights off the sands than on."

Anger darkened his face at the injuries.

"The other's a woman. She's one of the slaves and is not safe here."

Felix nodded. "She'd be the more difficult one to get out." He brushed off my look.

"She'd leave when the fighter does. Hopefully." From what Callista and Cyrus had said about each other, I wished them luck if they found freedom together outside the walls.

"Leaving you..."

"Leaving me," I said. "Just me, to risk an attempt."

"How long?"

"Three months."

Felix whistled softly. "That's cutting it close. We've been ordered to return to the front by year's end."

"You shouldn't even be thinking about risking it anyway," I said.

He gave me a pitying look. "You'd be here in my place, Commander. Would have already gotten me out, more than likely."

I doubted that. *I* had some sense.

A flash of gold caught my eye as a figure emerged from the stables. Cyrus paused, frustration twisting his face before he caught sight of me. He glanced around the courtyard before making straight for me. Even before he opened his mouth, I could tell something was wrong. Wrong enough that he'd risk us being seen together in public.

"We need to talk. Now." He looked over my shoulder at Felix, whose mouth had dropped open as soon as Cyrus came close enough for recognition. "Somewhere without anyone listening in."

It was my turn to smirk as I turned to Felix again. I'd pay money to see him tell the others about this. "Wait," I told him. He dumbly nodded, and I followed Cyrus to the infirmary courtyard. He stopped in the shelter of a grapevine trellis, eyes flickering around the arched entries as I joined him.

"What's wrong?"

"They're not planning on letting me go," he said abruptly, hands clenched into fists like he wished there was something he could fight. "They told me after my match that they'd consider retirement after I defeat you, but they're *lying*. I can tell." He started pacing under the trellis. "And everyone's talking about us being rivals. Sun and moon, light versus darkness—"

"Cyrus." I set my helmet on one of the planting beds. "Slow down." I reached out, gently resting a hand on his arm. It seemed like he might fly away without some sort of grounding touch. "How do you know for certain?"

Cyrus closed his eyes and took a deep breath, letting it out with a sigh. "I was talking with one of the scholars at the university last night. He was very enthusiastic about his studies, and told me about a celestial event that's going to happen later this summer." His arm tensed, and he turned to look at me. "He called it an 'eclipse,' where the moon's going to block out the sunlight. I counted the weeks. It's long before my three months are up."

A soft curse broke from me as the pieces fell into place. "Light versus darkness. How much do you want to bet we fight that day, and only one of us is supposed to walk away that time?"

"Those aren't odds I'd wager on." He pulled his arm free and went to sit on one of the benches beneath the trellis, bowing his head with fingertips going to the gold that pierced the top edge of his ear. "There's no way they'll let me walk out, even if I *were* to win. They've been planning this outcome ever since you hesitated that day."

Another curse hissed between my teeth, and I moved to sit next to him. It almost felt like I should apologize. "You think they'll want *me* as the next champion?" I tried to lighten my voice.

A humorless laugh broke from him. "They've been watching you since your first fight. Yes." He tipped his head to glance at me. "You're fierce and unknown, you fight like you don't notice the lives you're taking, and the crowds love the idea of someone who never pauses in the pursuit of glory."

Bitterness welled. "Glory," I scoffed. "Glory's nothing but empty sand and mud." Even if the faceless crowds thought one thing, I needed someone to know the truth. "And I notice."

"I know. You even notice the lives of those who *should* be your enemies." He shook his head. "I still don't understand that."

I scraped mud off my bracer. "We're all just flesh and blood in the end. Maybe all that matters is what we do when it seems like no one, not even the gods, are watching."

Cyrus laughed at that, a halfhearted sound but one that sounded lighter than his earlier tone. "I didn't think anyone was watching for the longest time." His gaze flicked to the beds of herbs, and he got up to snap a stem of rosemary from one of the bushes. "But maybe there's someone watching who might help me beat the odds."

I smiled, thinking I knew who he meant. "Someone who's looking even if you don't look back?"

"My father called him 'The One Who Sees,'" he offered. "I don't know what name you know him by." He resumed his seat beside me, sitting straighter this time.

"My mother only called him 'The First,'" I said. "We followed the goddess for most of my life. I had to lose my way a little before I found him in an unlikely place."

"Someone told me that we might see him in others before we gained the courage to meet his eye." Cyrus shrugged. "Maybe even in our ene-mies. Though"—he tipped his head sheepishly—"I wish it hadn't been with your sword against my chest."

"Someone else might not have hesitated." I nudged my elbow against his arm. "And maybe even enemies can become friends in the end."

He grimaced. "Well, that end might come sooner and bloodier than either of us want, if the board gets their way."

"And I was already having such a good day." I gestured to the mess of my clothes and armor.

Cyrus held out one of his arms to show me a sooty smear that could only be from a misfired trap. "You weren't dealing with explosives in addition to the mud."

"All right." I held up my hands. "You win. What new hell is the board planning?"

"They're putting us in the Arena to face each other to first injury. Next week." He smiled grimly. "I was told specifically *not* to kill you."

"That's a relief," I said wryly. My hands scrubbed together. Next week. Then a matter of weeks until the solar event, or whenever they planned to pit us against each other to the death. I didn't have a way out from where I sat, but I had a squad of loyal idiots on gryphons and someone beside me who'd know a thing or two about the Arena. I hesitated only a fraction of a breath. "What if neither of us were here for the last fight?"

"Sorry?"

I chuckled lightly. Defy the odds. "I have a wife outside who's desper-ate for me to get home. And a squad of gryphon riders who are willing to risk discharge at the least, death at worst, to try to get me out of here.

I'd just been telling one that I was planning to wait until you got out in a few months, but it seems like that's not happening anymore, so..." I lifted a shoulder. "Defy the odds?"

## CYRUS

A shiver went through my skin that had nothing to do with the rain. *Defiance.* That had rarely gone well for me in the past. Acutely so in the last several weeks.

"Escape," I said, almost unwilling to hear the pitch in my voice that said I hadn't given up hope. "Escape from *here*?"

"That is the idea," Bastian replied, voice keeping the lightness to it.

"No one escapes from here," I repeated numbly. "No. One. You really think it can be done?"

Recklessness edged his smile. "My men will tell you that I'd prefer a challenge." He sobered just as fast. "I've found no way out from the inside, which means we need a way for them to come to us. So you tell me. Is it possible?"

Gods, why was this insane idea taking root? I'd *tried* before, couldn't he guess that? But for all my attempts, from silly childhood schemes to full-grown plots, I hadn't managed it. I looked down at my hands, realizing that one had gone to where Octavian had lashed out with a riding crop the one time I'd made it to the forum.

I closed my hand into a fist. "Gryphons, you said?"

"I did. If we're escaping, I'd rather it be in the air than on foot."

"In the air..." I leaned forward to look up at the Arena, and the previous night's dreams invaded my thoughts in the gap between one word and the next.

Weightlessness. Air rushing past my face. Freedom.

"The roof," I said without hesitation. "How good are you at climbing?"

He followed my look, eyes narrowing in consideration. "If you're going to fly gryphons, you'd better be comfortable climbing anything," he said. "Over the barracks?"

"No, from the very top." I stood and walked far enough to be able to point at the Arena itself. "Up there."

Bastian stepped alongside me, one hand shielding his eyes from the rain. His gaze narrowed, lips moving silently. Then he turned to take in what he could of the surrounding walls. Tracked a path across the dull sky. "How broad is the roof?"

I turned to point at one of the planters before crossing the courtyard to stand by another. "From there...to about here. And the same again after a slight ridgeline."

He nodded. "Tile or stone?"

"Tiles," I answered instantly. "Knocked off plenty of them over the years. The others in the courtyard didn't even think to look up."

Bastian tilted an eyebrow at that, then studied the space I'd marked off again. Another glance at the sky. "They could come in one at a time. Be in and out within moments." He paused. "There's only one problem. Callista."

I groaned. "Callista." Sweet, gentle Callista, who would never be able to climb that distance. "I'm *not* leaving without her. We have to think of something else."

He scrubbed a hand across his jaw, leaving faint smears of mud. "Is she ever allowed to leave the Arena? Maybe we can arrange to get her to safety somehow."

I returned to the half-dry space beneath the trellis. "She doesn't visit the forums. Everything they get for the infirmary is brought in or grown here. And someone would notice if she tried slipping out...*unless* someone more important was with her." I waved a hand at Bastian's confused expression. "Not us. Atticus. He told me to let him know if he could help in any way."

"Then we ask him," Bastian said like it was done.

"He might say no," I warned. "I can't tell where his loyalties are."

He chuckled. It sounded closer to something actually *happy*. "Given how he looked one breath from feeding me piece by piece to a gryphon when I brought Callista to him weeks ago, I'd say his loyalty is to making sure she's protected."

"All right," I said. "I'll ask. Maybe it's a good thing you told your friend to wait." My laugh was faint, but the hope stirring beneath it couldn't be denied. "I feel like he might be relieved to hear what you have to say."

"Only because he's probably going to win a few bets with this." Bastian rolled his eyes. "Meet tomorrow night?"

I nodded, stepping from the shelter of the grapevines and into the rain. "Pray the rain stops. Otherwise we'll be this muddy again. I'm going to go visit the infirmary." I gave him a grin. "Training injury."

He scooped up his helmet. "I think I've forgotten something at the training courts."

"Give them my best," I called as I started for the infirmary.

He spun around. "If you don't show, I'll know Atticus finally smothered you."

I threw a rude gesture over my shoulder and kept walking, chased only by his laugh.

# CHAPTER XXV

CYRUS

T he corridor to the infirmary was lined with footprints etched in mud. As I approached the heavy door, it swung open to spit out a pair of newer arrivals, followed closely by their trainer. Both sported bruises, and one had a newly bandaged forearm. Rainy days made for plenty of opportunities to settle old scores.

I slipped inside the door before it closed. As expected, Atticus was in the main room, scrubbing his work table with emphatic strokes that spoke of a day filled with busywork. He straightened as he saw me. "Don't tell me..."

I held up my hands. "Not injured. Needed to talk to you."

Immediate concern filled his face, and I could understand why. The numbness brought on by understanding the truth of the board's plans had faded while I'd talked with Bastian, and now sharp, clear intensity had filled the emptiness—like the cold space in the middle of a fight. Some of it must have shown on my face, because Atticus set his cleaning supplies down and jerked his head toward the side door.

"This way."

The second room held a row of beds, currently empty of occupants. Atticus walked past all of them, opening another door and ushering me through. It was a long, narrow storeroom, its shelves lined with piles of linen, jars and bags of supplies, and boxes marked with the glowing green lettering used by alchemists. He closed the door and set a foot against it, leveling a stern look at me.

"What's wrong?"

I took a deep breath, then another. Then the story came out—all of it, from Bastian's and my chance meeting in the corridors, to the decision to ally to gain time, to the board skirting discussion of my retirement, to the eclipse... "And I must've been stupid to not see it earlier, but now it's clear. There's no way they'll let us go, so we need to escape. Him, me—" My voice faltered. "Callista."

I'd been pacing in the small space, but now I halted and locked eyes with the physician. "You said before that I should ask if I needed help. I'd never ask for myself, but I can't leave Callista here, and I won't be able to buy her freedom if I escape. But if she had someone to get her out of the Arena, there are people beyond who could bring her to safety."

Atticus nodded, icy blue eyes deadly serious. For a moment, I thought I could see what he'd been before coming here, and the shift in his posture, the way his face had composed itself, told me everything I needed to know.

"I've offered a means of escape to her before. She wouldn't leave," he said. "I didn't realize the depth of her feelings until the night you were taken to the Empress." He turned the full force of that serious expression on me. "And it seems you feel the same about her."

I nodded, straightening my shoulders under his scrutiny. "I do. And I know your protection is the reason she's been safe for the last few years. That's why I'm here. Can you see a way to get her out of the compound?"

"Yes," he immediately answered. "And if there's no other place to go, I have a haven where she could rest until another is prepared."

I'd thought I was past being surprised by him. "You...where? And why aren't you there, instead of here?"

Atticus gave a short laugh. "I took my discharge after twenty years with the army. It came with a small parcel of land and a farmhouse outside the city. There's vines, a small sheepfold, pastureland. I hired someone to keep it up, but I never visit. I was planning on returning there someday, but..." A shoulder lifted, then dropped. "The First God had other plans for me. If you get out of here—and *don't* tell me what you're planning—there's somewhere you can go."

I shook my head, dumbfounded. "How long have you had this in mind?"

"Long enough. This type of thing runs in my family. Like I said, defiance takes more than one form." Atticus hadn't moved from his position against the door. Now he folded his arms and a cunning look crossed his face. "I don't leave here often, though I'm free to come and go as I please. But there are times when I have to visit the alchemical workshops in the artisan district. I'll take her with me, and ensure she's left in the hands of whomever you send to meet us." He straightened from the door with a sigh. "But you have to tell Callista yourself."

My eyes widened and I took a step back. "I—I can't."

"You have to talk to her, Cyrus."

The storeroom suddenly felt too narrow, too crowded. "We haven't spoken since before the Sieneca fight. What if—"

"Cyrus." I hadn't realized I'd begun pacing again until his hand arrested my movement. "She's been worried sick. You have no idea how many times I've held her as she's cried over you." For someone so stern, Atticus's voice was unexpectedly gentle. "She doesn't care about what happened, she just wants to see you." He released my arm and opened the door. "Stay here. I'll get her."

He disappeared, leaving me in the storeroom. I immediately began looking for a way out. The only escape was the door through which he'd just left. I hurried through it, finding myself in the infirmary ward. Gods, there was only one way out of here, too.

Heart pounding, I made for the door, only to pull up short as Atticus returned with Callista behind him. As soon as she saw me, she pushed past Atticus to fling her arms around me. The force of the embrace knocked me back a pace in a way that no fighters' strike ever had.

"Callista, I—"

"Stop!" she all but shouted. "It wasn't your fault!"

"But I still *did* it!" Even as I said it, cold helplessness snared my heart. "I could've tried to stop them. I could've fought, or—or—*something*—"

"And then they would've killed you!" Callista grabbed two handfuls of my tunic. "Cyrus, please. I don't hate you for what you've done in order to survive." She turned a tearstained face up to me. "I just want you to stop running from me."

"Y-you can't mean that. With last week and the things that happened—"

"I don't care!" she exclaimed. Warmth streamed through my chest, replacing the cold as she insisted, "I love *you*. No matter what they've done to you."

I couldn't fight it anymore. My arms went around Callista, and I held her tighter than I'd ever dared to before, bowing my head over hers as she cried. It wasn't until cold air struck my face that I realized my own cheeks were wet with tears. "You're certain?"

She still hadn't let me go. "I'm certain."

I leaned back to run a thumb under her eye, brushing away tears before pulling her close again. "You might regret this when you hear what I'm planning."

"I don't care." A smile spread across her face, and she turned her head to rest it against my chest. "If it's something you're behind, I don't have any reason to be afraid."

"Well," Atticus said dryly from the doorway, "I don't know if I'd go *that* far." He walked to join us, pulling me into a strong one-armed hug as I let Callista go. "People do insane things when the odds are against them. But this, I feel, might actually be a time when it pays off."

"Thank you, sir," I said, standing to my full height and wiping the tears from my face. The clarity of battle was returning, but this time it was tempered by warmth unlike anything I'd felt in a long time. "Lis, I have some things I need to tell you."

## BASTIAN

Cyrus had once again beaten me to the stable training yard. He shifted between his feet, glance darting everywhere, only pausing once I emerged from the deeper shadows. I'd left the helmet behind, and its absence left an oddly empty shape at my side.

"Do you ever stand still?" I asked.

He looked down at his feet, then up at me. "No? I don't even realize I'm doing it. You'd be the same way if you'd grown up here."

I studied him for a moment. Growing up in the Arena explained a few more things about him. "You ever left?"

"When I was younger. My father was an armorer, and he'd take me with him when he left for supplies. Sometimes we'd go as far as the foundries outside the city. Mama worked in a laundry outside the Arena, but she never had spare time." He stilled for a moment, fingers individually tapping against his thumb as he counted. "Since they died and I started training, it's been...I don't know, a dozen times that I've left the city?"

I stepped closer to the gate, looking at the sandy expanse. The clouds had cleared by midday, but the time in the sun hadn't come close to drying the ground. "How old were you when you started?"

There was a pause before he answered, like he was watching for a threat in the question. "Twelve," he finally answered. "But I didn't take the sands till I was sixteen."

I jolted, the ages not what I'd expected. *Twelve?* But maybe worse was... "Gods, you were *sixteen* when you first fought?"

"...Yes?" He walked to the gate and knelt to put a hand to the ground. "A trainee match, like the first one you had. Then a lower-ranked team, then I won a spot on Dragonesque and fought with them for over a year."

A trainee match like the first one I'd had, where two of eight men walked away alive. But he stated it all like facts, like it was normal. "Cyrus...you realize the army doesn't even take men until they're eighteen?" I was nineteen before I'd finally convinced my father that I was meant for the army and not just training horses for the cavalry legion.

"This isn't the army." He straightened, brushing sand from his hands. "And I'd been watching the fights since I was eight or younger. Besides, it was that or keep getting singled out by the others." A sharp smile crossed his face. "They stopped once they realized I'd counterattack instead of retreating."

It sent a sharp ache through my chest. I'd seen the youngsters that skirted the courtyards and ran errands for the training staff, but it hadn't occurred to me what they'd grown up witnessing. I didn't want my son anywhere near this, and I'd throttle anyone who let their boy of *eight or younger* watch such violence. There was something else to the words, the same sharpness he carried with him. Always ready to counterattack.

"How long have you been on your own?" I asked softly.

Cyrus frowned, the expression almost lost in the shadows. "Twelve. Like I said. I was born here, but my parents weren't. So when the shivering fever reached the city..."

The plague hadn't struck the coasts as hard. Those cities weren't as densely packed with people as the capitol. And the farms where my father bred and trained horses were mostly safe. At least, my parents and I were. I couldn't imagine losing everything at twelve and being left in a place like this. It made me a little angry again that there was nothing left behind to make sure he'd been cared for. But how many others were the same all over the Empire? Especially after the Legions I was once a part of had swept through and raised Imperial banners.

"Nowhere else to go?" I asked.

"I didn't know where else *to* go. I already knew every inch of this place, so when there was the chance to be safe and famous, I took it."

He shrugged, the fall of his shoulders suggesting that he now had some regrets as to the decision. "It wasn't *all* bad. If things got really hard, I could always disappear." He returned to the alcove where he'd been waiting for me, and buckles rattled as he pulled off his practice armor. "It's too wet in there to spar. You want to see where I'd disappear to?"

"As long as you don't intend to murder me there." I tilted a smile.

"That'd be the end of both of us," he said. "Octavian would make certain of that." He emerged from the shadows and gestured for me to follow. I gratefully left the damp stables behind, no real wish to spend the rest of the night cleaning sand from my boots to pretend I'd done nothing but spend the night comfortably in bed.

Cyrus crossed to the main barracks building, softly stepping up the stairwell that led to the upper floors. Every now and then I caught his glance over his shoulder, checking to make sure I still followed, or wasn't going to give us away.

At the top of the stairwell that opened onto the third floor was an arched window—some vines gamely trying to cling to the lattice that allowed a patchwork look into the courtyard. Cyrus headed right for it, nudging the lattice aside and sliding through quicker than a cat.

I frowned and pushed on it. My shoulders were wider than his, and my frame a little bulkier. He was already out on a narrow ledge that wrapped the Arena itself. If I felt like betting, we were headed for the roofs, by a path that was ignored by all but one foolhardy young combatant. I shook my head and squeezed out, ignoring his quiet laugh. I cursed him under my breath and tilted my chin. *Lead on.*

He moved out over arches, then to a set of columns with rough detailing, using the textured surface to scale upward. I halted at the base of the column, hands on hips and studying the surface. Cyrus looked down from the top.

"This is supposed to hold someone?" I asked.

"Scared?" he whispered with a laugh.

"I'm not a wisp like you," I retorted and grabbed a handhold. Another ghostly chuckle was the only sound beside my boots scuffing against the surface. Not too terribly different from Laecanthum. Felix could sleep vindicated tonight.

Cyrus edged aside as I swung to the top. "Think you can keep up?" he asked.

I flicked his shoulder. "Respect your elders."

It was another few minutes of climbing and edging along a narrow surface, before one more swing over a crenelated edge to the roof of the Arena itself.

Cyrus's feet fell with hardly any sound as he straightened and picked his way over the rows of tiles. Once on the other side of the slightly pitched center, he dropped to a crouch and pointed over the edge. "Look down there."

I worked my way over, keeping a few feet of space between us to keep the weight distributed just in case. A smile crept over my face. A gryphon's eye view of the Arena itself. A light breeze kicked up over the edge, bringing with it dried leaves and the faint hint of salt again. It ruffled my hair and tugged my sleeves, reminding me of all the times I'd woven through it on a gryphon's back. A few half-alarmed *coos* and rustles from under the eaves marked doves. Movement down on the sand drew my attention. For a moment, I almost felt like a scout again.

"Setting up tomorrow's trials?" I pointed.

Cyrus shifted his weight to get a better look. "Looks like it." The wind stirred his hair as he turned to me. "It's your match tomorrow. You want an edge on your competition? This is how you get it."

It sent an almost dangerous thrill down my arms. I moved a little farther away, testing each tile before committing to it. Mounds of darker sand were displaced, and two men worked to bury something in a hole. They filled it in, and another came behind with fresh sand to cover any trace.

There was a pattern. Sets of three in small triangles.

"Traps," Cyrus muttered beside me. "See those ones?" He angled an arm at the topmost set. "There's jaws there. Metal to catch your feet or your opponents'. The placement is always the same, they just change which ones they activate."

I'd seen that particular trap my second fight. I didn't much care to see it again. "Do they change anything between matches?" I measured the distance between each set with my thumb. From this height, that would correspond to about thirty paces on the ground.

"The jaws and explosives are easy to reset, and there's multiple spots." He tipped his head to another set. "The acid...those they'll only use once tomorrow, then will have to set again overnight if they want to use them again."

I hummed understanding. "Octavian in his kindness told me he's throwing me in with three new arrivals."

"Must've failed training." Cyrus shifted position again. I was beginning to think he was never comfortable in one spot for long. "He's trying to see if you'll take the hint and make their ends spectacular."

I shook my head, fighting the nausea that came with being one step above an executioner. At least the condemned had a weapon and something of a chance. I just happened to want to live a little more than they did. I loosened the strap of my right bracer, sliding my left thumb underneath to work at a stubbornly tight muscle above the wrist. That, at least, predated the Arena.

"The day I make him happy is likely the day I die." I shifted back from the edge, starting to turn my attention to the roof itself. "Did you talk to Atticus?"

Cyrus nodded, getting to his feet and padding up to the ridgeline. "He never stops surprising me. Apparently he owns land and a house outside the city, and only stays here because he feels like it's where the gods have stationed him."

I arched an eyebrow, still glancing around at the peaks and tiles of the roof. "Did he say if it was punishment for anything in particular?"

"He said it was the One Who Sees." Cyrus balanced for a moment at the peak of the roof before lowering to a crouch and staring up at the sky. "He had the chance to find peace after twenty years of fighting, and he followed a forgotten god here."

Another breeze whisked over the edge, and I closed my eyes against the brush of freedom. Eight years of war, and maybe the god had sent me into the same misery for some sort of similar mission. Atticus was a better choice to be sure. "He willing to help get Callista out?" I asked.

"He's happy to help. Relieved, I think, to hear that we have something in mind other than killing each other in the Arena." Cyrus wobbled as the breeze sharpened, putting a hand out to balance against the tiles before continuing, "He suggested sending someone to meet him and Callista at the alchemists' workshops in the artisan district. Would your men know where to find that?"

"If the signs don't give it away, the unusual smells will," I said. "Taking her out will make it easier for them to get her to safety."

"That's what I thought as well. Atticus seemed to already have thought this through... He said he's offered her the chance to escape before, but she's never accepted." He ducked his head, voice dropping. "I wish she had. She's too perfect to stay here."

"Or is she just too stubborn to leave someone behind?" I smirked a little. It was no more than what Lyra was doing for me, and I could find no fault with it.

Cyrus let his feet slide down so he could lay with his back against the roof. "She's stubborn above everything else. I think that's the only reason she's stayed unchanged, even after so many years." He glanced up at me. "This place has a way of breaking things, but she's still whole."

"And you?" I asked quietly.

"I think I broke the first time that I faced someone to the death," he said, not meeting my eyes. "And a little more every time after that. When you grow up around it, it doesn't feel real until it's you or your opponent. And by that point, it's too late to make any other choice. Meeting Callista a few years ago started putting those broken pieces back together again."

"You can pretend it's a little different in a battle, but there's more chaos and less time to question," I said. My arms raised slightly against another gust, fingers spread like I could grab the wind itself before crouching out of its path. "And I know a little something about someone putting pieces back together." Callista had my secret, and I had theirs. I trusted Cyrus enough now to share it. "My wife has been coming to meet me at the wall. It's the only thing keeping me sane some days." A bitter half-laugh escaped.

Cyrus pushed himself to his elbows. "Callista said something about that. She *still* comes to find you? Is everyone related to you insane?"

A grin flitted across my face. "Felix, maybe. Lyra? Just stubborn. She reminded me I'd only do the same thing in her place, and she's right." I shrugged. Her stubbornness was really just the edge of a fierce, unyielding loyalty that I did my best to match every day. "We—*she* lives just on the outskirts of the standing encampments. Callista could go there once she's free of this place."

"She'd probably like that more than being somewhere by herself," Cyrus agreed. "She doesn't say much, but I think she misses being around other women."

"Probably desperate for a scrap of intelligent conversation." I pushed back to my feet and gently tapped my heel against the slate. A few pieces edged loose, and the doves rustled beneath us. Gryphons wouldn't like this. "I'll make sure Felix knows next time he comes."

Cyrus scrambled to his feet as well, gesturing at the roofline. "Will this space be enough for the gryphons to land?"

I rubbed my jaw, thumb skimming over the scar on my chin. "Space, yes. Sturdy enough?" I tilted my head, nudging at one of the tiles with a boot.

"It's sturdy under the tiles." Cyrus hopped up and down to demonstrate, somehow keeping his balance on the pitched roof. "They're just loose."

"Hmm. Wisp." I shook my head, allowing another faint smile.

"I could push you off right now," he retorted with a laugh, and my chuckle matched it. "Then who'd be the wisp?" He stopped bouncing to reassure me, "Trust me, the roof will hold. It's faced in stone beneath; the tiles are just to shed water."

I believed him if he'd been here his entire life. I'd just need to convince the others it was sturdy enough for the fifteen seconds it'd take to land and pull one of us up behind a rider. I turned and looked out over the city, flat roofs and stacked buildings of stone and wood spreading to the horizon. A faint break at the edge marked the city walls.

I oriented north. "The main encampments lie there." I pointed. "They're hopefully smart enough not to take off from the landing fields." *Hopefully.* My arm swept to the west. "Open hills with better cover. At least there *was* better cover, a year and three months ago when I left with the army." Who knew how much the city had grown since then? "Land, then fly east." I turned to face the opposite way. To the sea. "Up the coast. Unless there's somewhere else you wanted to go?"

I could disappear on my father's land or Leonis's, along with Lyra and August. Just as fast, I shoved down the thought. It felt too dangerous to even start thinking of such a thing just yet.

"Away," Cyrus said. "Just away. Though the coast sounds nice. I saw the sea once or twice, and I wished I could've stayed there."

"You and the sea can be restless together." I leaned closer to the edge again, taking one more look at the sands and committing the sight to memory.

"The times I dream, I'm always flying over it." He shook his head. "Even though I barely remember what it looked like." Cyrus balanced on one foot against the ridge of the roof for another moment before starting down the other side, toward the outbuildings. "You seen enough?"

Seen and learned enough about more than one thing tonight.

"Enough to know we'll have to get you on a gryphon someday." I followed him. "Get you in a helmet for once."

"Never." He swung his legs over the edge, slithered down a short distance, then disappeared into the darkness below. His voice floated up from the shadows. "Coming?"

I was tempted to stay longer. Just to keep feeling the wind on my face, boots treading a half step closer to freedom. But one more look over the city, up to the starry night with cold pinpricks feeling almost close enough to touch, and then I followed. It felt like climbing down into a suffocating pit even though open air still surrounded me. The arched stone fell back to solid walls to keep everything in.

*Soon.* I tried to hold on to the last bits of wind. I'd find freedom again. *Soon.*

# CHAPTER XXVI

BASTIAN

"**H**old still," Atticus reprimanded.

"Just take my arm off already," I retorted, trying to keep from jerking away from his hold.

"I will if you don't stop." He glared and kept working. One of the acid traps had triggered during the fight yesterday. I hoped it hadn't looked too much like I knew it was there as I drove my last opponent into it. The spray had still caught my left arm and hand. The crowd had seemed to love that, almost more than the killing. Especially as I'd been practically hauled into the tunnel for an infirmary attendant to pour solvent over the skin. The fight had also seemed to please Octavian enough that he'd left me alone.

My breath hissed between my teeth as Atticus dabbed ointment over the angry, reddened patches on my upper arm. He turned to grab a new bandage. "You've been having some interesting conversations recently," he stated in a low voice, brow arching as he started wrapping the cloth.

"You have too." I glanced up, keeping the same tone despite being in a smaller, private room off the main infirmary.

His smile flashed momentarily. "Cyrus seems to think you're confident your plan will work." The sternness deepened for a moment.

"It's more than just his life at play," I replied. It was an entire squad, me, Callista, possibly even Lyra. "I usually don't plan if I don't think it will work."

He snorted softly. "All right, Commander."

My brow arched as he let go of my arm. I hadn't told him *who* I'd been. Maybe he was just guessing. He curled his fingers and I lifted my hand for him to start treating the skin there.

The door opened, and Atticus glanced over his shoulder. "Ah, Callista. Perfect."

Her light footsteps crossed over and her smile faded as she took in the new bandages. It quickly turned to a soft laugh as I glared up at Atticus.

"You all right?" I asked her, trying to ignore the way the ointment stung and cooled all at once.

She nodded and pressed my shoulder. "Thank you." The fierce words tremored a little.

I reached up with my free hand and gently tapped her arm. "The First God showed me the reasons for being here," I said, and almost cursed the physician again. He made a rebuking noise and started wrapping a bandage around my hand and wrist.

"Are *you* all right?" Callista hadn't let up her hold on my shoulder.

"I'll survive. I think." I glanced at Atticus again. He only snorted and tied off the bandage, tucking the ends away. I cradled my left wrist in my other hand, gingerly flexing my fingers to check movement.

"Not too much," Atticus warned as he pulled up a stool. "Now," he said, getting my attention. "I have a place to send her if needed."

"I do too, if you both trust me enough," I said. "And I have men willing to get her to either place."

Felix would make sure she got somewhere safely, and Lyra would welcome her with open arms, those things I did know.

"I have a few things to set into place first," Atticus said. "And rumor is you and Cyrus will fight each other again."

Callista's hands worried together. I gave her a reassuring smile. The news had officially gone out, and rumors abounded. I hadn't heard it from Octavian yet. But as it was already announced, I doubted this would be the time he'd order me to kill Cyrus.

"Injury only. Don't worry."

"Too late for that," Atticus said wryly.

Callista gave him a fond look and touched my shoulder again. "Be careful. And thank you for...everything with Cyrus. He's..."

"He's not so bad," I said.

A blush suffused her cheeks. "He hasn't trusted anyone, not for a long time. But I think he trusts you."

I reached out and took one of her hands. "I'll watch his back," I reassured. I was even mostly sure he'd watch mine, if it came to it.

She whispered another thanks before putting the soiled bandages into a basket and taking them away.

"Anything else?" Atticus pointed at me.

I tipped my head against the wall. "No." Not yet, anyway.

A short breath filled my lungs, but I made no move to leave yet. Cyrus and I would meet again after nightfall, and thankfully I'd already done my training for the day. It was close enough to noon that I might dare to scan the courtyard wall for any familiar faces. Felix would be back today as we'd discussed, hoping that I'd have a chance to talk. But exhaustion had started to weigh me down, like it did any time I sat still for long enough.

Atticus's hand on my shoulder drew my surprised look to him. There was something fatherly in his eyes before he pulled me forward and wrapped an arm around me. My head rested against his shoulder, my next breath trying to shake.

"Courage, lad," he whispered. I nodded and pulled away. His hand pressed briefly against the side of my head. "Stay if you need to." He indicated the cot before leaving.

I did for a few minutes, closing my eyes and leaning my head back against the wall. Breathing in the soothing scent of herbs and ointment, listening to the rustle of vines at the window. If I tried hard enough, I could pretend I was home and that when I opened my eyes, it would be Lyra standing there instead of an empty room. Pretend I held my son instead of nothing. But I wouldn't. Not yet. Not today.

One more breath, then I pushed to my feet, slipping out of the infirmary and making my way to the courtyard.

As soon as I stepped out, I blessed the First God for sending Lyra. As before, I slowly made my way to her after buying some more shells. It was starting to feel wrong to place them at the First God's altar when they'd always been meant for the goddess, but the incense Callista had brought me weeks ago was in short supply, and the only other thing I had plenty of was desperate prayers.

Lyra reached through the bars and rested her hand against my cheek, the expression in her blue eyes almost unreadable as she studied my face.

"Have I changed that much?" I asked softly, half afraid of the answer.

"No," she said after a moment. Her thumb brushed softly over the scar on my chin. "I'm just ready to stop seeing you injured and tired."

I gently covered her hand with mine before kissing the inside of her wrist. She withdrew as I adjusted against the bars, keeping one eye on the courtyard and trying to block her from view.

"I'm also a little angry that you kept telling me no, but as soon as Felix came, there's something planned." A faint smile and brightness in her eyes belied the words.

"I have a new ally who knows more of this place," I told her.

"So he said."

A cooing marked August waking, and chubby arms fought free of the wrap. She tugged it away and settled him on her hip. His blue eyes locked on to me, and it felt like a fiery dagger through the heart. I slipped fingers through and tapped his hand. A smile chased across his face, and he clumsily reached back.

"He's gotten big," I said, fighting new tightness in my throat.

"Almost six months old." A slight tremor rocked Lyra's words.

August caught my fingers and pulled them immediately toward his mouth. Lyra *tsked* as a chuckle stirred my chest. I slipped my finger free, but he reached again.

"Lyra, if this works, you will need to leave. Go back to your parents," I told her. This time she didn't refuse, just nodded as I continued, "Felix and I will need to meet and plan."

"They were called to training last night. He barely was able to send a message to let me know."

Cyrus and I would fight in six days, and after that might have a better idea of how the terrain would lie. "Tell him to come in seven days if he can."

"How long, Bas?" She reached to take my left hand, pausing when she felt the bandage.

"Soon," I whispered, gently squeezing her hand and ignoring the pull of tender skin under the cloth. "The other fighter will be coming with me. And there's someone else we have to get out as well."

Lyra gave me a fond look through her threatening tears, and August tried to bite my finger again.

"She won't leave without him, and he won't leave her behind," I explained.

She laughed softly. "I can sympathize with her."

I freed my hand from my son's grip and tapped his nose, bringing another smile to his cheeks. "It's the young woman who met you here before."

"This is how I know you haven't changed." Lyra pressed her hand against my chest. "Your heart still beats strong and good."

I tipped my head against the bars, the dogged exhaustion that felt one breath from defeat invading again. "I don't know, Lyra. I'm just..." *so tired.*

"Soon, my love," she whispered.

I nodded, wanting to apologize. I hadn't meant for her to see this, for her to be the one comforting me.

"Can you take her in? For a little while at least?" I asked.

"Of course," she replied instantly, adjusting August on her hip. "And I'll take her with me to the coast."

My reply was cut off by a stir of red and a sharp, "Bastian?"

I pushed away, facing off with Phestus a few steps away. I heard Lyra's footsteps retreat as I made for my second.

"What are you doing?" he asked, suspicion narrowing his eyes.

I lifted the shells in answer, grateful I'd bought them first. It allayed some of his silent questions. "Asking for more prayers to be offered at the temples," I said. "Don't want to leave the coming fight all to chance."

I didn't know how much he believed me, but he said nothing more. And stayed close as I walked away from the wall without a backward glance.

## CYRUS

The courtyard dirt and Arena sands were nearly dry. In the wake of the rain, the complex had been almost subdued, like all the restlessness was temporarily washed away. I'd had time to train in the morning before getting dragged to a reception for a visiting dignitary, where the conversation made my stomach tangle into knots. Evidently, the warfront had become unstable, and the Senate was growing concerned. So concerned, in fact, that they'd called a session with the Empress herself presiding. I didn't care about the state of a military campaign, though Bastian might've. All that mattered was that the Empress was absent from Arena matches—a reprieve, though plenty of others were happy to share speculation and rumors in my hearing.

Too wound up to rest once I returned to the Arena, I'd waited until the shadows grew enough to cover movement and climbed to the roof, lying on my stomach at the edge and watching as workers reset the traps for tomorrow's matches.

At least the acid wasn't being reused. I'd seen Bastian's fight the day before, knots tightening in my stomach as he'd recoiled from the spray. Fortunately, he'd been pulled off the sands fast enough for neutralizing agents to have been applied, but I still guessed he'd have been cursing enough to bring down lightning at the unexpected pain.

I memorized the layout of the new traps, then scaled down to wait in my quarters until the Arena quieted. The quiet of the day persisted into night, and things settled much faster than usual once the first hour had passed. I'd never mention it to anyone else, but I was grateful. The early mornings training and late nights sparring with Bastian were so tiring that I'd begun napping each afternoon, much to the confusion and concern of my attendants.

If this escape attempt didn't work, perhaps I'd revolt by sleeping through every day until Octavian lost his patience and ended me himself.

Rustles and coos greeted my footsteps as I entered the stables. The gryphons were restless after too many damp days. The noises didn't rise beyond the limits of curiosity, though, and I dropped my practice armor in the shadows before turning to see if Bastian had gotten here before me. I didn't think he had—otherwise, he'd have been clucking back at the gryphons with no idea of how silly he sounded—but a closer look into the shadows proved me wrong.

"Bastian?" I stopped beneath a stack of crates and peered through the gloom. It was difficult to tell, but I thought I could see a huddled figure tucked in the space between ceiling and crates.

The crates rocked as I set my feet on them, and I gingerly scaled to the top to find him curled with his back against the wall, one arm wrapped in bandages and pressed tightly to his ribs.

He was fast asleep.

I held a forearm over my mouth to muffle my laugh. Maybe I wouldn't be the only one protesting via sleeping. The sound slipped out despite my caution, and Bastian stirred with an irritable growl. "Five more minutes."

"No." Another laugh escaped me, and I got a hand on one of his feet. "Get down or I'm *pulling* you down."

His hand found the side of my head and pushed as he tugged his boot free. I wobbled on the stack of crates before my reflexes engaged, and I jumped to the floor of the storeroom. "You want to go into this rematch unprepared?" I shot up at him. "I can walk away and let you sleep, but I won't be responsible for what happens..."

He peered over the edge of the crates before rubbing his eyes. "If you walk away I might actually *get* some sleep." He threw his legs over the side and jumped down.

"You can sleep when you're dead." I went to collect my gear and pull the barred door of the training pen open. "And you'll get that way fast if you don't train."

"You sound like my first cohort commander." He rolled his eyes. "Always grimly shouting and turning us out of bed at all hours."

"If that's what it takes for us both to survive this, I don't mind." I threw my armor over my head and began doing up the buckles. "Your arm feeling better today?"

He lifted his left arm and gingerly tightened the bracer. "Still stings, no matter the foul-smelling stuff Atticus has smeared over it."

"It'll be better tomorrow," I assured him. "The stuff they use for us works fast. That's why they keep putting those traps out there. They know we'll recover quickly even if we *do* get caught."

"One tiny bit of good." He yawned as he tugged the collar of his breastplate, testing the buckles. "You heard anything else about the rematch?"

"Other than what Octavian told me, no." I rolled my shoulders under my armor, working out the stiffness. "They spaced out our fights so we'll both have time to rest, which means they're really hoping we'll give them a good show." I laughed as Bastian spat into the sand at the word. "Which I did need to talk to you about."

We fell into what'd become a standard warm-up drill, alternating between striking and blocking while circling to gain advantage.

"Are they going to add in a chorus to make things look better?" he asked sarcastically, giving way before another strike. He closed the distance just as fast with a returning lunge.

I jumped out of the way, landing a smart tap on his back as he overshot. "I wouldn't put it past them, but no. I don't know what they're planning, but I suspect I'm meant to win this time."

He pivoted to face me, falling to guard position. "Two losses to the same opponent wouldn't look too good for you, would it?"

"Especially if they're planning for you to eventually kill me." I darted to the side and aimed for his knees, ducking as his sword passed over my head. "I expect Octavian will be having words with you, telling you to lose and make it look accidental. But it doesn't change the fact that they're expecting one of us to get hurt. And if I'm supposed to win, that means it'll be you."

"There isn't much of me that isn't bruised. But I could take a hit to my left arm." He lowered his sword and retreated out of range, shaking out the arm in question.

I frowned at the bandages wrapping his hand. "If you're certain..." I crossed to his other side, mentally calculating where a strike would do the least damage. "I have no idea what the terrain will look like, but I suppose..."

"I'll leave you an opening only if you promise not to prance around first," he said, a smirk threatening.

"There's no way I'm promising that. You know they're going to be watching for anything out of the ordinary. If this looks too contrived, they'll know." I swung my practice sword in a measured arc, stopping short of his forearm bracer. "If I can hit the edge of your armor, it might slow things enough that the wound looks messy, but isn't too deep."

He arched an eyebrow. "You're that good to nick but not chop my arm off in the middle of a fight?"

I tapped the outside of my own vambrace. "These do a better job than you think of stopping a blade." I tugged the buckle free and pulled the armor away to show him the scar that ran under it. "That would have taken off my arm if it hadn't been for the bracer. And I won't be swinging at full strength."

He hummed, casting a slightly doubtful look, but underneath was an expression enough like trust that I almost regretted what we knew would have to happen. "All right. We fight just long enough to appease the rich bastards, I'll leave you an opening, you *don't* remove my arm, and we part ways?"

I had to laugh at that. "Something like that. If you start your usual practice combination, I'll know you're about to leave an opening." I began moving as I said it, raising my sword as we began circling. A few moments later, Bastian turned a little too far after one of his swings and I struck, halting my sword just above his left arm. "And they'll have their injury." I stepped back and warned, "Just be certain you let me know when you're going to drop your guard. I don't want to accidentally hit you anywhere else."

He nodded, eyes sweeping the stirred-up sand like he was committing the moves to memory before his focus snapped back to me. "Just not my face."

"I wouldn't dream of it." I nodded to where his helmet sat at the edge of the training square. "Besides, you'll be trapped inside that."

Bastian huffed, an expression like amusement and exasperation tangled together crossing his face as he returned to a ready stance.

I caught his grateful look in the direction of the helmet, and an idea stirred in my head—something that could both give the crowds what they wanted *and* keep him out of the infirmary. Maybe I wouldn't have to risk his arm after all.

"I don't think I like that look," he said, eyes narrowing at me.

I laughed and brought my sword up to guard. "Don't worry. It'll be all right."

*It's better if you don't know what I'm planning.*

He only scoffed, and attacked.

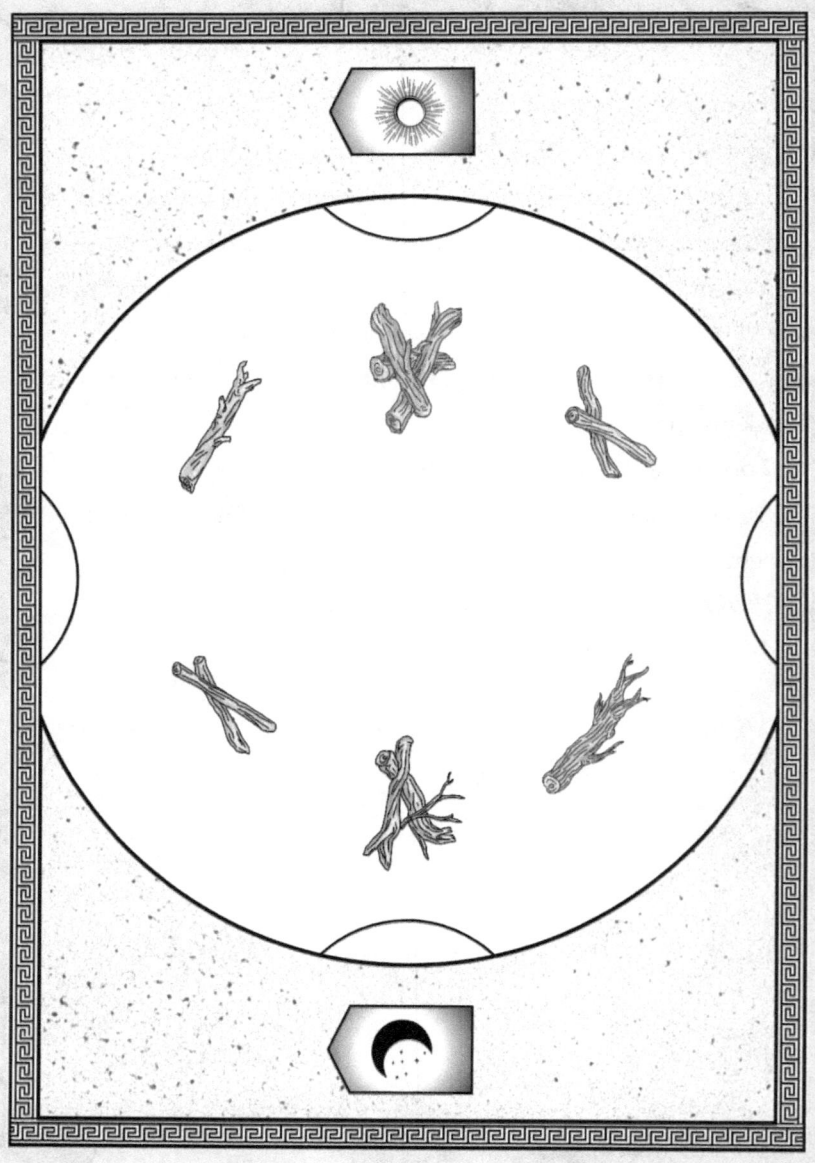

# CHAPTER XXVII

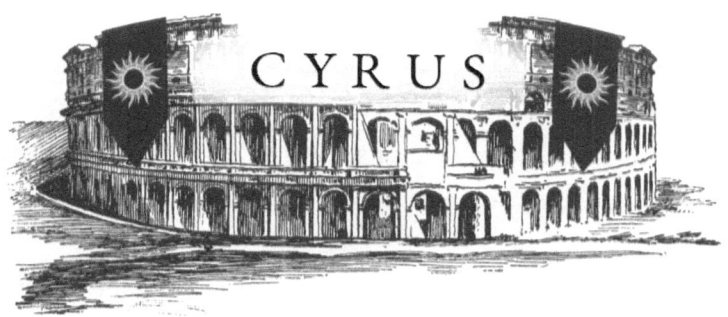

CYRUS

S craps of red, gold, black, and silver were already falling from the
stands. I could tell by the volume swelling the Arena to its limits
that the attendance from today would far outstrip any fights from the
previous month. The attendants had been tense as they'd gotten me
ready, and even my young second was quiet. I'd already spoken with
Octavian, the order simply given.

"Win. And make it look good."

I'd given a curt nod, my heart settling as I stood in the open mouth of
the tunnel. Unlike last time, when I'd faced an unknown enemy, today
I was taking the sands armed with certain knowledge that no one would
be dying today.

*Please.* I sent the prayer to the First God, hoping against all hope that he was watching. *Please keep us safe.*

Cheers greeted my appearance from the tunnel, matched by the shouts that heralded Bastian's appearance from his. Even across the ring, he was a foreboding figure in dark-stained armor and expression-concealing helmet. The space between us was littered with logs, stacked against each other and set at angles jutting into the sky. We'd seen the workers maneuvering each into place the previous night, after climbing to the roof and waiting in silence as the sky darkened above us.

At least the terrain wasn't a surprise. And Bastian was expecting to get hurt. I just hoped my new plan to keep him from severe injury would satisfy the crowds.

I sprinted for the closest set of crisscrossed logs and launched myself into the center of the ring. My feet landed in the sand and I was running again, readying my sword as Bastian charged from his side. The crowd roared as our blades met, the sound all but drowning out the clang of steel on steel.

It was just like the nights of practice—back and forth, dodging, cutting, sidestepping, ever circling. He still had the habit of trying to keep his distance, but by this point I was wise to it. By the third time around the sand, I started laughing. "Stop keeping your distance!" I let up the pressure in my strikes as I said it. "Counter! I'll back up!"

I thought I caught a scoff from behind his visor. "*You* wanted a show!"

"They'll get bored if we stay here the whole time!" I dropped my guard, twisting away as his sword fell behind where I'd been standing. "Press your advantage!"

This time he listened, altering his blows so they came with more power behind them. I gave ground until I sensed I was approaching one of the piles of logs, then counterattacked with a flurry of strikes that bought me enough space to scramble over the barrier.

"Follow!" I yelled over the noise, hoping he'd hear me. It seemed like he shook his head, but he jumped the log and readied his sword.

"Let's get this over with!" he called, sword flashing as he began circling into the pattern we usually began our training matches with.

I turned to engage, matching each blow like I did in practice and waiting for the moment when his guard would drop. Bastian brought his sword down against mine, then twisted away from my counterattack with his left arm going out to balance.

I should've swung then, let my sword cut through his bracer and into skin and muscle, but instead I ducked low and slammed my weight into him. The logs caught him behind the knees and he careened backward with a surprised curse to land in the dirt. I barely caught a glimpse of his eyes through the slit in his helmet before I jumped the logs, angling to get behind him as he struggled to a knee.

My fingers met the metal at his forehead, sliding down until they caught the top edge of the narrow eye slit. The edge dug into my fingers, but I curled them inside and pulled as hard as I could. Bastian toppled, sword falling from his hand as he flailed an arm to try to break my hold.

"Don't fight!" I tossed my own sword out of his reach and wrapped my hands around the straps, applying pressure against the space beneath Bastian's jaw—the same spot where, years ago, my own helmet strap had dug into my skin until I'd fallen unconscious at my own teammate's hands. "Just trust me!"

A strangled, hair-raising curse was my only answer. The noise of the crowd surged and I dug in my feet to pull harder, willing this to be over as fast as possible. A moment later, Bastian's hand fell slack, and I released him with my own heartbeat pounding in my ears.

The crowd hadn't calmed. Hadn't quieted. A chill struck me. *They don't consider this an injury. The match isn't over.*

Heart sinking, I crossed the few steps to retrieve my sword from the sand. A flicker of movement caught my eye as I turned—Bastian's hand curling into a fist as he regained consciousness.

My hand closed on my sword hilt. I reversed the weapon in my grip, stabbed down through his bracer, and stepped back as the crowd roared its approval.

## BASTIAN

The Arena had settled to silence. As much as it ever did. And I waited. The sliver of a cut along my forearm stung, but that wasn't what kept the restlessness stirred up inside. It was the way the plan had been disregarded and worse, how my helmet had been used against me. How I'd been helpless at the hands of someone I thought I could trust as he'd forced me into unconsciousness. The way I'd barely opened my eyes, automatically reaching for my sword, before Cyrus's blade had plunged down and pierced the upper edge of my bracer to catch skin.

I hadn't seen him since. And now I waited for him to return from the party he'd been spirited away to. Just to look him in the eye, and see if I could lay a bridge over the restlessness and back to trust.

The dark clothes they insisted I wear on and off the sands helped me blend into the shadows at the base of the stairs leading to the upper floors. Years of scout training gave me the patience to wait in stillness and silence. It was late when motion stirred, and he returned.

I waited until he was almost past me to move slightly and speak sharper than I'd intended. "Cyrus."

He flinched as I stepped closer, but before he could speak, I turned and made my way to the tunnels. It took a moment before his light tread followed. I didn't stop until we were deep enough to not be heard by anyone from the main floors. A single lamp cast a flickering circle on the ground. It felt more like a line drawn between us as I faced him.

"Did Atticus have to stitch it?" He nodded to my arm and the small bandage left behind.

My fingers curled into a fist before I extended them with an effort. "No. *That* injury wasn't the issue."

The harsh edge to my tone caught his attention. He stepped back, one foot falling outside the pool of light on the floor. "I told you to trust me. I didn't think I'd have to stab *at all* if they saw you were already out of the fight." He crossed his arms defensively. "No real injury. No lasting damage. I thought it was better that way."

My jaw worked and I shook my head. "Trust you? What happened to the plan, Cyrus? It would have ended the same way." I lifted my bandaged arm. "Instead, you changed it and didn't tell me a damn thing!"

"I didn't tell you because your reaction had to be real!" he insisted. "And I didn't want to injure you so badly that you might be at a disadvantage the next time you fight."

A scoff jarred my chest. "What happened to the confidence you had six nights ago? Was that a lie or did you always plan to make your own way *after we agreed*?" I jabbed a finger toward his chest. "How do I know you won't stab me through the heart next time?"

The shock that had grabbed hold the second his blade bit into my arm while I was powerless had sent doubt worming in alongside it. And right now, I didn't know what to make of the man in front of me, so used to surviving that he might turn on someone just for a chance to keep living.

He stared at me, shoulders tensing as I said, "I don't care about the injury, I *care* that you used my equipment against me without *telling me*. Allies...friends...the odds are only even if we're honest with each other. If we *work together*."

"Friends." He almost spat the word. "Forget hesitation, *friendship* is the fastest way to get someone killed here. And you have no idea what it costs to care." Cyrus dropped his arms, one hand going to a fist as he snapped, "I *had* friends, once. I was too smart for my own good, and now they're either dead or hate me. The moment I show any indication of caring about anyone, Octavian finds out and they disappear or—" His face pinched like he was trying to hold back tears. "Or a familiar face appears from the tunnel the next time I fight." He took another step out of the light, turning his shoulder as if to brace for a blow. "I did what I had to do in order to keep both of us safe. If you can't understand that, then I don't know what else I can say."

*Sorry.* The word ripped bitter through my head.

"If not friends, then wingmates, Cyrus. I can't keep you safe if I don't know what you're going to do next. I entered into this because you were my best chance of getting out, and I'm yours." My voice almost shook. It was anger, frustration—at Cyrus, the Arena, everyone and everything who'd put us here. "And if you think you're the only one who knows the cost of caring or has anything to lose, then you haven't been watching."

I pushed past him, making my way down the tunnel. He didn't call after me, and I didn't look back.

CAVE WYVERN

# CHAPTER XXVIII

I stood in the tunnel and checked my armor one last time. Phestus waited patiently, my helmet in one hand and a trident in the other. The crowd was already riled. The lower-level fight before me had gone spectacularly wrong. Or right, depending on which view you had.

I re-tightened the strap of my right bracer, ignoring the reddish line on my skin just beneath the leather. It had been one week. One week, and the wound had closed without issue despite training *and* another fight. I hadn't spoken to Cyrus since that night in the tunnels, and that was fine with me. The frustration and anger still whirled when I thought about it, not even lessened by the memory of his confession of the cost of friendship.

"You ready?" Phestus's question didn't settle me like normal. I gave a tight smile and reached for my helmet.

"You'll be on the sands already," I confirmed. He nodded as I pulled the helmet on. My fight today was a juvenile wyvern. The armorers had reassured me that full-grown wyverns were only given to teams, who'd wear masks soaked in an antidote against a wyvern's paralyzing smoke. Juveniles hadn't developed the glands yet, but were still a mess of muscle and spikes and crushing jaws to contend with.

"You'll have a gryphon, a chimera, and a wyvern on your victory lists." Phestus handed me the trident. I slid my sword in and out of the sheath with my left hand, hefting the trident in my right. My second took up his own spear, settling behind me as the trainer standing in for Octavian waved me forward.

Clouds were threatening again, and the sky above held a hazy glare. The Arena edges had been rimmed in spears with netting stretched between them to keep the wyvern from getting any ideas about easier meat than the armored men in front of it.

Phestus stopped five paces from the tunnel as the gate slid shut, and I kept on.

*They're eager to see you redeem yourself,* Octavian had told me hours before. Redeem myself from the "loss" to Cyrus. It sent bitterness to my tongue, and I gripped the spear haft tighter.

I'd met Felix the morning after I'd left Cyrus in the tunnels. Given him the dimensions of the roof, the schedule of the Arena. The squad would have to practice the maneuver a few times while pretending to be focused on their real training. He'd be back three days from now, and we'd set a date. I only answered with silence when asked about Cyrus, the anger still too fresh when face-to-face with a man who'd never let me down.

The creature gate creaked open, and a reverberating roar shook the sands.

Danger rippled over my arms, and I swept into a crouch, trident poised. That was no juvenile. That was a full-grown wyvern about to come through the gate.

Someone had lied to me. Again.

A hush fell over the Arena, broken only by the thudding of the creature fighting first in the tunnel. I'd faced cave wyverns before. But that had been on the back of a gryphon with four wingmates, barely keeping above the snapping jaws and noxious, paralyzing smoke after surprising a den in the mountains. Two days later, we'd driven the den right into enemy ranks—the maneuver breaking the last resistance and opening the way for Imperial rule. Something I might regret now.

"Bastian!" Phestus charged to my side, face white.

"Spear up!" I ordered. If this was a mistake, it wasn't going to be rectified in enough time for us to get off the sands. No one was calling us to retreat into the tunnel and send a team out instead. "If it breathes smoke, stay out of it."

Noise erupted from the stands as it emerged. Twice as long as a gryphon, just as tall, its sinuous grey-scaled body tinged with green and almost skeletal after months of captivity. Small, membranous wings flared from its sides to balance its quick movements. Thankfully, those weren't strong enough for flight. It saw us, and charged.

"Left!" I ordered Phestus, and raced toward the wyvern. Every bit of my body screamed against the foolish move. It roared and sped up. I swept up with the spear, intending to hook the trident points under its jaw. But it whisked to the side, tail flaring spikes and sweeping toward me. I threw myself to the ground, almost losing the spear as I hit sand

and the tail sliced the air above me.

A scream more terrified than warlike came from Phestus and he jabbed his spear at the wyvern, giving me enough time to get to my feet. Its hinged jaw gaped wide and I charged again, trying to get the mouth shut and keep the poison from spewing out.

It clacked its jaws together, a growl tremoring in its chest as it backed away, tail lashing. Saliva dripped between its teeth, and slitted eyes glanced between us.

"Steady," I told Phestus. But I could barely hear myself over the crowd.

I jabbed again, but the wyvern reared on hind legs and slammed claws down on the spear, ripping it from my grip. I lurched away, diving as the tail whipped toward me.

I scrambled to my feet, drawing my sword. Phestus had distracted it again, but it lunged and swiped with its claws. Its jaw clamped around his spear and tore it away. The gate *still* hadn't risen to let anyone emerge from the tunnels to help. We were on our own.

I charged with a shout, trying to come behind its head in its blind spot. It took the bait, whipping around close enough that its head slammed into me. I tried to stab as I fell, but missed. The sands blurred my vision as I rolled and dodged swiping claws. One hooked into the bottom edge of my breastplate, digging deep into my back as I was thrown forward.

"Bastian!" was the only warning before dull green smoke enveloped me. I clamped my mouth shut, desperately holding my breath as I slipped and scrambled forward.

A gasp shook my body as I stumbled free of the cloud. Phestus shouted again, swinging wildly with his sword but nowhere close to hitting it.

I gained my feet, stumbling as the wyvern swiped out and the claws caught Phestus, flinging him several feet away to lie in a twitching, bleeding mess. The wyvern prowled toward him. I raced to my second, not sure what I was going to do. Not by myself.

It struck Phestus again, and he stilled. A scream of rage reverberated through my helmet.

A new cloud of smoke rolled toward me, and I tried to change my course. Something *hit* my side and I gasped, inhaling the poison. I impacted the ground, dimly aware of the wyvern's jaw clamping around my left arm and chest. It pressed me against the ground as it ran, scraping me over the sands.

Dull sound hit my ears, my muscles heavy and confusion reigning until the wyvern stopped. I'd kept hold of my sword in an iron grip. Mustering strength from somewhere, I stabbed up at the eye. Over and over, until it dropped me with a furious sound.

The wyvern scrambled back, releasing another blast of smoke to sweep over me.

*Get out.* The thought slid through my fuzzy mind. I started trying to pull myself forward. Out. Breaths scraped raw with each inhale, drawing more poison into my lungs.

There was a change to the hazy sounds. I looked up to see a new figure running toward me, helmet obscuring his features. Only one man to help, and he might be too late. He pointed, and I slowly turned my head. The wyvern shook itself and locked eyes on to me again. My legs wouldn't move. I couldn't feel anything to explain the red staining the sands around me.

It charged.

I thought I heard my name. My vision swam, and all I could see was Lyra in front of me. I blinked and the wyvern was closer.

I couldn't die now.

Hands shaking, I raised my sword, daring those jaws. The blade wavered. The wyvern struck—and reeled back with my sword impaled through the top of its mouth. It shook its head, scraping at its face. It slammed its mouth shut, driving the blade deeper. The wyvern collapsed to its stomach, still writhing and fighting.

My head tipped against the ground. Weight pressed around and on my chest. One hand lay limply just in range of my ever-blurring vision. A breath fought for escape. I needed to get my helmet off. I needed to...

The unknown figure plunged a sword through the wyvern's neck, finally stilling it.

Something tugged at me, pulling me away from the lingering smoke. I heard my name before hands fumbled at the helmet and pulled it off. Cool hit my face, but it didn't bring any relief to my heavy lungs. I tried to pull a breath, but the air felt stuck.

Numbness settled over my entire body, panic flaring in my mind. *I can't breathe. I can't move.*

"Hold on, Bastian!"

I was weightless, my boots cutting paths in the sand as I was pulled. Darkness crept in, slowly swallowing me. I heard my name one more time, and my only answering thought was, *"...Cyrus?"*

CYRUS

Stab. Step, step. Block. Counter. Block. Sidestep, twist, strike.

The motions were rote, my opponent's moves easily marked, predicted, thwarted. Nothing like how I'd become used to training over this last month.

Domitian attacked again, sword locked against mine. Distraction had loosened my grip, and the weapon flew out of my hand before I could adjust my hold. A hefty blow landed between my shoulder blades as I tried to twist away.

"I know that one hurt!" he laughed. "It's about time I landed a hit on you."

I bent to retrieve my sword and gave him a salute. "Maybe we'll end it while you're at the top, then."

"You're done?"

"I'm done."

I sat beneath one of the olive trees, catching my breath and letting the adrenaline of getting hit subside. Domitian had fallen to talking with his team and the others hanging around the courts, but I didn't have it in me to join in the banter like I ordinarily would.

*You have no idea what it's cost me to care.*

Had I really said that? When I knew full well what had landed Bastian here in the first place? Gods, how stupid of me.

*How do I know you won't stab me through the heart next time?*

And the next time was coming fast. Less than a month till the eclipse, till the fight that was already being publicized through the whole city. Less than a month for me to decide if it was worth trying to make amends, or if I'd already missed my chance.

A building sound from the Arena caught my ear, and I tipped my head to look for the sun. Noon. Time for the biggest match of the day—I counted back in my mind and realized with a sour twist in my stomach that Bastian was about to step onto the sands. We hadn't spoken since the night of our rematch, a week ago, and I didn't know what my reception would be if I sought him out. The heat of that conversation had long died out, leaving confusion alongside certainty that—somehow—I'd been in the wrong.

"It's starting!" one of the others near Domitian said, pausing the conversation to gesture at the Arena. "They're *really* in for a show today."

I lifted my head from my circling thoughts to ask, "What do you mean?" The pitch from the crowd was increasing, its fervor meaning that while Bastian had taken the sands, his opponent hadn't.

I hadn't checked the lists today. Hadn't scouted the night before. But a change in the crowd's roar after the fighter emerged usually only meant one thing—

"Oh, it's nothing," he said. "Only, you may not have to worry about fighting that gryphon rider again. He's about to have his wings clipped permanently."

Sudden cold shot through my chest, and I got to my feet with urgency scattering into my limbs. "What. Do you. Mean."

"He's fighting a cave wyvern," the man explained, nods from his friends indicating they knew exactly what was happening—and were pleased with it. "They brought in a juvenile for him to take down, but he's about to realize it's a little bigger than he was originally told. Funny how a little gold applied in the right direction can change the odds."

A surge of noise came from the Arena, and I looked up with growing horror. A wyvern. Full-grown, if this fellow was to be believed, which meant a poison-breathing creature straight from nightmare tales. I didn't know what Bastian might think of me right now, but there was no way I could let him take on one of those creatures by himself. Forget wings being clipped—he'd be done for the moment it unleashed its poison.

If I intervened, I'd be showing everyone that there was something in me that cared about my rival. There'd be repercussions, and steep ones.

*If not friends, then wingmates, Cyrus.*

I wasn't sure what a friend would do. But wingmates wouldn't let each other fight alone.

I dropped my practice sword and started running, pushing past the others and pounding into the tunnels. There was no time to grab better armor, only seconds to grab a weapon from a rack and scoop a discarded helmet from a corner of the armory. Its weight settled against my head, strap cinching into place as I hurtled around the corner to the tunnel that sloped up to the Arena. It wouldn't do much, but it might buy me a moment against the wyvern smoke.

It was bedlam in the tunnel, men shouting and rushing back and forth. Beyond, the end of a barbed tail lashed in and out of view, and over it all came the exaltation from the crowd. Bloodthirsty cheers, like death was moments away. The gate was rattling upward, and I ducked my head to sprint out of the tunnel and onto the sand. There was the creature, its dulled charcoal scales iridescent with sickening greenish undertones and curving spines on its head catching the light.

A yell burst from me, desperate and almost lost in the cries from the crowd. Sunlight scorched the sand as the wyvern recoiled, dropping something—*someone*—on the ground. It scrambled back, shaking its head and roaring before opening its jaw to unleash a torrent of murky smoke against the figure crumpled on the ground.

Bastian. Alive, I thought.

I yelled again, hoping the thing would turn to face me, but it only roared again and focused on Bastian. He'd dragged himself halfway out of the smoke, but even at this distance I could see the slowness of his movements, the angle of his head, the shake in his arm as he pulled himself to an elbow.

It was all wrong. Either he didn't realize the wyvern was so close, or—more likely—the smoke was affecting him enough that he wouldn't notice when it killed him.

His name tore out of my throat as the creature recovered itself and charged. "BASTIAN!"

Somehow, he got his sword up as the wyvern's head descended into the lingering smoke. For a heart-stopping moment, I couldn't see if he'd struck first or the wyvern had. Then it recoiled, snapping its jaw and lashing its head in an effort to rid itself of a sword impaling its mouth. Sand rose in a cloud and mixed with the smoke as the wyvern fell, thrashing in agony and scraping at the blade with its claws. Beyond it, Bastian had been knocked to his back and was lying horribly still.

The crowd's noise had blurred in my ears, but a new surge of excitement came as I reached the wyvern. The sword in my hand was ill-balanced but sharp, and easily slashed through the creature's throat. I didn't wait to see if it would remain still, instead sprinting to Bastian's side. He lay immobile, limbs twitching as he fought the effects of the smoke. Even those movements were getting weaker, and I realized with a jolt of panic that he couldn't draw breath.

And this time, it wasn't my fault.

I looped my hands under his shoulders, dragging him away from the downed wyvern. Once clear, I fumbled for the straps on his helmet, ripping it free and sending it hurtling across the sand. Bastian's eyes were open but vacant, the pupils so small they were almost lost in the dark green of his irises.

He wasn't breathing.

"Hold on, Bastian!"

There was no response, no indication that he'd heard me as I grabbed the shoulder straps of his armor, dragging him across the Arena and to the tunnel. Behind and around me, the crowd was in a frenzy, the noise only growing as those who'd been too far gained recognition of his face.

By the time I made it to the tunnel, my own reflexes were growing slower and my vision was fogging. I'd drawn at least one or two breaths of the wyvern poison. The creeping dizziness reminded me all too starkly of another night, not too long ago, but the knowledge only made me tighten my hold on Bastian and hurry into the tunnel. A stretcher waited inside, and several onlookers rushed to help me lay Bastian on it.

"He's not breathing," I shouted over the din. "Get someone, quick!"

"Someone," in this case, meant Atticus. He appeared through the crush of people as if by the power of the First God himself and swore as he saw Bastian's eyes, half-open but staring at nothing.

"Infirmary, now!"

The attendants rushed to obey, as Atticus's gaze pierced the eye slit of the helmet I'd grabbed. He got his arm around me as my legs buckled. "Easy, Cyrus," he said softly, as outside the crowd began to quiet. "I've got you."

They took Bastian to the small medical facility I'd shown him a few weeks ago. He was lying on a table by the time I got there, eyes closed and complexion growing pale. Atticus released me as soon as we got into the room, pushing past the others and barking orders in a tone that demanded immediate compliance. My limbs were steadier now, but still trembled as I staggered to lean against the table where Bastian lay. A strangled gasp tore from his throat as Atticus tipped his head back, but no more followed.

Atticus swore, and his hands went to the buckles of Bastian's armor. "Get this off him. Hurry!"

Multiple people rushed to do his bidding, and within a moment, the punctured breastplate had been lifted away to reveal a tunic already soaked with blood. Atticus didn't seem to mind, balling up a fist and grinding his knuckles into Bastian's chest. "Breathe, damn it. Come on. Someone get me a cloth!" he shouted over his shoulder before taking a dark glass bottle from someone nearby.

"Is he—" I couldn't say it. My voice sounded funny to my own ears, muffled by the helmet I had yet to discard.

"Not yet." Atticus tipped Bastian's head to the side, then pried his mouth open. He soaked a cloth pad with amber-hued liquid before pressing it to the inside of Bastian's cheek. "But if he doesn't start breathing more than once a minute, he will be. Hold that there," he ordered, moving my hand to the cloth before stepping away.

I obeyed automatically, slipping a hand under Bastian's neck to stabilize his head as I pressed the cloth into his mouth. He'd struggle if he knew what I was doing, but at this point I just hoped he'd get the chance to fight back.

A long minute passed before Atticus returned. "Anything?"

I shook my head. "Not yet." Bastian hadn't stirred, a single gasp the barest indication he was still alive. His skin had gone even paler, almost ghostly under his tan.

"All right." Atticus swapped places with me and took the cloth pad, squeezing the liquid to pool inside Bastian's mouth before reaching down to rub his chest again. "Come on, breathe."

*Breathe,* I silently mouthed inside the helmet, my face growing damp with terrified tears. *Come on, Bastian. I'm sorry for what I said earlier. I'm sorry for what I* did—*just please breathe.*

I hadn't realized I'd been clutching Bastian's arm until it yanked from my grasp. A startled gasp issued from him, and his eyes flickered open.

"Gods all bless," Atticus sighed. His voice sharpened as Bastian jerked again under his hands. "Bastian, hold still. Breathe."

I leaned my weight against Bastian's erratic movements as his breathing normalized. His eyes had stayed open, but the distant look in them was chilling—like he couldn't see or recognize anyone in the room. From my own experience, I knew he probably wouldn't remember any of this, and the thought made me renew my grip on his arm. *Don't worry. No one's going to hurt you.*

"Let's get this tunic off," Atticus ordered. "I want to get the rest of these injuries taken care of before he wakes up all the way." He looked up at one of the attendants and said, "Go notify Octavian that he'll be all right. And"—his gaze sharpened—"that he's not allowed within a hundred paces of this room until he can prove this wasn't planned."

The man paled but obeyed, taking another attendant with him and leaving only a handful of us in the room. Atticus had returned his focus to Bastian, cutting the tunic and pulling the bloodstained fabric away to reveal a half-moon of punctures over his chest and shoulder. More scrapes and cuts marked Bastian's arm on the opposite side, and a gouge on his back bled sluggishly.

Atticus muttered under his breath at the sight, keeping a precautionary hand on Bastian's chest and calling, "Someone run upstairs and get the argentium salts solution. It's in the purple-marked flasks on the middle shelf in the work area. And the salve that's on the table. We're going to need both of them."

One of the others ran out the door, leaving Atticus, one assistant, Bastian, and myself. "Cyrus." Atticus's voice came quieter this time. "Take the helmet off."

I tipped my head to him in panic, and he repeated himself more firmly. "Take it off. No one here is going to tell anyone, not after I finish with them. And he needs to see you."

I numbly released Bastian's arm and my hands went to the helmet straps. "Are you sure? He—"

"I know you had an argument," the physician interrupted. "It doesn't matter. He needs you. And I need you to hold him still."

"If you insist..." I pulled the helmet off, pinning the one remaining assistant with a murderous look as his mouth gaped open. "What do you need me to do?"

Atticus moved my hands to a better grip on Bastian's arm—one that wouldn't irritate any of the scrapes or cuts—and gave me a grim nod as the man he'd sent to the infirmary returned with the disinfectants and salve. "Just hold him. And pray he doesn't wake fully until we're finished."

With that, he and the others turned to cleaning and disinfecting the punctures the wyvern's teeth had left on Bastian's chest and arm. I wasn't sure what was worse, the noise the disinfectant made as it bubbled in the wounds, or that Bastian didn't make a sound throughout. After the panic brought on by first waking, he'd lain still with his eyes closed, though his color had returned. It wasn't until the medical staff were finished wrapping the injuries and Atticus had gotten another measure of the amber-colored antidote into him that he began to come around. His eyes blinked open, and I breathed a sigh of relief as recognition lit them—albeit slowly.

"Cyrus?" He blinked hard, frowned like he couldn't believe what he was seeing. "You're...here?"

I had to smile. "Couldn't let you face it alone. That's not what a wingmate would do."

Something that might have been a laugh came from him. "...No, it's not." His eyes closed again, and the lines in his face relaxed.

I looked up at Atticus as he approached with a blanket. "He's sleeping?"

The physician nodded, tipping his head to examine the rise and fall of Bastian's chest. "Just sleeping." His hand squeezed my forearm, above the vambrace I had yet to remove. "I'll watch him. You'd better go before anyone else comes. I don't think Octavian knows it was you who intervened, and it's best he not find out so soon."

# CHAPTER XXIX

A wareness slipped in. I was alive. I thought. I floated, numbness soaking through my body, a rasping sound every few seconds keeping me anchored. Voices solidified.

"How long until he's up?" *Octavian*. "We have offers pouring in for him."

"Never, if that's what you have planned," the sharpness of Atticus's voice answered.

"Careful, physician. You take your wages from everything the Arena offers."

"It'll be days yet before he's ready to stand upright, much less training or anything else."

I tried to move, speak, tell them *no* again. But smothering *nothingness* held me prisoner.

"What's your plan if he refuses again?" A third voice with the deeper evenness of Tiberius came through.

Octavian scoffed. "Give him another taste of wyvern's breath."

"We can't dose him too many times, or rumors will start. Maybe a select few times at first. At least until he starts enjoying himself."

"There's some rumors he meets a woman at the gates."

This time my hand twitched against something soft.

"Keep an eye on him when he's up. Get rid of her or bring her in. Either way, he needs to start following orders."

*Lyra.*

"We'll need to get him back on the sand first anyway. Prove he's alive." The words faded out, no matter how hard I tried to fight.

I floated slowly to the surface, and dull light met my eyes finally opening. A blurred figure came into view. "Bastian." Atticus's voice soothed the rising terror.

"Octavian..." I barely formed the word.

The physician leaned closer. "He was here earlier. It's all right."

I tried to shake my head, clinging to some remembrance. "Offers..."

My focus sharpened enough to pick out his disgust. "I've bought you as much time as I can, Bastian. Just rest." His hand pressed against my cheek, then forehead. The dull pressure brought a terrifying realization to the surface.

"I can't...*feel*." The hitching sound picked up intensity as I *tried* to move. I *had* to be ready if they...

"Bastian." Atticus's hand settled against my face, something heavier on my chest. "Breathe."

An order. I tried to obey.

"The poison is working its way out. You'll be fine by morning."

I wanted to ask him about another voice, a reason I was here, but my eyes slid closed again.

Braided leather and a pinpoint of cool pressed into my palm.

"I brought it for you, Bastian," Callista's gentle voice reassured. My fingers twitched, trying to close around the scale necklace. *Lyra*. My eyes refused to open, exhaustion gleefully allying with the dullness still clinging to me. A few pinpricks of feeling had started all over. Something tentative brushed my forehead, then settled against my shoulder. "He's all right?"

"Slowly, but surely," came Atticus's reassurance.

Warmth clasped my hand around the leather, and my arm was moved, tucked under something woven and safe.

When I opened my eyes again it was to sand and the Arena. My heart fell. I was already back? A hazy glare clung to the edge of my vision, and I raised a hand to try to block it out.

A roar came from somewhere, and my heart raced. A cry sent me whipping around to see Lyra huddled on the sand, hunched over our son. My heart plummeted and I tried to get to her, but my legs were stuck, wrapped in ropes.

When I looked up, Cyrus stalked toward them, sword in hand.

"No!" I shouted.

He looked at me, face emotionless. "I have to."

"No!" I ripped free, but rope circled my neck, hauling me back. I thrashed, catching sight of Octavian from the corner of my eye.

"*Lyra!*" I lunged forward, breaking free for a moment before my legs tangled again. A wyvern burst out of the tunnel. Cyrus charged *me*, turning to a helmeted figure. The creature slammed into him, tearing him to pieces. Another scream fought free, bringing *pain* along with it. The sensation spread over my entire body, ramming into my chest as the wyvern circled and lunged at Lyra.

"NO!"

I was wrenched around, face-to-face with a helmeted figure. "Wake up, Bastian!"

I tried to fight, pull away, go help Lyra and August.

"Wake up! Gods, please wake up!"

My shoulders shook, and my hand met something *real*. I clutched it, pulling myself forward until my eyes opened to the infirmary and someone half-holding me, half-pinning me to a bed. I sucked in a breath, and feeling swept in with a sudden wish for the numbness to return.

"Atticus!" The sound of Cyrus's voice sent shock through me.

"I heard." Footsteps announced the physician. I glanced over my shoulder to see him bending over me. "I don't think he reopened anything." He gave me a faint smile. "Welcome back, Bastian." Then to Cyrus, "Let him up."

The pressure over me released, and Cyrus settled to a stool next to the bed. A guarded silence stretched between us, broken by Atticus's return. He straightened the blankets tangled around me, tilting my face toward him and holding a candle close to my eyes.

"What can you feel?" he asked, apparently satisfied by what he'd seen.

It only took a moment of consideration before I said, "*Everything*."

Atticus smiled and reached to grab a beaker. "This will help with the pain. Don't worry," he reassured as I tilted my head away. "No bit of a wyvern came near this."

He lifted my head and poured small sips between my parched lips. Then followed it with clear water before settling me on my side, with a look to Cyrus before an admonition to not move too much.

The silent threat was clear—don't move, but *start talking*.

## CYRUS

I hadn't expected to find Bastian awake. He hadn't been when I'd visited late last night, long after the complex had quieted. And I certainly hadn't expected to have to wake him myself. As soon as I'd realized what was happening, urgency had seized the part of me that recalled nightmares from several weeks ago, and I hadn't been able to stop myself from grabbing him in an effort to banish whatever horrors he was facing.

Atticus set the water cup within my reach before departing, a pointed look directed at me as he did so. Silence gathered in the room as he left, leaving me suddenly wanting to look anywhere except at Bastian. Even so, I couldn't escape the truth. I'd prayed for a chance to make amends, and here it was. Practically thrown my way, for that matter.

"I heard the wyvern wasn't supposed to be full-grown," I said, breaking the silence with the information that I knew I'd want, were I in Bastian's place. "But it wasn't Octavian who planned it that way. I think you might have more enemies than just him."

A muted version of his scoffing laugh came, and it relieved me more than I cared to admit. "Seems that way."

"I don't know if it makes a difference, but I suspect one of the men responsible might already be dead." I hadn't watched this morning's match, but word was spreading. A lower-class solo fighter had gone against one of the other elites and lost within minutes. No fanfare. No spectacle. Almost an execution. "I doubt anyone will try something like that again for a long time."

"Good. I doubt I'm up for facing another full-grown wyvern any time soon." He paused over some words, frustration pinching between his eyes. "Though...I think I had some help."

I dipped my head sheepishly. "I heard the others laughing about how fast you were going to die, and I realized I couldn't let you fight it by yourself. By the time I got out of the tunnel, you were already in its mouth." At his confused expression, I sat straighter and waved a hand in front of my face. "I took a helmet from the armory. The crowds didn't know it was me, and I don't think anyone else did either."

A smile quirked his mouth. "They come in handy, don't they?"

"It did what it needed to. At least, I didn't get more than a few breaths of the smoke." I shuddered at the memory superimposed over another, incense-laden and shameful. "And my identity was kept secret."

"Thank you," Bastian said slowly. "For coming. I didn't...didn't think I'd get any help."

"You didn't think I'd come for you," I said flatly. "Can't say I blame you." I shifted uneasily on the stool, wishing I could pace. "You were right. I should've told you what I was planning last week. I'm sorry. It was...stupid of me."

He studied me for a long moment. Then, "I'm sorry too. I was a little harsh." The mirthless smile crooked his mouth. "I don't like admitting I was shaken by it."

"I know the feeling. *Gods*, I know that feeling." I shook my head. "I never wore a helmet again after Flavius did that to me. It was where I got the idea, but I didn't stop to think how badly it'd shake anyone else. *Stupid*."

"Cyrus." Bastian reached out and grabbed my tunic, pulling me forward until his arm circled my shoulders. "It's all right."

I froze for a long moment before my arms went around him. This wasn't like hugging Callista, or even Atticus. It was more like the moments when we'd sparred, when he'd shoved my shoulder after I'd said something ridiculous, when he'd tipped his head to the sky atop the Arena like I'd so often done. Like the friendship I'd claimed would get both of us killed. Or like the word he'd used—wingmates—allies who'd be at each other's side no matter the odds.

"Wingmates tell each other what they're planning. And wingmates also forgive each other," he said quietly.

"I'm sorry for what I said, too," I said into his shoulder. "I...I forgot. You understand what it costs to care just as much as I do." I pulled myself free and sat back. "I'm sorry. This is all...different for me."

"What, wearing a helmet onto the sands?"

I laughed. "Caring enough to take risks."

"We'll make a gryphon rider out of you yet."

"Have to get out of here first." I dipped my head. "Assuming you still want me to come with you."

Bastian treated me to a flat look. "You think I'll just hug anyone around here? Yes, you're coming."

A relieved sigh escaped me. "Good, because otherwise I'm not certain how else I'd get away." I glanced at the door to the small room. "Does Atticus know anything more than what we already asked of him?"

"No, but..." He frowned again. "When did I fight? Everything is..."

"A blur? I know what you mean." Another shudder went through my stomach. "It was yesterday, but I imagine to you it's felt longer."

His fist tapped gently against my knee, and understanding flickered in his eyes. "I'd planned to meet my man again. Two days from now. But I don't..." He tried to move and immediately winced. "Don't know if I'm going to be able to."

"You won't if Atticus has anything to say about it," I chuckled. "I know we've seen him angry, but I don't think I've ever heard him deliver an ultimatum to Octavian like he did yesterday in the tunnels. If you can't go, I'll do it."

"They should be ready to set the day." His face twisted in frustration, like reaching for something just out of touch. "But there's something with Octavian...I don't..." A low curse escaped.

"Hmm." The stool legs scraped against the stone floor as I stood, sticking my head around the edge of the door to spy the physician folding linens. "Sir? If you have a moment..."

He set the linens down and returned to the room, giving both of us a stern look. "Everything all right now?"

"I think so," I said, grinning at Bastian as I resumed my seat. "But there's a few things that we might need you to fill in. *Someone* has a mind full of holes after yesterday."

"Respect your elders," Bastian said, moving his shoulder from beneath himself and wincing again. He looked to Atticus. "Everything from yesterday is...pieces. Was Octavian here?"

Atticus's jaw set angrily. "He was here. Him and Tiberius both. Apparently, the fact that the public finally saw your face is garnering plenty of attention from all the wrong quarters, and he's had a lot of *offers* for your company."

Bastian immediately stilled. Even though he was half-curled on his side in an infirmary bed, there was something dangerous about him. "They can *try*," he spat.

"Th-they *will* try," I stammered. My own limbs had locked at the thought, and all I could hear was a scream in my head that sounded nothing like an Arena crowd. "There's not much we can do—you saw what happened when you tried refusing. They put you in a fight you'd have no chance of winning!"

"And I'll keep fighting," he said, voice low and determined. "Because it's *wrong*, Cyrus. It's wrong. Everything they've done to you." He gripped my arm again. "Do you understand me?"

"I—yes. No. Yes, but there's nothing we can do!" I turned my face away, terror freezing in my chest. "That smoke yesterday...they could do it again. Make you or me or both of us unable to resist, and—"

"Cyrus." Atticus sank to a knee beside me, an arm going around my shoulder and a calm voice commanding me to listen. "I've done what I can to bargain for time. It doesn't have to end the way you're afraid it will. Breathe."

I closed my eyes. Focused only on the two men grounding me into reality. We'd already defied more odds than anyone had a right to, but were—somehow—still alive and able to continue fighting. And there was someone else, far older and more powerful than any of us, who'd been watching and intervened when Bastian stopped breathing yesterday.

If *he* was on our side, then maybe there was a slim chance.

A breath shivered through my chest. Then another. "All right." I glanced at Atticus. "How much time?"

"I told them he wouldn't be able to stand, much less anything else, for several days." Atticus squeezed my shoulder and let go. He reached across to ease Bastian back so he was no longer curled as tightly under the blanket, telling him, "And they want you fighting before they entertain any of these offers. I may have implied that it'd be longer than I expect you'll need."

Bastian chuckled softly. "I won't have to *pretend* to sleep for a week."

"That's not fair," I said. "Then I'll be the one covering all your matches." He looked up in surprise, and I gave him a sarcastic smile to cover the fact that my limbs had only just thawed. "You don't get to sleep the *whole* week."

"I fought a full-grown wyvern." He settled back against the pillow. "And I had mostly won by the time you got your slow self out there."

"Slow? Me?" Laughter dissipated the bits of cold remaining in my chest. "Just get into training again, I'll show you 'slow.'"

"Assuming the two of you are going to stop acting like new recruits in the mess hall..." Atticus rolled his eyes. "You'll need to move ahead with whatever it was you were planning. They *are* wanting you to fight as soon as you're able," he told Bastian. "To prove to the public you're alive. But you'll have to act quickly after that."

"Is everything ready with Callista?" Bastian asked.

Atticus nodded. "I'd recommend you send your men to the alchemists during one of your matches. All eyes will be on you, and hardly any on her." He angled a stern look between both Bastian and myself. "Just don't get hurt. I won't be here to put you back together."

Bastian lightly tapped a fist to his chest. "They'll take her to stay with my wife." He glanced at me as if checking.

I nodded immediately. "If she's half as crazy as you, Callista will be well cared for."

A distantly fond look fell over Bastian's face. "She is."

"Tell me the day," Atticus said. "I'll be ready." He leveled a hand at Bastian. "You need to rest. And you"—he looked at me—"need to leave. I don't trust him to stay put with you here."

I got to my feet, jokingly giving him the same salute I'd seen Bastian use. "As you command, sir." I glanced at Bastian. "I'll be back. And if you're not on your feet in two days, *I'll* go meet your man and tell him you're dead."

Bastian's curse, broken by a chuckle, followed me out of the infirmary.

Defy the odds? We'd have to. There was no going back from here.

# CHAPTER XXX

CYRUS

B astian didn't stand on his own until that evening, and the paleness under his complexion told me then and there that he'd be unable to meet with whomever his men would send. It only took a little pressing before he gave me a name, a description, and a phrase that he said would guarantee trust—or at least that the person I spoke with would let the conversation continue.

I had a match the following day, but three days after Bastian's fight against the wyvern, I finished training and went directly from there to the barred wall that separated the arrivals courtyard from the city. The usual hangers-on were all there: temple representatives selling prayers, merchants seeking to wring coin out of the desperate, and urchins trying to catch a glimpse of their heroes.

I stopped a dozen paces from the gate, praying no one would recognize me as I scanned for someone who matched the description Bastian had given. I'd almost given up hope, assuming I'd gotten the day wrong, when a figure near the edge of the crowd raised his head to look piercingly at me.

Red hair. Posture like Bastian's. Striking green eyes. And as he matched my course to the farthest end of the gate, I could see boots like my wingmate's. No doubt about it, this was Felix, who I'd been sent to meet.

"The golden sun himself," the man said with a rasp in his voice. "I didn't expect to see *you* here."

"It's Cyrus. Or at least, out here it is."

"Ah. Right." Felix looked over my shoulder, eyes narrowing like he was trying to see through the stonework of the Arena itself. "Where's—"

"Your commander from Laecanthum sends his regards," I said. "And he says to tell you that you were...right about it?"

Felix broke into a hoarse laugh. "As he should. I told him there was hope; guess it's just taken him a bit to remember. He's all right?"

"He's on his feet, at least." I hadn't seen Bastian yet today, but yesterday he'd been well enough to insult me several times. "Recovering as fast as can be expected."

Felix nodded grimly. "I was there during the fight. In the stands," he explained as I raised an eyebrow. "We've been laying odds and getting rich off both of your successes. But that thing—Gods all bless whoever that was that pulled him out."

"Me," I said shortly. "He needed someone, and I wasn't going to leave him there." I looked over my shoulder to make sure no one was paying attention to this edge of the wall. "He said to tell you to send someone trustworthy to the alchemists' workshops in the artisans' district, to the shop with a purple and crimson awning."

"For the woman." Felix nodded. "When?"

"Six days from now." I'd be on the sands again, the knowledge painful despite the fact that it would be the best way to keep attention off Atticus and Callista as they left.

"We'll be there." He gave me an understanding smile. "More than one of us, to be safe."

My hands tightened against the straps of my armor. "Make sure she gets far, far away," I said, desperation creeping into my voice. "Even if nothing else goes to plan, this has to."

"Easy, soldier." Felix reached through the bars to tap my shoulder with a fist. "We'll see her safely to the coast. And when it's time for *you* to take flight..." He withdrew his hand and reached into the satchel at his side, pulling out a folded square of bright turquoise cloth. "Put this on the Arena roof the night before you need us. We've been taking warmup flights over the Arena every morning. One of us will see it, and we'll be there the next night." He passed me the cloth. "Be on the roof by the end of the first watch, and there'll be no stopping us."

"They're matching Bastian and I against each other in less than two weeks," I said. "Will there be time?"

"There'll be time," he assured me. "We'll get your girl to safety, then you. Plan for eight days from now, but we'll wait for your signal to be sure."

"Thank you." I folded the flag tighter and tucked it under my practice armor, experimentally shifting to make sure it'd stay put. "Once we know Callista is safe, we'll signal you. Just pray we can keep out of sight from the coordinators until then."

"Speaking of…" He gestured behind me, and I cursed as I caught sight of Octavian, standing at the edge of the courtyard with the air of a man in search of something—or someone. I hadn't seen him since before Bastian's fight against the wyvern, though I knew he'd been rooting out those responsible for unleashing the full-grown animal on the Arena.

"I don't know faces," Felix said. "But that one looks like he's looking for someone."

"Me, probably," I said with a muttered curse. "You'd better go. I don't want either of us to get caught here."

"I don't blame you." Felix offered me a tap of fist to chest. His voice followed me as I turned away, tucking the flag more securely beneath my armor. "Gods all bless. And good luck."

I'd made it away from the wall and past the entry of the recruit barracks before I heard my name called behind me. "Cyrus!"

I turned to face Octavian with as neutral an expression as I could muster. The folded flag shifted under my armor as I did, and I prayed it would stay put long enough for me to get to my quarters. "Haven't seen you in a bit. What's wrong?"

Octavian stopped a pace or two away, an intense expression on his face. "Where were you on the day of the wyvern fight?"

A scoff broke from my lips. "Training. What, you think *I* had something to do with that?"

"I don't know, Cyrus." He tipped his head to the side, and for a moment I felt like I was eighteen again, under questioning after having evaded a trap that ought to have caught me. "He's *your* rival. Maybe you thought to take your competition out early."

"You think I'd need to do something like that?" I raised my head, not

319

even having to pretend to be offended. "I beat him once already. And I'll do it again. I know what's on the line for me, and I don't need to *cheat* in order to maintain my reputation."

"Did you watch the match?"

"Yes," I answered evenly. "Especially once I heard what he was facing." I couldn't resist adding, "I have to say I'm impressed. He had it in its death throes before whoever that was came to finish it off."

Octavian looked at me sharply. "I don't suppose you know who that was, either."

"Not me, if that's what you're implying." I gestured at my head. "Helmets, remember? I haven't worn one for years. You'd remember that."

He would, too. He'd been the one overseeing the training match when I'd lost consciousness against Flavius.

"I remember," he said, deceptively soft. Then, "But whoever that was, they might've acted to settle a debt. A life for a life. You wouldn't know anything about *that*, would you?"

I gave a bitter laugh. Some debts couldn't ever be repaid. "That sounds like a sense of honor, and you and I both know there's no place here for that." Gods, the flag beneath my armor was beginning to slip. I straightened my shoulders and settled my arms across my chest to hold it in place. "You're looking for answers in the wrong place, sir. I don't have any scores to settle or debts to repay. Just a future to earn."

"Keep it that way." He stepped around me and continued past the barracks. "More than one person interfered that day, and I'm going to find out who—and why. And you'd better watch yourself."

There was really nothing I could say to that. It wasn't until he stopped to talk with some of the trainers that I started walking again, doing my best to rein in the rising urgency that marked each footfall up the stairs.

One of my attendants was in my room, laying out the clothes I'd be wearing to a public appearance that night. At least this one promised to be relatively straightforward—attend, look stunning, regale guests with gory tales. All things I was well accustomed to doing. Hopefully it would keep Octavian's attention off me and my involvement with the wyvern fight. The attendant departed with a promise to bring wash water shortly, and I was left alone.

The flag folded small enough to slide between the padding of my bed and the wooden frame beneath. I prayed it was hidden enough that the attendants wouldn't find it—or mundane enough that they'd ignore its presence.

*Just over a week.* I counted the days in my head twice, then once more to be certain. *Just over a week, and so many things could go wrong.* A flutter had started in my chest, beating at my ribs with the insistence of a bird trapped and trying to fly away. *But if it doesn't go wrong—if we really can do this...*

I cast a look through the latticed window, and the flutter sharpened into longing. *If it works, I could be free.*

## BASTIAN

"These are healing well." Atticus's chilly hands pressed around the wounds from the wyvern's teeth on my back. "How do you feel?"

"Like I could keep sleeping," I said wryly. I sat on the edge of my bed, right arm propping myself up. My head still had a habit of swimming if I moved too fast.

"I can buy more time," he said, loosening the bandage around my waist to look at the wound on my lower back from the claw.

I shook my head. Octavian had been impatient, looking ready to drag me from bed and to the training courts himself. "No, I need to get up. I need my strength for later anyway."

In five days, when we'd climb to the top of the Arena and meet the gryphons. Just the thought had my heart racing again. Five days and then I could be free. But before then, I had to get up and moving. Get back to fighting. And—my throat tightened—keep avoiding the board's plans for me.

"Octavian already has you listed on the sands in two days." Atticus replaced the bandage. "He won't be persuaded otherwise."

"Well." I huffed a sharp laugh. "Another reason for me to get back up."

Atticus circled the bed to look down at me as he wiped his hands on a cloth. "I'll make sure I'm there when you get off the sands. Maybe with something that'll have you needing to stay here for a few days more."

My jaw clenched tighter before I forced a smile. "Let's see if I can make it into my armor and outside first. You might not need it."

The physician gave me a grim once-over. "Any more nightmares?" he asked.

No real point in denying it. Not when Cyrus had woken me the first morning, and Atticus took his turn the afternoon after. "A few."

Every night. Any time I dreamed. It was always on the Arena sands, always watching people I loved and cared about die. Sometimes by my hand.

"Give it another few days. Sometimes the mind takes longer to heal than the body does."

I nodded. Cyrus had cautiously asked me the same two nights ago, and I'd talked around it, not wanting to say anything else that would bring back that spooked look in his eyes. Just like I hadn't said anything about Octavian's threat again.

Atticus handed me my tunic, helping me get it over my head. My attendant had been in earlier, rather mercilessly helping me wash and get halfway dressed before the physician arrived.

"Don't overdo it." Atticus leveled an admonishing finger at me. "You lost enough blood to keep you dizzy for another few days if you don't take care."

"*You* want to tell Octavian that?" I asked.

"Tell me what?" The trainer prowled into the room and Atticus matched my immediate defensive posture.

"That he shouldn't be up yet," the physician growled.

Octavian sneered softly. "He's had plenty of time. Besides, his match can't be moved." He looked to me, eyes slitted and daring. Calculating. Seeing if I would shatter before this.

I hadn't broken yet, and I still had plenty of defiance to give. I matched his stare as I rose to my feet. His lip curled again and his gaze swept over me. "Five minutes, Bastian. Training and assessing a new second." He spun on his heel and was gone.

I didn't particularly miss Phestus, but no one should have had an end like that. I'd yet to burn some incense for him, still unable to make it all the way to the altar niches. But I'd sent up a prayer or two in hopes that it could weigh his scales in favor of a better afterlife. Atticus looked at me, but I brushed him off as my attendant scuttled in and started handing me training armor.

"Thank you," I told the physician. He reached out to gently press my shoulder before gathering his things and leaving.

It was more than five minutes before I was armed and had slowly made my way to the sheltered training courts. More men than normal were gathered around, some in groups whispering in low speculation. Octavian waited on the sand with that same challenging look as I went to meet him. My helmet tucked against my side, new padding inside.

"The full-grown wyvern was an accident," Octavian said. "Those responsible for it have been dealt with." His voice seemed louder than needed, and a quick glance around showed it wasn't for my benefit.

"What a relief," I replied. He smiled thinly and lunged forward. I swept back, keeping space between us.

"You impressed a lot of people." He came again, and I circled. Testing my reflexes and footwork before he put a sword in my hand. "Even Cyrus." It came probing along with another feint, this time to my right.

"Should I be honored that he pays attention to anything lower than him?" I returned.

Octavian chuckled. "I wouldn't say 'lower,' Bastian. In fact, after that performance, you're well on your way to surpassing him."

I pushed forward, and he gave only for a moment before lunging. My foot finally stumbled as I retreated. Octavian swept my legs from under me, hand on my chest pushing me into the ground as I impacted the sand with a breathless grunt.

He knelt over me, pressing harder. "Only if you start listening," he hissed. *This* was just for me. "You're poised to become something great, Bastian. Something enduring."

If he was looking to flatter my pride, he'd missed the mark.

"But understand." He ground harder into my chest and panic flared at the weight on my lungs, the way he was right on top of one of the puncture wounds. "One way or another, you *will* follow orders." He let up and stepped away before I could move.

I slowly rose to my feet, brushing sand from my armor. Another trainer passed me a sword.

"Helmet," Octavian ordered. I pulled it on, blinking hard and sucking in a short breath between my teeth to calm the reflexive memory of smoke trapped underneath. One breath out, one in, and out again. Everything stayed clear. My heart steadied, settling into rhythm as I tested the weight of the practice sword and moved into the first sequence.

Two days later, I stood on bloody sands, the dull roar of an almost cheerful crowd ringing in my ears. My fingers fumbled with my helmet strap.

"Take it off at the end. Let everyone see your face," Octavian had ordered. I'd thought about refusing until the Arena had started tilting.

I squinted against the sun as I pulled the helmet off. The cheers took on a new pitch. I'd killed scraps and the spectators knew it, but I was giving something in return. Something that would bring them and their money back. Octavian hadn't mentioned *offers* yet, but given how I'd reacted last time, he probably wouldn't until he had me pinned.

Scraps of cloth fluttered down, their edges frayed and blurry. A hard blink and they settled on the ground as neatly edged strips. I needed to get back to the tunnel. Get back before I ended this like I had the last two days of training. On my hands and knees, vomiting whatever I'd managed to eat that morning.

One foot dragged forward, then another. My banner flapped idly above the tunnel entrance, the dark mouth twisting.

I stumbled in, dropping my helmet from trembling fingers. One more step and I hit my knees, palms scraping the rough ground.

"Bastian?" The man they'd picked as my second hovered worriedly. He didn't know me and I didn't know him. Bile threatened and I clenched my jaw, trying to get breath into my lungs.

"Get up," Octavian snarled. I didn't want to be on the ground anywhere near him, so I blindly reached for the tunnel wall to steady myself. And my body revolted, dry heaving before I collapsed again.

"Move," Atticus snapped. Steady hands rested on my shoulders. "Bastian, breathe."

He'd told me that too many times in the last six days. I squeezed my eyes shut and did as he ordered until the nausea passed.

"What's wrong with him?" Octavian asked dispassionately. I pushed up, Atticus helping me sit against the wall.

The physician glared over his shoulder. "Perhaps fighting almost a week sooner than he should've."

Octavian smiled thinly. "How do I know this isn't an act?"

I ground my hand against the floor, trying to find something steady to center around as everything tilted again.

"Look at him. He's not going anywhere other than to bed," Atticus said. "You want him in fighting shape? He needs to rest. Nothing else."

"Fine. Half day rest tomorrow, Bastian, then light training."

I could hear Atticus's teeth grinding, but I managed a look at the trainer and tapped my fist to my chest. He glowered down at me, then walked away. I didn't care. I was safe for at least one day more.

"Well." Atticus turned to me, pressing a hand against my temple, studying my eyes and face that felt entirely drained of blood. "Let's get you back to bed."

My new second had to help him get me to my feet. Atticus waved the man off, keeping one arm around me as I stumbled forward. I think he kept me propped up as the attendants divested my armor in quick movements. Then slowly through the tunnels, pausing for a long moment at the base of the stairs to my room. I collapsed onto the bed, eyes already closing. If he stayed to check bandages or anything else, I didn't know.

# CHAPTER XXXI

CYRUS

The longing hadn't subsided over the last few days. I'd avoided looking at the flag Felix had brought, but its presence under my bed was a constant reminder of how close freedom might be. And with me due on the sands this afternoon, the feeling was even sharper.

I'd climbed the Arena last night to scout the new array of obstacles. I ended up staying there through the second watch of the night, swinging my feet over the edge like I was twelve again. Only the knowledge that I hadn't checked on Bastian since the previous night had sent me down again, dropping to the ledge outside his quarters and finding them dark and still.

He'd been sleeping a lot lately. The fact worried me, even though everyone knew how he'd collapsed after his most recent match. The whispers were mostly concerned, but each rumor had its own way of crawling under my skin. The gossips wouldn't have to climb the Arena, and he and I would.

But first, Callista had to get to safety.

That morning, I stopped in the corridor of altars, ducking my head around the corner to check for observers before approaching the altar belonging to the First God. The offerings around his feet were familiar now—shells from Bastian, herbs from Callista, the candle that I now suspected was from Atticus.

I pulled a pure-white dove feather from my tunic, laying it at the feet of the statue before settling to my knees. I wasn't sure what to say to him, or if he'd care to listen, but soon I found myself letting all the concerns of the last few weeks spill out to fill the silence with prayer.

"...not sure how often you look down to see us, but I hope you're still taking an interest," I finished, rubbing a hand through my hair with frustration. "This could go so wrong, and I don't know what I'll do if it does. It's so *new* to me, all this, when I've only ever thought of surviving till now. I—" I sighed, glad no one else could hear me. "I've been cautious my whole life, but I've left that behind in so many ways. Like the ones who lay all their odds on one fight. If I lose now, I'll have lost everything."

A soft noise came from nearby, and I looked up to see Bastian standing a dozen feet away. He walked over, laying a new blue-painted shell at the feet of the god before kneeling next to me with a hand on my shoulder.

"You get an answer?" He tilted his chin toward the altar.

"Don't know if I'm looking for one. Not really." I laughed halfheartedly. "Just want to know that he's watching. Though"—I slipped free from Bastian's arm—"I think he might be."

Bastian huffed quietly. "It's been my experience these last few weeks that he is, and he'll let you know in the strangest of moments or places." His elbow came to nudge my side.

My gaze fell on the feather I'd placed on the altar. Doves here were mostly grey, but I'd seen a scrap of white caught between two tiles and had hardly believed my eyes to find it whole and clean, despite having been swept up by the wind.

Almost like the god knew what my dreams had been lately.

"They're here!" Callista's soft voice broke into my thoughts, and both Bastian and I turned as she and Atticus came down the corridor. She was still in her grey dress, but a woven shawl hung around her shoulders in subtle colors of blue and darker grey. She carried a basket under one arm.

I got to my feet, taking in the sight of her with warmth stirring in my chest. Gods, I'd never seen anyone so beautiful, even in a worn-out dress. Then, something caught my attention as my gaze fell on her face. Or rather, the *lack* of something.

"Lis. Your earring—" My hand drifted to the top of my own ear, where cold metal met my fingers. "Where..."

"My record of sale is cleared, thanks to Atticus." Her eyes sparkled as she looked up at me. "I'm free."

I gaped at the physician. "You—Sir? Really? You'd do that?"

For someone so stoic, Atticus actually looked *sheepish*. "I didn't want her to be in any danger once she got out of the city. This seemed like the best way to handle things. And don't worry." He straightened, and his voice took on its usual dry tone. "The office isn't going to say a word, not with as much extra as they were paid."

Behind me, Bastian gave a low laugh. He'd gained his feet and rested one shoulder against the wall. "Someday I want the story of how a soldier turned physician has enough money to do all that."

Atticus almost smiled. "Maybe someday. After you two are long gone and I don't have to work myself to the bone keeping you intact."

Bastian only chuckled again. I ignored him, turning back to Callista. "Freedom looks beautiful on you."

She blushed, and I did as well before telling Atticus, "Thank you, sir. For this—for *everything*. I'll try to stay out of trouble today, so you don't have to fret about leaving in the middle of a match."

"Be sure you do," he warned with a glint in his eye that might have been tears. "I'd hate to see your lady to safety only to come back and find you half-dead." He looked over my shoulder to Bastian. "Your men will be there?"

"Look for a gryphon rider by the name of Felix with red hair and less common sense than me," Bastian said, smirking as Atticus arched an eyebrow. "They might wait to make sure of you before approaching, but they'll be there. Lyra will take you with her to her parents," he told Callista. "It's on the coast, far from here. You'll be safe with them."

"And gods all bless that we'll be joining you there soon," I said, shifting from foot to foot. "If all goes well."

"I'll be praying it will." Callista's earnest gaze swept from me to Bastian.

My wingmate stepped closer, holding something in his hand. "Will you give this to Lyra? I don't want to risk losing it in the next few days, and if anything..." He forced a smile. "I just want to make sure she has it."

Callista took the object and I glimpsed braided leather and the brightness of a dragon scale. A marriage token. It made the fluttering in my chest grow again, thinking of giving one to Callista once both of us were free. Until now, it hadn't been something I'd allowed myself to think about.

"I'll make sure she gets it," Callista promised, tucking it into the basket.

"Thank you." Bastian crooked a smile. "Tell her I'll see her soon. And don't..." He swallowed, blinking hard for a moment. "Don't let her overwhelm you."

It didn't seem exactly like what he'd meant to say, but Callista nodded seriously.

"And congratulations." Bastian gently tapped her arm.

Callista smiled, then wrapped her arms around him. "Thank you for..." Her voice caught, muffled against his training armor.

He patted her shoulder and pulled away. "You're welcome. Be safe." He sounded almost admonishing before stepping around us both, swiping her basket and shoving Atticus down the hall. As they walked away, I caught him saying something about another training injury.

"'Training injury,'" I scoffed. "He's been asleep for four days, there's no way he—" I stopped and rolled my eyes before reaching down to take Callista's hand. "I meant what I said. Freedom is beautiful on you." My other hand went to cup the side of her face, fingertips brushing where the mark of slavery had now vanished. "Just give it a few days, and we'll have our whole lives in front of us to spend as we please."

Tears filled her eyes. "I wouldn't spend it with anyone but you," she whispered, standing on tiptoes to touch my cheek, then pull me closer to kiss me on the lips.

I froze for a moment, then my arms were around her, scooping her off the ground and holding her tight. Time stretched, and I wasn't sure how long it was before I set her down and pulled away to wipe tears from my eyes.

"I—" A laugh broke from my chest, the first really joyful sound I'd made in what felt like forever. "I still have to fight today, Lis. How am I supposed to focus now?"

Callista giggled, pink to the ends of her ears. "I'm sure Bastian will be happy to shake you around until you get angry and punch him." She grabbed my hand, towing me to the end of the corridor. Atticus and Bastian were several dozen feet down the hall, doing their best to act like they were talking about something extremely important. "Take care of him please," she said, putting a hand on my back and gently pushing me in Bastian's direction. "And don't let him do anything foolish."

Bastian *tsked*. "I didn't think you'd be asking impossible tasks of me before you left."

"I notice you're not telling me to keep *him* out of trouble," I said. "He's the one you need to be careful of."

Atticus sighed. "Unfortunately true."

Bastian lifted one hand in muted protest, but didn't make much of a denial.

"You'd better go." I wrapped my arm around Callista's shoulders, planting another kiss on the top of her head before pulling up the shawl to hide her hair. "I have to warm up soon, and no one will be paying attention to anything other than the fights if you leave now."

Atticus nodded, holding a hand out to Callista. "Gods all bless. Don't get killed."

Bastian tapped fist to chest with a smirk. "I'll keep an eye on him." He pushed my shoulder, turning me away as Atticus and Callista began walking the opposite direction. "You should probably stop grinning like an idiot," he told me, "or Octavian might think you've been kissing a girl

C.M. BANSCHBACH, BRIGITTE CROMEY

down here."

I rubbed my face. "With any luck, he won't notice. And in two days, I won't have to worry about him ever again."

"Just don't start kissing her when I'm there, or else you'll have to start worrying about *me*." He pushed my shoulder again, and I let the momentum send me spinning.

"That'll be the one time you don't hesitate," I laughed. "At least I'll die happy." I righted my gait and began walking up the stairs that led toward the courtyard. "Wait a few minutes before leaving. Just in case."

"I will." He nodded. "Be careful, Cyrus. I'll be watching." He tilted his chin in the direction of the Arena floor.

I waved over my shoulder, increasing my pace toward the courtyard and open air. My hand went to the ring piercing the top of my ear, and I couldn't help the smile that insisted on lingering.

*Soon.*

BASTIAN

Quiet hovered in my room, at odds with the jittering filling my muscles. It had been there since I'd woken after my last match in the dead of night. Ever since then, my strength and energy had rapidly returned—either due to the sour medicine Atticus had been giving me or my appetite finally returning. My attendant had been raising an eyebrow and bringing extra food every day like I was some starving child. I only cared that my head didn't spin when I stood up, and I could make it through training without feeling one breath from losing consciousness or breakfast.

My knees bounced, and not even leaning my elbows atop them could

334

still them for long. Cyrus was planting the flag tonight. Likely scaling the Arena heights as I sat on my bed and practically fretted. He'd been climbing that wall for years, so he said. I knew he wouldn't put a foot wrong tonight.

My left thumb pressed against my opposite palm, working along the base of my fingers and the callouses there. One day. One more day if the First God was watching. I was scheduled to fight tomorrow and then...

Hopefully leaving before Octavian could do anything else. He'd been practically friendly and caring the past few days, and it only made a sickening knot form in my chest.

Some bits and pieces from the hours after the wyvern fight had come back. Fragmented conversation that perhaps had happened or that my mind was all too happy to conjure into a nightmare.

I'd foiled his plans days ago by collapsing in the tunnel, but with how well I was moving now, I didn't think he—or the board—would stay patient for long. And I didn't know what I could do to refuse or resist this time if they came for me.

My fingers curled into a fist and back out. My men would be watching for the flag, to let them know everything was proceeding as planned. *Please let this work.* I closed my eyes. *Cyrus needs to get out. And I...* My fists clenched and stacked atop each other. *I just want to see Lyra and August again...* Stinging hit my eyes and I forced them open as a soft thump sounded outside the window.

At this hour, it could only be the wingmate I'd decided to claim. He was more half-feral gryphon than anything, but he was showing himself just as loyal as any other soldier I'd fought with.

Another thump came, then Cyrus's blond hair came into view around the edge of the window. His feet landed on the sill and he dropped into the room with hardly a sound. "You're awake? That's different."

"There's a perfectly good door, by the way," I replied, ignoring some of the unease I still had from *missing* parts of days since the fight, and not knowing how many times he'd come by.

"Only if I want to be seen." He settled on the floor, gesturing beyond the ceiling toward the Arena. "And it was easy to drop onto the roof. The banner's in place now; I weighed the edges down with loose tiles. I just hope nothing happens to blow it off the roof, not that it'll change the plan too much. They still fly overhead each morning?"

"They do," I reassured. "I heard gryphons this morning before the sun." I'd been wide awake for an hour at least by then. "Did Atticus tell you Callista's off safe?"

He nodded, the same dreamy expression as yesterday crossing his face. "I heard. She's well out of the city by now. He told me he followed them long enough to see them out of the gates."

My thumb worried across my hand again. Watching him and Callista yesterday had only added more urgency. They both needed to escape this place, needed to be able to live and love freely. If this didn't work...I wasn't sure what either would do. Lyra would mourn me, and perhaps eventually move on. But Cyrus? I'd make sure he made it, that much I would promise myself and him.

"Good," was all I had to say. The tremoring in my muscles seemed to be stealing my words, and I was about to mimic Cyrus's usual pacing if I wasn't careful. "You haven't heard anything else about the upcoming fight?" My new second was less inclined toward gossip, or maybe just sharing it with me, than Phestus had been. And most seemed to be avoiding me on the training courts.

"Nothing about the eclipse, if that's what you mean." Cyrus narrowed his eyes. "I don't think they want it to be public knowledge—it would ruin the drama of everything. But I did take note of the layout for your match tomorrow." He got up and crossed the room to take a cup of water from a side table, returning with it and using the dampness to sketch a rough map on the stone floor. "Here. At least you won't be caught off guard."

I allowed a faint smile as I studied the markings. "Thank you."

"Gods grant it'll be the last time either of us has to memorize where the traps are."

I nodded in silent agreement, watching the lines slowly fade against the stone. "I'll be at the gryphon stables by mid-watch," I said, palms now scraping against each other as I debated my next words. "My attendant tried to hide it, but some new clothes arrived today." I tilted my head toward the closet. "*Very* fine clothes. I think my days of anonymity are at an end." I barely mustered a smile.

Cyrus clenched his jaw, and his shoulders stiffened. "Given the uproar now that everyone's seen your face, I suspect so. Nobody told you to expect anything? No party invitations or events scheduled that you know of?"

I shook my head, unease bitter in the back of my mouth. "Octavian hasn't been very forthcoming in the past, and it seems like he might keep it that way."

"He *really* doesn't like you," Cyrus answered. "We knew he didn't, but this means he's trying to keep you guessing." A shuttered look had come over his face. "He's trying to remind you who's in control. Maybe we need to meet earlier than mid-watch."

I shook my head. "Too early and the attendants might get suspicious. But if I catch wind of anything, I'll be putting some of my scout training to work." Another whisper of a smile tilted my lips. I wouldn't have a weapon to slide between Octavian's ribs in a dark corner, but I still might be able to avoid him with what I'd learned of the Arena in the last few months.

A hint of a smile stole through the tension in Cyrus's expression. "If they can't find you, they can't hurt you. Just keep to the shadows, and remember they never look up."

"No one ever does," I replied. Something that had come in handy more than once on scouting runs. I pushed to my feet as Cyrus rose and started making for the window. "Cyrus." I snagged his shoulder and pulled him into a hug. This time he didn't freeze before returning it. "Be careful." I tapped his shoulder.

"You too." He stepped back. "And tomorrow, don't hesitate."

He turned and slid out the window, disappearing into the blackness. I made sure the shutters were snugly shut again before turning away. I drew in a short breath, the restlessness held at bay for a few minutes now surging back. Tomorrow. It would be over tomorrow, one way or another.

# CHAPTER XXXII

BASTIAN

T he gryphons were restless. There was a shift in the air, I could feel
how it held an edge of extra warmth to drive away the moisture
that had been clinging the last few days. It was that, or they could pick
up *my* shifting through the stable walls.

I was early.

My fight had gone smoothly, and Octavian had met me in the arming
room, looking pleased. He still hadn't said anything other than a veiled
instruction to make sure I kept resting. I'd barely eaten any dinner, wary
when it was brought earlier than normal. My suspicions were confirmed
when the attendant had drawn a bath with strongly scented oils. He
hadn't said anything either, and the absence of his normal chatter as he

laid out the new clothes had been another signal.

He was busy and hadn't noticed me coming behind him. He'd wake later, likely panicked to be bound and gagged in the closet, but I needed him out of the way so I could vanish.

A gryphon warbled again and another answered sulkily. They wanted freedom just as badly as I did.

"Bastian?" Cyrus's low voice alerted me and I edged out of the shadows. His hair was a beacon, even with him wearing a tunic in a darker red than most of his other clothes.

"I'm here," I said. "And we need to go now. The attendant was trying to get me ready to go somewhere, so he's stuffed in the closet. We don't have much time."

"It's still busy out there," he said, coming to join me at the edge of the barred pen where we'd first trained. "I had to make it look like I was taking a walk. There's no way climbing the wall will go unnoticed. We have to wait."

I glanced at the sky through the courtyard entry. Dregs of sunlight held out, but dusk was making ready headway. "A quarter hour, and that might even be too long," I said, trying to stay between nervous anticipation and the steadier commander somewhere still inside who could make decisions in a wings-beat.

"We need to wait," he repeated. "If they were getting you ready, there's still time."

"I don't know when—or how—they planned to take me," I replied, not wanting to give voice to where I thought I'd be going. There was no doubt in my mind that an *offer* had been accepted and Octavian would happily make sure I was *compliant* this time.

"I wish I could answer, but I don't know either." Cyrus ran a frustrated hand through his hair. "The times when this happened to me, I'd already said yes. I don't know what Octavian would do—" He stopped talking, raising his head as tension spread through his shoulders.

I heard the same change in sounds, a call from somewhere within the courts. "We need to go."

"Fast," Cyrus agreed. He spun, and I followed him back the way from which he'd come, out of the training courtyard and toward the wide, arched corridor that spanned the width of the stables and connected the courtyards on either side.

"Stay close," I murmured, glancing down each path before we moved again, sliding into the shadows clustering along the wall. More shouts echoed behind, coming from the direction of my room. "Go." I tapped his shoulder, checking over mine as we picked up the pace. Lights flashed on the other side of the narrowed arch of the tunnel.

The main arrivals courtyard held its normal late-evening activity until another stir rose in front of us. Cyrus hissed under his breath as the light from two more torches spilled from the main barracks.

"Keep going." I shoved his shoulder. We just needed to make it to the barracks stairs and from there to his room, where the lattice would give us access to the Arena walls and a straight path upward.

Calls and answers started, and we kept moving. Nothing much to give us cover along the curving wall itself. Another glance showed men in the courtyard now, more torches gathering in clustering groups. The gryphons shrieked, muffled by the stable walls. No answer from above, but it was early yet.

*Too early.*

"There!" Octavian's snarl whipped across the courtyard. I cursed in answer and we broke into a run, all care and caution forgotten. Get up the stairs to the wall, climb as fast as we could. Pray to the gods somewhere in between.

We never got the chance. Three men raced to head us off, and the heavy sounds of pursuit picked up behind. Cyrus skidded to a halt a half-pace away, twisting away from the blunted edge of a spear.

I pulled him back, trying to angle him away from the solid wall. Another staff swung out and I ducked, pushing forward and coming up under it to drive a fist into the man's gut. He buckled with a wheezing cry. To my right, Cyrus had grabbed another spear and swung it to crack against its former wielder's side.

A hole opened up. "Go!" I pointed, urging Cyrus through. He obeyed, dodging another lunge and making for the wall. I made to follow, but my feet tangled beneath me. I pitched to the ground with a surprised cry, palms stinging on impact. A bolas was wrapped around my ankles, resisting all attempts to kick free.

I barked a desperate curse as two more men circled cautiously. I rolled, grabbing for the staff I'd used only moments ago. I came up with the weapon and locked eyes with Cyrus. He'd frozen a few feet from the wall, poised mid-stride with horror in his face.

"*GO!*" I screamed, twisting to swing at a pursuer. The bolas loosened enough for me to kick a foot free. It became half-wild lunges from my knees, trying to get up and moving again.

A *crack* of wood against wood pulled my glance that way. The idiot was fighting and *not running*.

"Cyrus!" I surged to my feet.

He whipped the spear around with furrowed intensity, smashing it under the slower guard's spear. The man crumpled, grabbing at his leg. Stubbornness filled Cyrus's look at me, replaced quickly by warning.

I spun, my own staff impacting a sword. The steel cut into the wood, cracking it beyond use. Octavian snarled and threw his weight against me. Another spear caught my ankles, and he threw me to the ground.

A curse from Cyrus announced he was also down, another bolas tangled around his knees. Torchlight glinted off the points of spears hovering dangerously close to my chest. I tried to find Cyrus again, only to see his former second lash out in a kick, clipping him across the forehead. Despite the spearhead pressed firmly against my ribs, I jolted toward Cyrus, cursing Flavius. Octavian pressed his boot against my arm, pinning me to the ground. He loomed overhead, fury contorting his face before it smoothed into something cold and unreadable.

"Restrain them both, and take them upstairs."

As guards grabbed me and wrestled arms behind me, a wild cry drew my gaze to the Arena roof. A gryphon had landed on the tiles, wings spread wide. A rider crouched on its back, helmet and darkened armor encasing him. The gryphon screamed again and the rider raised one hand, waving twice before clenching a fist in silent promise. *We'll be back.*

But there was nothing left to hope with as I was dragged toward the barracks, Cyrus similarly restrained and surrounded. Maybe I'd have a chance to tell him I was sorry. He'd been right. There was no way out.

No way except death.

CYRUS

Light stung my eyes, rope burned against my wrists, and the stone walls had never seemed closer as we stood in an office lined with nooks for scrolls and tablets. The cut over my eye throbbed, stickiness against my face telling me that the bleeding had subsided. Guards on either side of me kept firm grips on my shoulders and arms, as if having me bound wasn't assurance enough. An experimental twist against their weight resulted in a cuff to the back of my head, and I subsided with a muttered curse.

The silence in the room stretched. I cast a glance at Bastian, whose head drooped between his shoulders. Defeated, like I'd never seen him before. Anger surged through my veins, and I twisted again, managing to wrench a shoulder free before a punch to the stomach made me double over with a groan.

"Cyrus, stop before I make you," Octavian said as he came in, followed by another man who I recognized as belonging to the board.

I spat a curse at him, only to be silenced by another blow. This time the wind went out of my lungs, and only the guards' hands kept me upright. Bastian looked over, concern showing through his eyes. I thought I caught a warning in them.

*Be still. Just be still.*

He had a point, not that I planned to listen. If they were going to kill us, I was going to make them work for it. This wasn't going to be like the last time I was surrounded by Octavian's men. Another wrench, and I had an arm free. The rope around my wrists cut into skin as I twisted to slam my elbow into one of the guards' ribs. Their grips had weakened with surprise, and I yanked free only to stop short.

One of Bastian's guards had clamped an arm around him, pinning his already bound hands and pulling him off-balance. The other hand leveled a knife at his throat.

I immediately froze. *Stop. Don't.*

"Well, if I had any doubts, you've very effectively erased them," Octavian said, a malicious smile twisting his face. "At what point did *this* happen?"

"It was my idea," Bastian said tightly. "He didn't have anything to do with it."

"Hmm. That I seriously doubt." Octavian waved a hand at the men holding Bastian. "Leave it."

The one holding the knife withdrew it, releasing Bastian with enough of a push that he stumbled and would have fallen were it not for the other guards grabbing his arms. With a quick step, Octavian was in front of him, and a hand fell across my wingmate's face with a crack that could have split the stone.

"Leave him alone!" I shouted. "It was *my* idea. All of it! I—" I let my eyes fall to the ground, unwilling to meet Octavian's disbelieving stare or Bastian's cautioning one. "I had a debt to pay."

"That sounds awfully like a sense of honor, Cyrus." I caught sight of Octavian's feet in my periphery before his hand caught my chin, pulling my gaze to his. "I did have my suspicions after your stunt during the wyvern fight—did you think no one would notice that the mystery fighter was wearing old Dragonesque armor?—but I didn't expect you'd take it to such ridiculous lengths. You *know* that type of thing comes with consequences."

"I know." I looked over his shoulder at Bastian. If we were about to die, I needed him, at least, to hear this. "But someone believed I was worth sparing, and I couldn't leave him to die when he needed someone at his wing. I don't regret it."

Octavian's features contorted with barely contained anger. "Such a pity. The golden sun, the Arena champion. You could've been my greatest triumph, and *now* you'll weaken?" He scoffed. "What a waste of potential."

My eyes opened wide at the word. "Potential," I repeated, something hot gathering inside of me. "Not a person, just 'potential.' Something to shape, to wield, to use, for *twelve years* that's all I've been to you."

Twelve years since the day when I'd been surrounded by enemies, counterattacked instead of cowered, and attracted the attention of someone who'd seen potential in a golden-haired boy who covered fear with ferocity. Twelve years of hiding tears, winning fights, breaking little by little until I'd become the weapon Octavian had foreseen.

I raised my head to look him in the eye. "You never cared about me. Didn't care whether I lived or died, only if I lived up to my *potential*." I threw the word in his face. "You taught me to be vicious. To be fast, strong, *merciless*. You had me flinching at every footfall, so scared of disappointing you that I'd do *anything* if it got me a 'well done.'" I stopped and took a deep breath, the pressure in my chest shattering my voice. "I...I was never going to be enough for you, and now the only value I have in your eyes is to die spectacularly so your own legend can continue."

A slight movement caught my eye. Across the room, Bastian had lifted his head. The corner of his mouth turned up in a faint, proud smile as our eyes met.

The sight settled the cracking in my heart, and the clarity of battle steadied my voice as I turned back to my former trainer. "Hear this, *sir*." I tugged my shoulder free and stood straight, meeting his mocking gaze without flinching. "I'm finished. No matter what happens, you're never going to have me pinned again. You can decide to kill me now, and I won't be able to stop you. But you'll *always* know I died unafraid, and I'll take that triumph to the gods with me." I spat on the floor at his feet.

"Let them weigh your actions when it's time."

"If you're so willing to die, I can oblige," Octavian said with a sneer, like my words had gone past him unheard. "But not yet. Not here." He nodded toward the Arena. "There's still fate to satisfy."

"Fate," Bastian said scornfully. "Don't call it that when everyone knows you've planned the outcome."

"Sometimes fate is clearly written," Octavian said. "I just help it along. So here's how it's going to be. You care about him?" he demanded of Bastian, a hand shooting out to point at me. "You want to see him trapped here for the rest of his life?"

"No."

"Then end him." The words cracked through the room. "End him on the sands and take his place."

"And you'll have your new champion." Bastian's eyes glittered dangerously. *Defiantly.* "What happens when the people realize I won't be controlled?"

"You will," Octavian said softly. "Sooner or later, you'll break. They always do."

Bastian didn't flinch, didn't look away from Octavian's surety until the trainer glanced back at me.

"And you. You're so unafraid now, but do you think he'll last as long as you have? With all your newfound honor and restraint, have you considered what will become of him after he kills you? The things I'll visit on him, the *lessons* he'll have to learn?"

Blood hammered in my ears. I'd gotten used to this life, but each new revelation had made Bastian recoil with horror in his eyes. *Would* he survive the life victory would bring him? Or would it consume him the way it'd almost consumed me?

"Cyrus, don't," Bastian warned, pulled back by the men holding him. *Don't worry about me.*

I looked away.

Gods, I had to look away.

"Sorry, Bas." The words choked in my throat. "I can't let him do that to you." Fury strengthened my voice, and I looked straight into Octavian's eyes. "You'll get your fight. But whichever one of us survives is going to become your worst nightmare."

Octavian's smile thinned, and for a moment I saw uncertainty flit through his eyes. "*Everyone* breaks in the end. Neither of you will be any different." He looked over my shoulder to the guards. "Get him to his quarters. Keep him there. Don't let him out of your sight." He turned to the men holding Bastian. "Lock *him* up downstairs."

I only had time to catch sight of Bastian's face, stunned and panicked, before he was pulled out of the room.

"I'm sorry!" I screamed. "Bas, I'm so sorry!"

Then the door closed on the echoes of my words, and he was gone.

# CHAPTER XXXIII

BASTIAN

The guards shoved me down the stairwell, passing a few shocked slaves and lower-level fighters. I could almost hear the whispers spreading over the pounding of my heartbeat. We entered the tunnels, winding deeper until my frantic heart threatened to make itself heard. A guard pushed past and swung open a barred door, returning to shove me in. He pinned me against the wall as something cold clamped around my right wrist. The ropes were untied, and I was released in a rush.

The door clanged shut and the flickering torchlight retreated slightly. I turned, chain clinking softly as I did. The restraint allowed four feet of movement, but there wasn't much more space within the narrow cell.

The guards stood a few paces down the hall, waiting for something.

I refused to let them see how the closeness of the stone already weighed around me. An even tread had the guards standing at attention before Octavian came into view. He unlocked the door and stepped inside.

"Well." He studied me. As before, I held his gaze, anger and helpless fury driving away any fear I'd had. Echoes of Cyrus's pained *I can't let him do that to you* hung in the still air. "I'm impressed. You almost managed to get out. And turned Cyrus while you were at it."

I didn't respond, didn't flinch when he lunged. Cyrus had told me before to not be defiant. Others had warned me. But defiance was all I'd had left since being brought through the gates for the first time. The only way I had of making sure some part of *me* still existed. I wouldn't give it up now, especially not to the man who'd tried to break me, and had broken Cyrus in so many ways.

"Do you know how much you cost the Arena tonight?" he asked. The shadows draped across his face, turning his eyes into dark pits.

"Hopefully a fortune," I responded with a slight sneer.

He struck quicker than a viper. A fist to my stomach sent me staggering. I was too slow to block another strike to my still-throbbing face that threw me off-balance. He swept my legs out from under me and kicked twice, three times with a furious shout.

A wheezing gasp tore from me. Octavian hauled me up by the front of my tunic and struck my face again. Dampness trickled down my cheek and the salty sweetness of blood filled my mouth. His hand closed around my throat, pushing me into the wall.

"Defy me for now, keep pretending to care. You'll walk off the sands in four days as the new champion and this?" Octavian released me and swept a hand around the cell. "This will be only the beginning."

He stepped away. "You could have been something great."

I spat blood toward his feet. "Not of your making."

His jaw worked for a moment before he slammed and locked the door, leaving me a slouched heap on the floor. Octavian turned to regard me one more time before taking the torch. Whatever he saw in the faint light made him smile thinly. He ordered the guards to follow, then left.

I clenched my jaw against the sudden lurch of panic as the torchlight faded and I was plunged into pitch darkness. It was a childish thing, but some small part of me had hated the deep dark ever since my first night on the mainland, far from the familiar sea I'd known for all my five years. Surrounded by strange noises and missing home. But at least there had been the wind, nighttime noise, the soft familiar noises of horses.

Here, it felt like one breath away from a cave-in, even though these walls had stood for years and would for generations more. No air, no sound, just suffocating stillness.

I pushed my back against the wall and drew my knees up, forcing one breath after another until they came more easily. A humming ran through the chain, tied to the tremors in my hands. I clenched my fists together and it gradually quieted again.

The only reassurance I had was that I wouldn't be left in this cell to die. Not yet. I'd have to take the sands in four days, fight Cyrus... My hands tightened around each other.

*Bas, I'm so sorry!*

The idiot really thought it was his fault. A bit of anger reared up. Why had he hesitated for the first time in his life? He could have gotten away, could have been picked up by the advance scout.

It was *my* fault. I'd all but promised him freedom, then failed. We were more trapped than before, physically *and* by the cruel ultimatum from Octavian. Kill your friend to spare them misery, and take it upon yourself instead.

"I'm sorry," I whispered to the darkness, even though he couldn't hear me. "I'm so sorry."

The anger faded, leaving me cold instead. I buried my hands in my hair, compressing over my aching stomach. I'd failed Lyra and August too. My men might try to come again, but there was no way to meet them. Not if this was my future. And if it was, I didn't want my wife and son to see what I might become in the end.

Dampness eased from my eyes, stinging the fresh cut on my cheek. I'd finally dared to imagine holding Lyra again, bringing her close without bars between us. Holding August.

The ache stabbed deeper into my heart. One of my first memories was my small hands clutching the wiry salt-crusted manes of the stocky island ponies, my father's calloused hands wrapped around leathers and mine as we raced the wind-swept beaches and chased seagulls across the tide lines. That would be August's memory too. My father, not me, teaching him to ride. Lyra's father, not me, teaching him to ride a gryphon. At least Lyra had my scale necklace. Something to remember me by, something to pass to August if he wanted.

And with the dark the only witness to the tears streaking my face, I made a promise. I'd do what I could to still try to protect Cyrus. If I did survive in four days, I'd stay defiant for as long as I could.

And I prayed, *begged*, that the First God still watched.

 CYRUS

Three days. Three days of pacing my rooms, of training in an underground court, of staring at the light changing beyond the latticed windows. The wooden slats and doors had never felt more solid, the outside air never farther away than in the hours after I'd been thrown to the floor in my quarters and the ropes cut free. The guards had stationed themselves at each door, their eyes barely leaving me for a moment.

And there I'd stayed.

For three days.

Plenty of time to hear my own voice over and over, screaming Bastian's name as he was dragged out of the office with panic in his eyes. I'd tried asking about him, even tried asking Octavian the one time he'd come to ensure that I was following orders.

"He's alive," my former trainer had coldly answered. "And if you care at all about him, these are his last few days."

The words sank into my heart colder than ice. *I have to do it.* I'd never seen Octavian so angry, so desperate. If I didn't somehow manage to kill Bastian myself, I didn't know what his fate would be.

I threw everything I had into training, craning my neck each time I was ushered through the underground on the chance that I'd be able to catch a glimpse of Bastian in some intersection or tunnel. They must've been careful to keep us apart, however, and all I gained was a clip to the head and a more strenuous training session.

And now the sun was rising on the morning of the fourth day, the hum of daily life already building in the courtyard beyond the windows. The guard slouched, bored, in his place at the door. I'd already eaten—food was unappetizing, but I knew better than to refuse—and one of the physicians was present to give me a last check before the match. It wasn't Atticus. Something told me that Octavian didn't trust him any more than he trusted me or Bastian.

"Let's make sure you're all fit for today," the man said. His fingers probed the spot on my forehead where Flavius had kicked me three nights ago. "This bothering you at all?"

I shook my head. "It closed on its own." And even if it hadn't, I suspected no one would have really cared. "It's fine."

The physician frowned. "That's so. I don't think it'll trouble you." He continued his exam, asking more questions as I sat on the edge of a bench below the window. The words struck a strange knell in my heart, and I rubbed sweaty palms against the worn linen that covered the horsehair padding. It didn't matter what happened to me today, so long as Bastian was forever safe from Octavian's schemes.

The physician had finished his exam when the door opened and Flavius walked in alongside two of his friends—cronies, really.

"What are you doing here?" I growled. After he'd recovered from his broken arm and joined the trainers, I hadn't seen much of him, though the poisonous looks when our paths *did* cross had kept me wary.

"Me?" He tucked his hands behind his back innocently. "Nothing. Just making sure you were ready for this." He shrugged. "It's not every day you get to see one of your old friends get publicly flattened."

I stood and grabbed my tunic as the physician slipped out the door. "We're not friends," I snapped. "I'm not sure we ever were."

My head was halfway through the neck of the tunic when someone grabbed me. I thrashed an arm free of the fabric, and there was a crash—the side table falling over—before I was slammed against the wall. I wrestled my head into the light to see Flavius pulling a translucent bottle from the bag slung over his shoulder, shooting a malicious grin at the men restraining me. Inside the vessel, something small and brightly colored skittered, its panicked movements matching the pulse in my throat.

"We *were* friends, once," Flavius commented, loosening the wooden stopper on the bottle as I struggled to break free. The men holding me weren't top-ranked fighters by any means, but they were strong—and had the element of surprise. The guard across the room met my eyes but ignored the panic in them, turning his head away as Flavius added, "That was before you became a god and the rest of us stayed mortal."

I'd forgotten how fast he could move. In one quick motion, he'd seized a flailing arm and upended the vial. A stabbing sensation streaked across my arm as the creature within sank a stinger into my skin.

I yelled, yanking my arm free and sending the bottle—and its contents—flying to smash on the floor. Flavius's friends may have been strong, but this time *I* was the one with the element of surprise. I twisted under the arm of the one still holding me, driving my fist into his ribs and sending him staggering backward as the other swung ineffectively at me. Another several blows to their ribs and jaws, and they backed off, eyeing me fearfully and the door longingly.

I took advantage of their uncertainty to run a hand over my arm. It felt fine until my fingers brushed where the mouth of the bottle had sat. A burning tingle spread through my skin, and I could see a tiny puncture when I looked closer.

"What did you do?" I demanded.

"Call me an agent of fate." Flavius straightened from examining the wreckage of the bottle, crushing something under his sandal as he did. "Don't worry, you'll be fine. I'm certain no one will notice that the golden sun is a little slower than usual today." Malice glittered in his smile. "And fate will have its way. An immortal, brought low at last. I'm just glad I get to see it." Flavius winked over his shoulder as he went out the door. "Gods all bless, Cyrus. Destiny's waiting."

The door fell shut on him and his minions, leaving me staring at the wound in my forearm. I knew I wasn't imagining things as the tingle spread, my limbs growing heavier and reflexes slowing. And soon I'd have to step onto the sands and kill my only friend. A sinking feeling swallowed me and I had to sit down, head falling into my hands. An effect of the venom, perhaps, but awfully close to despair.

*I was always going to lose today.*

*Gods grant that I can still do what needs to be done.*

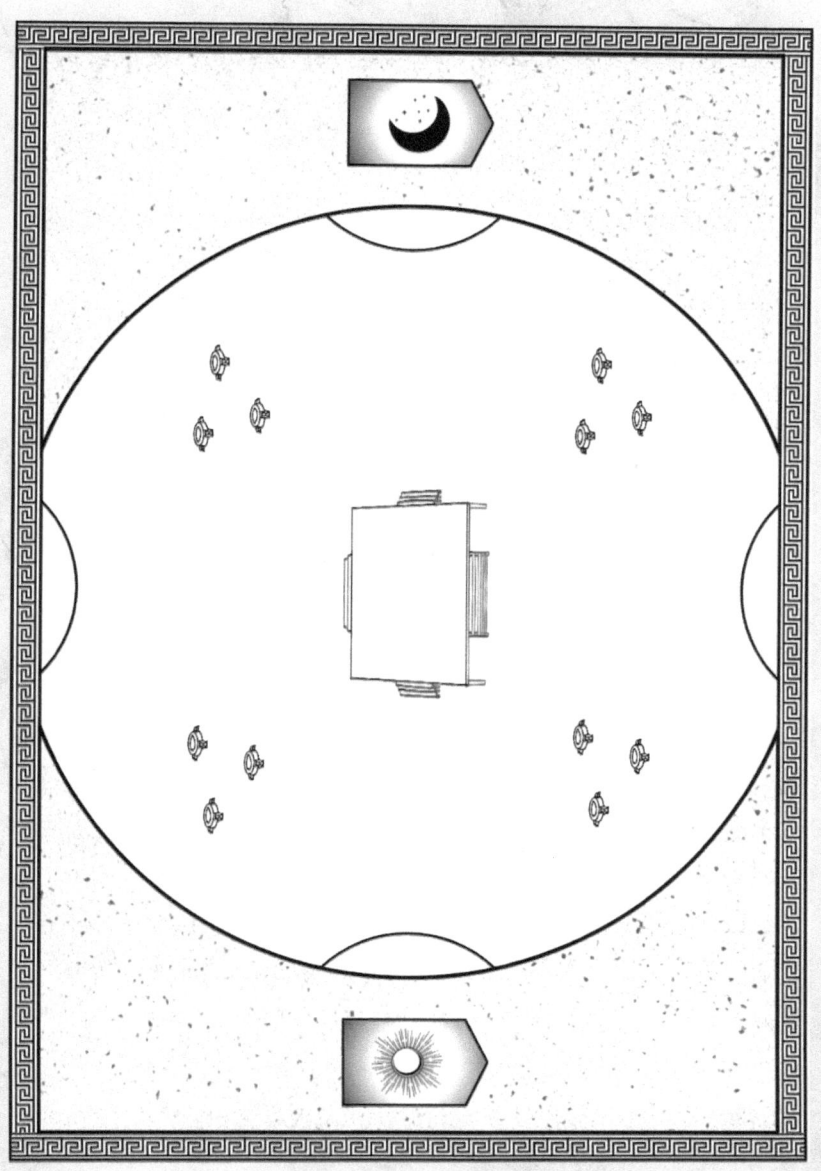

# CHAPTER XXXIV

BASTIAN

Absolute quiet marked the armory. The attendants said nothing about the array of bruises and welts on my face and arms as they slid armor into place. They said nothing about the conspicuous lack of my second. And said nothing about the lingering guards.

After the first day literally in the dark, a small torch had been left. More because of how long it had taken my eyes to adjust to the light in the underground training courts than any shred of decency. There had been no sight or sound of Cyrus. No friendly face of Atticus. Nothing other than the continued silence in the underground cell and my own churning thoughts. Live or die? Kill or be killed?

No more time to think, or pray.

I took my helmet, turning it over in my hands, inspecting it like I always did as they belted on my sword.

"Bastian."

I forced myself to look at Octavian. As they'd dragged me, limping and battered, back to the cell from the training court yesterday, I'd caught a glimpse of triumph in the man's eyes. He thought he was already breaking me.

He stepped closer and I held still. The attendants rapidly gave space, sensing the brewing storm faster than an airborne gryphon.

"This is it," he said. "The day you rise, or the day you fall."

I checked the release of my sword in the sheath. He raised an eyebrow, not threatened by the whisper of steel on leather.

"You might still be weighing a choice, but the board has made their decision." He tugged the helmet from my hands, turning it over and inspecting it. "Cyrus is taken care of. He won't leave the sands, one way or another." He shoved the helmet into my chest. "Make it spectacular and buy yourself a little more time."

He gestured to the door. I pushed past him without a word, striding up the Arena tunnel. Even paces back, the brilliance of natural light stung my vision.

The board may have chosen, but so had I.

If Cyrus lived, he might have a chance to grasp for freedom again. And me? I just had to make it look spectacular, and buy him a little more time.

I pulled the helmet on and did up the strap. The crowd was already working to a frenzy. I unsheathed my sword, and took the sands.

The corresponding roar felt like it would bring the stones down around me. For a terrifying moment, everything was too loud and bright. My starved senses adjusted enough to see a golden sun unfurling over the entrance opposite, heralding Cyrus's appearance. A platform sat in the center of the Arena, a few feet off the ground. Suspiciously empty sands surrounded it. There would be plenty of surprises for us under the finely combed grains.

I sent one more prayer heavenward. Whispered one more goodbye to Lyra and August, and moved to meet him.

Cyrus raced for the platform, gaining the surface as I cleared the last step. He didn't hesitate, lunging forward to cross blades. The screams and shouts from the crowd nearly drowned out the clash of steel.

We circled, hammering away at each other like the first time we'd fought. Cyrus's face had sharpened to grim concentration—no trace of the quick laughter or friendly jibes I'd become accustomed to. No recognition. The feral edge was back.

Or so I thought.

He took an extra second to pull out of a lunge. I left my side exposed for a moment as he did, daring him to take the opening. End this all sooner. But he didn't. I pushed forward, driving him back. Even over the deafening sounds, his sandals scuffed the boards.

*Cyrus is taken care of.*

A curse rose to my lips, having nothing to do with the new attack he launched. This was different than the first fight, different than his victory that we'd planned together. This was labored, with no dramatic feinting or frustration around his eyes as he tried to draw out a fight.

I backpedaled, risking one glance over my shoulder to check the distance. No extra attack came, even though that moment would have been enough for him. Risking it, I jumped off the platform to the sands.

He followed, stumbling an extra step as he landed.

"Cyrus!" I shouted, hoping he'd hear me. Somehow. "What did they do?"

He didn't answer, just charged again with his lips clamped grimly shut. I let him drive me back a few paces, then blocked a strike, sliding my blade to lock against the hilt of his as I crowded dangerously close.

"What did he do to you?" I yelled before disengaging. Forget Octavian and the board and the impossible choices they'd given. Forget what I'd decided in the darkness and silence. Even if Cyrus replied, there was nothing I could do to Octavian right now. But I could still find some way to protect my wingmate.

Cyrus's next swing faltered for a heartbeat. A flicker of frustration crossed his face, and he bit out, "Flavius and his friends. Venom of some kind. Probably Octavian was behind it." He put more power into his next blow, shoving me backward another step. "Everything is...slow."

I barked a curse and kept retreating. We were close to the southern rim of the Arena, scraps of cloth fluttering around us—gold and silver. They'd slowed him down and ordered me to finish him off.

But I hadn't agreed to that.

My feet swept back and back until I felt a *click* under my heel. A harsher curse escaped with my "Run!"

I sprinted away from the trigger, hoping Cyrus had heard. Then the ground shook, and sand rained down around me.

CYRUS

I was almost too slow.

Like everything else since this morning, *too slow*. Bastian's warning had barely registered before the ground erupted, a reverberation going through my chest and sending me stumbling. I shook sand from my eyes, coughing and spluttering as the dust settled.

Bastian had also escaped the blast, circling to the foot of the platform's eastern steps. He was already settled into a guarded stance, and the pitch of the crowd overhead proclaimed that I'd taken a moment too long to recover from the blast. My head rang, and my skin stung where sand had scorched it. And gods, I was *tired*.

For a moment, I considered dropping my sword, letting Bastian walk out victorious as the board had planned. Then his furious curse from a moment ago flashed through my mind. If just *hearing* what Octavian had done to even the odds made him react that way, what would the days of victory bring?

Cold sealed over my heart, and I sprinted toward him.

Our blades met with a screech of metal, and he stumbled with how fast I'd crashed into him. Just like that, we were back to circling, his height versus my speed—only, I could still feel the half-heartbeat of hesitation coating each muscle, slowing each strike, capturing each thought just long enough to make me afraid.

He was holding back. I could feel it. But what if he actually fought like I knew he was capable of? What if he succeeded in killing me, only to face the life that both of us had tried so desperately to escape? A stab of pain went through my chest that had nothing to do with injury or exertion. He'd saved me more than once, but now all I could do was make sure he'd never have to suffer the way I had.

In the serpentine pattern of strike versus block, counter versus dodge, we'd circled halfway around the platform that dominated the center of the Arena. My eyes scanned the open area behind Bastian that mirrored the spot on the other side of the platform where the ground had exploded beneath us. Memory returned in a flash.

*They're always in the same spot,* I'd told him weeks ago. *It's a pattern, see?*

Bastian might not remember, but I'd had years memorizing this field. The roar of the crowd shifted to something excited and eager as I put more strength into my strikes, pushing him back, back, back toward the innocuous square of sand that held several explosive charges.

A last furious push, and he stood among them, readying his sword to counterattack. I'd seen the trigger plate etched in the sand, and wasted no time in stamping my foot on it.

"I'm sorry!" I shouted.

*I'm sorry for all of it.*

Bastian was sent flying by the explosion, thrown from his feet to land with his shoulder taking most of the impact. His left hand clutched at his side, and for one moment he lay still. Long enough for me to lunge. My knee scraped the sand and a hand darted out to pin his sword arm to the ground, blade poised to plunge through his throat and end the misery for at least one of us.

But despite every instinct screaming at me to do it, I couldn't.

And he knew it.

"It's all right, Cyrus," Bastian said, tilting his chin up to expose more of his throat. "I'd rather it be you."

A pained gasp—almost a sob—tore out of my chest. "Bas, I'm sorry. I can't."

The crowd overhead was a distant noise in my ears. Bastian's eyes widened behind his visor as I dropped my sword, releasing the pressure against his arm and pulling him to his feet instead.

"Cyrus, what—"

He didn't have time to say anything else before I threw my arms around him. "I can't do this, Bas," I said over the confused sounds from the crowd. "They're going to have to contend with both of us now."

A short laugh came from him, and he let me go before reaching up to undo the straps of his helmet and pull it off. My stomach flipped at the new bruising all over his face, the cut in his hairline, the swelling across his jaw.

"You idiot," he said, then pulled me into another hug.

"Me? *You're* the idiot." I thumped his back before pulling away and grabbing my sword from the sand. "You were just going to let me kill you?"

He shrugged. "Felt like if you were alive, you'd have another chance to get out."

The venom from a few hours ago must've been wearing off. Even amid all the noise, I caught a screech of metal—the tunnel grates creaking open. I tipped my head to hear better, then drew into a defensive stance as shouts came from both Bastian's tunnel and mine. "Well, we're going to have to settle it later. If we're given the chance. Ready?"

Bastian flashed a crooked smile. "To defy the odds? Always." He spun toward the board's box, holding up one hand in a gesture that sent a new pitch through the crowd before he pulled on his helmet and scooped up his sword.

I drew closer to him, angling so each of us could keep our opponents in view. "They wanted a show, huh?" A reckless laugh filled my chest. "Let's give them a show."

# CHAPTER XXXV

BASTIAN

A quick scan of the Arena showed five opponents coming our way. Three from Cyrus's tunnel, and two from mine.

"Do you feel up for this?" I asked over my shoulder.

Cyrus rolled his neck and settled his sword in his hand. "I think it's wearing off. At least I noticed them coming." He gave me a dangerous grin. "Don't worry about me."

"Too late." I dropped to a crouch. "Wingmates, Cyrus," I reminded him as the fighters charged. "I've got your back."

"I'll watch yours." He pivoted to face the tunnel he'd originally run through, keeping a shoulder to me as the first fighter reached him.

I trusted my back to him as I crossed blades with one of the men—a lower-level solo fighter I'd trained against days ago. The look in his eyes mirrored his strikes—desperate. Until his fellow joined him.

I wove away from their joint attacks, trying to keep space but not abandon Cyrus. The gaping hole in the sand loomed in my periphery. *Sets of three.* I kicked up dust, startling them enough to give me space to head for the corner. They followed, circling as I did, putting their backs to the wall.

I allowed a faint smile as I backed up and they advanced. One found the trigger based on his pause, mouth opening in a shout before the ground heaved again. He was thrown into the wall, where he lay twisted and still. The other was sent to his knees, stunned enough for me to deal a killing blow and retreat to Cyrus.

Cyrus was moving quicker than he had been earlier, even as his opponents tried to wedge him toward the wall. But he didn't see the third man circling, keeping the others between him and Cyrus until he was ready to strike.

*Flavius.*

Cold fury gave me speed, and I sprinted toward the former second. He barely saw me coming, whipping toward me with a sloppy block. I hammered the sword from his grip, dodged the fist he threw, and rammed my sword through his throat.

I pivoted toward Cyrus to find him pulling his bloody sword free. The other two men were dead or dying on the sands. He crossed to my side, shaking blood from his sword and pushing sweaty hair from his face. "Was that Flavius?"

"It was. May his scales weigh toward damnation," I spat.

Something like relief crossed Cyrus's face, and for a moment I saw the youth he'd once been, thrown into this too early with no one to watch his back. "He's better off this way. You're all right?"

"Only sorry I didn't do it sooner," I replied. But my ribs were protesting after being hurled to the ground, and we faced a fight that was likely far from done. I turned a slow circle, watching for the next strike. There would be one.

The crowd was uncertain. Some were still cheering, others watching in grim silence. A disconcerting chill hit my arms. They felt the change in temperature too, based on their shifting and the new murmurs starting.

And we had other concerns. The third gate was creaking open, roaring filling the tunnel. Now *that* sounded like the juvenile wyvern I was originally meant to fight.

Cyrus's head whipped around, fear lighting his face. "Wyvern."

A flash of color distracted me as a strip of bright turquoise fluttered to the sands. My squad's colors. The color of the flag Cyrus had planted to let my men know all was well. My heart froze before freeing itself to race in a frantic pattern that felt a little like hope. More and more fell, and I scanned the crowd, unable to find a familiar face.

But gryphon riders wouldn't be coming from the ground.

I turned to Cyrus, gripping his arm. "They're coming, Cyrus." I pointed at the ribbons. "We just have to hold on a little longer."

Understanding broke over his face, and dangerous hope flared to life in his eyes.

The tunnel stood open, and another furious roar echoed out. We had swords against a wyvern, and gods grant this one didn't have smoke yet. We exchanged one look and readied our blades before the creature burst onto the sands.

## CYRUS

A chill went through my limbs as the wyvern surged out of the tunnel. Fear, maybe, or venom working its way out of my body, but it also felt like the air was growing colder. As the creature lashed around, snapping at whomever had driven it from the tunnel, I cast about on the sand for anything else I could use to defend against it. One of the men I'd just sent to the gods was still clutching a spear in bloodied hands, and I dashed to pry it from his grip.

"Here!" I tossed the spear to Bastian. "Try to keep it busy. Blind it if you can!"

I caught his shout of agreement before we both took off running toward the center platform, the wyvern twisting in the space between it and the gate it'd exited from. Scraps of bright blue fabric were still falling into the Arena, and I wondered how many people the riders had handed them out to. The wooden platform echoed as my feet fell on the steps, reverberations twinned by another roar as the wyvern noticed us sprinting at it. This one *was* smaller than the adult Bastian had taken on a week and a half ago, its wings barely developed and scales a duller color. Hopefully, it wouldn't be able to poison us.

Bastian cut away to the left, yelling and brandishing the spear to force the wyvern's attention toward him. I veered the opposite way, jumping from the platform to land in the dust near one of the hind legs. Wickedly sharp claws cut through the air as it reared, avoiding the spear in Bastian's hand, and I took the moment when its weight was farther back to drive my sword through one of its hind feet.

The wyvern screeched, forefeet falling to the ground as it wheeled to snap in my direction. I dodged, skipping over the lashing tail and swinging my sword to lop off the barbed end. The wyvern screamed again, then shuddered as Bastian thrust the spearpoint into its exposed shoulder. Teeth snapping, it whirled on him, mouth closing on the spear haft as its tail lashed around to counterbalance.

Scales impacted my shins and I toppled to hit the ground, a heavy buffet landing against my shoulder as the tail struck again. I swore and rolled to an elbow, cutting outward and carving another gash in the tail before regaining my feet.

A splintering crunch announced that the wyvern had made quick work of the spear haft, and a shout from Bastian warned that it was slithering up to place its forefeet on the platform where he was standing. It struck out at him, and he dodged its teeth before a clawed foreleg caught his right side. A cry of pain broke from him, and I glanced up to see several furrows dragged across the moon and stars design on his breastplate.

The wyvern shifted again, gathering its weight to clamber fully onto the platform, and I seized the moment to slide beneath it and stab up into its belly. Thick blood poured from the wound as I withdrew my blade, dodging the torrent and getting as much distance as I could while it contorted around the injury. The shadows shifted strangely as I did, like my eyes were seeing everything with a mirror image trailing behind.

"Get out of there!" Bastian shouted, swinging his sword to deflect another bite.

I turned to obey, but a claw caught my side and sent shooting pain through the gap between breastplate and backplate. I hurtled to the sand, air leaving my lungs in a startled gasp. The wyvern shifted, claws trapped in the buckles of my armor, and I reached up to hack at the scales with desperate motions.

A dark blur went past as I struggled, pale light catching on a helmet, and Bastian stood between me and the wyvern. With a wordless shout, he drove his sword into its belly, close to the spot where I'd wounded it. With a last screech, the creature collapsed, its head and neck flopping to the platform surface before it slid into a shuddering mess on the sand. I was wrenched sideways as the thing fell, claws twisting against my side and threatening to pull the straps of my armor apart. A moment later, Bastian was kneeling beside me, and within a few seconds of prying and pulling I was free.

I caught my breath, staggering to my feet and glancing at the damage done to my armor. "Thank you."

"Did the claws cut you?"

I winced and nodded. "I'm not certain how badly." I pulled the armor away enough to reach beneath it. My hand came away coated in blood. Bastian swore at the sight, and I gritted my teeth against a wave of pain. "Maybe it's not as bad as it looks."

He gently clapped my shoulder. "Let's hope, since I doubt that's the last Octavian has to offer."

I spat in the sand. "You said we had to hold on. Any idea for how long?" I looked up at the sky. The sunlight was chilly, and even the bright ribbons littering the sand looked drained of their color.

Bastian shook his head. "This is the eclipse?" He pointed at the wavering shadows with a hollow laugh. "It feels cursed."

I shivered, the cold unnatural in contrast to the warmth of blood against my skin. My hand went to the wound again. There were at least *two* spots where claws had gouged my side. And my shoulder ached from being hit by the creature's tail. "Any guesses as to what they'll throw at us next? And how soon?"

No sooner had I asked than another trumpet sounded, and shouts came from the tunnels. Bastian had been squinting at the sky, but now he straightened and turned to peer over the platform. "I don't think it's going to slow. Let's get up there. At least then we'll be able to see it coming."

I accepted his hand up onto the platform, side cramping as he pulled me after him. Between the wavering shadows, the uncanny cold, and the subdued crowd as more and more things went unexpectedly, the Arena felt like it'd been cast into twilight.

Or a nightmare.

*The sun's light will be blotted out.*

Suddenly, the design on my breastplate felt like a target. And as a new wave of opponents rushed from the tunnels to face us, I prayed we could hold on long enough to see freedom emerging from the darkness.

## BASTIAN

As we gained the higher surface, I glanced at the Arena roofs. Hoping. And finding nothing. A flock of doves darted under the eaves, daring the noise of the crowds. Simmering unease felt weighty in the air.

*Come on, Felix.* It felt more like a prayer.

Sweat stung the corners of my eyes, and a stabbing sensation hit my ribs. We weren't the only ones looking toward the entry gates. Some onlookers shouted and pointed, a pitch in their voices like they were trying to warn us of oncoming danger. A figure stood in the tunnel still marked by my banner—Octavian.

Even yards away, he met my glare. Anger stretched taut between us, and I slowly, deliberately, stepped in front of Cyrus.

Octavian shook his head. *What a waste.* I could see him thinking it. Only to him.

He rested a hand on his sword, and for a moment it seemed like he might take the sands against us himself. Then he paused, likely knowing we'd be no more merciful to him than he had been to us, and made way for a new wave of opponents.

These seemed eager and impetuous, armed with spears and thick, metal-studded staffs usually used for subduing young dragons. I glanced over my shoulder to where Cyrus faced down swords and more spears. As one, we took a step toward the center of the platform, drawing closer together.

"Ten or more total," I reported.

"Same," was his grim estimate. "They are coming, right? Your men?"

I shifted the leather grip in my palm. The ribbons weren't an accident. They'd promised they'd be back, and I should have believed them. "They're coming."

We set our backs to each other one more time. Even with the numbers against us, our opponents still had to make it up the narrow stairs. Two staff wielders charged first, and I strode toward the west steps. They had to come up one at a time, making it easier for me to cut them off before they reached the top. The first man twisted out of the way of my sword, losing his balance and falling off the steps. The man behind was caught off guard by his sudden disappearance and my quick descent and blade.

I retreated with his staff in hand.

Unfortunately, the rest learned from that. A spearman flanked another staff holder, striking up at me from the ground as his fellow climbed. I managed to block a prodding sweep with my staff, but not with enough time to prevent the second man from reaching the platform.

A whistling sound keened around the metal studs with each swing of the staff. I chucked mine at him and charged as he batted it out of the air. I moved in behind it, getting in close before he had a chance to recover. He stumbled, and I let his momentum take us closer to the edge before I pulled the sword free and he fell to earth.

Cyrus had a spear, sweeping clear the eastern steps before him. The wyvern's body blocked the southern steps, but the north was clear, a swordsman making his way up.

"Cyrus! Left!" I shouted. He didn't hesitate, spinning in a tight circle with spear raised. A cry was all I heard as I faced off with two more men coming up the west steps. The shadows were growing, the chill at odds with the fight surging through my veins. The shouts of opponents were louder than they ever had been, the crowd still caught in the uncertainty of everything that was happening. Even some of the fighters had paused, pointing up at the sky. A few backed away, wide-eyed fear crossing their faces.

I ducked a swing from a staff, but this man was quicker, stronger than those before. He'd held back to evaluate the field first. We traded blows, and I twisted and dodged away from his sweeping strike, sharpened steel points coming close to cutting me a few times. It gave another man enough time to climb to the top.

Some signal passed between them, and their tactics changed. I cursed as the newcomer started sweeping at my feet, while the smarter one swung high at my head. There was enough noise from Cyrus and his opponents that I couldn't yell for help.

They drove me toward the edge of the platform. I caught the higher staff against my sword, trying to trap the other beneath a foot. It worked for a split second before the pressure against my sword let up, sending me lurching forward against the lack of resistance. The weapon under my foot heaved, further throwing me off-balance. And I caught the hissing sound too late.

Bright, nauseating pain hit my left arm as I tried to block. Numbness chased after it as I went to a knee under the force of the impact. A foot hit my chest, throwing me back. Darkness threatened the corners of my vision, clearing just enough for me to see the men looming overhead.

Enough alertness remained for me to roll, finding the edge of the platform and falling.

"Bastian!" Cyrus's yell was dim. I coughed and tried to get to my feet. One of the men jumped after me and I lunged upward, felling him. Another spearman had seen my fall and charged. He thrust and I tried to twist, but the point caught my breastplate, right on one of the grooves torn by the wyvern.

The pain in my ribs now had competition from the spear tip pushing through the weakened leather. He pushed me into the platform, its edge arresting my motion. My shout was half pain, half helpless fury as he hauled on the spear, yanking me forward as it ripped from the leather. Before he could thrust again, there was a familiar yell and a spear impacted my opponent, hurling him to the ground.

"Bas!"

I unsteadily put my back to the platform again. Two men with yellow-splotched breastplates circled toward me on my left. I recognized neither from my first days of fighting on the same team. The surviving staff-wielder edged closer to my right.

Numbness clung to my arm despite the blood oozing from torn skin above my bracer. My breath came short, and the darkness was growing.

A flash of gold and red, oddly muted now, descended in my periphery to take the staff-wielder down with a shout.

"What are you doing?" A wheeze coated my shout.

"Helping!" Cyrus called as he gained his feet and attacked a new oncoming spearman.

The yellow team charged as one. Time moved slower for me now, my balance off with my left arm hanging uselessly at my side.

A sword sliced my thigh. I stabbed in return, as another strike hit my unguarded left side. The leather turned the sword point, but the impact still sent me to the ground. I swept at the nearest legs, slicing deep and sending the man hobbling back.

I got halfway up before steel hit my helmet, pitching me forward. Pain slashed across my shoulder as I tried to roll again, to get away from both of them. Then into my hip just below my breastplate.

My name barely echoed over the reverberations still clinging to the helmet. Darkness had swallowed the sky, and was pressing down around me. I caught a glimpse of Cyrus standing over me, and above him...*wings*.

# CHAPTER XXXVI

CYRUS

I freed my sword and spun to help Bastian as the Arena grew tinged with the cast of night. Eerie silence had filled the air, so much so that the only thing I heard was his scream as a blade bit into his hip. I yelled his name frantically and charged the two men, finishing one with a blade through the side and bringing the other to the ground with a strike to the side of the head.

In those short seconds, darkness had fallen completely. There weren't any more opponents—not that I could tell—and the hush over the Arena reminded me of the dead of night. I tipped my head up to look for the sun, and froze at the sight of a ring of fiery light surrounding a pitch-black orb.

*The sun's...gone.*

At that moment, I caught a sound as unexpected as the darkness. A rustling, whooshing sound, reminiscent of the doves that had fled for shelter only minutes before. And at the edge of the ring of light, a shadow flickered past the sun. Somewhere nearby, Bastian gasped, and the realization came as clearly as if I'd seen it with my eyes.

Gryphons. Here. Now.

In the Arena.

The ground vibrated beneath my feet as first one, then another, then two more massive creatures landed nearby. I shook myself from the immediate instinct to strike and ran toward where I'd last seen Bastian. The pale band across his armor glowed in the darkness, as panicked cries rang from the stands above.

"Bastian!" I dropped to a knee beside him, my hands finding the straps of his armor and hauling him to sit against the platform. My side hadn't stopped aching since we'd first climbed onto the platform and my armor was sticky with blood, but even the brief glance I'd had of Bastian's injuries told me that the gouges in my side were the least of our worries.

Voices came from all around me, confident and laced with danger.

"Commander's hurt bad."

"Someone grab the tethers. He'll have to ride in front."

I tightened my hold under Bastian's arms and stood, assisted by someone else at his feet. A dark shape loomed above on the platform, resolving into a gryphon crouched with its belly almost touching the ground. Before I could panic, the other riders had gotten Bastian into the saddle and were securing him in front of the still-mounted rider.

A hand caught my shoulder, and I wheeled to see a figure wearing a familiar helmet, his shape flanked by the bulk of another gryphon. "Let's get you two out of here."

"Hang on, I need to stay with him!" I pulled away from the rider holding my arm. "He's hurt, and—"

A raspy laugh came through the darkness. "He'll be all right. Trust us. We know what we're doing." He tapped my shoulder again. "Here. Ride with me."

I was about to argue again, when a ray of light streaked from behind the moon.

*No time.*

I grabbed Felix's hand and clambered up behind him, the gryphon shifting its weight and adjusting its wings impatiently. His arm snaked around me for a moment, looping a tether to secure me in the saddle. The sky was already lightening, and now I could see Bastian atop the gryphon on the platform, the rider's arm around his chest. He wasn't moving, and worry snared my heart.

*Hold on, Bas. Just hold on.*

A rush of sound came with the sunlight, as the crowds above realized what was happening below. Sand flew as the remaining riders returned to their mounts, the creatures unfurling massive wings and leaping into the air.

"Hold on!" Felix ordered, and the ground fell away beneath us, the Arena shrinking faster than I'd ever believed possible as true sunlight spilled into the air.

Astonished cries faded behind us, the ever-present hum of the place I'd lived my whole life giving way to the rushing of feathers, cool wind blowing against my face, and an unmistakable but completely foreign feeling of weightlessness.

Just like in my dreams.

I twisted to look back at the Arena, its tiled roof already diminishing behind us. "Where are we going?" I yelled over the wind.

Felix's answer came instantly. "We're taking you home."

# CHAPTER XXXVII

BASTIAN

T he soft sound of singing drew me out of the darkness, bringing me to warmth and hazy golden light. Softness surrounded me, beckoning me back toward sleep. I shifted slightly, and the scent of lavender crept through. The voice sang a lullaby, the melody rising and falling with another gentle *shushing* in the distance.

The sea.

Home.

My eyes opened, blinking a few times against the pouring sunlight. I lay on my side, blankets tucked around me. I looked first to my left arm resting on the bed, bandaged and splinted. To my relief, my fingers were warm and moved clumsily. Then I tracked up to find the owner of the voice.

Lyra sat a few paces away, leaning forward over a cradle. A dark braid fell over her shoulder, a smile on her face as she sang while she gently rocked our son.

Emotion hit my chest so hard it felt like the spear wedging through my armor again. The sunlight gathered around her in a halo, making me feel for a moment like it wasn't real. Like I'd been granted some last vision of Lyra happy and content before I passed on into the afterlife. If it weren't for the splint on my arm and the awareness of injury all over, I might have believed it.

Lyra glanced over, and a smile bloomed across her face. She crossed to the bed in a heartbeat, sitting and taking my uninjured hand in hers.

"Bastian." The blue of her eyes brightened with threatening tears. I freed my hand to touch her face, just to make sure she was real. She reclaimed her hold, brushing her other hand against my forehead. "How do you feel?" she asked.

"Alive," I said, voice hoarse.

"Good," she said, barely above a whisper.

I tugged her hand. "Come here."

"Bastian, you're hurt," she protested, but leaned closer.

"I can still kiss you."

She laughed softly and pressed her lips to mine. Her caution vanished in a moment as something desperate took us both. Desperation, longing, the loneliness of a year and a month an Empire apart, of three more months with bars between us. She braced her arms on either side of me as I wrapped mine around her.

"I thought I was hurt?" I said between one kiss and another.

"Hush." She kissed away my laugh until her arm gently bumped my shoulder, causing me to pull back slightly with a hissing breath. I fore-stalled her apology with another kiss.

She sat back, though still bent close. "I was starting to think I'd nev-er..." She didn't finish, chin trembling and tears beading her dark lashes. I gently nudged her arm and she curled up next to me, head against my chest. Her fingers clutched my soft linen tunic. "It's been...*so long*..."

"One year, three months, and three weeks," I whispered against her forehead.

"And six days." Her words hitched.

I tightened my arms around her. I'd lost two days somewhere. "I'm here now."

"If you even *think* about leaving again..." A sob still laced her voice.

I pressed a kiss to the top of her head. "You'll be sick of me by next week." I tried to keep the words light, but the way we tucked closer to each other belied them. Her warmth felt enough to keep the darkness of the last days and months at bay for a little while longer. This wouldn't be the first time I'd brought some home with me. She hadn't flinched when it'd woken me in the middle of the night before, and I knew she wouldn't now. Not even when I eventually told her some of what had happened.

"I'm sorry," I said softly.

"You couldn't have lived with yourself if you'd followed those orders months ago, Bas. Don't be sorry." She tilted her head up to look me in the eye.

I managed a faint smile. An unfamiliar sound broke, and the cradle rocked slightly, drawing another happy coo. It brought a new pang to my heart.

Lyra smiled and carefully lifted herself out of my arms. She went to the cradle and bent over it, nose scrunching up with her smile as tiny arms waved. She scooped August up in a bundle of blankets and brought him over. I managed to push myself a little taller against the pillows.

Lyra settled him between us as she reclaimed a seat on the bed. August's bright blue eyes settled on me and an echo of his mother's smile flashed as I brushed a finger against his cheek. He grabbed my finger, making another happy sound.

"Your grandfather hasn't put you on a gryphon yet, has he?" I asked. He grinned like he understood, trying to eat my finger a moment after.

"No," Lyra said. "Father said that was for you to do. He'll be glad to see you awake. He and I paced grooves in the tiles until they brought you in last night."

August leaned forward precariously, trying to grab my hand again. He half tumbled from sitting, seeming surprised to end up on his stomach.

"He could have finally been rid of me," I said, and Lyra pursed her lips. "You could have remarried any one of the—how many was it? One hundred and eight other suitors?"

She laughed. "One hundred and nine, I think." She reached over to the low table and picked up braided leather and dragon scale. I lifted my head enough for her to loop the leather around my neck and fasten it like she had on our wedding day. "And you're the only one I ever wanted."

I kissed her hand as she pulled away, leaving the scale to settle right under my collarbone, its slight weight enough to fill up at least one of the small pieces of emptiness. The way her fingers skimmed the rim of my right ear, telling me the slave earring was gone, softened another fracture inside.

Lyra's hand combed through my hair as she studied me another moment. It made me painfully aware of every bruise and cut I could feel all over my body. A shaky inhale came before she pressed her lips tightly together.

"I'll be all right," I whispered softly.

"I know," she replied in kind.

August got hands against my chest and started reaching, intently focused on the scale. I shifted to keep him off my tender ribs, but let him lean against me as he started tugging at the cord. I brushed his dark hair, not stopping him except to make sure he didn't grip the scale too hard. I'd missed almost six months of his life and I wouldn't miss a moment more.

"Your father had to go check the stables. Father is with him to make sure he actually went." Lyra chuckled. "They'll be back soon."

I smiled. It had been well over a year since I'd seen my father. I'd be glad to see him again. "Does he have a colt picked out for August yet?"

"Of course he does." She laughed. August beamed, and I settled my hand against his back.

"Soon," I promised him. "We'll race the winds."

Lyra just shook her head, but didn't argue. Her own father had taken her up on gryphons as a child.

I had another promise to keep, too.

"How's Cyrus?" I asked.

"He slept until mid-morning, then I think he's been outside," she replied. "He's been on edge."

Pacing, more than likely, to try to ward off uncertainty. But if he was allowed outside, that meant his injuries weren't too bad. I dug my elbow into the bed, but August's protest and Lyra's hand against my chest stopped me.

"Don't even think about it, Bastian."

I lowered back and raised my hands in surrender. My son tried to shove a fistful of my tunic into his mouth next.

"Could you find him for me?" I asked. She nodded, giving a soft smile and leaving August with me.

CYRUS

It was so quiet here.

Granted, there were a few familiar sounds—squawks and clucks and shrieks of gryphons, the encouraging shouts of trainers, and thumps from the rings where riders practiced maneuvers on foot before trying them in the air.

But everything else? It was all different. The sun shone over an infinite sea, casting serene rays across rolling green hills. Breezes off the water brought smells of salt and moisture, and I'd yet to hear even a single voice raised in anger. The hum of the Arena was gone, leaving an echoing space that I wasn't sure how to fill.

After our arrival late the previous night, I'd collapsed into sleep after being reunited with a tearful Callista and having my injuries tended by the riders' medics. A cut on my left forearm would heal with barely the need of stitches. The gouges in my side from the wyvern's claws would take longer, but both I and the medic knew they hadn't been the most pressing injuries sustained in our escape.

I still hadn't seen Bastian. Hadn't heard anything beyond that he was asleep and would recover with enough rest. The news didn't settle the restlessness that'd set in almost as soon as I'd woken close to midday. By the time I'd eaten and met the others in the house—including a woman with dark hair and blue eyes who'd hugged me strongly enough that she *had* to be Bastian's wife—I was aching for a chance to disappear into the heights.

Only, here the heights were barely three stories tall, and everyone knew to look up.

Callista found me outside, pacing in tight circles around a garden where herbs intermingled with flowers in messy beds. "You're awake! Why didn't you come find me?"

I stopped pacing and reached out to her, the sound of her voice doing something to quiet the restlessness. "I don't know. Habit, I suppose."

Habit, to not seek her out. To not draw attention to the way she calmed my restlessness, steadied my heart, put surety in my steps.

A habit that—gods, I could hardly believe it—might no longer serve me.

I tightened my arms around her. "I'm sorry. I'm not used to being somewhere where it's safe to acknowledge you openly. It's..." I swallowed hard and looked over the top of her head toward the sea. "It might take me some time to get used to it."

Callista nodded and slipped from my embrace. "We'll both have to learn." She bent to pick a purple flower from the shade of a taller plant. "But we have the rest of our lives now."

"We do." The admission felt almost foreign in my mouth, so I tried again. "We do, but... Lis, I don't know if you feel differently now that—"

I stopped as Callista gave me a severe look.

"Don't." She tucked the flower behind her ear. "Don't you dare. I loved you when you were trapped in a golden prison, and I love you now that you're free to fly." She nodded toward the entrance of the garden, where a fig tree guarded a path that wound around the house. "Go let the place settle. I'll find you in a bit."

"All right..." I began walking, then stopped to look over my shoulder. "You're certain?"

Callista laughed. "I'm certain. Just go for a walk!"

I did as she said, following the path until it ended at a well, then continuing until I found myself under several old trees within sight of the road. Hills stretched beyond to meet the sea, the vast sky opened over all of it, and I stopped with the sight itself threatening to overwhelm.

*Everything's so...big. So open.* I tucked my arms tight to my ribs. *Too open.*

I eyed the road that led inland toward the capital. For a moment, I almost wanted to go back. Face the familiarity and misery of what I'd left behind, instead of the uncertain future. Then a voice broke the echoing silence, and I caught sight of Lyra approaching from the house.

"Cyrus! He's awake!"

That news was enough to shatter the tension, and I hurried past her to re-enter the house. They'd put Bastian in a room on the ground floor, and the door stood open to allow the sounds of laughter into the rest of the house. It was strange to hear his voice pitched that way, after so many months of tension. And the warbling gurgle that answered him was entirely unknown. I stepped through the door and almost jumped out of my skin at the sight of my wingmate with a baby balanced on his chest. Another shocked glance confirmed my suspicions—the little boy had hair just like Bastian's, and I'd wager anything that the blue eyes had come from Lyra.

"When were you planning on telling me about this?" I gasped, falling to a seat at the edge of the bed.

"I barely let *myself* think about it since finding out he existed three months ago," Bastian replied, wincing as he shifted the boy on his chest.

*Three months.* I blinked hard as the knowledge slid into place, stammering, "No wonder you were being so gods-touched stubborn! You didn't—Bas, why didn't you *say* something?"

"Lyra would argue that I'm *always* stubborn." He crooked a smile past me.

"You are," she said from the doorway, crossing to scoop the baby from her husband's chest and give him a stern look. "I told you to keep him *off* your ribs."

"Did you?" he asked innocently.

She pursed her lips and bent to kiss him before touching my shoulder with a smile. "Do *not* let him get up."

"Don't worry," I said. "He's not going anywhere."

She left with the baby draped over her shoulder, his delighted gurgles fading as she let the door fall closed behind her.

"Are you all right?" I asked immediately. "It was such chaos when we got here—I didn't know anything. And right at the end—Bas, I'm so sorry I wasn't fast enough."

"Cyrus." He reached out with his splinted arm, still managing to tap my hand. "It's all right. You couldn't have done anything. Not with how many men there were."

"I lost count. I think they must've told anyone that wanted a chance to stab us to take the sands." I buried my face in my hands. "Gods, I never want to be that scared again. We fought a *wyvern*. And half the Arena."

A grunt of pain marked Bastian pushing himself upright. He lifted a hand to forestall my protest. "I'm not getting *out* of bed," he said before leaning forward and pulling me into a hug. "We're probably immortal by now."

A laugh shook my chest, and I wrapped my arms around him. "Octavian's going to be *furious*. All this time, he wanted to be remembered as the man who created legends, and we created an even better one on our own."

His soft laugh sounded so free. "He can choke and die on the legend for all I care." He tapped my shoulder and let me help him back to the pillows. "Now, how are *you*?" The assessing look he gave was so different from Octavian and anyone before that. Like he cared enough to really *see*.

I sighed, letting my hands fall to my lap. "It's...different here. Quiet. *Too* quiet. I don't..." My fingers tightened into fists. "I don't know what to do. Where I fit." A thought struck me, and I raised my head. "You've been a soldier for years. Did it ever feel like this when you'd come home?"

"Every time," he said softly. "Sometimes it only took days to settle, sometimes weeks. It's a little easier when someone who knows what you fought is around. Don't worry if it takes some time. And I'll be here if you still want a wingmate."

The simple statement sent tears to my eyes, and I ducked my head to scrub them away. "Sorry. I'd..." I took a deep breath. "I think I still need someone watching my back. And the gods know you're stubborn enough to knock me flat if I try anything stupid."

He chuckled. "And I'll help you up after. And, Cyrus, rule number one. Don't apologize unless you've done something wrong."

"I'm terrible with rules." I laughed and raised a hand to wipe the last few tears away. "Thank you."

"You're welcome," he said simply. "And you'd better get used to a few rules. Leonis has a whole list for riders, and we still need to get you properly in the air on a gryphon."

I nodded. After clearing the city's borders, the riders had set down near an abandoned shepherd's hut on the edge of some woods. We'd hidden there for several hours, seeing to Bastian's injuries and waiting for nightfall before taking off again. The rest of the journey had been fraught with tension even with the reassurance that Bastian would survive, and I'd barely paid attention to the weightlessness of flight.

"Once you're recovered," I told him. "*Fully* recovered. I can wait until then. For now"—I forced my shoulders to relax and lightness to return to my voice—"I think I need to learn how to handle a baby. Since apparently you're a father now."

Bastian smiled. "I didn't say anything only because I could barely stand to think about losing Lyra. I couldn't think about losing a son I hadn't even been able to hold yet. I was gone for a year on campaign before coming to the Arena. I..." He shook his head. "I had to keep fighting as long as I could for a chance to see them again."

"And you won," I told him quietly. I looked around the small room, the quiet not bothering me as much as it had before. "We both did. Maybe someday I'll actually understand how."

"Someone was watching."

"I think so." A smile tugged at my mouth. So many years in the public eye, and it had all come down to someone *seeing* me. "I'm glad I looked back."

# CHAPTER XXXVIII

It was another week before Lyra let Bastian out of the house, and several days after that before his father-in-law let him near the gryphons. After that, every day saw us in the stables, him showing me everything I'd never known about the majestic animals. Bit by bit, the restlessness in my blood settled, shushed by the whisper of waves against the shore, until the remembered drone of the Arena only visited in nightmares.

It was about three weeks later that the visitor came. Bastian and I were coming back from watching Leonis train a fledgling to its first harness, and had just stepped onto the wide patio of Lyra's childhood home when her mother came around the corner with a concerned expression.

"Bastian—oh! Cyrus, you too." She gestured toward the front of the house. "There's someone here from the capital, with a message for you."

Fear immediately flared in my heart, and I looked at Bastian to see the same reflected in his eyes. We hadn't heard a single thing from the Arena or the capital since the riders had departed and returned to their unit commanders. Only a brief note reassuring Bastian that their involvement wasn't known and their lives and ranks were safe. Not a word, not a threat—nothing. I'd thought the silence was worse than anything, but now I feared it had been the false calm before a terrible onslaught of retribution.

Bastian and I rounded the corner as one, poised to attack, then stopped. Bastian started laughing first, and a wash of relief broke through me with the sound. The newcomer was a grey-haired man, dressed for travel, bending to chuck August under the chin as Lyra smiled at him.

"He's perfect," Atticus informed her as he straightened. "Takes after you, thank the gods. I—oof!" The rest of whatever he'd been about to say got cut off by me crashing into him. For a moment, things were happy chaos as he hugged both of us fiercely, then cuffed our heads and admonished, "I know I said 'don't tell me your plans,' but you didn't have to take me that seriously! What were you thinking? You could've both been killed, and not even I would've been able to save you!"

Bastian held up his hands innocently. "I know better than to disobey my superiors. You gave me an order."

"He's got you, sir." I hadn't been able to stop smiling since seeing him, and the look on his face was enough to send me into laughter once more. "I'm just glad you didn't get pulled in with us."

The expression on Atticus's face sobered. "Octavian had his suspicions, but couldn't prove anything. He's been furious, but I suspect he has more than enough on his hands with both of you gone and the public wondering what's next." He raised an eyebrow as I stilled, my muscles locking up at the mention of Octavian's name.

"What's...*next*?" I managed, voice hoarse. "Are they coming after us?"

Relief dissipated the frozen feeling as Atticus shook his head. "That would cause even more of a stir, and I suspect they can't afford it. They're taking the events surrounding your escape and letting them be the catalyst for changes in how things are run. I saw some new events going onto the schedule for next month—team trials in combination with riders from the gryphon races."

"That'll be a change. Rely on skill instead of ruthlessness to entertain the crowds?" Bastian said with a scoff as he took August from Lyra. The baby immediately began gnawing on the cord of his marriage necklace, and he rotated it enough to keep the scale out of August's mouth. "The gods must be laughing, but maybe it'll mean less work for you."

"Gods all grant it," Atticus agreed. "It's a gamble for everyone involved, but I suspect it'll turn out well. Still, there's been enough suspicion thrown my way for my involvement with you two that I thought it was time I took some of the leave they've owed me for the last three years." He turned to dig through a bag, handing me a sealed document tube. "And I wanted to bring this to you in person."

I frowned as I took the container, more questions poised at the base of my tongue. Before I had the chance to let any of them fly, a delighted squeal came from the house and Callista pelted out to throw herself into Atticus's arms.

"You're here!" She wrapped her arms around him, tears shining in her eyes as he returned the embrace. "I've missed you so much! Look!" She stepped back, smoothing the front of her lilac dress with a glowing smile. "No more grey! And oh—did you meet Lyra?"

Both Bastian and I laughed at Atticus's bemused expression as Callista kept chattering. Freedom had settled on her much easier than it had on me, and it was a beautiful thing to see how readily Atticus softened in her presence. I'd almost forgotten the document tube in my hand until Bastian gently knocked against my elbow.

"You going to open it?"

"Oh." I flipped the tube over, running my finger under the seal and popping it loose. A document slid out, thick paper with the words transcribed in ink that held a distinctive coppery sheen. An *official* document, written in a clear hand that meant it'd been penned by an actual scribe.

Easy to read.

Not easy to understand.

Bastian noticed me shaking as the words sank in. He immediately passed August to Lyra, and his hand caught my elbow. "Cyrus, what's wrong?"

I raised my head. Handed Bastian the paper, and locked eyes with Atticus across the patio. My heartbeat was pounding in my ears like it did in battle, but this time there was nothing to fight.

There never would be again.

He smiled, and the gesture was all it took to send me crumpling to my knees with tears filling my eyes. Callista immediately rushed to my side, putting an arm around my shoulder. "What is it?"

Bastian passed the paper to her before taking a knee beside me. "Freedom is a new experience, isn't it?" He chuckled as I leaned my head against his shoulder, still trembling with shock.

Callista gasped, and her hands tensed around the paper. "...house of Apelles, with all the rights and dues thereof... Atticus!"

The physician knelt in front of me, Bastian moving aside to let him have space. One hand cupped the side of my head. "I couldn't think of any better way to ensure they'll never have a hold over you again. As a citizen, I'm within my rights to name whomever I want as my heir, and I couldn't be happier with my choice." His hands shifted to the top of my ear, prying open the thinned spot of my earring where the solder had long worn away. The gold band slid free, and he closed his fingers tightly over it. "Cyrus Apelles, you don't have to keep looking over your shoulder anymore."

"Atticus..." My voice broke. I'd never had a family name, or if I had, it'd been lost the day that I entered Arena service as a twelve-year-old orphan. "I can't."

"It's already done, son." He pulled me to my feet and wrapped his arms around me. "There's nothing you have to do, nothing you have to earn. It's yours. Besides"—he drew back to command my full attention—"anyone who's defied as many odds as you have deserves to have a certain future."

"I..." I stepped back, tremors rocking my stomach. "Thank you. I never—thank you." Callista slid her arm around my waist, and I stood taller. "You've done so much, and we owe you everything."

"Nonsense," he snorted, a smile quirking his mouth. "And if you keep being ridiculous about this, I'll start worrying that the years of fighting have done permanent damage to your mind."

"Might not be too late to wonder," Bastian cut in with a smirk.

I freed my hand from Callista's shoulder to gesture rudely in his direction. He only laughed and went to reclaim his son, tossing him in the air and ignoring Lyra's shaking head and fond smile.

"Will you stay?" Callista asked Atticus. "Surely you didn't come all this way only to leave again."

Atticus gave her an affectionate smile. "I have to return to the Arena soon. For whatever reason, the First God still has work for me there. But I can stay a little while." He tilted a sarcastic look at Bastian, who'd just winced after catching August. "I might be needed here, as well."

Bastian gave him an offended look and deliberately handed the baby to Lyra. "Not if anyone here has anything to say about it." He looked over my head toward the stables, and his face brightened. "Cyrus, let's go."

I straightened and released Callista. "Go? Where—"

He'd already walked past me. I rolled my eyes and bent to press a kiss into Callista's temple. "I'll be back. I think."

"Go," she urged, light dancing in her eyes. "I'll be here."

I stepped away, quickening my pace after Bastian. He rounded the stables, making for the side that faced the sea. In the space where sand turned to grass, a gryphon with feathers that glowed like sunlight through honey crouched with stable hands checking its harness. I stopped for a moment, certain that this was some kind of joke. Bastian had been recovered for weeks, yet had never mentioned a coming flight.

He stopped at the gryphon's head, raising a hand to its beak and muttering softly. Then he called over his shoulder, "You coming?"

My feet moved on their own, bringing me alongside him. The gryphon tipped its head to regard me with fierce amber eyes, its beak clacking softly.

"I think he likes you," Bastian said with a smile. He bent to a pile of gear on the grass, holding a helmet out to me. "Here."

I shook my head. "Not on your life."

"You'll need it," he warned.

"Not this time." Not the first time. If I was going to fly—*really* fly—I didn't want anything between me and the sun.

He rolled his eyes, but pulled on his own helmet. Before I knew it, I was atop the gryphon, harnessed in and holding tight to Bastian with something between panic and excitement stirring in my stomach.

"Hang on," Bastian called, then whistled a high-pitched, sharp command. Muscles bunched beneath us, the massive wings snapped open, then weight dropped into my stomach as the ground hurtled away from us. A startled yell broke from me as we climbed, then leveled out, Bastian guiding the gryphon in a wide circle around the house. Callista and Atticus had come out from beneath the patio, her purple dress and his traveling cloak a patch of color against the path as they waved. They disappeared behind the house as we climbed higher, circling the stables before angling toward the sea.

Water stretched before us in unbroken waves, the afternoon sun casting a brilliant path on its rippling surface. Air rushed past my face, almost too fast for comfort, as Bastian whistled again and took us into a climb. Force dragged us down, the sensation immediately erased as, with a flip of its wings, the gryphon dove.

Weightless. I was weightless.

And as we leveled off to skim the waves, I found myself whooping with exhilaration, Bastian's laugh sounding behind it. Sunlight gilded every single wave crest, turning the water to gold. And for the first time in years, I wasn't afraid. Not of the past, not of my present, and no longer of the future.

Freedom?

It was in trust. In friendship. In flight.

Maybe the next time, I'd even wear a helmet.

# ACKNOWLEDGMENTS

I've had "write *Fates Defiant* acknowledgments" on my to-do list for two months now, because to *acknowledge* something is to accept or admit the truth of it, and this book has had a whole lot of that.

The fact is, I couldn't have written this story by myself. "I don't understand," a certain POV character says on multiple occasions...and it's not just Cyrus talking. Once it sank in why this story, why *him*, I was terrified—but not alone. And that's the thing, isn't it? In writing with someone who'd already faced her share of monsters, I didn't have to be afraid of what we might encounter as the story unfolded.

So let's thank some people.

Laurel, who looked over the first outline, then exercised absolutely heartbreaking discretion by keeping it a secret for years. Your enthusiasm conceals such sharp intuition, and I treasure your input.

Robin for making up the tail of a make-believe lizard during writing retreat, providing excellent feedback on the beta draft, and being a most reliable sounding board when it comes to my hare-brained schemes.

Elisabeth—cartographer, drawer-of-monsters, harshest critic & strongest believer, best beloved soul-bound sister. This project creatively stretched us both, yet here we are. I couldn't be happier to have had you with me through it all.

Jenni, for being Jenni. You make more out of 60% effort than anyone I know. Without you, this story wouldn't have as strong an emotional core, which would've been a travesty. Thanks for helping pinpoint the why behind Cyrus. He's so much better for it.

I put off this last bit. For quite a while, actually.

Because how do you acknowledge—how do you *thank*—the wing-mate who stood at your back, slew monsters when you couldn't, patched your broken edges with snark and understanding, and still has the *audacity* to say that no debt is owed…

I can't. But I'm going to try anyway.

Thank you, Claire. For the late nights, the long talks, the ice cream you sent when I'd been kicked down by life. Thanks for the deadpan humor in chat, the time, the *kindness*. For making me yell, and making me cry, and making me swear out loud at inopportune moments. I don't think I've ever had so much fun writing a book.

Thanks for trusting me. Thanks for saying yes.

~BCC

Well now I have to follow that up.

When Brigitte pitched this idea, and the idea of co-writing, to me a few years ago, I was just coming out of a grueling book release. Still working through some other hard book news of a publisher closing. And more projects lined up further than it seemed like I could see. Not yet, I told her. And she patiently waited. Fast-forward to Fall, 2024. I'd just finished drafting a final book in a series, should have been ready to take a break, but instead was still humming with creative energy. So Brigitte threw the ball to my court. Ready? she asked. I looked over the outline again, asked a few more world/character questions, and then Bastian's voice popped into my head, clear as crystal. Ready, I said.

I don't know if I'd quite anticipated the late night writing sessions, the laughs, the oofs, the "do it scareds". But I wouldn't change it.

And no, Brigitte, you didn't cause my cold as we pushed one more session to finish the book and debriefed into the late night hours afterward. I'm pretty sure it was the patient who'd coughed directly on my eyeballs.

That was the writing, and now there's a few people to thank for getting here today.

Thanks to all the beta readers – Robin, Laurel, Elisabeth, and Jenni. The feedback and reactions made this book even better. And thanks for keeping this project a secret. To Deborah for the amazing copy edits, comments, and Bastian love.

Thanks to Mollie and Gillian for the constant support in life and writing and this crazy author journey we're all on together.

Thanks to my parents who didn't mind when they were staying and I disappeared into my room to "go write with my friend" like I was a teenager.

I adopted my cat Omega halfway through the drafting, and I'm only sorry you didn't get to see her incredible contributions to the text. Sadly strings of 8's and asterisks didn't quite fit thematically.

And one more thanks to Brigitte. I'd never done anything like this before, but I couldn't imagine a better person to do it with. I'm truly honored you invited me to come play in your sandbox, and I'm so proud of this story we created and the monsters you battled. Friends, and wingmates.

Thanks also to the First and Only God Who brought us together as friends first, co-conspirators second.

And thanks to you, reader, for coming this far. I hope you found some courage, healing, and maybe just some stubbornness to keep going within these pages. Stay courageous, friend.

~Claire

# THE AUTHORS

Brigitte Cromey can best be described as the cat who lives beneath the stairs—she may take a bit of time to warm up, bites if provoked, and is fiercely loyal to those she loves. She lives with her family in southern Arizona, where she wrangles a horde of small barbarians by day, drinks tea by night, and writes stabby books that feel like home the rest of the time. She loves to feed others, and her door in the desert will always be open to those needing a home-cooked meal and a hug.

Facebook/Instagram – @yarrowleafauthor

Website – wordsinmyblood.com

C. M. Banschbach is a native Texan and would make an excellent hobbit if she wasn't so tall. She's an overall dork, ice cream addict, and fangirl. When not writing fantasy stories packed full of adventure and snark, she works as a pediatric Physical Therapist where she happily embraces the fact that she never actually has to grow up.

She writes clean YA/MG fantasy-adventure as Claire M. Banschbach.

Facebook/Instagram – @cmbanschbach

Website – clairembanschbach.com

# BORDERLANDS PUBLISHING CO.

B orderlands Publishing Co. is a traditional press that seeks to publish stories that venture off charted paths and call to the hero in all of us. Find them at @borderlands.publishing or at borderlandspublishing.com